The Dead of Midnight

Other titles by Catherine Hunter:

Where Shadows Burn
(a thriller from Ravenstone)

Lunar Wake
(poetry from Turnstone Press)

Latent Heat
(poetry from Signature Editions)

Necessary Crimes
(poetry from The Muses' Company)

Rush Hour
(spoken poems on CD from Cyclops Press)

The Dead of Midnight

a thriller by

CATHERINE HUNTER

RaveN
STONE

published by Ravenstone
an imprint of Turnstone Press
607–100 Arthur Street
Artspace Building
Winnipeg, Manitoba
R3B 1H3 Canada
www.TurnstonePress.com

Turnstone Press gratefully acknowledges the assistance of the
Canada Council for the Arts, the Manitoba Arts Council and
the Government of Manitoba through the Book Publishing
Industry Development Program for our publishing activities.

The Canada Council | Le Conseil des Arts
for the Arts | du Canada

Canadä

Original cover photograph:
Midnight over Wolseley House, by Karen Barry
Design: Manuela Dias
Author photograph: Melody Morrissette

This book was printed and bound in Canada
by Friesens for Turnstone Press.

Canadian Cataloguing in Publication Data

Hunter, Catherine, 1957–
The dead of midnight

ISBN 0-88801-261-6

I. Title.

PS8565.U5783D4 2001   C813'.54   C2001-910816-8
PR9199.3.H8255D4 2001

Acknowledgements

Special thanks to Michael Dudley for the title, and to Karen Barry for the cover photo.

Many thanks to my editors, Jennifer Glossop and Pat Sanders. I'm also grateful to Henry Resta, Jack Montgomery, Frank Weiss, and Maggie Dwyer for answering all my weird questions, and to Melody Morrissette, Karen Zoppa, Brian Janzen, Marnie Woodrow, and Anne Marie Resta for reading earlier versions and providing advice. Any mistakes are my own. I could not have written this book without the support of the fabulous Manuela Dias. And thanks to Ron Schneider for the boat rides, among other things.

I dedicate this book to those who suffered neglect while I was writing it. You know who you are, and you probably shouldn't put up with it.

Better go down upon your marrow-bones
And scrub a kitchen pavement, or break stones
Like an old pauper, in all kinds of weather

—W.B. Yeats, "Adam's Curse"

Chapter One

PERPHAPS IT WAS MERELY THE BOOK she was reading, but Sarah Petursson felt uneasy. She turned a page and tried to ignore the sensation that she was being watched. She didn't usually let her imagination get the best of her like this, but sometimes the cracking floorboards and rattling window frames in this hundred-year-old house set her nerves on edge, especially when she was into a good thriller like the one she was reading now. Tonight, every irritating creak and moan seemed magnified. And there was a peculiar little scritching sound from upstairs, or was it outside—what was that? Sarah sighed. For what seemed like the tenth time, she rose from her comfortable chair and peered out the window into the darkness of her back yard. What was making those noises?

Nothing unusual out there. Just a cool night in May with a slight wind from the south. The white blossoms of the crabapple tree bobbed delicately in the breeze, and the bed-sheets on the clothesline swayed back and forth. Otherwise all was still. The bedsheets reminded Sarah of the loads of

1

laundry still unwashed and waiting for her in the basement, but she was certainly in no mood to venture down there tonight.

From the corner of her eye she saw a swift movement in the alley, and she swung her head quickly to see what it was. A cat. It was only a cat, leaping up onto the trash cans, looking for a midnight snack. Sarah smiled and returned to her chair. The presence of the cat comforted her. It was the cat, of course, or cats, making those bothersome scrapes and scratches out there. She thought briefly and with sorrow of her own cat, Max, who had died this past winter, Max who had consoled her after her marriage disintegrated last summer, Max who had been the one and only other living creature in this big old house. Now she wandered around in it all alone, and every sound made her jumpy.

She twisted in the chair, seeking a more comfortable position. The whole point of taking a vacation, she reminded herself, was to relax. She opened the book again. Where was she? Oh yes. The hero was trailing his suspect through a deserted amusement park, but Sarah knew he was following the wrong man. The amusement park was a red herring. Had to be. There were still a hundred pages left in the novel, so the hero couldn't possibly have solved the mystery yet.

It was a gruesome story about a serial killer who stalked his female victims for weeks, sending them a series of expensive presents in the mail—emerald necklaces, jeweled combs, and finally a diamond ring. The ring was the ultimate mark of doom. After that, he would sneak into their houses when they were alone, cut the telephone line with a pair of pinking shears, and throw the switches on the fuse box, plunging the hapless women into utter terror. Then he would play a game of cat and mouse in the dark house—before brutally murdering them. At the stroke of midnight. With a silver letter opener, of all things.

Sarah knew there would be some psychological explanation for all these weird details. She couldn't wait to analyze the killer's motivation tomorrow night with her cousin Morgan and the other members of her book club. But so far she hadn't figured out who the killer could be. All she knew was that he must be somebody wealthy; he had sent thousands of dollars' worth of jewelry to his victims. But there were numerous wealthy characters in the novel. It could be any one of a number of them.

She began a new chapter: *The full moon was rising over the abandoned park, illuminating the silhouette of the roller coaster tracks that loomed like the skeletal spine of some monstrous—*

Suddenly the entire room went black. Sarah froze in her chair, clutching the book. Her eyes were wide open, staring into the darkness. Her mouth was open, too, but she was too surprised to scream.

THE NEW CHIEF of police in Winnipeg had instituted several changes to the way things were done in this town, and one of his most popular innovations was to restore the presence of a cop on the beat in every neighborhood.

Morgan Wakeford thought this was an excellent idea, and she admired the new chief's initiative more and more every time she saw the handsome blond officer assigned to her own Wolseley neighborhood. He was walking past her right now as she sat at the window of Zina's Mystery Au Lait Café. Morgan checked her reflection in the dark glass of the windowpane. She tugged at the embroidered neckline of her peasant blouse and swept her thick, auburn hair off her bare shoulders. Then she raised her fist and knocked lightly on the glass.

The cop turned in her direction. Morgan waved at him, and his serious expression brightened when he saw her. He waved back and tipped his cap. His deep blue eyes were strikingly luminous in the light from the café. Morgan smiled warmly, then returned to the novel she was reading. It wouldn't do to pay too much attention to him. She grinned to herself behind the cover of the book.

"Who are you waving at?" Zina asked. "Is that Alfred coming in?" Zina stood behind Morgan's chair with a broom in one hand and a dustpan in the other. Her Mystery Au Lait Café, a combination bookstore and restaurant, had been busy tonight, but now it was quarter past eleven, and the customers were long gone, except for her friend Morgan and, naturally, the ever-present Byron Hunt, who had left his notebook and papers scattered across his table while he went to make a phone call.

"No. It's that new cop," Morgan said.

"Who?"

"Oh, wait till you see him," Morgan said. "He can serve and protect me any time."

Zina laughed. "You're incorrigible." She shook her head, tossing her silver-streaked braids and making her long earrings jangle. "Almost thirty and you're still a teenager at heart."

"Well, at least I'm still alive. Look at you—forty-two and acting like it's all over," Morgan teased.

"Hey," Zina said. "When it's over, it's over."

"You should take a look in the mirror sometime," Morgan told her. "It is *far* from over, my dear."

Despite the hectic evening, Zina still looked great, Morgan thought, and Morgan took most of the credit for that herself. She congratulated herself on her exquisite taste. Tonight Zina was wearing a choice treasure from Morgan's vintage clothing store. An original flower-print sundress, circa 1967, in mint condition, and a red fringed gypsy shawl from the same era—the summer of love. Morgan had chosen it for her, knowing it was perfect for Zina's role as hostess to the second-generation hippies of the Wolseley neighborhood, the "granola belt" of Winnipeg.

Zina rolled her eyes and returned to her sweeping. Long ago, she had painted the hardwood floor like a night sky, deep blue, with white and yellow stars scattered across it. This theme was repeated on the curtains that hung at the large windows set deep into the red brick walls, and repeated again on the tablecloths that graced the twelve small tables at the front of the café near the windows, where Morgan was sitting. Pine bookshelves, packed with hundreds of mystery novels, were crowded into the back of the café, along with a couple of cosy chairs for reading and an antique wooden telephone booth, from which Byron Hunt was now emerging. He returned to his table and surveyed his papers with a serious air. Under his frizzy curls, his round, freckled face glowed with exertion, though he hadn't done anything all day, Morgan thought, except scribble and sigh.

"Closin' time," Zina told him.

"I know." Byron made a notation with his pencil, then frowned and crossed it out.

Zina turned her attention to the large display shelf by the front counter. Every Saturday night, she changed the display to feature a new thriller for the Sunday night Mystery Book Club meeting. She picked up a felt marker and printed the words "NEWCOMERS ALWAYS WELCOME" at the top of a sign advertising the Mystery Book Club. Summer was the season for selling mystery novels, and Zina didn't want any new customers to think the club was exclusive. She wanted it to be an informal gathering, with no distinctions made between casual members and the die-hard regulars.

Morgan, like her cousin Sarah, was a die-hard regular, and she awaited the new books every Saturday night with eager anticipation.

"Where's the new book of the week?" Morgan asked. "Aren't you going to put it out?"

"I don't even know what it is yet," Zina said. "Alfred was supposed to bring it by tonight." She held up the two remaining copies of *Bloody Midnight*, which would be discussed tomorrow. "This one was sure popular," she said.

"Oh yeah." Morgan held up her own copy. "It's a real page-turner. I'll be finished it tonight."

"I couldn't get into it myself," Zina admitted. "I was so busy this week, and the book was a bit too—"

5

"Too stupid," Byron interrupted, as he plunked his empty coffee cup on the counter. "I don't know how you can read that garbage."

"This is a good one," Morgan told him. "It's more—I don't know—it's better than the usual ones. More description. And it's Canadian. It's set right here in Manitoba. In the Whiteshell."

"It's Canadian?" Byron picked up the book and examined it. "Walter White? I never heard of him."

"If you like that one, you'll like the next one," Zina told Morgan. "It's by the same guy. Alfred convinced me to take the whole series."

There were five books in the series. Five weeks of Walter White. Zina knew she was taking a risk, but Alfred had offered such a huge discount, she couldn't resist.

"Canadian, eh?" Byron muttered. He opened the book and began to read.

IN SARAH'S HOUSE, the sudden darkness was not complete, only relative. She realized after a few seconds that she could still see the glow from the desk lamp in her office across the hall. So the electricity was still functioning. She slumped in her chair for a second, as the tension left her body. Then she pulled the switch on the lamp beside her chair. Once. Twice. Three times. No light. The bulb must have simply burned out.

She rose and unscrewed it. There were fresh lightbulbs in her office drawer, and she went to retrieve one. "What a fool you are," she said, and she laughed out loud. But the effort was feeble, and the result was hollow.

Why in the world, her husband Peter used to ask, would an intelligent girl like Sarah indulge in mystery novels to the point of near hysteria? When Peter and Sarah first met in college, Peter assumed she was high-minded and artistically inclined. After all, Sarah's grandfather had been a well-known sculptor and her mother had been a poet with a small but loyal following. This made Sarah a minor celebrity in Peter's eyes. He always introduced her to his friends as the daughter of Carolyn Yeats. Sarah was surprised to learn that this impressed many of them, especially Peter's best friend, Byron Hunt, who was an aspiring poet himself. But Sarah was not interested in art or poetry. As far as she was concerned, poetry had ruined her mother's life. Peter and Byron thought Carolyn's life was terribly romantic. But Sarah took a different view. Carolyn had never married. She'd raised Sarah on her own, out on Persephone Island, trying to make ends meet with the pitiful earnings from her poetry. Then, when Sarah was only a little girl, Carolyn had died in an act of carelessness that Sarah still couldn't forgive. No, there was nothing romantic about Carolyn's life. It was a reckless, foolhardy life, and by the time Sarah reached college, she'd succeeded in forgetting almost everything about it. She studied accounting and joined the track team to keep in shape. After graduation, she started her own business and buried herself in her work. She kept a tight rein on her imagination and prided herself on her practical nature. Her only diversion from routine was reading mystery novels, a habit she'd picked up from Morgan and managed to conceal from Peter until after their wedding.

At first, Peter had tolerated Sarah's love of mysteries as an endearing quirk. When his usually calm young wife let herself get unnerved by an exciting thriller, he would merely shake his head in fond amusement. But near the end of the marriage, when his music career was failing, his mean streak started to show. He began to torment her whenever she was reading a scary book. He took advantage of the huge house, exploiting the fact that she couldn't always tell exactly where he was hiding. Sometimes he'd wait around a corner, the kitchen was his favorite spot, and wait until she was deep into her reading. Then he'd jump out at her, yelling boo! just to hear her shriek.

But it was his phony ghost story that had been the last

straw for Sarah. One day, when she was in the middle of reading a novel about a haunted house, she found Peter standing stock still on the third floor, his face pale as a cake of soap. He had seen a woman, he told her, walking up the stairs toward the attic, a woman in a white, old-fashioned dress, carrying a large book in her hands. She had floated right through the closed attic door. Peter was mocking her, she knew. Gaslighting her. Taking childish pleasure in her fear. He was a bully, she realized now, a bit sadistic.

Yet his face had been convincingly white, and when she touched his arm, he was cold as snow. Sarah shivered, remembering. Don't let him get to you, she reminded herself. He's out of your life now, and it's for the best.

She entered her office and found the lightbulbs easily. The office was excessively tidy at the moment. Sarah had suspended her home accounting business for the summer, taking her first vacation in three whole years. Tax season had been no more hectic than usual this April, but it had left her feeling stressed and exhausted, and she'd resolved not to take on any more work until she felt better. She planned to read and relax and most of all to run. The Manitoba Marathon was only a month away, and Sarah was in serious training, running ten miles a day and planning to break her personal record this year.

She tossed the burned-out lightbulb in the wastebasket and carried the new one into the hall. She paused at the bottom of the stairs, listening. What was that scratching sound? It sounded for all the world as though someone was up there. Way up there. It was probably water in the rusty pipes. Or the wind tugging at the loose shingles. Or a hundred other possible problems. The paint peeling off the walls.

Sometimes Sarah hated this ancient house. Not that she believed Peter's ghost story. It was just that the place was too big and burdensome. What did she need with three stories, six bedrooms, three baths, and a front and back staircase? She had wanted to sell it ever since she first learned, at the age of eighteen, that she'd inherited it from her grandfather's estate. But her cousins, Morgan and Sam, had made her promise to keep it in the family. Although there were three grandchildren, Sarah had inherited everything. No serious money, but a lot of real estate—this house and the place where she grew up on Lake of the Woods. She now owned the whole of Persephone Island and all its property—or what was left of it—though she'd never go back there.

It was Peter who'd convinced her to live in this house. Sometimes Sarah wondered if it was the house that made Peter propose to her in the first place. When she'd first inherited it, she'd taken Peter and Byron to see it, and they had been captivated. Byron had wandered about the rooms in awe, touching her grandfather's sculptures and her mother's books with a reverence that Sarah found ridiculous. Peter marveled at the architecture, the gables and quaint shuttered windows, the spacious rooms full of family heirlooms. Sarah argued that the house was too big and drafty and in need of repairs, but Peter had taken her aside and whispered in her ear. If she would only marry him, he would take care of the repairs, he promised. The house wasn't too big. Someday they would fill it with children, and besides, he needed to roam about freely while he was composing in his head. He was a hopeless dreamer, Sarah realized now. She should have known better than to marry a musician. But Peter had convinced her. She'd wanted to make him happy.

Now, of course, Peter wanted her to sell the house. Now that they were talking about a divorce agreement, now that it was time to split up their assets legally, he'd suddenly changed his tune and was advising her to sell, citing all her own complaints about the upkeep, using all her own old arguments against her.

Sarah screwed in the new bulb, turned on the lamp and settled back in her chair, adjusting the pillows for maximum comfort. There was no need to think about her real-estate problems tonight—not when she had a good mystery to get into. She found her place once again and began to read.

In her back yard, the upper branches of the crabapple tree tapped and squeaked against the upstairs bathroom window. Sarah deliberately ignored the sound. She was determined to get lost again in her story.

What would happen next? The hero was following the suspect into the dark tunnel of a fun house. Sarah curled up and prepared to enjoy whatever horrors he might encounter there.

Chapter Two

"WHERE IS ALFRED, ANYWAY?" Morgan asked.

Zina looked at the clock. "He's two hours late. He was supposed to be here before ten. I can't wait around much longer."

Byron remained standing by the front counter, turning the pages of *Bloody Midnight*.

"You going to buy that?" Zina asked.

"What? Oh no. I don't read this kind of stuff." He turned another page.

"Well, you better put it back then," Zina said. "And pay your bill, 'cause I'm cashing out in a minute."

"Okay. Okay." Byron paid her. "Can I get a quarter in my change? I need to make another call."

"Make it short," Zina said. "I'm closing up."

"Five minutes," he promised, as he headed back to the phone booth.

"I'll clean up after myself," Morgan offered. She pushed open the swinging doors to the kitchen and made her way to one of the gleaming double sinks to wash her cup and spoon. The kitchen was spotless, thanks to Zina's new dishwasher, Javier, a musician from Guatemala, who spoke very little but sang in the kitchen all day long in Spanish. She had enjoyed listening to him sing earlier this evening as he stacked the chairs on the patio and brought them inside for the night, carefully wiping them clean, before going home. Morgan paused on her way out and put her hand on the telephone that hung on the wall. Should she? It was getting late. She had a tentative date tonight, and she wanted to know if it was still on. She knew she shouldn't call the house, but she was growing anxious. She lifted the receiver. There was no one around to see her, and the sound of the cash register adding up the day's receipts would surely drown out her voice.

WHEN THE TELEPHONE rang in the kitchen, Sarah jumped out of her chair, and her book landed on the floor. She picked it up, smoothed out the bent pages, and went to answer the phone. Only one person could be calling at this hour. Peter. Drunk and apologetic and full of promises to change his ways. Well, she wasn't going to be sucked in by him ever again. She had taken him back into her bed twice this winter when he showed up on her doorstep in the middle of the night, and both times she ended up regretting it.

"Hello?"

There was no answer.

"Peter, come on. Don't play games with me."

But the line was curiously silent, no breathing or static. Sarah pressed the button to disconnect and listened again. No dial tone. Nothing. The line was dead.

A tingle ran down her spine. The line had been cut! From outside—with a pair of pinking shears, just like in the book!

She gasped and whirled around suddenly as a movement

across the room caught her eye. Her heart leaped, but it was only her own reflection she had seen in the mirror above the sideboard. She stared at herself. Her blue eyes were wild, and her thin face so pale that the light freckles stood out on the bridge of her nose. She looked like a crazed victim from a horror movie.

You're being ridiculous, she scolded herself. She hung up the phone and went back to the living room. You're reading too many murder mysteries. No husband, no children. Tomorrow you'll be twenty-five years old, and you don't even have a lover. Not even a cat to keep you warm. Getting your thrills from a paperback novel. You're pathetic. And what's worse, you're starting to believe what you read. She turned the novel over and studied the glossy cover. It was embossed with the silhouette of a frightened woman, her hand across her mouth, a shadow looming above her. Red ink dripped like blood from the letters of the title, staining the woman's dress. It was trash. No doubt about it.

Yes, she was being ridiculous. She'd call the phone company tomorrow and get a repairman out, and that was that.

And she'd read something else. A magazine maybe. Then she wouldn't be so jittery. But she hesitated. Creepy as the story was, she couldn't put it down.

She returned to her chair, found her place again, and started a new chapter. While the hero swaggered bravely through the deserted funhouse, his girlfriend was at home, opening her mail. Oh no. Sarah knew what was going to happen next. Sure enough, the first package the girlfriend opened contained a necklace—a single emerald on a gold chain. There was no card enclosed, but the girlfriend merely shrugged. A minor oversight. She knew the hero was busy these days on an important case and was often absent-minded. She didn't want to bother him with trivialities. The hero had told his girlfriend nothing about the case he was working. He said the details would only give her nightmares, so she asked him no questions. Sarah gritted her teeth in frustration. Why hadn't the hero warned her? Typical male. By trying to protect her, he had sealed her doom.

AS SOON AS she got home, Betty Carriere performed a quick sweep of her house, turning on every light and looking inside every room, not even stopping to answer the ringing telephone. Then she checked the doors and windows. All securely locked. Everything in order. The house was empty, which was good, but unexpected. Where was Alfred? Had that been him on the phone? She checked for a message, but whoever called had hung up without leaving one.

Where *was* Alfred? He should be home at this hour of the night. Betty let a brief concern for her husband flit through her mind, but the truth was, she was glad he wasn't home. She had other things to worry about.

Like money.

She walked across her spotless kitchen floor and opened one of the glass doors in her brand-new cupboards. Tucked neatly between her cookbooks, she found her account book and drew it out. She poured herself a glass of wine and sat at the kitchen table with a pencil, trying to figure out how much extra cash she could spare for Anna this time.

There were twelve days left in May and just enough money in the account to cover household supplies. Then there was the dinner party on June the second. She knew Alfred would give her some extra money to cover that, but she'd have to use it for the party. If she scrimped there, he'd notice right away. But maybe if she was extra frugal until then....

She stood up and made an efficient inspection of her cupboards and pantry. They needed groceries, that was obvious. Alfred's assistant, Gregory Restall, had been here all day, helping Alfred send out press releases and eating everything in Betty's fridge. The broom closet revealed a shortage of floor wax, the expensive kind—floor wax was not the place to pinch pennies—and a shortage of vacuum bags. She was also low on silver polish, lightbulbs, bleach, and a dozen other necessities—and she hadn't even checked the bathrooms. It was all her sister's fault. Why couldn't Anna manage her life? Betty had given her two hundred dollars just two weeks ago, leaving herself short. And now Anna wanted more.

Betty finished the wine in her glass and took it to the sink, where she washed and rinsed it and left it to dry in the stainless steel dish rack. Then she headed upstairs to search through her husband's dresser drawers and the pockets of his pants. She hated doing it, but if Anna didn't pay her rent in full, she'd be evicted again, and there was no way Betty wanted her sister landing on her doorstep. There was no telling what Anna might say in front of Alfred.

ZINA WAS RELIEVED when Alfred Carriere finally arrived, carrying a heavy box and announcing, "New books," in a hearty voice.

"About time!" Morgan said, as she came out of the kitchen. "Zina's ready to fall asleep. She's actually been here longer than Byron tonight."

"Very funny," Byron said. He had finished his phone calls and was packed and ready to leave. But he didn't seem to be going anywhere.

"Yeah, sorry, Zina," Alfred said. He set the box on the counter. "I got held up. Bad day."

Although he was over fifty now, Alfred still worked long, grueling hours, keeping his business going. Ever since his brother Quinn moved away, Alfred did most of the work himself. It seemed to agree with him, though, Zina had to admit. Although Alfred's sixties-style ponytail and mustache had long ago turned gray, he kept himself as muscular and trim as most men half his age.

"Hand me a knife, will you?" he asked.

Zina gave him a sharp utility knife, and he slit the box open. "The second one in the series," he said proudly. He held a copy up for them to see. "*A Chill at Midnight.*"

Zina wasn't sure she liked the cover. It was almost more melodramatic than the first. A slender blonde in a filmy nightgown stood cowering outside in a snowy landscape at the edge of a frozen river. From beyond the frame, a gloved hand reached for her throat. The title, in white letters, was hung with long icicles.

"Brrr," said Morgan.

Byron merely rolled his eyes. He dismissed them all with a wave as he left the café.

Zina was well aware that Byron didn't approve of Alfred Carriere. Byron didn't try very hard to conceal it. He had little respect for Alfred's business, which he described as "mercenary." Alfred pandered to the basest instincts, in Byron's opinion. He published nothing but cookbooks and celebrity bios and popular crime novels, with never a hint of real literature in the catalogue. Byron had submitted several of his own poetry manuscripts to Carriere Press and had been rejected every time, but that had nothing to do with his dislike of the man, Byron often insisted to Zina. It wasn't personal. It was a matter of principle.

Once, Zina knew, Carriere Press had been a respectable venture, a small literary press with a strong commitment to the arts. In the seventies, Alfred and Quinn Carriere enjoyed a reputation as Canada's most innovative editors, willing to take risks on promising young talents. But in the eighties, the business ran into financial trouble. Quinn, who had a young family to support, took a more stable job with a bigger publisher in Toronto, and Alfred found he had to change his business practices to keep afloat. The Carriere Press backlist still boasted the first novels and early volumes of poetry of many of the country's finest authors. But Alfred couldn't keep those authors. As soon as they made a name for themselves, they hired agents who demanded advances Alfred couldn't afford. Gradually, Alfred began to publish less literature and more best-sellers. But in Canada, even a best-seller barely brought in enough to cover production and advertising costs. Alfred's latest venture was not even publishing, exactly, but promotion and distribution. The Walter White mysteries were all mass-market pocket books. Published years ago in the States, they were long out of print, and Alfred had acquired the rights for a song.

In Byron's opinion, Alfred was a sell-out. But Zina sympathized with Alfred. She admired the way he changed with the times and kept his company thriving. She knew what it meant to run your own business. Hard decisions had to be made all the time, and sometimes principles had to be compromised.

Alfred handed Zina an invoice. "I'll see you tomorrow," he said, as he headed toward the door.

Morgan followed him out. "Me too!" she called. "Good night, Zina!"

"Don't you want me to walk you—" Zina began. But the door banged shut. They were gone.

Zina took the last two copies of *Bloody Midnight* off the shelf and began to stock *A Chill at Midnight*. Although the cover images were different, the design of the two books was similar enough to mark them as part of the same series. A clever marketing ploy, Zina thought. In the upper left-hand corner, both books carried the same logo: a little gold clock, both its hands standing straight up at twelve, and the words "A Midnight Mystery."

Zina fussed with the display, procrastinating. She dreaded walking home alone at this dark hour, when Westminster Avenue was deserted. Why hadn't Morgan waited for her?

THE CRABAPPLE BRANCHES were now scraping heavily against Sarah's bathroom window. It sounded almost as if the window was sliding open. Sarah put her book down and listened.

A subtle but unmistakable grating sound could be heard at

intervals, as if someone was ever so slowly forcing the upstairs window open. Impossible. Sarah held her breath and listened harder. She didn't dare to move. If she still had Max, she could say to herself, *it's only the cat*, and forget about it. But there was no cat, now. No little Max to blame for the clunks and creaks that emanated from the far corners of this cavernous, drafty old house. Maybe it really was haunted.

Or maybe someone really was upstairs. Someone with a silver letter opener. And it was almost midnight.

Upstairs, a soft bang sounded in the bathroom, and Sarah leaped out of her chair. This was crazy. She paced the floor, hugging her own shoulders. Maybe she should light a fire. Yes. She placed a log in the fireplace and began to stack kindling. The house wasn't exactly cold, she thought, as she struck a match. It was psychological warmth she craved. She should put on some music too, to mask these little sounds. They were only very tiny sounds, she told herself. The size of the house, and her own loneliness, were amplifying them out of all proportion.

As she crossed to the stereo, she glanced out the window and saw that the freshly laundered sheets on the line were now swinging vigorously under the apple tree. The wind was picking up. You see? she said to herself. It was only the wind causing the shutters to bang. She chose a Mozart concerto and slipped the CD into the machine. Sweet violins began to fill the room. She turned the volume louder. If the house was going to make noises, she didn't want to hear them.

Settling back in her chair, she quickly lost herself once again in the novel. She heard nothing but Mozart. Not even the crackling of the flames in the fireplace could be heard above the music.

AT THE SALS restaurant on Broadway, Officer Daniel Bradley rejoined his partner Marnie for a last cup of coffee and a chance to compare notes before their shift was over.

They chatted about the new software Marnie was buying for her foster son's birthday, and the boy's unusual talent with computers. Then Daniel changed the subject to his new car, a 2001 Jetta, which he couldn't afford but couldn't resist, either. He'd parked it in the Sals lot during his shift tonight, and paid a waiter ten dollars to watch it for him, just for the pleasure of driving it fast through the empty streets when he got off in the early hours of the morning.

"Can I take it for a spin sometime?" Marnie asked.

"Sometime," Daniel promised. "Not just yet."

Marnie laughed. "Well, let me know when you're through bonding with it." She took Daniel's empty cup. "One more for the road?" He nodded, and she went to the counter for refills.

Daniel reviewed his notes. It had been an uneventful night. As usual, they'd taken turns walking through the neighborhood, up the front streets and down the back alleys, sometimes together and sometimes apart, in order to cover more territory. They kept in radio contact when apart, in case of emergency, but in the two months since Daniel had been assigned to Wolseley, he hadn't encountered any emergencies.

Tonight was typical: a store clerk selling aerosol cleaner to addicts, an attempted arson, an epidemic of bicycle thefts, and one lost kid, quickly found at the local arcade. There was also an incident Daniel regarded as grave, but as usual it was downgraded to simple assault at the station. Daniel and Marnie had arrived at the parking lot of the Big Sky Tavern to find one drunk lying on the ground and another drunk kicking his head in with steel-toed cowboy boots, while a crowd of twenty people stood and watched, as if they were spectators at a ball game.

As he reread his notes on the incident, he could still visualize the blood that gushed from the victim's mouth and trickled into a dark pool in the parking lot. His stomach turned over again. Violence made Daniel physically ill, and he tried hard to hide it. He didn't ever want a repeat of the humiliation he experienced on his first big case, when he was a rookie. He'd disgraced himself back then by fainting at the sight of the blood. He keeled right over, bashing his forehead on a metal sewer grate, when he and his partner discovered a body in a dumpster. The guys took to calling him "Waffle-Head," because of the corrugated bruise he'd received from the sewer grate, and it took Daniel years to live that down. But he didn't faint any more. Violence still made him feel ill, but when he felt ill, he didn't pass out. He got angry.

Marnie brought two refills of the strong Sals coffee to the table and began filling hers up with the usual three spoons of sugar. Daniel snapped his notebook shut. "Quiet night," he remarked.

"Yeah," Marnie said. "Not much going on tonight."

THE MOZART CONCERTO rose to a brilliant crescendo, a grand finale, and then the house fell silent. Sarah jerked awake. She'd nodded off over her book, despite the suspense. She looked up and saw that the fire was nothing but smoldering ashes. In a minute, as soon as she finished this chapter, she'd get ready for bed, put on her flannel pyjamas, and crawl under the quilt to read. She knew she was going to end up finishing this thriller tonight, no matter how sleepy she felt. She was hooked. She had to find out who the villain was.

The hero had long since realized he'd been on the wrong track at the amusement park, but he remained unaware of the danger to his girlfriend. By this time she had received several gifts of jewelry and interpreted them as the hero's feeble attempts to make up for the way he was neglecting her lately. She hadn't been impressed. But when the diamond ring arrived, she forgave him everything. She naturally assumed it was his romantic way of proposing marriage. At this moment, she was setting the table for a candlelight dinner and rehearsing her acceptance speech, unaware that the villain—who could he be?—had left a fake message for the hero, canceling their date, and was at this very moment outside her house, armed with his letter opener, spying on her through a window as she arranged fresh flowers in a vase. The chapter ended. Only thirty pages left.

Well, now the author would cut to the chase. Sarah yawned. She'd better go upstairs before she drifted off again in her chair. She would enjoy the rest of the story in bed. She poked the fire, to make sure it would die safely, and switched off the lamp. She moved to the window to draw the curtains closed. The white sheets on the line were dancing like celebrating phantoms in the night breeze. As Sarah watched, a sudden gust of wind lifted one of the sheets high into the air, and she glimpsed what lay behind it.

She let out a scream.

Right under the apple tree, she could clearly see the rungs of a tall wooden ladder leaning against the trunk.

Chapter Three

SARAH CLAPPED HER HANDS over her mouth, but it was too late. The sound of her scream seemed to echo through the whole house. Then she heard the footsteps on the upstairs hallway. God! Her nightmare was coming true. Someone was in the house. She had to get out, fast. The back door!

She tore through the kitchen and unlatched the chain on the storm door. Footsteps pounded down the front stairs. She grabbed the doorknob, turned it violently, and pulled. The door would not open. In her panic, she had forgotten the double deadbolt locks that were supposed to keep her safe. But the footsteps were descending rapidly now. She didn't have time to deal with the locks. She raced for the back staircase and flew up the steps two at a time, still clutching the mystery novel in one hand. She paused for a moment on the second floor, wondering wildly which way to turn. Her own bedroom? The bathroom? She heard a thump from the kitchen below and bolted up the next flight of stairs.

Sarah was not thinking straight. When she reached the third floor, she ran into the guest bedroom and tried desperately to dial 911. She spent entirely too much time jiggling the receiver and cursing before she remembered it was dead. The lines to the house must have been cut. For real. She felt helpless, as though she were a character in one of the thrillers she had read. Which one? They were all the same. Madman in the house, the telephone wires cut. No way out. Except, except . . . she remembered the ladder and the sounds from the second-story bathroom. If she could climb out the window. . . . She tore across the hall toward the back staircase. But then she heard the footsteps again, coming up. She would never make it in time.

She slipped into the linen closet and drew the door close, but didn't risk making a sound by shutting it completely. She listened intently. The footsteps had paused at the top of the stairs. Nothing but silence. Crouching low in the semi-darkness, Sarah tried to breathe quietly, but her heart was pounding and her lungs gasped for air. The laminated paperback in her hand was slippery with sweat. She was still gripping the stupid book! A thin ray of light seeped through the crack of the closet door, illuminating the cover. Sarah stared at the figure of the cowering woman. The lurid drawing seemed to mock her own terror. Why oh why had she held on to the book and not grabbed some kind of weapon? She was completely unarmed.

For the next few minutes, an eerie silence enveloped the house. Even the usual creaks and rattles fell still. Sarah could hear nothing but her own ragged breathing. What was happening? Where were the footsteps she had heard so clearly? She was *sure* she'd heard them. Hadn't she? She thought of the ghost that Peter said he'd seen up here. The hairs on her arms and the back of her neck began to rise.

Then she heard it again—somebody walking, softly this time, creeping down the hall. Yes. Someone was definitely moving toward the bathroom. She thought she heard the bathroom door open. Should she try to slip out now? Make a run for it, down to the front door?

Too late. Whoever it was, ghost or madman, was back in the hall. No time to do anything but wait, pray that she would not be found. But someone was intent on finding her. Someone was opening doors, searching. She recognized the squeal of the unoiled hinge on the guest bedroom door. Then the rattling knob on the sunroom. The linen closet was next. Sarah stepped away from the door, toward the back of the closet. She dropped the book, but it landed on a soft pile of laundry and made no sound to give her away.

The laundry!

Sarah backed up one more step and slid her foot along the floor. There! She could feel the trap door to the laundry chute. She bent down and fumbled blindly with the catch. Then she pulled the trap door open and climbed inside. She barely squeezed through, feet first. Gripping the rim tightly with her fingers, she lowered herself into the chute, until only her hands and the top of her head were visible above the floor. Her body dangled in the void below. *Please don't see me*, she prayed. But the crack of light widened. The closet door opened.

With a wild sense of futility, Sarah let go.

Before she lost consciousness, she felt the swift, sweet rush of adrenaline, like the wings of a large bird beating through her body, as she dropped three stories into utter darkness.

Chapter Four

ZINA CLOSED HER COPY OF *Bloody Midnight* and shivered under the bedcovers. Every time she came to one of those terrifying chase scenes, she had to put the book down. She'd intended to finish it for tomorrow's book club discussion, but it was just too disturbing. Zina hated violence. She preferred the bloodless crimes of the older writers—the tidy, unseen murders of Agatha Christie or the intellectual puzzles of Doyle's Sherlock Holmes. The modern mysteries were too realistic. And this one in particular seemed too vivid, too close to home. To Zina's mind, the whole point of reading a mystery novel was to *escape* from reality.

She placed the book on her bedside table and switched off her reading lamp. But light from a street lamp streamed in between the curtains, and she moved to close them.

She peered out the window. Someone was riding a bicycle down the middle of Lipton Street.

She recognized the bike. It was one she had seen many times before, distinctive with its large, unwieldy metal carrier full of old leather satchels and overstuffed plastic bags. The rider was Byron Hunt, his frazzled mop of hair bobbling up and down as he pedaled.

Zina grinned. That bike! It must have been twenty years old, at least! But of course Byron could not afford a new one. He had never, as far as Zina knew, held down a real job for longer than a couple of months. He spent all his time revising his unpublished collection of poems and song lyrics. If he hadn't inherited his mother's house, over on Ruby Street, he would probably be homeless.

Byron turned the corner, and the bicycle tires wobbled under the weight of the bags in the carrier. Zina knew exactly what was in there. Byron's hoards of notebooks and reams of loose-leaf paper. He unloaded them all every morning in Zina's café, where he scribbled and chewed on his pen for hours, in between huge mugs of the Colombian coffee he was addicted to. She laughed. No wonder he was awake in the middle of the night.

Zina closed the curtains and climbed back under the covers, letting her mind turn to the day ahead. On Sundays, she didn't open the café until noon, so she'd be able to get some paperwork done before she started cooking. She ran through her menu: potato soup and the usual slate of sandwiches for the afternoon crowd. For dinner, a choice of vegetarian chili or curried chickpeas, with fresh pita bread. That would be easy. Zina could make those stand-by dishes in her sleep. But of course there was always the Sunday baking. The Mystery Book Club members were, without exception, avid chocolate addicts. Zina wanted to make something special for tomorrow night. Cady Brown, the reporter who was writing a story about the book club, would be there, and Cady loved sweets. Maybe Zina should try that new recipe for cherry brownies. She wanted to make a good impression. The story would be great publicity for the café, if Cady would ever finish it.

SARAH WAS WALKING *through the woods down a crooked path lined on both sides with wild, ripe raspberries. She was very small and carried in her hand a yellow tin pail, the size of a child's beach toy. Far above her head, the tall pines swayed, and poplar trees rustled like whispering human voices. The air was cool. Although the sun above the trees was bright, only thin, scattered patches of light skipped and shimmered on the path before her and danced across the green leaves of the berry bushes. Ahead, Sarah could see only the twists and turns of the path. But she wasn't lost. She knew her way. Her feet, in their little buckled sandals, kept slipping and sliding in the soft sand and thick cover of pine needles as she trudged along.*

She reached the end of the path. In the clearing ahead, she could see the outline of a woman sitting on the grass beneath the sheltering shade of two enormous maple trees. Sarah stepped closer. The woman did not raise her head. She did not move at all. She was focused intently on something—she was reading. Sarah stood before the woman and looked into her perfectly still, concentrating face. With no sense of surprise, she realized she was looking at herself. She could see herself clearly. Her head was bent forward, fair hair covering her freckled face, completely absorbed in the large open book that lay spread across her lap.

The crash and tinkle of breaking glass somewhere far, far above roused Sarah toward awareness. She remembered, dimly, a sense of danger. A threat to her life. She had to wake up, get moving. But her knees were welded together with pain. Her legs were two dead weights. A woman's voice whispered in her ear, "Sleep, now. Go back to sleep." The voice was soothing and strangely familiar, but Sarah resisted. As she struggled to throw off the heavy blanket of sleep that bound her, the pain flared through her ankles, up through her left knee, and pierced her hip. Although she knew she was not moving, she felt her whole body spinning in the empty space that surrounded her. Dizzy and sick, she wanted nothing more than to sink back into blackness, to feel nothing.

"Just rest now."

Sarah let the voice convince her. It could have been her own voice, she thought vaguely. What she wanted more than anything was to sleep. She sank back into the depths of the dream and lost consciousness again.

IN THE SECOND-FLOOR bedroom of the house next door, Dr. Adele Allard sat up straight, suddenly wide awake and alert. What had she heard? Was that furnace acting up again? She cursed. She had paid a fortune, just this winter, to have it repaired.

She listened for a while. Nothing but the occasional sound of distant traffic from Westminster Avenue. It was still the middle of the night. Dr. Allard lay down, but she couldn't get back to sleep. The abrupt awakening had unnerved her. She turned over on her side and tried to relax by thinking of her bank account. Not the checking account for the bills and the day-to-day expenses, but the savings account. The one that had been growing since she started her private counseling practice. Every extra dollar went straight in, and never a dime came out. Now, thanks to her new tenant, the account was growing faster than ever. Adding the extra two hundred a month would bring in twenty-four hundred a year . . . all undeclared and completely tax-free. . . .

A sudden crash, like smashed glass. Dr. Allard sat bolt upright again. What a fool she'd been to try to lull herself back into sleep. Something was definitely wrong. She eased herself to the edge of the bed and pulled on her dressing gown. A faint clatter came from the dining room directly below her bedroom. A burglar! After her china collections! Her silver! Her precious rare books! Furious, she knotted the belt of her dressing gown and reached for her spectacles.

Dr. Allard kept a baseball bat in her bedroom in case of just such an eventuality. It had cost her forty-eight fifty at the Bay, but it would be worth every penny if she could protect her property with it. She crept down the stairs, gripping the bat tightly, pausing now and then to listen. She was small, but she was fearless.

She reached the main floor without hearing anything more, but she could see a light from the dining room. She waited, bat raised and ready to strike, between the grandfather clock and the tall glass-paneled cabinet that held her rare book collection. All was silent. Then a sudden burst of sound. The unmistakable clickety-clack of typewriter keys. She lowered the bat and stepped into the dining room. Yes, it was only her new tenant, Mark Curtis, working on an overdue essay.

"You woke me up," she said.

He turned, flashed her a rueful grin. "I'm sorry," he said. Then, seeing her pallor, "I hope I didn't scare you. Here, sit down." He rose and pulled another chair out from the table. "I've made a pot of tea. Let me get you a cup."

Dr. Allard sank gratefully into the chair. She set the baseball bat down beneath the table, hoping he hadn't seen it. "Tea would be nice," she said. Now that her rage was calmed, her hands began to shake. She concealed them in her lap.

Mark walked slowly into the kitchen. He saw the bat, and though he made no comment, he felt a twinge of uneasiness as he poured the tea. His new landlady was eccentric. He was lucky she hadn't taken a crack at his skull.

"I should get myself a computer," he remarked as he set a cup before her. "Quieter."

"Oh, it wasn't the typing that woke me," Dr. Allard said, perfectly composed now. "It was—did you hear a—sort of a clanging? And breaking glass?"

Mark shook his head.

"I thought it was—oh well. Kids drinking in the lane, maybe, knocking over garbage cans, smashing beer bottles." She smiled grimly and sipped her tea. "This neighborhood's not what it used to be."

"I didn't hear a thing. I've been kind of obsessed with this paper."

Dr. Allard picked up a page and skimmed it quickly.

29

"*Problems in Psychological Profiling?* I thought you were studying family therapy."

"It's a required course," he said. "Methods in Psychological Testing. And believe me, writing is not my strong point." He moaned. "This paper is six weeks late!"

"Six weeks?" Dr. Allard frowned. "What seems to be the problem?"

"The whole paper is one big problem." Mark ripped a sheet from the typewriter and crumpled it in his fist. "I'm totally blocked."

"You're just frustrated," Dr. Allard said calmly. "And you're no doubt exhausted. Why don't you get some sleep?"

Mark sighed. "Maybe you're right." He rose from the table.

She began to gather his notes into a neat pile. "I'll read over what you've done so far and make some suggestions. In the morning, when you're fresh, we'll work on it together. How would that be?"

Mark brightened. "That would be great. That's what my dad used to do for me and my brother in high school. He checked over our homework every night."

Dr. Allard smiled as she watched him head upstairs to his room. For two hundred a month, she didn't mind doing a little homework.

SARAH FELT SOFT *arms around her shoulders, a gentle hand stroking her temples. "It's all right now. You can wake up. You can face it, Sarah."*

"Mum?" The sound of her own voice roused her. Pain flooded back through her lower limbs and she groaned.

"Sarah? Are you there?" A man's voice. She opened her eyes. Across the dim room she could make out the figure of her husband, Peter, coming toward her. Scenes of her recent terror flashed through her memory. The cut telephone cord, the ladder. The letter opener—no, wasn't that in the book?

The pain confused her. She remembered hiding in the closet. The footsteps, that awful, hopeless fear as she let herself drop down the chute.

"Peter? Help me, I—" She gasped. She could see him rushing at her with a long blade glinting in his hand. No!

She summoned all her available strength and began to scream as loudly as she could.

Peter backed away. "Sarah, what's the matter? What's happened?" He looked down at the object in his hand and, shocked, thrust it away from himself. It clattered across the basement floor, far from them both. "For God's sake, I'm not going to hurt you," he cried. "I was only—"

But Sarah continued to scream.

DR. ALLARD WAS still up, poring over Mark's notes on the dining-room table, fascinated by the forensic applications of psychological profiling. She heard the scream distinctly—a prolonged, wrenching cry of pain and terror that made the blood stand still in her heart. Dr. Allard didn't need her hard-earned Ph.D. in psychology to tell her someone was experiencing deep trauma. This time she didn't even consider her baseball bat. She reached for the telephone and dialed 911.

Chapter Five

DANIEL BRADLEY MADE A SHARP U-turn on Broadway when the call came through on the radio. His shift was over, but he was only two blocks away from the address.

He radioed Marnie, who, he knew, would also be close by. He had left her at the Sals not five minutes ago.

"I'm at Broadway and Main," Marnie radioed back. "Be there right away. Over and out."

Daniel heard her siren begin to wail before she signed off. Marnie was driving the black and white. Daniel was in the Jetta. But he was still in uniform, and he was still armed. He pulled onto Home Street. The nearest street lamp was dark, burned out. But he knew by the address the house must be near the river. There! One porch light glowed near the end of the block. He sped up. He could see a tiny woman, about sixty years old, standing on the curb, dressed in a threadbare housecoat and slippers. She frantically waved him over.

"It's my neighbor!" Dr. Allard blurted. She pointed at the house next door.

Daniel got out of his car. "What's the trouble, ma'am?"

"I heard screams. From that house, there! Something is horribly wrong."

Daniel listened. He heard nothing but the wind rustling in the branches of the elm trees. He drew his flashlight out of his belt and, almost unconsciously, unsnapped the holster of his gun. Then he heard it, high pitched and hysterical, as if someone was being murdered. Lights turned on in several windows across the street. Daniel moved swiftly toward the house.

As he approached, the front door flew open and a man came tearing out, straight at him. Daniel drew his gun.

"Freeze!"

The man froze.

"Put your hands up, in front of you. Open them! I want to see the palms of your hands. Now!"

The man complied. One of his hands was dark with blood. Daniel kept his weapon aimed at the guy, but let his eyes wander briefly in a quick sweep of the periphery.

"My wife!" the guy cried. "She needs help."

"Down on the ground," Daniel ordered. "Hands behind your back." The guy dropped to the lawn and Daniel approached cautiously. The blood on the man's hands was obviously his own. His right palm was sliced up badly, and he cried out when Daniel grabbed it. Nevertheless, Daniel cuffed him tightly and told him to stay put.

Marnie pulled up and rushed out, her hand on her holster. Dr. Allard backed away, toward the safety of her own porch. She saw Mark standing at the open front door in his bathrobe. She motioned urgently for him to get back into the house.

"You watch him," Daniel told Marnie. "I'm going inside."

"In the basement," the cuffed man said. "Go straight through to the kitchen and down the stairs. She's hurt bad."

SARAH TRIED TO scream again when she saw the huge shadow of Daniel Bradley coming at her, but her throat was so hoarse she could barely croak. His flashlight shone on a thin chain hanging above him, and he pulled the cord. The bare bulb revealed her fully to him. She lay in an enormous heap of laundry up against the rough cement wall. Her face was scratched and bruised, and she had her eyes screwed tightly shut, whether from the sudden light or from fear, he wasn't sure.

In such a situation, Daniel would normally bark, "Winnipeg Police!" But instead he heard himself say gently, "It's okay. I'm a cop. I'm here to help you. See? Open your eyes."

Sarah peeked, and when she saw the uniform, she let herself faint.

MORGAN WOKE TO the stuttering long-distance ring of the telephone. Sam!

She jumped up and headed for the kitchen phone, so she could make coffee while she chatted with her brother.

"Hey, Sam," she said as she snatched up the receiver.

"Hey, Morgie. You up?"

"Up now. What's new in Vancouver? How's Mum?"

"Good. She's good. We took her out for a stroll on the sea-wall yesterday."

"See any whales?" Morgan measured generous spoonsful of French dark roast into her coffee maker.

"No whales, just sail-boarders. Mum loves to watch them, you know. I think it reminds her of sailing on Lake of the Woods."

"Those were the days," Morgan said wistfully.

"We have a sailboat, you know. Any time you want to come, we'll take you out on the ocean."

"I have a business to run here, as you seem to forget."

"So chuck it." Sam laughed. "Open a scuba-diving emporium on Galiano Island."

"Ha. Ha," Morgan said. Her tendency to "chuck" things was a running joke with Sam. In college, she'd flitted from fine arts to home economics to fashion design, without ever earning a degree. Then she had opened a series of short-lived businesses—a jewelry kiosk, a doomed art gallery, and now the clothing shop. "I'm committed to Vintage," she told him.

"Right," he said. "How is business, anyway?"

They chatted for twenty minutes, and Morgan caught up on the latest news of the family. Their mother, Darlene, was "about the same," Sam said. Shortly after their father's death five years ago, Darlene had suffered a stroke that robbed her of her memory and left her easily confused. That was why Sam had moved to Vancouver, to care for her. But Darlene's physical health was good. Sam's wife, Didi, looked in on her daily to make sure she was eating well and walking regularly. Morgan suppressed a surge of guilt by reminding herself that her mother barely knew the difference, any more, between Didi and Morgan.

"How's Sarah?" Sam asked. "I called her just now, but she's not answering."

"She must be sleeping in. Why'd you call her? Oh yeah, it's the twentieth today."

"Have you made any plans?"

"No," Morgan admitted. "I forgot all about it." She knew Sam wouldn't approve. He'd always been protective of Sarah, ever since Sarah had come to live with them at the age of six and taken Morgan's place as the cherished baby of the family.

"Make sure you call her today," Sam said. "Remember, you're the only family she's got."

"I know, I know," she said lightly. "We're more than cousins, we're sisters, to quote Mum."

"Do the sisterly thing, then. Show her she's loved."

"I do love her, Sammy. You know I do. But face it, she's not very much fun!"

Then to forestall any more nagging from her brother, she asked about her two nephews and enjoyed hearing Sam brag about their growing skill as sailors and their music lessons and the marathon races they entered to raise money for the Humane Society.

Long after she hung up, Morgan continued to sip coffee and muse about Sam's family. She could hardly believe the boys were learning to sail. The last time she'd seen her nephews, the youngest was just learning to tie his shoelaces. She indulged herself in a daydream of taking Sam up on his offer to take her sailing. They had sailed often when they were children. Sam, especially, was addicted to the water. As a boy, he'd lived for summer, lived to get out on the boat.

Yes, those were the days. When Aunt Carolyn, Sarah's mother, was alive, they visited her and Sarah every summer at their place on Lake of the Woods. Sam and Sarah and Morgan would play for hours on the sandy beach of Persephone Island. They swam and explored the little island, taking picnic lunches to eat in the woods, and at night they stayed up long past bedtime in the little green cabin their grandfather built at the edge of the woods, away from the main house. Out of earshot of the grown-ups, they giggled and played Twenty Questions until they couldn't keep their eyes open any longer. Or Sam would spook his younger sister and cousin with ghost stories until they were afraid to close their eyes at all.

Morgan shuddered. But it wasn't the memory of the ghost stories that shook her. It was the memory of the night those happy summers came to an end for good. Those tall, flickering shadows, the choking, tear-wrenching smoke. Morgan broke into a thin sweat and felt the skin on her back begin to prickle, as if her body, too, were remembering the intensity of the heat. And Sarah's screams. Those awful screams.

A WEEK'S ACCUMULATION of dirty laundry at the bottom of the chute had probably saved Sarah's life. But her left leg was fractured below the knee, and the left ankle badly sprained.

Her face and arms were scraped, and her head throbbed, despite the pain medication that kept her so groggy she could barely stay conscious. Her throat was raw from screaming.

She lay in bed at the St. Boniface Hospital, her leg, with the calf encased in white plaster, propped on a pillow. She stared at the clock on the wall. Four in the afternoon. The nurse arrived with another pill in a paper cup.

"Someone to see you," he said. "You feeling up to it?"

"Who is it?" Sarah asked. She winced. Then she saw the police officer in the doorway. The one who came to her house this morning when she was screaming. The one who calmed her, held her hand as they carried her to the ambulance on a stretcher. "Yes," she said weakly. "Let him in."

"She's all yours," the nurse told Daniel, and he left to attend to other patients.

Daniel crossed the room to stand beside her bed. "How are you?"

"I'm . . . okay. Thank you. Thank you so much. You rescued me."

"That's my job," he said. He pulled up a chair. "Mind if I sit down?" Without waiting for an answer, he sat and opened his notebook. "I'm Daniel Bradley, your local beat officer. Can you tell me what happened last night?"

"I don't really know," Sarah said. She barely remembered the weird events of the night before. Surreal images flickered and wavered in her memory, jumbled together—a ladder, a pail of raspberries, a long blade gleaming in the darkness. Every time she closed her eyes, the silhouette of the woman on the book cover loomed above her, dripping blood, and over and over again, she relived the sensation of hurtling through the narrow metal laundry chute, the soft clang of the sheet metal vibrating in the air.

"Your husband said—"

"My ex-husband."

"You're divorced?"

"Separated."

"Well, your estranged husband, then. Peter Petursson. He said he found you on the floor in the basement."

"I fell—I escaped down the laundry chute," she said. "Someone broke into the house. Someone was chasing me through the house."

"Petursson broke in," the officer said. "He admitted it."

"It *was* Peter!" Sarah covered her face with her hands. "What is he doing? He's gone mad!"

"You don't need to be afraid of him," Daniel said. "We're holding him downtown until we get your statement."

"He's in jail? Oh my God!" What was happening to Peter? To her life?

"He broke your living room window and climbed into the house. He assaulted you?" Daniel pointed at her leg with his pen.

"No—I mean, yes, but—he didn't break—he didn't come in through the living room. There was a ladder."

"A ladder?" Daniel had seen no ladder.

"Against the crab tree in back. He must have climbed in through the second floor. The bathroom window."

The officer consulted his notebook. "I see. A ladder."

"I saw it," said Sarah. "I saw it out there."

"Peter said he broke in through the living room window. He searched the house and found you unconscious on the basement floor."

"No—no, he was upstairs. He climbed up to the second story."

"The panes on the living room window *are* broken," Daniel said. "I was at your house just an hour ago. Your next-door neighbor was boarding them up."

"That's—well. What?" Sarah knew she'd been sitting in the living room when she heard the footsteps upstairs. If the living-room window had been broken, she would have seen and heard it. "I don't understand," she mumbled.

Daniel continued to question her, but her story didn't make much sense. If she'd leaped down the laundry chute voluntarily, he thought, that was hardly grounds for an assault charge. Especially if she hadn't even *seen* Peter Petursson before she jumped. And her talk of a letter opener seemed, frankly, just crazy. She hadn't been cut.

After twenty minutes, he gave up. He'd have to question Peter Petursson again, down at the station. He thanked her for her time, wished her a speedy recovery, and rose to leave.

"I'll check in on you again in the next day or so," he promised. He had already stepped into the corridor when he heard her quiet voice again. He turned. "What's that?"

"It's my birthday," Sarah said. "I just remembered it's my birthday today."

"Well," said Daniel. He looked back at the small figure on the bed, with her bruised face and her eyes shining with unshed tears. "Well. Happy birthday, then."

He shook his head as he left the hospital. That was one confused lady. And she didn't even seem to recognize him.

Chapter Six

ZINA WAS HAPPY. IT WAS AN excellent turnout. At least thirty people filled the café, and she had fed them all. She rested her back against the counter for a moment and surveyed the faces.

Lots of women. All the original Mystery Book Club members were women, but gradually a few husbands and boyfriends had dropped by to "check it out"—and had gotten hooked. Over the past year, the number of men had increased. Zina counted ten males in attendance tonight. Some were strangers—a good sign that her business was growing—but most were regulars from the neighborhood.

Alfred Carriere was here with his young assistant, Gregory, to help push his Midnight Mystery series. He'd also brought his wife, Betty, along. Zina doubted that Betty was interested, but Alfred dragged her everywhere. He rarely let her out of his sight. Betty sat demurely beside him in her usual drab ensemble—a beige pantsuit tonight, with a baby-pink ruffled blouse. Ugh. And that hairdo! Betty's tightly permed brown curls were clustered stiffly on top of her head like a bed of fossilized sea-cabbage. Alfred sat with his chair pushed right up against Betty's and one arm tightly fixed around her shoulder, while he leaned away from her to whisper in Gregory's ear. Zina saw Gregory nod and smile as if Alfred had said something earth-shakingly brilliant. Zina found Gregory irritating. Either he worshiped Alfred, or he was an expert at sucking up to the boss.

Byron Hunt was present—not for the meeting, but because he never went home. Joe Delaney was there, too. It was Joe's turn to lead discussion, but Zina doubted he'd be prepared. The only thing Joe was usually prepared for was fooling around. He rarely took the books seriously. He viewed these Sunday meetings as a social club, not that he'd be the only one. . . . Oh. Hello. That charming graduate student she'd met recently had shown up. What was his name? Mark? When he'd purchased *Bloody Midnight* last week, Zina gave him a copy of the club newsletter and invited him to come tonight. He was standing uneasily near the door, and Zina decided she should make him feel welcome and encourage him to order something.

She crossed the room and, smiling brightly, offered him her hand. "Mark, isn't it?"

"Yes. Hello," he said. "You've got quite a crowd here. I'm wondering where to sit."

"Staying for supper? Or just for the book club?"

"Both. Your special sounds great, and I want to hear the talk." He held up his copy of *Bloody Midnight*. "I enjoyed the book."

Zina noticed an empty chair at Alfred's table. "Come on over here. I'll introduce you to some friends."

He followed her as she wove between the small tables and squeezed past the chairs where Morgan was sitting with Linda Rain, who ran the Hand-Made Harmony shop next door. The place was so crowded that Linda's dog had to sit in the aisle, and Zina tried not to step on her paws.

"Alfred, do you have room for a fourth?"

"Sure," he said. He reached up to shake Mark's hand without removing his left arm from Betty's shoulder. "Alfred Carriere," he said. "Carriere Publishing. My wife Betty, and this is Gregory."

"This is Mark," Zina said. "He's a new neighbor and, I hope, a new member of the club, as well. He loved the book."

"Glad to hear it," Alfred said. "It's one of ours. The first in a dynamite series."

"It's a fascinating story," Mark said, as he sat down. "I don't usually read mysteries, but from a psychological point of view, it's very sophisticated."

"Do you think so?" Morgan put in. She leaned over from the next table. Alfred introduced Morgan and Linda to Mark, and a general conversation began between the two tables.

"From what I know about psychological profiling," Mark went on, "the author is bang on with his description of this type of obsession. Was he a psychiatrist, by any chance?"

"Just a good researcher," Alfred said.

"And a good writer," Linda added. "The killer's obsession is a sort of metonymy, don't you think, for the destructive nature of human desire in general? I mean, the lengths he goes to, the unstoppable—"

Morgan ignored Linda's analysis. "Are you a psychologist or a psychiatrist or something?" she asked Mark.

Mark laughed. "Not yet. I'm still a student."

"Gregory's also a student," Alfred said. "University of Manitoba."

"I'm at the U of M, too." Mark smiled at Gregory. "What are you studying?"

Gregory stopped chewing his sandwich long enough to say, "English," and then wiped his mouth on one of Zina's blue napkins and took another bite.

"Greg works for Alfred," Betty told Mark. It was the first thing she'd said.

"Oh, great job for a student!" Mark said to Gregory. "I'm

just a lab assistant—pays a pittance. So you're in publishing? What do you do? Editing?"

Gregory's mouth was full, so Morgan answered for him. "Greg's a sort of go-fer," she said. "Aren't you, Greg? He's an all-round ribbon-changer and envelope-licker." Gregory had once remarked that Morgan dressed like an oversexed bag lady, and Morgan had never forgiven him.

Gregory shot her a dirty look, and Alfred said, "Gregory's a lot more valuable than that, Morgan."

"So don't you agree that the killer is just an exaggerated negative exemplum of the universal—" Linda was interrupted by Zina, who placed a generous portion of the special, a chickpea curry, in front of Mark and told them all to quiet down because the meeting was about to begin.

Zina rang her little bell to announce to all that it was seven o'clock and Joe Delaney would be speaking momentarily. Then she squeezed past Linda's dog again and found a seat beside Cady Brown, the reporter who was supposed to be covering the book club for a story.

"Great novel," Cady remarked. "Kept me up all night."

"I didn't get through it," Zina confessed. "It was a little too—"

"Oh, you have to read it, Zina!" cried Linda. "It's stunning!"

Zina suppressed a smile. Linda used that adjective about every second book she read, and it crossed her mind to say so. But Zina didn't want to offend her. Linda was probably Zina's number-one customer. She was totally blind, but that didn't stop her from indulging her mystery novel addiction. Most of the best-sellers were available as talking books, and when they weren't, the other club members took turns reading chapters into Linda's well-traveled tape recorder.

"What did you think, Cady?" Linda asked. "Doesn't the novel have a stunning symbolic structure?"

"Don't ask me," Cady said. "I just read to find out who dunnit. What did you make for dessert, Zina? Something smells great."

"Wait and see." Zina laughed. Cady was so slight she seemed almost dangerously frail, but Zina had seen her put away half a chocolate cake in one sitting. Maybe that's why she was taking so long to write the article. She didn't want to give up the free treats.

"Good evening, everyone." Joe Delaney stood at the front of the store and clapped his hands to attract the group's attention. "Good evening, and welcome to any new members. I'm Joe Delaney, your host this Sunday, and I'll start off with my own review of *Bloody Midnight*, just to get the discussion going." He reached into the pocket of his blue jeans and pulled out a much-folded piece of paper.

He actually *is* prepared, Zina thought. As Joe read his review, she was even more impressed. He had obviously put a lot of thought into it. True, he had taken a light, ironic tone, which wasn't really appropriate for such a grim book. But she could tell by the laughs he was getting that his audience appreciated his sense of humor.

After Joe's presentation, the club broke up into small groups and people began to mingle. Zina and Javier went into the kitchen to cut and serve the cherry brownies.

"This *Bloody Midnight* book," Javier began, and then he stopped.

"Yes?" Zina slid an extra-large slice onto a plate for Joe, who deserved it.

"How is it that midnight could be bloody—this is twelve o'clock at night, correct?"

"That's right." Zina wondered how much of Joe's review Javier could follow. "It's sometimes called the witching hour—the time when ghosts and spirits roam the earth."

"But Canadians—they don't believe in that."

Zina laughed. "Well, they do and they don't," she said. "They don't, but they do."

"Ah," said Javier, as if he understood this.

"That's why these books are so popular here," Zina explained. "We're bored, so we love a thrill. People love to be

scared. In our ordinary lives, there's nothing to be afraid of."
She lifted the tray of desserts and carried it through the
swinging doors.

"There is crime," Javier said. "There is car accidents,
sickness. There is death."

But Zina did not hear him.

"WHAT IRRITATED ME," Mark Curtis was saying, "was the
way the detective didn't talk to his fiancée. I mean, if he'd just
said something. . . ."

"Sexist," Morgan interrupted. "He assumed she couldn't
handle it. He assumed he could handle everything himself."

"And she assumed he was sending her the jewelry," Joe
said. "That's sexist, too."

"That's different," Morgan objected. "Don't go blaming
the victim!"

"That diamond ring, as the final warning. Don't you think
that's a feminist message?" Cady asked. "I mean, you know,
marriage as a power struggle?"

"It didn't read like a feminist book to me!" Morgan
exclaimed. "All those poor dead women!"

"But you're missing the irony," Linda countered. "It's the
detective's sexist attitude that's clearly the cause—"

"Treats?" Zina asked, and the argument was abandoned as
everyone helped themselves to brownies.

"How is the article coming along?" Zina asked Cady.

"Fine," Cady said. "All I need now is a kind of angle, you
know."

"An angle?"

"Yeah, you know, something to grab the reader's attention,
a slant. Something to focus on."

"How about this new series?" Zina suggested. "See?" She
pointed at the rack full of *A Chill at Midnight*. "It's being
released one book a week."

Cady picked up a book and began to read the back cover.

"Hey," she cried, "*the dead cold of a Winnipeg winter*! It's set right here in town! Now there's an angle!"

"Set in Winnipeg?" Zina wished she had paid more attention to the publicity materials Alfred had supplied. She peered over Cady's shoulder and read: *Sub-zero suspense stalks the residents of a northern town paralyzed by a freak blizzard.*

"This will definitely strike a chord around here!" Cady exclaimed. "Who is this Walter White? Does he live in Winnipeg?"

"Ask Alfred," Zina advised. "That's Alfred Carriere, over by the phone booth. He's the one who's re-issued the series. He's distributing it locally." Zina turned to Morgan. "Isn't Sarah coming tonight?"

"Yeah, where is Sarah?" Byron asked. "She's usually the first to arrive at the Sunday Night Trash Club."

"Shut up, Byron." Morgan searched the crowd, though she was pretty sure Sarah wasn't there. "I should have called her," she admitted. "Today is her birthday and I forgot all about her."

"If it's her birthday, she's probably doing something special," Zina suggested. "Maybe she has a date."

"Sarah?" said Morgan. "I doubt it."

Chapter Seven

"WE CAN'T HOLD HIM," the staff sergeant told Daniel and Marnie. "Not on what you've got here. The lady sounds like a nut." He leaned back in his chair and put his feet up on his desk. He did not invite the two young officers to sit down.

"She's afraid of him," Marnie argued. "She told Dan he came at her with a letter opener or something."

"There was no blade on him, and no weapon of that description in the house," the sergeant said. "His story is weird, but it's believable. She calls him in the middle of the night, makes some muffled kind of noise, and hangs up. He star 69s her, and she answers, sounding upset. Then her line goes dead—"

"But he broke into her house," Marnie insisted.

"Of course he broke in. Makes sense to me. He's worried about her. Can't reach her by phone, so he drives across town. Bangs on the door. No answer, so he breaks in. Cuts his hand—you saw it. Then he finds her in the basement screaming like a banshee, and he tries to call 911. The phone's dead, so he rushes outside, and *you*"—he pointed at Daniel—"you pull a gun on him."

Daniel said nothing. He'd already been reprimanded severely for drawing his weapon.

"The guy sounds legit," the sergeant finished up. "And her side of the story is completely—" He shook his head. "Maybe she had a nightmare. But we can't arrest a guy every time his ex has a nightmare about him." He chuckled. "I'd be in jail myself."

SARAH SAT GLUMLY in a wheelchair by the glass doors of the St. Boniface Hospital with her rented crutches across her lap, waiting for her cousin. The damage to her leg was not serious, the doctor said. He'd applied a "light cast" that left Sarah's foot free and said she'd be able to walk once her swollen ankle healed. He'd pronounced her strong enough to go home. But she didn't feel strong at all. What was she going to tell Morgan? She recalled Daniel Bradley's skeptical face as she'd tried to explain what happened on Saturday night. His look of doubt—not about her honesty, but her sanity. Was she really losing it? She tried not to think about her grandmother, who was confined to a psychiatric hospital at the age of twenty-five. Since yesterday, she reminded herself, she was twenty-five years old, too.

Sarah wouldn't have called Morgan if she didn't have to. She knew the sight of Sarah in a wheelchair would send Morgan into a fit of excessive fussing. Sarah didn't feel up to Morgan and her emotions today. Normally, Sarah was the voice of reason, counseling Morgan to settle down and think things through. But today, Sarah could barely string two thoughts together. Even her eyesight was bleary; the view from the window seemed distorted. She watched as Morgan's battered brown sedan pulled to a stop and Morgan came dashing out. Morgan's wavy red hair looked to Sarah like a mass of molten copper in the sun, and her face was nothing but a smudge. But Sarah could easily imagine the expression of panicky concern. She resigned herself to the onslaught. Morgan was family. Sarah loved her dearly, and right now Sarah needed her.

Morgan rushed toward her. "Sarah! My God! What on earth happened?"

"It's a long story," Sarah said.

"Tell me! Are you all right? Is it broken? What happened?"

"It's not a bad break. A hairline fracture, the doctor said. But my ankle is sprained. Right now I just want to get out of here. Give me a hand, will you?"

Morgan helped her cousin to stand and lurch out the doors into the hot sunshine. The heat was intense. Summer had arrived, very suddenly, during Sarah's brief hospital stay.

"Wait here," Morgan ordered, as if Sarah could do anything else. "I'll bring the car around." She left Sarah standing on the sidewalk, balanced precariously on her new crutches. Sarah sighed. She wasn't sure what had happened to her, or what might happen next, but she knew she was glad to be out of the hospital. A cool breeze ran through her hair and lifted her spirits slightly. Yes—it was good to be outside and to be free.

ACROSS TOWN, PETER Petursson was also free. He stood on Broadway, waiting for a cab, examining his bandaged hand and flexing his wrist, trying to keep it from stiffening up. The rush-hour traffic annoyed him. Even the sunshine annoyed him. He was hungry, tired, and most of all furious. He'd spent all of Sunday and most of today in the lock-up, waiting for his mother to get back from the lake and arrange for bail. He hadn't dared call Cady. But as it turned out, he didn't need bail. After all that fuss, they decided to drop the charges. Idiots!

He'd need to make up a good excuse to explain to Cady why he stood her up yesterday. He'd promised to pick her up yesterday at noon to take her on a riverboat cruise. What excuse could he invent—wait—she was likely to find out anyway. It was impossible to keep anything secret in this town. Maybe he'd better tell her himself, before she heard it from someone else.

He tried not to think about the way that female cop had glared at him. With disgust. As if he weren't even human. And that Daniel Bradley character! What a madman! You'd think he was personally involved, the way he acted. Once again, Peter felt the inner trembling that had gripped him when he saw Bradley's gun pointed at him. He could be dead right now, thanks to that trigger-happy maniac. That's the cops for you—shoot first, ask questions later.

What in the world kind of tale had Sarah told them? He imagined her embellishing it with all sorts of evil details. Recounting all his faults. She probably got completely carried away, thrilled to be talking to the cops—like a victim in one of her beloved detective novels! Peter was sorry Sarah seemed so unbalanced, but he had to admit that her nervous break-down—or whatever it was—had probably helped him out this time. Evidently, her weird behavior had swayed the cops in his favor, because, finally, they'd believed his entire story—even the lies.

SARAH'S HOUSE LOOKED different to her, and it wasn't just the plywood nailed over the broken living-room window. The barn-shaped roof seemed to loom above the upper gables, casting warped shadows across the blank, shuttered windows that stared blindly down at her. Below, the high stone foundation seemed cold and formidable, the wooden steps to the front porch nearly unscalable. She leaned on Morgan as she drew herself up the steps and crossed the porch to the front door. Even the familiar scrape of her key in the lock sounded sinister, alien. She limped awkwardly down the polished wooden hall, casting a wary glance up the front staircase where she had first heard the intruder. Morgan followed, solicitous and falsely cheerful, chattering about dinner and a nice cold drink.

Sarah paused at the doorway to the living room and studied every detail, as if taking inventory. The smell of dead ashes from the stone fireplace permeated the room. And the slipcover of the overstuffed chair where she had been reading was askew, the rose-patterned pillows scattered on the floor. Otherwise, all was in order. The room had changed very little since Saturday. In fact, the house had changed very little since her grandparents' day. For years it had been rented as a furnished home, so her grandparents' things had remained virtually undisturbed. When Sarah and Peter first moved in, Sarah painted the walls a cool forest green, to bring out the rich, warm colors of the oak trim and the walnut furniture. She hung modern white curtains and replaced the worn throw rugs with a deep red wall-to-wall carpet. But she kept everything else the same. Her grandfather's books still filled the shelves, and the row of his stone animal sculptures still graced the mantel, the black raven eyeing his domain with his usual air of propriety. But now—Sarah cocked her head slightly, trying to identify the difference. It was—cold in here, somehow. Uncomfortable.

"I'll open a window," Morgan offered. "We'll get you settled on the sofa and I'll clean out the fireplace later."

"You don't have to—"

"Yes I do. You sit. I'll get us a drink."

Morgan took charge. She plied Sarah with pillows, a sandwich, and a glass of iced tea. She opened the envelope containing the two painkillers the doctor had given Sarah to take home, and she tapped them both into Sarah's palm. She used her cellphone to arrange for repairs to Sarah's telephone. She found a bottle of white wine in the fridge, poured herself a brimming glass, and lit a cigarette. Then she insisted on hearing the whole story.

Sarah couldn't bring herself to speak of the bizarre details—the ladder, the laundry chute, the letter opener—

even if she *could* remember them coherently. She was feeling even more thick-headed than before. Thick-headed and terribly drowsy.

"I fell," she said. "Down the stairs."

"But how? In the house?"

"Yes. Morgan? I don't think I can stay awake."

"Well, you rest then. We'll talk tomorrow. I'm staying here tonight," Morgan said. "I'll be staying for a few days. No arguments. I'm not leaving you."

Sarah didn't protest. "It *would* be just like Peter to try to scare me," she said sleepily.

"Shhhh," Morgan said. She tucked a pillow under Sarah's head and covered her with a quilt. "Peter's not here."

"I don't know why he cut the phone line," Sarah mumbled. "That's going too far, even for him."

"No one cut the phone line, honey. It's just a downed wire or something."

"Maybe," said Sarah.

"I'll be right upstairs in the guestroom." Morgan turned out the light. "Just call if you need anything."

"Good night," Sarah said. She really was exhausted. She closed her eyes and prepared to drift off. But as she listened to Morgan's ascending footsteps, she felt a chill run through her body and she was suddenly afraid.

"Morgan!"

Morgan raced back down. "What is it?"

"Could you leave on a light? In the hall?"

"Sure." Morgan switched a light on.

"And maybe that lamp? In here?"

"Okay." Morgan turned it on. She looked down at Sarah and smiled. "Don't worry. You're going to be fine." She kissed her cousin and climbed back upstairs, where she read *A Chill at Midnight* until she fell into a deep sleep, oblivious to the creaking floorboards and rattling shutters that haunted Sarah's dreams throughout the night.

NEXT DOOR, MARK Curtis was finding it difficult to concentrate on his psychology paper. Just before midnight, Mark heard a vehicle pull up and saw the headlights reflected on his bedroom wall. The motor shut off, and the lights went out. He waited for the slam of a car door, but heard nothing. After a few minutes of silence, Mark became curious. He snapped off his lamp, walked to the window, and peered out from behind the curtains. After what happened Saturday night, he was cautious. He didn't want to be caught up in any more drama.

As his eyes adjusted to the night, he could make out a man sitting in a darkened black Jetta. He recognized the car, and he recognized the man's profile. It was that cop—the same one who pulled his gun on Saturday night. Obviously, he was keeping an eye on Sarah's house. But why? Mark had seen them arrest the husband. They took him away in handcuffs. So why would they still be watching the house?

He returned to his desk, turned the lamp back on, and tried to rewrite the conclusion to his essay. But he couldn't focus. Every few minutes, he returned to the window. This cop was persistent. He was still sitting there at three o'clock when Mark finally gave up and went to sleep.

IN THE MORNING, Sarah woke to the sounds of Morgan bustling in the kitchen, brewing coffee and making pancakes. She stumbled to the bathroom and managed to shower, using a garbage bag to protect her cast, as the nurse had instructed. The ordeal was clumsy and tiresome, but the shower left her refreshed. She was smiling as she sat down to breakfast.

"Good morning," said Morgan. "You're looking better."

"I'm feeling better," Sarah agreed. "I think those painkillers were clouding my head."

"I'll fill that prescription for you this afternoon," Morgan said. "I have to go in to the shop today. I hate to leave you alone, but the spring fashions have to come off the racks. Will you be okay by yourself?"

"Of course. I'm really much better—and don't bother with the prescription, okay? Those pills made me feel as though my brain was stuffed with cotton. Frankly, I'd rather have the pain."

After Morgan left, with a reminder to call if Sarah needed anything, Sarah lay down on the couch under the quilt and slept for two hours. When she woke, she felt even better. The sharp edges had returned to the room around her, and to her mind. She felt like herself again. She was stiff and sore, but her head was perfectly clear. She vowed to stick to aspirin from now on. She took two with a glass of lemonade and hobbled out to the porch to collect the daily newspaper.

The sun was shining brightly, and Sarah realized she didn't want to go back inside alone to brood all day. She studied the three wide steps down to the sidewalk. She had made it up these steps yesterday with Morgan's help, but going down seemed harder, more awkward. She angled herself sideways and grasped the railing with her right hand. Her right crutch slid out from under her arm and landed in the flower bed below. Damn. Sarah maneuvered her left crutch onto the second step. Slowly, she lowered her right leg, then swung her left leg, in its rigid plaster, down after her. She teetered for a second, then caught her balance. There. She had made it. Now two more steps.

"Hello there!"

She looked up to see a tanned, rugged face with dark curly hair, peering over the hedge next door. Dr. Allard's new tenant, a young man Sarah's age.

"You look like you need a hand." He quickly skirted the hedge and jogged across the yard. Before she could protest, he was standing beside her, extending a muscular arm for her to lean on.

"I want to try this myself," Sarah told him.

"Well, okay. But I'm right here. I'll spot you."

Carefully, she made her way down and insisted on retrieving her crutch without his help. Once she was steady again, safe on flat ground, she smiled and extended her hand. "You're my new neighbor."

"Mark Curtis," he said. He shook her hand warmly. "You're Sarah, right?"

"Sarah Petursson."

They stood foolishly smiling at each other, holding hands. Sarah felt an immediate connection to Mark, as she looked into his dark brown eyes. There was concern there, she thought, and something else. Curiosity.

Oh.

Sarah colored, realizing that Mark must have been the neighbor who boarded up her broken window. He must have heard the commotion on Saturday night. Yes. She could tell. Otherwise, he would have mentioned her injury, asked questions. She felt an apology was due. Reluctantly, she removed her hand from his.

"You fixed my window, didn't you?"

He nodded.

"I'm sorry about the other night. It was—"

He held up a hand to silence her. "Hey—none of my business." He smiled. "I'm just glad you're okay."

"Yes, well. Sort of." She laughed. "I think I'll try to walk a bit." She headed toward the sidewalk. "Thanks for your help."

"No problem. You want me to come with you?"

"No. Thanks. I'm just going up and down the block." She left him standing in her yard and forged ahead. She wanted to get some exercise, keep limber, and stay out of the house.

Sarah kept her eyes on the ground, watching for cracks in the cement. At some point during the weekend, the neighborhood children had decorated the sidewalk with colored chalk. Messages were scrawled across driveways: *Chelsea loves Jason. Alanna is the best!!!!* Pink and yellow hopscotch games, their large crooked numbers barely contained in their little squares, covered half the block. The cramped front gardens were carefully tended and filled with shrubs, mostly bleeding hearts and azaleas. Here in Wolseley, the tall houses were built so closely together that their upper eaves overlapped, and the huge American elms on either side of the street had spread so wide that their branches touched each other high above the middle of the road. Sunlight was at a premium, and every available patch of sunny ground was crowded with plantings. Avid gardeners, frustrated with their own shady yards, would plant anywhere they could. They dug up the wide grass boulevards between the sidewalk and the road, and seeded them with marigolds and oregano and sometimes even tomatoes, though that was risky—too tempting for passersby. Tulips and daffodils bloomed around the bus stop, and a morning-glory vine was beginning its long climb up the bus stop sign. Along the curb Sarah recognized the green shoots of peonies, shasta daisies, and day lilies. Yes, summer was coming to Winnipeg. Summer, and the Manitoba Marathon, which Sarah wouldn't be running. Her arms ached, but she pressed on, determined to make it to Westminster Avenue.

She surprised herself by walking all the way to Zina's Café, where she endured the sympathies of Zina and her customers for a few minutes. Thanks to Morgan, they had heard all about her "fall down the stairs," and she was grateful she didn't have to explain. She stopped just long enough to pick up a copy of *A Chill at Midnight*. She was going to need something to read in the long, empty days ahead.

Chapter Eight

PETER PETURSSON WRAPPED HIS ARMS around the warm, naked body of Cady Brown and buried his face in her neck. "I missed you so much," he whispered. She was so warm— and so sweet. When he'd told her the whole story, she had instantly taken his side. She was horrified by his false arrest and ready to write an exposé of the police bungling for the newspaper. Luckily, he had talked her out of that plan. The less said about the whole affair the better, as far as he was concerned. He was just happy she believed him.

"Kiss me again," he said, and she did. He moved his hands over her tiny back and pressed her breasts close against his chest. "I'm so sorry about standing you up on Sunday," he whispered. "I'll make it up to you."

"You couldn't help it, honey," she said. "It's your ex-wife. She's vindictive. Do you think she's setting you up?"

He raised himself on one elbow and looked down at her, surprised. "For what?"

"For the divorce case. Alimony. Maybe she's heard about your recording contract, and she wants a take."

Peter highly doubted this possibility, since there was no recording contract. The contract was a figment of his imagination, inspired to life a few weeks ago by too much beer and a keen desire to get Cady Brown into bed.

"Maybe," he said carefully. He sat up, suddenly unwilling to be close to her, and walked naked across the thick plush carpet of her bedroom floor toward the kitchen. "Should I open the champagne?"

"That's what they do, you know," Cady called.

"What? Who?" He was searching through her shelves for a couple of champagne flutes.

"Women. In a divorce. They claim abuse, just to squeeze more money out of their ex-husbands. They do it all the time. I did a story on it last year. Maybe Sarah is setting you up for that."

"Forget about Sarah," he said. He returned to the bedroom and placed the glasses on the night stand. Then he stood above her and admired the lithe curves of her white little body on the flowered satin sheets. He popped the cork, so that the cold spray sizzled across her skin.

She shrieked. Then smiled up at him. "Pour me a glass," she said. "And I'll let you make it up to me."

He poured, and they toasted. "To making up," he said. "Seriously, I really am sorry, baby. What did you think on Sunday when I didn't show up?"

"Oh, honey," she murmured, as she drew him down on the bed. "I was so worried about you." But she was lying. On Sunday afternoon, she'd been so engrossed in *Bloody Midnight* that she'd completely forgotten about her date with Peter.

BETTY CARRIERE WATCHED her sister suspiciously across the glasses of beer that littered the terry-cloth–covered table of the dark Big Sky Tavern. As usual, Anna looked as if her

wardrobe had been selected by a class of mischievous kindergarten children. Her short brown hair was uncombed and
decorated with plastic barrettes in four different colors. Her
tight yellow T-shirt bore the motto of the defunct Winnipeg
Jets. Tattered denim cut-offs rode high on the thighs of her
yellow tights, which disappeared far below into white leather
disco boots. Betty knew they were disco boots because she'd
seen them in the window of Morgan's clothing store with a
sign on them saying "disco boots."

Anna was waving with both arms at the waiter, ordering
more beer. She showed no signs of leaving to meet with her
landlord.

"I thought this was urgent," Betty said. "I thought he was
going to evict you if you didn't pay him by noon."

"Oh, he'll wait," Anna said. "He likes me." She paid for
the beer from the thick roll of bills Betty had just given her
and told the waiter to keep the change. "Just one more for
the road." Anna grinned at her sister, but received only a dis-
approving frown in return. "Aw, Betty, come on, I gotta
live!"

"We have to live, too. I took that money out of Alfred's
petty cash in the office, and—"

"Really?" Anna clinked her glass against Betty's in a toast.
"Tell Alfred thanks for me."

"He doesn't know," Betty said. "For goodness' sakes, he
doesn't know about it. If he did, he'd blow his top."

Anna opened her eyes wide. "You mean you pinched it?"

"I borrowed it."

"Right." Anna's eyes scanned the pub, darting from the
pool players to the shuffleboard.

"And I'll have to pay it back," Betty said. "It's Alfred's
money, and he's—"

"He's stingy."

"He is very generous! He gives me a very generous
allowance, and he likes to see that I spend it well. We have an
agreement." Betty sniffed and pushed the glass of beer away

from her. "It's called marriage," she added. Then she changed her mind and took a drink.

"I don't know why you're so loyal to that guy. I told you he's no good. My old man said—"

"And I told you I don't want to hear it again. Just because you've never met a faithful man doesn't mean they don't exist, Anna."

Anna shrugged. "Suit yourself, then. Believe what you wanna believe. But I'm telling you, my old man saw your old man with some redhead in that fancy Greek restaurant on Osborne Street, the night it opened—just last month."

"That's hardly a reliable source," Betty said.

"Listen, I gotta go." Anna stood up, staggering as she pushed her arms through the sleeves of her threadbare jean jacket. "Thanks for the money. You know what? Maybe one of these days I should tell old Alfred the true facts about you, Betty."

"No! Anna! You know he'd never accept it. You know he'd leave me—"

"Put you out of your misery," Anna said.

"Anna! No!" Betty reached for her sister's arm, but Anna pulled away. All Betty could do was watch her as she walked away, swinging her hips provocatively for every loser in the place to see.

SARAH LOOKED THROUGH the peephole before she opened the door, because Daniel Bradley had been by to tell her that Peter was out of jail. She was relieved to see it was only Linda Rain.

"Linda! What a nice surprise! Thank you." Sarah took the bouquet of daffodils and opened the door wide for Linda and her dog to enter. "Hi, Buttercup," she said. The retriever wagged her tail expectantly, but Sarah knew she shouldn't pat Buttercup while she was working. "Come on in."

She led the way into the kitchen and filled an empty

peanut-butter jar for the flowers. Every vase she owned was already full of flowers from neighbors and clients and mystery-club members. Even her cousin Sam had sent roses from Vancouver, with a card reading, "Happy Birthday, Get well soon." Two for the price of one.

"Would you like a drink?" Sarah asked Linda.

"Please don't bother. I just stopped by for a minute, just to see how you are."

"I'm fine." Sarah was getting tired of repeating this phrase. "I have to wear an awful cast on my leg for a few weeks, but I'm getting used to it. I hobbled all the way to Zina's yesterday on my crutches."

"Good for you! Did you pick up the new book?"

"Yes. But I haven't started it yet." Sarah noticed that Linda had her little tape recorder strapped to her wrist. "Is that what you're listening to today?"

"No, unfortunately. I just picked up my recorder from Cady Brown, but the tape's still empty. I was so disappointed! Cady promised to have it read by today, but she didn't get it done. Too busy."

"Cady is busy?" Sarah laughed. Zina had recently been complaining about Cady's procrastination and laziness.

"She's chasing some big story, apparently. Some big feature. 'Investigative reporting,' she called it."

"Did she start reading it, at least?"

"Not a word. And I'm supposed to give the review on Sunday! And it's supposed to be a great book! Joe Delaney told me it's even scarier than *Bloody Midnight*."

"That's hard to believe."

"He said the climax is even more shocking. And there's a real surprise twist. Don't you love his twists? Didn't you love it in *Bloody Midnight* when she saw the ladder out the window?"

"The ladder!"

"Yeah. When he climbs up a ladder at the end of the book, gets in through the window while the hero's girlfriend is reading. Remember?"

"I—I never finished it." Sarah felt dizzy. "I don't think I got to that part."

"It's a great ending," Linda continued. "He has the letter opener in his teeth, and he's climbing—"

"Stop it!" Sarah cried out. "Stop!"

Buttercup growled.

"Oh—sorry." Linda giggled, a little nervously. "Down, girl," she whispered to Buttercup. "It's all right. Down, now."

"I still have the book," Sarah said, slowly. "Up—upstairs." She forced herself to sound calm. She was glad Linda couldn't see her face. "Maybe I should read the end for myself."

"Sorry, I have a bad habit of giving away—"

"Don't worry about it," Sarah said quickly. "I'm just—I'm a little on edge these days. Sorry."

"Maybe we should go," Linda said. "I guess you need to rest."

Sarah walked Linda to the door, feeling guilty. After all, none of this was Linda's fault. "Say, Linda, why don't you leave the recorder with me? I can read *A Chill at Midnight* on tape."

"Oh, Sarah, I don't want to—"

"No, really. I'd love to. Besides—" She faked a laugh. "I'm not going anywhere. I've got nothing but time on my hands."

"Well, thanks, then." Linda handed the recorder over. "I hate to fall behind in my reading."

Sarah barely made it back to the living room before her legs, or leg, gave way. She sank into the sofa, her hands shaking. He climbed up a ladder! While she was reading! It was too much. Was Linda making it up? But how could Linda know what had happened? Sarah thought of *Bloody Midnight* lying crumpled on the floor of her linen closet. Three stories above her. Out of reach.

BETTY TORE A few leaves off the mint plant in her yard and stuffed them into her mouth before she entered the house, chewing as fast as she could. She didn't want Alfred to smell beer on her breath at one in the afternoon.

She was dismayed to find two hundred cardboard cartons of books stacked on her kitchen floor, with no space to walk except for a crooked, narrow pathway leading from the back door through into the dining room. She followed it, cursing softly. She couldn't even see the stove. How was she going to make dinner? It was bad enough that the basement had become a warehouse since Alfred started distributing American paperbacks. But now that he'd bought the rights to these bloody mystery novels, the whole house was overrun with books.

She headed upstairs to Alfred's office, trying to work up her nerve to ask him to clear out her kitchen. If his operation was getting this big, she'd suggest, he should rent storage space somewhere. She was just about to knock on his door when she heard a strange voice from within his office. An angry voice. A woman's voice. She pressed her ear against the door and listened.

"I can't wait any longer," a woman was saying desperately. "If you can't get it together by the weekend—"

Betty could not make out Alfred's answer, but whatever it was, it seemed to calm the woman down. They spoke in quiet tones for a minute, then Betty heard the scraping of chairs and footsteps coming toward the door. She crept quickly down to the front hall and fixed an unsuspecting smile on her face.

"We'll talk this evening, then," Alfred said. A petite blonde woman, wiry as a ballet dancer, was clutching his arm as they came downstairs. "And I'll tell you—Oh. Betty! I didn't hear you come in. You're home early."

"My sister had a headache," Betty explained. "Poor Anna. She went home straight after lunch."

"This is my wife Betty," Alfred said. "Betty, this is Cady Brown. She's doing a story on Zina's Mystery Club and the new Midnight series."

"Oh, you're the reporter," Betty said coolly. "I think I saw you at Zina's the other night."

"Yes. I'm hoping your husband will give me a scoop." She smiled sweetly at Alfred.

I'll give you a scoop, Betty thought.

"I have to run now and check out some other leads." Cady let herself out the front door. "Bye-bye. So nice to meet you!"

"Wait!" Alfred called. "What other leads?" But Cady closed the door behind her without answering. He turned to Betty and smiled absently. "So, you had lunch with your sister? Where did you go?"

"Oh, to the—" Betty couldn't admit to entering the sleazy Big Sky Tavern. But she had forgotten to prepare a lie. Then she had an idea. "That new Greek restaurant on Osborne Street," she said. "What's the name of that place again?" She watched Alfred's reaction carefully, but he merely shrugged.

He pointed at her mouth. "Well, you got something stuck in your teeth," he said. "Spinach or something."

SARAH STARED AGAIN at page 301 of the book and again she felt the tingle of fear throughout her body.

When Morgan had returned from work, she'd wanted to rush right out again for groceries, but Sarah had asked her to do a favor first. "Would you mind fetching my copy of *Bloody Midnight* for me? I dropped it on the floor in the linen closet Saturday night."

"No problem. I'll run up for it now."

Sarah had tried not to dwell on the sound of Morgan's footsteps echoing through the house or on the sound of the whoosh she heard from behind the wall as Morgan sent the rest of the laundry tumbling down the chute.

As soon as Morgan left, Sarah had found the chapter where she'd left off reading and skimmed at top speed through to the end.

Linda was telling the truth. The murderer in the novel gained entrance to the house of the hero's girlfriend by propping a ladder against a tree and stealthily climbing up. To the bathroom window! And his unsuspecting victim had been too absorbed in reading her book to hear him.

But there was one major difference. In the novel, the villain had stabbed the woman to death.

Chapter Nine

GREGORY RESTALL WASN'T SURE whether he should be flattered or suspicious, but he decided he might as well enjoy himself. This little reporter was cute, and she was buying, so he pretended to listen earnestly as he thrust his steak knife into the sirloin tip.

Cady was too small to lean across the massive wooden table, but she stretched out her hand and managed to touch Gregory's wrist. As the waiter passed by, he smiled indulgently at this apparent show of affection, which wasn't unusual in the darkened steak house at six o'clock in the evening. It was one of the most popular romantic spots in the city. Gregory moved his hand away and reached for a roll from the bread basket. Cady sighed and continued her appeal. "Fran Dreisler from the *Washington Post* said the same thing. The editor of the *L.A. Times*, too. If I can get an interview with Walter White, they'll print it."

Gregory ladled sour cream onto his baked potato and

nodded gravely. He was pretty sure he knew where this was leading, and he wanted to draw it out as long as he could.

"It's the chance of a lifetime," she continued. "Six major dailies and maybe—if the books really take off as Alfred says they will—I can do a longer feature for, say, *People* or maybe *Time*." She paused, waiting for a reaction, but Gregory was concentrating on his food. "I'll make a lot of money," she said.

Gregory looked up.

"But I have to get it by the weekend," she rushed on. "If I miss the deadline, who knows what'll happen? Someone else will snag him first. I'll lose my exclusive, and the interview won't be worth peanuts."

Gregory swallowed. "I told you," he said. "I don't know where he is. I never met the guy. When Alfred gets back from Toronto—"

"When Alfred gets back from Toronto it'll be too late. He promised to introduce me to Walter White tonight, and then he got called away...." Cady arranged her lips in a pout.

Gregory smiled sympathetically. He knew she was lying. Alfred had promised no such thing, or if he had, he'd been leading her on. Alfred had told Gregory very specifically that he was not to answer any questions concerning the whereabouts of Mr. White. Mr. White valued his privacy highly, and Alfred had guaranteed him there would be absolutely no publicity. In fact, Gregory knew, Alfred was planning to use the author's reclusive nature as a gimmick later in his advertising campaign. It would add extra mystique to the Midnight books.

"I'm sorry," he told her. "I don't have any information on Walter White."

"But there must be contracts," Cady said. "There must be papers with his address on them, correspondence, stuff like that—maybe a photograph?"

"That'd all be in Alfred's business files, up in his private office on the third floor. I don't work up there. I don't have access to the business end of things. I don't deal with the published authors—just the rejects."

"But you want to learn the business, don't you? Alfred tells me you're very bright. Shouldn't he be letting you in on the real business of the company? Why, does he think just because you're only a student you can't deal with real authors? Doesn't he trust you?"

"He trusts me," Gregory said quickly. "He gave me a key to his private office before he left town—in case of emergency."

"This is an emergency," Cady said. "If I don't get hold of White—"

"I wouldn't know where to start looking," Gregory protested.

"Couldn't you *try*, though?" she pleaded. "Couldn't you look through the files?"

"Wait." Gregory held up both hands. "Just stop for a minute, will you? Let me think."

"I'd make it worth your while."

"Let me think," he said.

WHEN MORGAN RETURNED from the supermarket, Sarah was sitting perfectly still on the couch with *Bloody Midnight* in her lap open to its final page.

"This book," she said to Morgan.

"Isn't it great?" Morgan carried the groceries past the living room into the kitchen and put them away. She picked up the telephone, discovered it still wasn't working, and called the phone company on her cell to give them a piece of her mind. Then she popped two frozen dinners into the oven and grabbed a bottle of wine and two glasses.

When she returned to the living room, Sarah was still motionless with the book open before her.

"Did it freak you out?" Morgan asked. "It nearly did me in." She poured herself a glass of wine. "Want some? It'll settle your nerves."

"Morgan," Sarah said slowly. "This book—the plot—"

"What?" Morgan looked more carefully at her cousin. "For God's sake, what's wrong?"

Sarah told her.

"ARE YOU SURE you didn't fall asleep reading? It wasn't a nightmare caused by the book? I mean, you used to walk in your sleep, and maybe—"

"I told you, I never finished the book! He broke in before I was finished reading it."

"Who, Sarah? Who could possibly have broken in?"

"There was someone in here. I swear it! I don't know who it was. But he was here. He was literally pounding up the back stairs. Chasing after me!"

"But you didn't see anyone?"

"I *heard* someone."

"Are you sure you—"

Sarah grabbed Morgan's hand. "I did!"

"Okay. Okay." Morgan fell silent. She drained her glass and went to the kitchen, returning with a second bottle. Sarah shook her head, refusing. Morgan poured herself another large dose.

"He must have been watching me for days," Sarah said. "Think of it! Watching me through the window. Waiting till I started reading that very book. And—oh my God—when the light went out!"

"The light went out?"

"Yes, the bulb in my lamp."

"You never mentioned that."

"It didn't seem important. But now that I've read the end of the book, it makes sense. He was trying to recreate the power blackout in the book. He probably came in earlier and put an old bulb in there."

Morgan sighed as if her heart were breaking. "Sarah, honey, don't you think that's a bit paranoid?"

Sarah shook her head vehemently. "No, I don't," she said.

"I felt all night as if someone was watching me. It's almost like—"

"It's almost like you fell asleep reading, Sarah." Morgan's tone was gentle. Too gentle. Almost sad. "Don't you see? You wove the elements of the plot into your dream. You must have been so stressed out that you had a nightmare. You walked in your sleep. You must have left the trap door open and—I hate to think what might have happened. Thank God Peter came when he did." Morgan lit another cigarette, although her previous one was still burning in the ashtray. "What did you say Peter was holding when you saw him?"

"Well, it *looked* like a letter opener, a shiny blade of some— but that's the thing, I'm not *sure*—I thought—I don't know."

The cousins sat in silence for a while. Morgan sipped her wine between drags of her cigarette. Sarah stared at the ceiling. She sighed. If even Morgan, the most gullible person she knew, wouldn't believe her, then no one would believe her.

"Morgan—don't tell anyone what I said, okay?"

"Don't worry. I won't say a word."

"Not even to Zina?"

Morgan hesitated for a second. "Not even to Zina," she promised. "I already told her you fell down the stairs. We'll stick with that. But listen, I'm just going to say this once. I think you're mistaken. You mixed up the events in the book with your own dream, and I don't think there was anyone in the house at all, except Peter. You were sleepwalking and you fell." Morgan leaned over and hugged her. "You were in shock when Peter got here," she said. "You were lying there with a broken leg. You were probably delirious."

Sarah tried to smile. "I *did* have some pretty weird dreams," she admitted. But she didn't tell Morgan about them. For some reason, she didn't want to share that dream of the forest and the reading woman who looked so much like herself. The dream tugged at her from some private place deep within, and she wanted to be alone to revisit it later. Much later.

Chapter Ten

ANNA'S HINTS ABOUT ALFRED'S INFIDELITY were the least of Betty's worries. Anna understood nothing of normal relationships, Betty thought. Their father had cheated continually on their mother, and although Betty had broken the cycle in her own life, Anna was still inside it. Betty pushed the squeeze mop hard across the parquet floor of her vestibule. Squeak, squeak. She pictured her sister as a little hamster going round and round inside an exercise wheel. Every man or woman Anna had ever been involved with had betrayed her in some way. And the pattern would continue forever, Betty thought, as long as Anna kept her mind clouded with booze.

But Betty was different. She had quit drinking. Well, almost. And she and Alfred were happily married. At least they were faithful. Of course, when Betty first met Alfred up at the lake, he had still been married to his second wife—Daniel Bradley's mother. But Betty didn't count that. That was more than ten years ago.

She wrung out the mop and carried the pail outside to dash the rinse water on the patio. Although the day was surprisingly cool, a red Sunbeam convertible sat parked at the curb with its top down as if ready for a summer joyride. Betty admired the car for a minute, wondering who it belonged to. Then she walked around the back of the house, to avoid stepping on her newly washed floor, and entered the kitchen.

She threaded through the stacks of boxed books to the broom closet and put away her cleaning supplies. Alfred was in Toronto for some publishing meeting and wouldn't be back until Sunday. Gregory was working upstairs, typesetting a new cookbook, and Betty had the rest of the house to herself. She lugged the vacuum into the living room and was about to turn it on when the telephone rang. She moved through the labyrinth in the kitchen as fast as she could, but by the time she picked up, Gregory had already answered the upstairs extension. Betty was about to hang up when she heard the name "Cady Brown." She covered her mouth with her hand and listened.

"How the hell did she get Quinn's phone number?" Betty recognized her husband's voice. What was he talking about? Why was Cady Brown calling Alfred in Toronto?

"I have no idea," Gregory said. "I certainly didn't tell her you were staying with Quinn."

"Well, don't tell her anything," Alfred said.

Betty's anxiety eased a bit as she listened to the rest of the conversation. It was only business. Cady was trying to contact Walter White, and Alfred was telling Gregory to stall her until he returned.

"Who's there? Is someone there in the office with you?" Alfred asked.

"No. I'm here by myself."

"I can hear someone."

Betty moved the receiver away from her mouth.

"Anyway, Alfred," Gregory said. "I've been looking for

Walter White's address. Some letters have come for him. Fan mail, I guess. I should forward it to him. Where does he live?"

"His agent's listed in my address book," Alfred said. "I'll take care of it when I get back."

"If you could tell me where your book is—"

"It can wait," Alfred said.

Betty knew where the address book was, but she could hardly interrupt now and confess she'd been eavesdropping. She hung up as softly as she could and returned to her vacuum.

WHEN THE TELEPHONE repairman arrived, he spent a mere ten minutes outside Sarah's house before returning to test the phone and announce that it was working.

"What was wrong with it?" Morgan asked.

"Broken."

"Broken?" Sarah asked. "Or cut?"

He shrugged. He was busy repacking bolts and wires into an old metal tool box.

"Did it look as though it had been cut?" Morgan asked.

"Coulda been."

"Didn't you look at the edges?" Sarah asked. "Was it cut with something sharp? A blade, maybe?"

The repairman stood up and began scribbling something on a work order.

"Or shears?" Sarah persisted. "Pinking shears?"

He calmly tucked his pencil and notebook in his overalls pocket. He raised the battered tool box and held it up for their inspection. "What does this look like to you?" he asked. "An FBI lab?"

He left.

THE ONLY ROOM of Cady Brown's small apartment that was not prettily furnished was her study. The paint was the same monotonous landlord white that it had been when she moved in five years ago, except that it was a shade grubbier. No plants or ornaments of any kind decorated the dusty surfaces. The drab blinds served only to shut out the sunlight, and plain, functional bookshelves lined the walls. A hazardous web of wires criss-crossed the floor, connecting two televisions, two VCRs, two telephones, and two computer terminals. She was busy at one of these terminals now, searching out information on the Internet.

A general search for the Midnight books had revealed what she already knew. The first two books in the series were receiving plenty of media attention and rave reviews, but so far not a word had been written about the author, Walter White. She had already searched the major North American library holdings and found seventeen different authors named Walter White with a wide variety of different birthdates. None of them sounded promising.

But Cady had finally convinced Gregory to snoop through Alfred's files, and now he'd come through with a lead—the name of Walter White's agent. So she was hot on the trail again. According to Gregory, White was represented by a Bill Wesley of the Pen and Ink literary agency, but Cady quickly discovered that Pen and Ink was out of business. There was no Bill Wesley listed on staff at any of the other Canadian agencies she had looked up. He might work for an American firm, but it would be foolish to search through the endless list of American agencies when she had a much more promising clue to follow up. She had only one clue about Bill Wesley, besides his distressingly common name. He taught at the University of Manitoba, right here at home. That was all Gregory had found out so far, but with a little luck, it might be enough.

She accessed the University of Manitoba website and clicked on "Faculty." No Bill Wesley. She had a sudden inspiration and typed in "Walter White," but there was no Walter White, either. She couldn't decide which department Wesley might be in. If he was a literary agent, he was probably in English. But if he was in English, wouldn't Gregory know him? Oh well, it was a big university, and Gregory wasn't exactly the brightest guy she'd ever met. She looked up the number for the chair of the department and dialed it.

Professor Dawson was busy and sounded distracted, but he said he vaguely remembered Wesley, who was long retired. Wesley was no longer in Winnipeg, as far as he knew. He gave her Wesley's last-known mailing address and wished her luck. Cady looked at the address, then looked out the window. Too late to drive out there tonight. But she could make an early start tomorrow. If only it would warm up, she could drive all the way there with the top down on the Sunbeam.

NOW THAT HER telephone was working, Sarah dialed in her code to retrieve the messages in her voice mailbox. Lots of birthday greetings. A frantic client with a late tax return, begging for help. And three progressively more concerned messages from Mr. Knight.

"Oh, no," she said out loud. "I forgot about Mr. Knight!"

"Who's Mr. Knight?" Morgan asked.

"My lawyer. In Kenora. I had an appointment with him for Monday. It totally slipped my mind."

"Mr. Knight? The guy who handled your mum's estate? He's still your lawyer?"

"I never see him any more, but he still manages the trust." Sarah's mother had left a small monthly income, barely enough to cover the gas bill.

"Oh, yeah," said Morgan. "The trust-fund guy. I remember him—with the little mustache! He must be 101 years old!"

Sarah laughed. "Not quite. But he's—"

"Wait! He wanted to see you Monday? You'd better call him right away."

"He made the appointment months ago, Morgan. I don't think a few days is going to matter."

"But *Monday*, Sarah! Monday was the first working day after your twenty-fifth birthday!"

"So?"

"It can't be coincidence. There must be something in the will—Aunt Carolyn must have held something back until you turned twenty-five. Like Grampa did with the house and the island, waiting till you turned eighteen."

"I never thought of that," Sarah said slowly.

"Let's call him and reschedule. You've got to go as soon as possible."

"How?" Sarah pointed at the cast on her leg. "I can't drive out there like this. It's a three-hour trip."

"Two hours. And I'll drive. Where's Knight's number?" Morgan flipped through Sarah's phone book, her voice rising with excitement. "Maybe Aunt Carolyn left you a fortune!"

"You live in a fantasy world, Morgan," Sarah remarked. But she called and spoke to her lawyer's receptionist. Surprisingly, Mr. Knight wanted to see her as soon as possible. They made an appointment for tomorrow at four.

AFTER MORGAN WENT to work, Sarah spent the rest of the afternoon in her home office, trying not to think about *Bloody Midnight*. She called the client with the late tax return and told him to courier it over. It was routine, and she couriered it back to him within an hour. She spent the next hour tidying her desk and rearranging files until she had to admit there was nothing left for her to do. She had deliberately cleared her calendar so that she could take some time off, and now time off was the last thing she wanted.

Morgan called three times during the evening to check on Sarah and to apologize for working so late. Each time Sarah assured her that she was just fine. She would make herself some scrambled eggs and toast for dinner, she said, and spend the evening reading the new mystery. No, she didn't need any painkillers. No, she wasn't afraid. She was perfectly fine.

She had convinced herself she had nothing to worry about. She knew she hadn't dreamed or imagined her intruder. But she didn't think he was a stranger. Some maniac who followed women home from bookstores and libraries, noting the titles of their thrillers, doing his research and then committing copycat crimes? It was a ludicrous idea. No. It had to be Peter, and if it was Peter, she was safe.

It was quite possible, even likely, that Peter had read the book and set up the whole scenario on purpose. It matched his previous behavior, except it was more extreme. Far too extreme. But why? To scare her into selling the house, no doubt. But he certainly hadn't planned that her terror would be so acute she'd leap down the laundry chute and break her leg. And given that she'd hurt herself so badly, he could hardly confess to his crazy plot now.

No, he wouldn't be confessing. But she was pretty confident he wouldn't try it again, either.

Despite the logic of her theory, however, Sarah found she couldn't bring herself to read in her usual chair by the fire after dinner. She took the tape recorder and book into her home office, where two whole walls were filled with windows. It was much brighter in here, more open, and she felt safer. The office was on the north side of her house, within easy shouting distance of Dr. Allard. In fact, she believed she could probably reach out one of her windows and ring Dr. Allard's side doorbell, if she had to.

The nearby street lamp was still out of order. But tonight was cloudless and crisp, and the thin crescent moon shone brightly through the windows. Sarah gazed outside at the yard next door. The leaves of the scraggly honeysuckle hedge between the houses seemed silver-tipped, and the lawn glowed with pale light. Dr. Allard had covered her plants to protect them from night frost, and her green garden had been transformed into a ghostly landscape. The strange, irregular shapes of the tomatoes, all bundled in white cloth, gleamed mysteriously in the moonlight like little snow-capped tombstones. Sarah closed the curtains.

She turned on the tape recorder and opened the book. "*A*

Chill at Midnight by Walter White, Chapter One," she said. Her own voice sounded tinny and seemed to bounce around the room and echo strangely against the high ceiling. She resolved to relax. The trick to making a good tape, she knew, was to forget about her own voice and let herself get caught up in the story. That way, her expression would come across naturally. She took a deep breath and began the first page.

"When the first innocent snowflakes came drifting from the sky on Christmas morning, nobody suspected that they were only the first sign of the worst storm to hit the city in a hundred years. Adults smiled indulgently as delighted children ran out into the streets with their toboggans. People turned up their thermostats, unconcerned about conserving energy. They didn't know that, by nightfall, the escalating blizzard would cause a power blackout, and that every road in the city—and every road out—would be completely impassable." Sarah paused and hit the *rewind* button. She played the tape over to make sure it was recording properly. Her voice sounded clear enough. She stopped it at the words *"completely impassable"* and pressed *record* again. She continued to read: *"They didn't know that someone was stalking the winter streets. . . ."*

Outside, in the early summer evening of Wolseley, the temperature suddenly dropped to zero.

Chapter Eleven

On Thursday morning, Morgan made herself breakfast in Sarah's kitchen as quietly as she could. Sarah was still sleeping on the sofa. Morgan scribbled a note, asking her cousin to be packed and ready by noon, so they could stop at Zina's for lunch before they left town. She drove to the shop, where she gave detailed instructions to the two young women she employed and hoped she could trust them to run the shop for two days. Then she went home to pack for the trip. She fretted over what to take. She'd booked a Kenora motel room for the night, hoping they could spend Friday at the beach. But now it was so cool, she wondered if they would be able to enjoy a day at the beach. The radio announcer predicted a prolonged cold spell, but Morgan never relied on the forecast. No one could tell what the weather might do in this part of the country. Ever optimistic, she stuffed sunscreen, sunglasses, and beach wear into her bag.

AT HOME, SARAH was folding a thick sweater when the doorbell chimed. She placed the sweater carefully on top of the rain jacket in her overnight bag and clambered down the hall. She was getting more nimble on her crutches, though her arms were still stiff from her adventurous walk the other day. She was faster now, but still not fast enough to stop the visitor from ringing again. She heaved a small sigh of exasperation. She should be grateful for the concern of her friends and neighbors, but she was a little weary of repeating reassurances of her well-being.

Officer Daniel Bradley stood on her porch with his arms crossed over his chest. "Just came to see how you are," he said.

"I'm fine," she said automatically.

"How's the leg?"

"In a cast."

Daniel smiled. "Well, if there's anything I can do. . . ."

"Nothing I can think of." She wondered if she should mention the strange coincidence of the novel, but decided against it. Daniel already thought she'd imagined the intruder. Throwing a fictional madman into her story would only make things worse.

"You want me to drop in on you tonight?"

"Thanks, but we're going to Kenora for the night, my cousin and I."

"Going to the lake? That's great."

"Well, it's business."

They stood in uneasy silence for a few seconds, and then Daniel spoke softly. "You don't remember me, do you?"

Sarah shook her head.

"I played football with your cousin Sam in high school."

Sarah looked more closely. There was something about those eyes, such a dark blue, unusual. "You're Danny? Danny Carriere?"

"Dan Bradley," he said. "But, yeah, Alfred Carriere was my stepfather. He was married to my mum—very briefly."

"Yes, I remember. Say, you were practically the star of the football team—well, you and Sam. I remember when you won the city cup."

Daniel could remember further back than that. He'd first seen Sarah at Sam's fourteenth birthday party. She was only about seven years old then, and so shy she wouldn't speak at all. She'd helped Sam's mother serve cake, but her eyes never left the ground. He remembered Sam telling him the story of how Sarah came to live with his family. How she'd been raised on some remote island with an eccentric mother and no father. How she'd been orphaned and left dependent on Sam's mother. Daniel had been struck by the strange, romantic story. He'd never seen an actual orphan before. For years he would think of the story every time he saw her in the school-yard, hanging back from the other kids, as if she didn't even know how to play.

"Imagine!" Sarah exclaimed. "And here you are, assigned to your own old neighborhood. What a coincidence!"

Daniel had worked hard and pulled a lot of strings to get himself assigned to this neighborhood, but he didn't mention that.

He was waving good-bye as Morgan arrived to pick Sarah up.

"My favorite cop," Morgan said to Sarah, as they watched him walk away. "What's he doing here?"

"He's the one who took me to the hospital. Did you know he grew up around here? He knows your brother."

"He knows Sam? Oh, wow. Well, that's Winnipeg for you." Morgan laughed. "One degree of separation."

BYRON HUNT LOOKED up from his notebook long enough to nod at Morgan and Sarah when they entered Zina's café. He didn't ask about Sarah's leg, and she was grateful. He's probably heard the whole story six times already, she thought. As she contemplated the menu on the chalkboard, she noticed the pile of Walter White's new novel was depleting rapidly. The whole neighborhood was getting hooked on this series.

Zina was doing a brisk lunch-hour business, but managed to stop by their table to serve them personally. She was wearing an embroidered cotton dress, made in India in 1977, with dozens of little mirrors sewn into the bodice. Another one of Morgan's great finds, which she had saved especially for Zina. Despite its age, it was still a deep, unfaded scarlet, as bright red as the borscht Zina was serving today.

"So you're off to the lake," Zina said, as she placed two steaming bowls in front of Morgan and Sarah. "You lucky girls."

"It's business," Sarah said.

"Sarah's inheritance," Morgan said. "Something to do with her mum's estate."

Byron looked up. "Lake of the Woods?"

"Yeah," said Morgan.

"The lake of the woods grows green with waiting," Byron said.

"What's that?" asked Morgan.

Byron smiled. "Tell her, Sarah."

"Tell her what?"

"The lake of the woods grows green with waiting," he repeated. *"And every whitecap speaks of your arrival."*

"I don't know what you're talking about," Sarah said.

"You don't know those lines? That's your own mother's poem!"

"Her mother?" Zina asked.

"Carolyn Yeats. Only the best Canadian poet of the twentieth century."

Sarah and Morgan exchanged a look. Byron's hero-worship of Carolyn had long been a source of irritation to them.

"I hardly think she was considered the *best*—" Sarah began.

"She should have been," Byron declared. He seemed almost angry.

Zina, intrigued, turned to Sarah. "Your mother was a writer?"

"A poet," Byron said. "She wrote five books of poetry. But does anybody read them? No! God forbid their brains might start functioning! They might *feel* something!"

"Your mother wrote five books?" Zina asked.

"Five brilliant, beautifully crafted volumes," Byron proclaimed sadly. "They sank like stones, unnoticed." He sighed and looked out the window, letting his eyes glaze over. "I always wanted to meet her. In my first year of college, I wrote an essay about her nature imagery. I even got up the nerve to write her a letter. But then I learned she'd been dead for years. Damn it! What an opportunity missed—" He looked up. "Oh. Sorry," he said.

Sarah was white.

"Sorry, it's just that I've always felt that I knew her."

"Well, you didn't," Morgan said. This was creepy. As if her Aunt Carolyn would have given a nut like Byron Hunt the time of day. Or would she? Byron had called her "brilliant." Morgan felt suddenly that she hadn't known her aunt at all.

"Byron's kind of a romantic," Zina said, trying to repair the atmosphere. "He reads a lot of poetry."

Sarah remained silent.

Byron stood and stuffed his notebook in his satchel. "I'd better go. What do I owe you, Zina?"

Morgan and Sarah watched them walk to the counter. "What an insensitive jerk," Morgan whispered.

As she gave Byron his change, Zina also spoke in a low voice. "What's her name again? Sarah's mother?"

"Carolyn Yeats."

"And she was famous? I never heard of her."

Byron looked around the bookstore. "What poets *have* you heard of?" he asked.

"Was she rich?"

Byron snorted. He took his change and left.

Chapter Twelve

"LITERARY EXECUTOR?" SARAH ASKED. "What does that mean, exactly?"

She and Morgan were sitting across from Mr. Knight's paper-strewn desk in his crowded, oak-paneled law office overlooking Lake of the Woods. Mr. Knight peered sternly over his glasses at them and then began to cough. He seemed smaller than ever, Sarah thought. Shriveled. His shoulders barely reached the top of the desk.

"Does that mean money?" Morgan asked. "From Aunt Carolyn's books?"

Mr. Knight was still coughing, but he managed to shake his head no.

Morgan sighed. She gazed out at the lake. The colored sails of the boats shimmered in the harbor, and the lake sparkled invitingly. Across the water, she could see the edge of Coney Beach jutting out into the lake. It would be too cool to swim, but it was sunny. The day had turned beautiful, and Morgan imagined all the lucky people without appointments lazing about on their bright towels on the sand, listening to the lapping waves, far, far away from their lawyers.

"A literary executor," Mr. Knight was explaining, "is the person responsible for overseeing the literary estate of the deceased. This includes protecting copyright, collecting royalties—"

Morgan swung her head toward Mr. Knight and started paying attention again. "Royalties?"

"Well, they don't amount to much," he said. He opened one of the files in front of him. "The total royalties since Carolyn's death have been kept in trust, and they amount so far to four thousand dollars."

"That's good news," Morgan said to Sarah. Sarah remained quiet. She was trying to process this information.

"Unfortunately," Mr. Knight continued, "sales are so few and far between these days that royalties have slowed to a trickle."

"So there's not much for me to look after, then," Sarah said. "If there's only a trickle."

"There are a few other things," Mr. Knight said. "Your mother's papers, for example. That's the main thing. Most writers name a trusted and, uh, competent literary executor, usually an experienced editor. But your mother's will instructed me to keep the papers in storage until you reached the age of twenty-five and then to turn them over to you." He coughed again. "Obviously, she didn't expect to die so young."

"What papers?" Sarah asked. "How many papers?"

Mr. Knight pressed a button on his desktop intercom. "Nancy? Bring in the Yeats papers, will you?"

"What am I supposed to do with them?" Sarah asked.

"Normally, the literary executor would sort through them, determine what is suitable for publication. Sometimes there are unfinished manuscripts that are salvageable. Or, in the case of a famous writer, letters that are publishable, or of interest to a university library—"

"You could sell them to a library!" Morgan said. "I've heard about that. Alfred sold a lot of correspondence from Carriere Press to the university archives. He made a bundle—"

"What are you talking about?" Sarah asked her cousin. But they were interrupted by Mr. Knight's assistant Nancy, straining to push a long cart laden with a dozen cardboard cartons.

Sarah pulled herself up by one crutch and stood. "Not all these?"

"Yes."

She approached the cart. Each box was sealed and stamped with the imprint of Knight and Knight Law Offices. Sarah ran her fingers lightly across a box and read the writing on the seal: "*Property of Carolyn Yeats. Received June 21, 1982.* Oh my God. That's the date of her—"

"The date of her death," Morgan finished. "How could that be?" Both women looked to Mr. Knight for an explanation.

He consulted his file again. "Carolyn Yeats turned these boxes over to us for safekeeping on the morning of her death," he said. "It was unusual luck—I mean—I don't mean luck, of course. Just—shall we say—fortunate timing. Otherwise—"

"Otherwise—" repeated Morgan.

The word hung in the air. Morgan and Sarah stared at each other. Morgan remembered the flames and the smoke and her brother Sam holding six-year-old Sarah while she screamed. Sarah remembered only the morning after. The dawn light pale and weak, filtered through smoke. Her mother's cabin burned to the ground. It was her only conscious image of Persephone Island, and usually she kept it tucked tightly in the dark, unreachable, inner pocket of her memory. But now, running her hand across her mother's name on the sealing tape, she could see the scene clearly. The image was so vivid and so utterly bleak. . . .

"Sarah, sit down." Morgan held her cousin's arm and nearly pushed her back into her chair. "Are you okay?"

"Nancy, bring some water," Mr. Knight ordered. He had not moved from his seat behind his desk. Nancy hurried out.

"I'm all right," Sarah told Morgan. She turned to Mr. Knight. "My mother brought these papers over that morning?" she asked. "With instructions to keep them till I turned twenty-five?"

"Yes."

"That very morning? Don't you.... You don't even seem to think that's odd."

"Perhaps a little odd," Mr. Knight replied. "But we had already discussed Carolyn's wishes at length. Originally, she named her father as literary executor, but after his death, she changed it to you. Wanted to keep it in the family, I suppose. So on that day the only detail remaining was the delivery of her actual papers. The legal work was drawn up in advance. Carolyn's request was unusual, in that we don't normally undertake the storage of so many documents. But her father—your grandfather—was a dear friend. I felt a responsibility—"

"The only detail remaining!" Sarah repeated. She looked at Morgan. "Isn't that weird?"

Morgan nodded. It was weird. But Mr. Knight continued to downplay the coincidence and refused to speculate on it. "Carolyn had wanted to get these papers off the island for some time," he explained. "She worried about dampness, rot...."

Sarah stopped listening. She was mentally counting the boxes, wondering what on earth she was going to do with them all.

"CAROLYN YEATS, 1952-1982," Byron read aloud. He passed the book across the table to Zina. "This was her first volume, *Island Songs*, 1973. A little sentimental, but you might like it."

Zina pushed her plate aside. She had eaten an early dinner of spinach pie and borscht, and now she was trying to relax for a few minutes before the evening rush began. She turned the book over in her hands. "She wrote a book when she was only twenty-one," Zina marveled. "Wow. Look at her!"

They both looked at the faded photograph on the back cover. At twenty-one, Carolyn Yeats had been an ethereal beauty, with slightly bucked teeth, a timid smile, and wild, wispy blonde hair, only partially tamed by two thin braids that encircled her head like a halo.

"Alfred Carriere reprinted this after her death," Byron said. "Trying to cash in on the tragedy."

"1952-1982. Only thirty," Zina said. "How did she die so young?" She leafed through the pages, but did not read.

"A fire," Byron said. "She lived on a little island on Lake on the Woods. Log cabin, wood stove, no fire department. Pioneer style, real back-to-the-land stuff. Her father was Luke Yeats, you know, the artist?"

Zina shook her head.

Byron rolled his eyes. "Luke Yeats was a great sculptor," he said. "You should know that. Some of his pieces are in Assiniboine Park. You know that one of the Minotaur?"

"Minotaur?"

"The beast. The man with the head of the bull? By the gates to the zoo?"

"Oh, yeah. Sarah's grandfather did that?"

"Yes! He lived right here in Wolseley with his wife and two little daughters. He was well respected. Very successful artist. He had this vacation place on the lake, not far from my parents' cottage. My parents met him, actually. They bought some of his work. Anyway, his wife got sick, ended up in the mental hospital, leaving him with two little girls. He just couldn't handle it. He dropped right out of the art scene. Quit selling his work. Just lived off his savings, I guess. He rented out the house in Wolseley—the house Sarah lives in now—and took the girls to the island. That's where Carolyn Yeats grew up, and that's where she died. Read the poems. There are some brilliant descriptions of the island."

Zina turned the pages more slowly, pausing to read a few lines here and there.

Byron continued with his story. "The older sister, Darlene, got married young and moved to Winnipeg—"

"Morgan's mum!" Zina said.

"Right. And Carolyn stayed on with her father. She never married. Never left the island. Well, she must have left once in a while. I mean, she toured the country a few times, doing poetry readings, promoting her books."

"And she got pregnant," Zina added.

"She got pregnant," Byron agreed. "Gave birth to baby Sarah right there on the island, with a local midwife attending. The story goes that Luke Yeats nearly drowned that night. Carolyn went into labor early. Luke left her there all alone and took the speedboat up to Kenora to fetch the midwife in the middle of a lightning storm."

"How do you know all this?" Zina asked. "I never heard Morgan or Sarah talk about any of this."

"I know the story of Carolyn Yeats," Byron said. "I've been a fan for a long, long time. There were a few biographical sketches in magazines shortly after her death. A brief flurry of interest, some reprints, and then—nothing. Nobody reads her work any more, except a few graduate students."

Zina closed the book and gazed again at the photograph of Carolyn. "She was so romantic-looking," she said. "I wonder what ended her love affair. Where is Sarah's father, now?"

"You mean *who* is Sarah's father," Byron said. "Nobody knows."

"Nobody?"

"Luke might have known, I suppose," Byron said. "But he didn't tell. And he died of a heart attack a couple of years after Sarah was born. Carolyn kept that secret well. Not a single biographer could ferret it out. So nobody knows."

"Not even Sarah?"

"Not even Sarah."

WHEN THE CANVAS top of the little Sunbeam was up, the car was claustrophobic, but it was far too cool today to drive with it open. After her long, cramped trip, Cady was looking forward to hopping out and stretching her legs. She found the street she wanted on the map. It was a long, winding road that began in town and then ran for miles along the shore. Nice view, but Cady wasn't in the mood for a nice view. She was in a hurry.

When she reached the house, she pulled to a stop and stared up at it.

"Holy jackpot," she said under her breath.

She double-checked the address. Could this mansion on the hill possibly be the home of an English prof? He must have made a fortune as an agent. She turned the wheel and steered slowly up the circular drive. The house was built at the top of a rocky incline, and the grounds were studded with massive outcroppings of granite and scattered with little rock gardens. The wide-tiered lawns were immaculate and green. Not a dandelion in sight. Cady parked and got out. She could see the lake shimmering through the trees below.

The stone steps and heavy wooden door with its brass knocker intimidated her a little. She took a deep breath and started toward the house. Then she saw a woman walking toward her. The woman wore gardening gloves and carried a basket of lilies and a pair of secateurs, but she was no landscaper. Her posture, her raised chin, and the perfect cut of her dress all spoke of wealth. The soft red fabric flowed stylishly around her legs as she crossed the lawn toward Cady. She was in her late fifties, Cady guessed, a beautiful woman with a kindly smile. The lady of the house.

"May I help you?" she asked.

"Yes, I'm looking for Professor Bill Wesley. Have I found the right place?"

"May I ask who is calling?"

Cady pulled her business cards from her purse and presented one.

The lady studied the card. "A reporter? I confess, I'm perplexed. Why do you want to speak with Bill?"

"For a story I'm working on," Cady explained. "I'm actually looking for the author Walter White. I understand Professor Wesley represents him."

"Oh, I'm sorry, dear. My husband is very ill. You won't be able to speak with him."

"Perhaps I could come back tomorrow, when he's feeling better?"

"I'm terribly sorry," Mrs. Wesley said. "But it's not that kind of illness. He will not be feeling better tomorrow. He may not live the night."

Cady gaped. She didn't mean to be rude, but this woman, with her gracious manner and her fashionable clothes, did not seem like a woman whose husband was dying.

"Cancer," Mrs. Wesley said softly. "He's barely conscious. It's been dragging on for months now, the poor man."

"Oh, I see. I'm sorry."

The woman bent her head, as if studying Cady's business card intently. She was not the type to show emotion, Cady thought. She was probably brought up that way. Be polite, even in a crisis. Well, Cady could use that to her advantage. She hadn't won her credentials as a journalist by practicing compassion.

"Is there someone else I could talk to? A business associate? Yourself, perhaps? Do you know where I might find Walter White?"

Mrs. Wesley shook her head.

"Because I have some important information for him," Cady improvised. "About the auctioning of foreign rights. Something he needs to know."

"Foreign rights? His novels will be translated?"

Ah ha, Cady thought. She *does* know who he is. "Germany, France, Japan," she rattled off.

"Come and sit a moment," Mrs. Wesley offered. She tucked Cady's business card into her flower basket and led the way to a flagstone patio with wrought-iron garden furniture.

Cady sat down and affected a friendly interest. "So you know Walter White?"

"I remember Mr. White," she answered. "He was an odd man, really, rather quiet and, well, almost surly at times. And his books! Such unpleasant stories!"

"They're very popular," Cady said. "They're selling very well."

"Is that so?" Mrs. Wesley looked up with interest. "And how is it you know so much about Walter White's books and so little about Walter himself?"

"My story is about his books," Cady explained. "But now I want to talk to him, as a writer. Interview him. And, of course, uh, give him the information about the foreign rights sales. You see"—she thought rapidly, trying to calculate how much this woman might know about the publishing industry—"I've learned that there's a fierce bidding war going on for the foreign rights. It's part of my story. And Mr. White's publisher, Alfred Carriere, is out of town at the moment, so I'd hoped to reach Mr. White through his agent. But obviously. . . . Is there an address, perhaps, in your husband's office? Your husband must have a partner, especially if he's so terribly—" She hoped she hadn't gone too far.

"Alfred Carriere is his only partner, as far as I know."

"Oh." This was news to Cady. Useless news, but news.

Mrs. Wesley rose from her chair. The interview was being cut short for some reason. Perhaps Cady had not been convincing enough. "Why don't you wait until Mr. Carriere returns and write your story then? I'm sure he can help you more than I can."

"But I have a deadline."

"I'll walk you to your car," Mrs. Wesley said, and there was nothing for Cady to do but follow her.

"So, you say he was quiet?" Cady tried. "A bit surly?" She hurried along to keep up with Mrs. Wesley's brisk pace. "He was, what did you say? Odd?"

"Anyone who can come out with six such perfectly dreadful tales can only be described as odd," Mrs. Wesley remarked. "Really, I don't know how Bill ever found a readership for them. It's astonishing what people consider entertainment these days. And the movies! It's to the point now where I won't set foot in the cinema."

"Yes," Cady agreed, trying to drag the conversation out, hoping for more information. "It's shocking, really. Hollywood—"

But they had reached the car, and Mrs. Wesley was waving a gloved hand as she retreated rapidly toward her house.

"All best wishes for success with your story, dear," she called.

Cady stood staring at the formidable door after it closed. She wondered if Bill Wesley was in there, somewhere— languishing in the master bedroom, probably. Barely conscious, she'd said. Well, that didn't necessarily mean he couldn't speak. And maybe he was not as sick as his wife implied. If Cady could come by sometime when she was out. . . .

Trying to plot her next move, she roared down the driveway. She had dinner in town and checked into an upscale hotel, charging it to her local paper. All through her dinner of roast beef and dumplings, her dessert of apple pie and ice cream, the shower she took, and the movies she watched in her room, Cady felt something nagging at her. Was it something she'd seen at the house? Or something she'd heard? Cady had the feeling she had overlooked some detail she should have pursued. It was like that time she gave a lecture at the convention center, not knowing that a pair of pink panties, charged with static electricity, was clinging to the shoulder of her dress the whole time she was standing there.

SARAH SAT ALONE in Mr. Knight's office, gazing out at the lake. She could see the five o'clock water taxi returning from Coney Island, its passengers huddled together against the wind. The weather, which had hovered between warm and cold all day, had decided on cold. The lake was dark with the shadows of clouds, and the waves were high. Morgan would not be getting her day at the beach, after all.

Morgan and Mr. Knight had gone downstairs to arrange for the transfer of Carolyn's papers into Morgan's car. By the time they finished, Sarah knew, it would be time to retreat to the motel for dinner. She turned her attention from the lake to the Kenora streets, which climbed steeply from the harbor up toward the law office. Traffic was increasing as rush hour approached—or what passed for rush hour in this small town. The sidewalks seemed more crowded than the roads, and Sarah guessed that many residents walked to work.

She amused herself by people-watching, noting that no one was dressed warmly enough. The morning's promise of summer had been false, and now pedestrians scurried home or for other shelter from the biting wind.

A tall man in a loose-fitting, gray summer suit hurried along the sidewalk below, clutching a briefcase and simultaneously trying to keep his hat from blowing off and his light jacket from flying open. Sarah watched him approach, struggling against the wind. She was startled when he stopped directly below her and looked up at the window, holding his hat on his head with one hand. Their eyes met briefly before he ducked into the entrance to the law office. Perhaps he worked in the building.

Sarah leaned forward and peered farther down the street. A small after-work crowd was trickling into the Tyndall stone pub on the corner. But nobody else caught her interest. She watched a yellow float plane cruise in over the lake and land in the harbor. She looked at her watch. Five-thirty. Then, slowly, she was overcome by the feeling that she was being watched herself. She turned in her chair and there he was, the man from the street. He was leaning in the office doorway, his black hair disheveled, his hands in the pockets of his gray suit, as casually as if he were home in his own living room. He smiled again, and Sarah found herself smiling back, though she didn't know why.

"Sarah Yeats," he said. "I'm glad I caught you. No—don't get up." He straightened his long frame and came forward, extending his right hand.

Sarah shook his hand and found it warm, though he'd just been out in the cold a minute ago.

He glanced down at her cast. "Looks like you've had a bit of an accident there," he said.

"It's not so bad." Who was this man and why was he here to see her? Why did he seem so glad to see her?

He settled himself familiarly on the edge of Mr. Knight's desk, adjusted his rimless glasses, and gazed at her with interested brown eyes. "You're just as I imagined you," he said. "Exactly."

"Excuse me?"

"How long are you in town?" he asked. "I hope you're coming for dinner. I have so much to show you—"

"Excuse me," Sarah said again. "Do I know you?"

"Oh." He dropped his head, disappointed. "No, I guess you don't. Sorry," He looked up. "I'm Jacob Knight. I somehow thought you'd recognize me."

"You're a lawyer here?"

"Yes." He was smiling again. "I'm the other Knight in Knight and Knight. Evan's grandson."

"Oh, I see." So, he was only here on business after all. "Are there some more papers I have to sign?"

"No, no. My grandfather's taking care of every detail of your case. You are his very last case, by the way. He's been retired for years, but he just had to come in and handle this one by himself. Luke's granddaughter and all. He had to make sure it was all done right. Now he can die happy."

"Die?"

Jacob laughed. "Just a figure of speech, I assure you. He's strong as a bull. Now, seriously, how long are you staying? My mother can't wait to see you. She was very upset when you didn't make it here Monday."

"Your mother?"

Jacob folded his arms across his chest and leaned back to observe her. "You don't know what I'm talking about, do you?" he asked. "You haven't got a clue who I am."

Embarrassed, Sarah could only shake her head.

"Well, you must know my grandfather Evan was great friends with your grandfather Luke."

Sarah nodded.

"Did you know my mother was also a great friend of your mother's?"

"No, I didn't. Who is your mother?"

"Mary Knight. You haven't heard of her? She was your mother's best friend."

"I never knew—" Sarah couldn't continue. Her throat ached. She turned her head and gazed out the window again.

"Of course." His voice softened. He leaned forward and clasped his hands together. "When my mother married my father, she was only twenty—the same age as Carolyn. My dad used to take her along to Persephone Island with my grandfather, when they went to visit Luke. My mum was glad to have someone her own age to talk to, and she says Carolyn was glad to have any friend at all, stuck out there all alone with no one but her dad. My mum would bring her books to read, and they'd cook together while the guys went on their fishing trips. After a while they got so close my mum started taking the boat over there by herself when my dad was working. She'd take me over in the boat when I was a baby, just to visit Carolyn. The two of them were like that." He held up two crossed fingers.

"And where is your mother now?" Sarah's heart began to beat a little faster. She didn't like this conversation. The thought of her mother, young and alive, was too painful.

Jacob gestured toward the window. "Just across the bay in Keewatin. She's waiting for me to bring you home to dinner. She has photographs and. . . ."

Sarah's heart was pounding now. She wasn't listening to Jacob at all. To think there was someone who knew her mother—knew her mother well—just across the next bay, a few minutes' drive away, waiting for her, wanting to talk about Carolyn—

"There's a funny one of you and me making mudpies," he was saying. "She has a whole envelope of stuff she's been saving for you. She's been looking forward to this for— What's the matter?"

"Nothing," she managed. "It's just that, um, I promised my cousin that I'd—that we'd go out for dinner tonight."

"Your cousin Morgan? All the better! Bring her along."

"No—really—we can't. It's—we have reservations. And we're only here the one night. Some other time, maybe."

He was studying her even more closely now. "I see," he said slowly. "Reservations. Well."

"Yes," she went on. "Morgan's probably waiting for me right now." She stood up. "I really must be going. It's been nice to meet you." She started toward the door, but as she passed him by, he reached out and touched her shoulder. The warmth of his hand stopped her in her tracks.

He slid off the desk and stood beside her, looking down into her face. "Won't you change your mind?"

"I really can't."

"How about tomorrow?"

"No," she said. "We have to leave early tomorrow, because. . . ." She gave up. She was past making excuses. She could tell he didn't believe them anyway.

"I'll tell you what," he said. "How about you drop by the office on your way out of town tomorrow? I'll bring the envelope from my mother, and you can at least take it home with you."

"Oh, I don't know—" she began.

"You can at least do that for her," he said very firmly. "And you will."

"I will," she promised. She wasn't sure who she was doing it for, but she promised.

"I'M TOO TIRED and hungry to enjoy the beach anyway," Morgan said. The cousins had picked up pizza and beer and were sharing it out on the patio in front of their motel unit, wrapped in blankets and curled up in Adirondack chairs. Despite the cold, the evening was clear, and they anticipated a good view of the sunset over the lake.

"Yuck," Sarah said, when she tasted the beer. "Warm."

Morgan shrugged. "It does the job." She took a large drink from the bottle. "I can use it right now. What a shock!"

"I know. Literary executor!"

"What could have made her choose you? You were only six years old! And I can't get over that date. June 21. God! June 21, 1982. Do you—" Morgan hesitated. They had a long habit of avoiding this subject. "How much do you remember, Sarah?"

"Not much. I remember you and Sam were there. Where was Aunt Darlene?"

"My mum and dad had gone back to Winnipeg to work," Morgan said. "Carolyn took them in to Kenora by boat early that morning. My gosh! She must have had those very papers with her! Of course we were too little to pay any attention to that. Sam and I stayed with you on the island. I remember we'd begged to be allowed to stay a few more days on Persephone Island with you and Carolyn. I remember because it was Sam's birthday, and we were having such a wonderful time. So our parents let us stay. And then that night Aunt Carolyn put us all to bed in the little green cabin. She slept in the big one—remember the big log cabin?"

"Vaguely." Sarah imagined a tiny white bed beside a window. White curtains, a teddy bear. Then the image vanished. All she could see were the charred and broken logs, thin smoke wavering over the horrible stillness. An old sense of despair rose in her throat and threatened to choke her.

Morgan's voice took on a nostalgic tone. "Sam had just turned thirteen. Aunt Carolyn baked him a chocolate cake. She let us take the leftovers to the green cabin for a midnight snack. Remember the ghost stories Sam used to tell us?"

"Not really," Sarah said. She was thinking of the ruined log cabin. If Sam and Morgan had not been visiting that night, Sarah would have been in the big cabin with her mother—sound asleep in the little white bed when the fire started. These past nineteen years would not have existed.

They fell silent for a long while and watched the lake turn golden, then darken as the last rays of the sun played across the water. They faced south, their gaze turned in the direction of Persephone Island, which lay far beyond their scope of vision. Sarah knew where it was, miles past the islands she could see from here, down the southeast channel, beyond Devil's Gap, among the Hades Islands. She had seen it on the marine chart, an unnamed dot surrounded by blue space. Her property. But she could not reconcile that geographical place with the brief images that were starting to flicker to life in her memory. A wooden boat. The creaking of a dock. The scratchy branches of berry bushes.

"It's getting dark," she said finally. "Do these patio lights work? Maybe we could read a bit."

"I'll check it out." Morgan cleared the table and carried the remains of their dinner into the motel room. She flipped a switch inside the room and the two patio lanterns came on, creating a small pool of light. She returned with two more blankets and her copy of *A Chill at Midnight*. "I'm dying to get back into this story," she said. She dropped a blanket in Sarah's lap. "Do you want me to fetch you a book?"

"I've got it here." Sarah took the tape recorder out of her bag, opened *A Chill at Midnight* and found her place. "Linda picked up the first tape this morning. She'll be dying to hear the end."

"Wait a minute—you're reading it out loud? I don't want to hear the end before I finish it!"

"You can go inside to read," Sarah suggested. "I'll read out here."

"Deal. It's getting too cold out here, anyway." Morgan picked up her novel and the box of beer with its three remaining bottles. But on her way to the door, she turned and said, "What are you going to do with Aunt Carolyn's papers? Sell them?"

"To who?"

"A library, maybe, or a university. Like I said, Alfred's done it. Carriere Press's papers are at the U of M, now. In their Canadian Literature Collection. There are letters from a lot of well-known authors in there. People do research, you know, and—"

"How do you know so much about Alfred's business?"

Morgan shrugged. "We talk. Anyway, you should ask him what to do. He knows all about this literary stuff."

Sarah was wrapping herself in the blanket. "I'd have to read them first," she said slowly. "See what's in there. She must have had a reason for keeping these papers in the family. They might be too personal."

"Yeah." Morgan turned to go, then suddenly wheeled around again. "Yeah! There must be all *kinds* of personal stuff. Diaries and letters and all kinds of family history. There might be clues in there about—about your father!" Morgan's voice rose in excitement. "And maybe—"

"Maybe nothing," Sarah interrupted. "This isn't a mystery novel, Morgan. This is my life."

She turned her back on her cousin and pulled Linda's tape recorder out of her bag. "I promised Linda I'd give her the last tape tomorrow." She turned on the tape recorder and, ignoring Morgan, began to read aloud: *"The windows were opaque with frost. Leaf-like swirls and patterns of thick crystals completely obscured the view outside. Nobody could see him coming as he crept across the front yard with his face concealed behind his ski mask and his ice-pick gripped tightly in his mittened hand."*

Morgan shivered. She entered the motel room and closed the door behind her.

IN THE MORNING, Morgan piled all their bags in her back seat, on top of the two last boxes of Carolyn's papers that wouldn't fit in the trunk—and hoped she'd be able to see out her back window on the highway. She pulled Sarah's brown cardigan over her emerald green sundress, got in the driver's seat and waited as Sarah clumsily got in beside her.

"We have to stop at Knight's office," Sarah told her as she buckled her seat belt.

"Again? What for?"

"I have to sign some more papers."

"You never mentioned that. Why didn't you do it yesterday?"

"It won't take long. You can wait in the car." Sarah didn't want Morgan meeting Jacob. She was certain Morgan would insist on going to see Mary and turning the whole visit into a trip down memory lane. Not a place Sarah wanted to go.

Morgan asked no more questions. She drove slowly through the streets of Kenora, pointing out the beauty of the fountains and the gardens along the harborfront, the old brick post office, a bakery she remembered. She parked in front of Knight and Knight, apparently content to wait in the car and watch the seaplanes taking off.

Nancy was typing at the reception desk. "Oh, hello, Sarah. Jacob said you'd be in. He left this for you." She handed Sarah a bulky manilla envelope.

"He's not here?"

"No. He's with a client in Keewatin."

"Oh." Sarah felt inexplicably abandoned. "All right. I'll just—take this then." She smiled brightly at Nancy, stuffed the envelope in her bag, and left the building.

"That was quick," Morgan said. She pulled away from the curb too swiftly, narrowly missing a little red sports car that was speeding north on Main Street.

IT WASN'T HARD to figure out that the Wesleys, with a house like that, would be well known around town, and in a place the size of Kenora, it wasn't hard to find people willing to talk about them.

In the coffee shop at the biggest hotel in town, Cady had gotten lucky on her first try and learned that Mrs. Wesley volunteered at the Lake of the Woods Hospital every Friday afternoon. Paydirt. The coast would be clear. But how to get into the house? Flower delivery? No, she had to get past the servants, for there were bound to be plenty of servants, and into his room. Doctor? Too risky. She roamed the downtown district, poking around in drugstores and gift shops, chatting up the clerks and customers, stopping for coffee so often her stomach churned, garnering bits of information about the Wesleys. There was a lot of envy toward them among the locals, and Cady sensed that they were regarded as snobs. Bill Wesley was fifteen years older than his wife, and this was a source of much gossip. They'd met when he was one of the "summer people" with a cabin on the lake, and she was a young nurse, still living at home with her parents. It had caused a stir, apparently, this older professor marrying such an inexperienced girl. They'd had two sons, and Cady heard wild tales of their troubled youth, involving stolen cars and rumors of drugs. These long-ago scandals did not interest her. Her story wasn't about Bill Wesley. She only wanted to find a way to ask him about Walter White.

"But Mr. Wesley is so nice," one waitress told her. "He goes to my church—First Presbyterian—or at least he did until he got sick. Attended every Sunday."

This gave Cady an idea. She drove down to the First Presbyterian Church, which was just filling up with wedding guests in preparation for a ceremony. She grabbed a church newsletter from a stand in the foyer, smiled broadly at everyone, walked confidently to the bride's side, sat in a pew, and slipped a Bible into her purse.

Ten minutes later she was speeding toward Bill Wesley's house.

"BIBLE READING?" THE maid was puzzled. "Mrs. Wesley did not say anything about Bible reading."

"Reverend James specifically asked me to come today," Cady said in a meek voice. She had pulled her hair back into a severe ponytail and left her sports car parked out of sight below. She wore her raincoat over her clothes, which were a little too sexy for the part she was playing.

"Well, all right." The maid, who wore a gold cross prominently around her neck, smiled and ushered Cady up the broad spiral staircase to the sick room where Bill Wesley lay.

It was a dimly lit and overheated room, suffocatingly close, and smelled of mothballs and medicine. Cady approached the bed, Bible in hand, and gently called Bill Wesley's name. He snored softly, but his shallow breaths did not raise the heavy quilts that covered him.

"Mr. Wesley?" Cady touched his forehead lightly. His cheeks were hollow, and his eyelids sunken. Meager wisps of white hair barely covered his pink scalp. He was sweating under all these covers and seemed too frail to withstand their weight.

"Mr. Wesley?" She took his hand, then tried to rouse him by shaking his shoulder gently. No response.

She shook a little harder, and his eyelids fluttered. It was hard to tell if he was actually unconscious or simply conserving his energy. She pulled a chair close to the bed and began to talk to him, telling him what she wanted to know. At one point he opened his rheumy blue eyes and seemed to look right at her.

"Do you know Walter White?" Cady asked.

He closed his eyes again. The rhythm of his breathing changed and became raspy. He worked his lips, as if trying to moisten his mouth, and Cady noticed they were cracked and dry. Why wasn't that maid taking care of him?

"Here," she said. A glass of water with a hospital straw sat on the bedside table, but it looked bubbly and stale. She entered the ensuite bathroom to rinse and refill it. A rack of plush, expensive towels caught her eye, and she grabbed a washcloth. "What the hell," she said as she ran it beneath the tap.

She returned and offered him fresh, cool water from the hospital straw. He sucked greedily, but inefficiently, and the effort of drinking a few ounces seemed to drain him. Cady bathed the fragile skin of his face with the wet washcloth and removed the top layers of blankets. Then she opened the curtains and raised the sash to let in some light and air. A fine collection of classical music lay gathering dust on the dresser, and Cady selected some Handel and slipped a CD in the player. She checked her watch. Mrs. Wesley would be home in half an hour. Cady was getting nowhere.

She tried again. "Mr. Wesley? Can you talk to me for a few minutes?"

She thought she saw a faint smile cross his lips, but she wasn't sure.

"Do you know where I can find him?" she asked. "Even just the name of the city where he lives? The names of any relatives?"

After five more minutes of shaking and calling him, she gave up. She sat back down in the chair and opened the Bible to the Song of Songs.

"Let him kiss me with the kisses of his mouth," she began. *"For your love is better than wine."*

Chapter Thirteen

By THE TIME MORGAN PARKED in front of Sarah's house, it was warm enough to take off the sweater. Forgetting it belonged to her cousin, she tossed it on top of her bags and the boxes in the back seat and went around to pop the trunk, while Sarah gathered her crutches and wriggled out of the car.

Morgan hefted one of the boxes in her arms and groaned. "Feels like it's full of bricks," she said. She staggered as she followed Sarah up the front walk.

Mark Curtis was digging in Dr. Allard's garden next door. "Whoa," he said. "That looks heavy." He dropped his shovel and crossed the yard.

"Thanks," Morgan said as Mark took the box out of her arms. He winked at her and grinned as he carried it easily up the steps to the porch.

Sarah opened the door. "Let's just set them on the porch for now," she said.

Mark lowered the box onto the floor.

"There're a lot more where that came from," Morgan told him. She pointed toward her car. "You up for it?"

"Anything for the ladies."

Sarah smiled at him. "Thanks, Mark. I'm obviously no use at the moment." She went inside and phoned Linda to tell her the *Chill at Midnight* tape was ready to be picked up. Then she listened to her messages.

"Hello Sarah, this is Cady Brown. As you might already know, I'm working on a story about Zina's Mystery Book Club, and I understand you're one of the faithful. I was wondering if you could fill me in on—"

As she listened absent-mindedly to Cady's voice, Sarah watched Morgan and Mark unloading the trunk and carrying in the boxes. Morgan was laughing and tossing her golden red hair and, it appeared, telling Mark her whole life story. The two of them seemed to be enjoying themselves as they moved back and forth from the car to the house. Back and forth. Back and forth. Sarah sighed. It would take months to read through all those papers.

"So if you could give me a call at 772—"

Sarah quickly picked up a pen and jotted down Cady's number before she erased the message. Morgan's laughter drifted in through the window. Sarah turned to see Morgan pulling up the loose sleeve of her sundress to show Mark her muscles. She struck a comical pose and flexed her biceps. Mark put down the box he was carrying to feel her muscle and pretended to be mightily impressed. Morgan flashed him one of her famous smiles. Sarah shook her head in affection-ate exasperation. Morgan never quit.

CADY STEPPED HEAVILY on her brakes as she suddenly saw the red light ahead of her. The car lurched and the cell phone slipped from her grasp. She picked it up and shoved it be-tween her shoulder and her ear. Waiting at the intersection, she listened with skepticism to Gregory's claim that he had some new information for her.

"That last little tip you gave me was a bust," she said. "I still need to find White's agent."

"Bill Wesley is his agent."

"I'm telling you it can't be Wesley. I just talked to him this afternoon. He's seventy-five years old and practically comatose. He can't even speak."

Wesley actually had uttered one word that afternoon, so she knew he *could* speak. As she'd crossed the carpet to exit his room, she'd heard him breathe a faint "Thank you." She smiled, thinking of it. It was good to know he'd appreciated her small efforts. The poor guy must be horribly lonely.

"His name's on the paperwork," Gregory was saying. "I saw the contract with my own eyes."

"Maybe it's an old contract, then. What was the date on it?"

Gregory's silence told her he had not checked, or had forgotten. "Look," she said. "Wesley's wife mentioned he'd been partners with Alfred. Is it possible Alfred is representing White now?"

Gregory whistled. "Unlikely," he said. "Representing White to who? To himself?"

"But is it possible?"

"I never saw any evidence of that. You'll have to ask Alfred."

"But Alfred won't tell me anything! That's the whole problem!" Cady reminded him. "Listen, Gregory. Time is running out for me here. Can't you take another look? Find a more recent contract?"

"Well, yes, but there's something else. Since Alfred's been away, I've discovered a few more things of interest about Walter White and his books."

"Yeah? Like what?"

"I thought we could go back to that steak place," Gregory said. "It's quiet in there, we could have a little dinner. . . ."

"That would be great. That would be fun. But Gregory, can't you just tell me?"

"You really have to see it to believe it," he told her. "You'll pick up the tab?"

"I'll tell you what. I'll pick up the tab *after* I see it and believe it," she said. "It's in Alfred's office?"

"Yeah. Can you meet me there tonight?"

"No way. I have an article to write this weekend. Walter White or no Walter White, I still have to write the Mystery Au Lait story for the local paper." The light turned green and Cady made a left-hand turn onto the Perimeter Highway. "In the meantime, keep trying to find White's agent. Even if I can't reach him by deadline, I still want to be first to reach him when he does surface. I'll be honest with you," she said. "If I get an exclusive interview with this weirdo, I'll be able to sell it all over the States. Big money. I'll cut you in."

"When can we meet, then?"

"I'll call you." She disconnected.

ON SATURDAY MORNING, Morgan and Sarah took their coffee out on the porch. The sun was shining, and the neighbors were all out early, tending to their yard work, removing the sheets and buckets that covered their delicate plants overnight, and stacking them close to their gardens, where they could be easily reached when needed again. The danger of night frost was not yet past.

Mark Curtis was hauling Dr. Allard's lawn mower out of her shed. Morgan watched his broad back as he bent over the mower to fill it with gasoline.

"He's a sweet guy," Morgan whispered. "You sure kept *him* a secret!"

Sarah busied herself with counting the boxes. "They're not all here!" she cried.

"Oh, I forgot," Morgan said. "There are still two more in the back seat. Let's get them later. I want to open these up. Where should we start?"

"I'm not going to look at them now," Sarah said.

"Why not? Aren't you dying to read this stuff?" Morgan began to pick at the sealing tape on one of the boxes. "I'll get some scissors." She disappeared into the house.

Sarah sat down in the armchair and rubbed her temples. She could feel a headache coming on. Next door, Mark started up the power mower, and she winced at the sound. Too much had happened in the past week. Her plans for a stress-free vacation of running and light reading were ruined. Twelve cartons of a dead poet's papers could hardly be considered light summer reading at the best of times. The fact that the dead poet was her own mother, a woman she could barely remember, a woman who had taken the secret of Sarah's father to her grave, was more than she could bear at the moment.

Sarah watched as Morgan returned and opened a box.

"Oh my—Sarah, look!"

Morgan placed the open box at Sarah's feet and Sarah folded back the flaps to discover a tightly packed jumble of paper. Several thick Hilroy scribblers, their covers stained and discolored, had been shoved haphazardly into one corner. The rest was chaos—loose pages, manilla envelopes, brown-paper bags, and crumpled file folders were crammed together indiscriminately.

"There's no order at all!" Sarah cried.

"God, she was disorganized!"

"Either that or she was in a terrible hurry," Sarah said.

The sound of the power mower grew louder, and the women looked up to see Mark pass by the porch, pushing the machine across Sarah's front lawn.

Morgan waved at him. "He's cutting your grass for you," she said. "What a sweetheart." She pulled out an orange Hilroy scribbler and opened it carefully. "*August 10, 1967.* At least it's dated." She began to peruse the first page. "And her handwriting is legible enough." She read silently while Sarah surveyed the boxes with a heavy heart. Would they all be such a mess inside? The task before her was daunting.

"You should read this, Sarah," Morgan said. She held the journal toward her cousin. "It's like a travel journal, sort of— about different boat trips around the lake. Look at all the maps—my brother would love these!"

Sarah took the journal. It was bulging with extra pages, some of them folded thickly inside envelopes attached to the inside covers, some of them glued directly onto the inner pages. They were all maps, showing various parts of the lake—Yellow Girl Bay, Devil's Gap, Massacre Island. Many were drawn in ink on onion-skin paper, as if traced from a marine chart. Each one illustrated the record of a particular trip. Sarah's eyes traveled rapidly across the pages as she turned, picking out phrases here and there. "Four bass today," she read. "Saw two eagles. . . . Caught in rainstorm." She kept turning, without ever completing a sentence.

Morgan was busy with other things. She dug out a brown paper bag and discovered it was full of loose scraps, which she pulled out one by one. "Hey—these are poems . . . I think. *When day breaks with cold light. . . .*"

But Sarah wasn't listening. And she wasn't reading. Her eyes were blind with tears.

PETER WAS BEGGING now, and he loathed himself for it. He had begun this relationship with a strong upper hand, playing it cool, always letting her come to him. He wasn't certain exactly when his edge had started to slip away, but he wanted it back. He sat fully clothed on Cady's unmade bed while she lay with her head in his lap, telling him of her plans. He stroked her hair as if patting a cat and tried to keep his tone light, as if her silly plans amused him.

"Cady, you *can't* talk to Sarah. You said yourself we shouldn't let her find out about us."

"Look, she'll never know. I told her I want some background info on the book club—that's the truth, actually. I can use her. I can even quote her. She's one of the founding members. And meanwhile I'll get friendly. Tell her about my greedy ex and how he screwed me in the divorce—"

"The divorce? You were married?"

"Of course not. It's just to get her to open up. Make her identify with me. Oldest trick in the book."

"Oh." Peter didn't like this casual admission. If Cady was an expert at deception, he'd rather not know about it.

"Then I can find out what she's up to."

"I'm sure she's not up to anything."

"I'm telling you, Peter, I saw her coming out of a law office in Kenora, just yesterday. With that cousin of hers." Cady lifted Peter's shirt and kissed his bare belly. "She's planning something. That story of hers, that you assaulted her, is just the beginning."

"Sarah isn't the scheming type," Peter said reasonably.

Cady paid no attention. She was unzipping his jeans and searching inside his underwear.

Peter lay back and tried to relax. But all he could think of was Cady and Sarah talking together. He envisioned them seated in Sarah's comfortable living room, cosily sharing a pot of tea. The last thing he wanted! He closed his eyes and made vague murmurs of appreciation for Cady's caresses.

"Come on, honey," she coaxed. She slipped a hand under him and slid his jeans down over his hips.

Peter buried his face in the flowered pillowcase and cringed as he imagined an intimate conversation between Cady and his ex-wife. A conversation about ex-husbands and money! He imagined Sarah filling Cady in on his pathetic financial history. Telling Cady how she had supported Peter for years. Listing his failures. Undoing all the elaborate lies he had told about his success as a musician.

"Come on, honey. What's the matter?" Cady rubbed and stroked with her smooth, experienced hands, but nothing was happening.

Chapter Fourteen

SARAH STOOD ALONE ON HER PORCH, surrounded by boxes of papers, and watched Morgan drive away. They had agreed to meet at the book-club meeting tonight and then spend the night together at Morgan's apartment. Morgan needed to go home for a while, which was understandable, and neither she nor Sarah was comfortable with the idea of Sarah's spending a night alone in her house.

"Not yet, anyway," Morgan had said. She'd spent yesterday and most of today poring over Carolyn's notebooks, especially the orange one with the maps, and talking so much about Lake of the Woods and how much she missed it that Sarah had escaped to the kitchen, where she'd baked two cakes and enough casseroles to last the summer.

"Why won't you even *look* at this stuff?" Morgan had asked. "It's full of family history. It's fascinating."

Sarah didn't feel ready. Not yet. But now that Morgan was gone, she decided to look at the envelope from Jacob. Sitting down on the rocker, she drew the envelope from her bag and opened it. She sorted through it quickly and was disappointed to find no message from Jacob. Only a short note from his mother, Mary, with her address and phone number and an invitation to visit any time. There were autographed copies of three of Carolyn's books. Sarah was moved to see that they were signed for Mary. From what Jacob had told her, Sarah guessed it had cost Mary dearly to part with them, and she was struck by the woman's generosity. Sarah was, after all, a stranger to her. She resolved to return them. Sarah already had several copies of Carolyn's books in the house, though she never read them. There was some jewelry in the envelope, too—nothing expensive, but it was pretty. A coral necklace and a silver ring. And there were photographs.

Sarah's heart ached suddenly when she saw the first one. It was her own self, about four years old, with her mother. An outdoor shot. Winter. Carolyn and Sarah were decorating a live pine tree with strands of something—probably popcorn, though the tree was out of focus. Carolyn was lifting Sarah up to reach a high branch, and she was laughing. She was looking straight at the photographer, probably Mary, and laughing as if she'd never had a care in her life. Sarah stared at her mother's face. There were no pictures of Carolyn displayed in the house, and it had been a long time since she'd seen one. But there she was—looking very much like Sarah herself—the same high forehead and unruly blonde hair, the same narrow face and wide mouth. But Carolyn was much more—Sarah couldn't quite put her finger on it—more *alive*, somehow.

She flipped through the remaining photos, finding several of her mother in various poses, and a few of herself—one with a little boy who must be Jacob. He was only about eight years old, but she recognized his baffled smile. Sarah, age four, was beaning him on the head with a plastic beach pail. She supposed she'd done much the same thing to him the other day in the law office. What was the matter with her? Jacob and his mother were only trying to be kind. And so was

Morgan. They only wanted to reacquaint her with her mother.

Maybe they were right. Sarah reached into the open carton before her and chose a small blue notebook. Taking a deep breath, she opened it and began to read.

Christmas Eve, 1968, the entry began, *Our first Christmas without Darlene. It's lonely. But peaceful. We're to go to the Knights' for Christmas dinner tomorrow, if the ice holds. Dad gave me a present tonight, a little carving of a loon. He's put another present under the tree, all wrapped up, but it's obviously books, and a good thing too, 'cause I've nothing left to read. I finished* Uncle Tom's Cabin *last night, and already I'm halfway through* A Tale of Two Cities. *I want something lighter for a change. I'm hoping he's listened to all of my hints!*

I French-braided my hair all by myself tonight. It was hard without Darlene, but I managed. It's a bit lopsided and frizzy, but I'll do a better job tomorrow. I want to wear the red wool dress and Mum's gold earrings, if Dad will let me. Oh I hope the ice holds! The thought of people and conversation and even the traffic in the streets seems miraculous. Anything but snow, snow, snow, and Dad moping around, missing Darlene. I tried on the dress with the earrings today and I think I look at least twenty. If only I had some lipstick.

In Sarah's imagination, a picture of the young writer of these words began to form. She could see her standing before a mirror, turning her head this way and that, examining her own image, dreaming of a Christmas party. While outside the cabin, nothing but snow. . . .

"Hi, there!"

Sarah looked up. It was Mark Curtis again, standing on the steps beyond the screen door to the porch.

"Is Morgan still around?"

"You missed her. But come on in. Thanks for cutting my lawn."

"Nothing to it." He entered, then hesitated, taking in the

open boxes of papers, the notebook in Sarah's lap. "So that's what's in there? Looks like you're busy."

"It's okay. Sit. I'm just looking through my mother's old diaries and things. She was—" Sarah decided against explaining about the will, the literary executorship. She had learned long ago not to mention her mother was a poet. It was too offbeat for most people.

But Mark seemed interested. "She was a writer?"

"Why yes." Sarah smiled. "She was."

ON SUNDAY EVENING, Zina's Café was filled to capacity. Javier brought in all the patio furniture and set up a row of the extra folding chairs Zina kept in the back. A teaser in today's *Manitoba Daily* promised Cady Brown's feature on the book club in next Sunday's literary section, and even that one small paragraph brought in a crowd.

"Imagine what will happen next Sunday," Zina said to Alfred. "When that feature comes out, we'll be swamped."

Alfred looked up from the dish of vegetable stew he was enjoying. "Hmmm. Yes. We'll have to increase your book order."

"I'll make a note of that," Gregory said. He pulled out his fountain pen and checked the display rack. The third book in the series, *Midnight Feast*, was already selling briskly, though he'd only brought it in this afternoon.

"Have you seen the article?" Alfred asked Zina.

Zina shook her head. "Cady's still working on it. That's why she's not here tonight. She's the type who puts everything off to the last minute."

"I'd like to give it a once-over before it goes to press," Alfred said. "Check the details. Make sure it's accurate."

Gregory cast a worried glance at his boss, and Zina said, "You really *are* a control freak, Alf." She crossed the starry floor of the café to speak to Betty, who was perusing the menu on the blackboard.

"Greg," Alfred said. "Did she call back, that reporter? Did she grill you for any more facts about Walter White?"

"Haven't heard from her," Gregory said quickly.

"Good. You have to watch these media types. They're unscrupulous." Byron Hunt passed by the table, and Alfred lowered his voice. "Remember—Walter White is not to be contacted. It's part of the marketing plan. The higher the interest in the Midnight books, the higher the interest in the author. That's the thing nowadays. Personality. So we let public curiosity grow—maybe plant a few stories to help it along. Then, when it reaches a peak, we unveil him, so to speak. Send him on tour. TV talk-shows—" He stopped as Zina returned with the coffee pot.

"My, my," Zina said, as she poured. "What are you two up to? Plotting the overthrow of the book industry?"

"Something like that," Alfred said.

AT SEVEN, ZINA rang her little bell, and Linda Rain walked to the front of the room with Buttercup at her side. She set her braille notes on the podium and ran her fingers across them. As she greeted the audience and introduced herself, many of the newcomers craned their necks to stare, as if surprised to be addressed by a blind woman. But they quickly settled down to listen as Linda began her review of *A Chill at Midnight*.

"The winter setting is obviously highly symbolic," Linda began.

In the audience, Joe Delaney poked Morgan in the ribs and whispered, "obviously," in a mock-intellectual tone.

Morgan hushed him. She turned in her seat to scan the crowd again for Sarah. Where was she?

Linda explained the metaphorical implications of ice, and Morgan tried to follow her. Something about existential loneliness and the void. Morgan remembered that Linda had a Master's degree in English from the University of

Manitoba, which, you would think, would make her *good* at communicating. Oh well. She turned around again just in time to see Sarah entering the café with Mark. And Mark was carrying Sarah's suitcase. Good.

"The hour of midnight, of course, fits into the symbolic pattern," Linda concluded. "It is the darkest hour, just as December is the darkest month. Judging from the titles in the series so far, it is tempting to predict that the motif of alienation from the light is a significant recurring theme in White's work."

Polite applause greeted this conclusion, along with a great deal of puzzlement. Then the usual buzz of discussion rose steadily as the mingling began. Zina and Javier disappeared into the kitchen to dish up the chocolate ice cream.

Morgan made her way through the chattering crowd to find Sarah. All around her, everyone was discussing *A Chill at Midnight*.

"Linda is right," a young woman remarked to Joe Delaney. "The theme of the first two Midnight books is definitely similar. All those references to disguises and masks! And both books have a detective with a secret in his past."

"True," Joe agreed. "And some of the minor characters are the same, too. That artist in the first book shows up in the second book as well. Did you notice that?"

Morgan pushed past Joe toward the front counter, where Sarah and Betty were listening to Mark's critique of *A Chill at Midnight*.

"What I don't get," Mark was saying, "is how could the door be locked from the inside, if the murderer is gone?"

"Maybe the killer had a key?" Betty suggested timidly.

"It was a chain, Betty," Morgan said. It was obvious Betty hadn't even read the book. She never read anything.

"Well, it's a mistake on the author's part," Mark continued. "He never explains that detail."

Morgan turned to Sarah. "Glad you made it."

"Yeah, we got talking, and then I had to pack.... I'm sorry I missed most of Linda's review. She's always so original."

"She was . . . interesting," Morgan said quietly. "She has a different way of reading. Looking at the little details and that. Me, I just thought it was a great thriller. Anyway, she went on and on. It's late. You want to head home?"

"Sure. Let's just pick up a copy of the new book first."

"Beat you to it," Morgan said. She patted her purse. "One for me and one for you." She picked up Sarah's suitcase and headed for the door. "Ouch, this is heavy. What did you put in here?"

Sarah smiled. "Just some reading materials."

As they passed by Byron, they heard what he was saying to Linda. "Fascinating theory. I like your notion that the prairie is a kind of Wasteland, à la T.S. Eliot. But didn't you think that the body in the freezer was overkill? I mean, if death is metaphorical . . ."

Morgan had to laugh. Was it possible that Byron Hunt, literary snob *par excellence*, was actually reading mystery novels? Or was he just hitting on Linda?

MORGAN'S COUCH PULLED out into a lumpy double bed, and both cousins sat on it, wearing pyjamas and watching the late news.

"See? It's a slumber party," Morgan joked. "I told you you'd love it here."

"I have to admit, I don't know when I'll be able to sleep alone in my house again."

"You'll get over it," Morgan said, with a little too much confidence. "What have you got in there?" she asked, as Sarah opened her suitcase.

Sarah smiled. "My mum's diaries."

"You decided to read them!"

"I started today and I just got hooked," Sarah said. "It's as if she's talking to me, you know."

"Can you remember the sound of her voice?" Morgan asked.

he Dead of Midnight

"Not really. Sometimes I think I imagine it, but—no. Not really."

"You remind me of her," Morgan said. "The way you speak. She had a low voice, like yours. And your laugh. You should laugh more often. When you laugh, I remember her."

Sarah looked at Morgan, amazed. "You never told me any of that."

"You never wanted to talk about her," Morgan said.

Sarah nodded. "That's true. I guess I thought it was better to forget. Unfortunately, I did forget."

"You were only six," Morgan said. "It's natural to forget."

"I suppose so. Still, it feels like I've left her behind. Gone off somewhere without her. Reading her words, I feel as though I'm getting a little bit of her back again. Do you know what I mean?"

Morgan was watching her cousin with interest. "Sure. I can understand that."

"And also—you were right, Morgan—there's all sorts of family stuff in here."

"Anything about—"

"No. Not yet. But she wrote down practically everything. Listen to this: *Sixty-eight degrees today. Dad planted sunflowers along the back fence, and we saw two robins gathering threads from our towels on the clothesline. Red and yellow and blue. They will have the most colorful nest on the island.* That was, let's see, when she was only sixteen she wrote that. She recorded everything."

"If you can find the diaries for the time of your conception—" Morgan stopped to count on her fingers. "Around the fall of 1975. She must mention him!"

"That's the trouble with these papers," Sarah said. "They're in no order whatsoever." She sighed. "I have no idea what she was doing in the fall of '75. Years ago I tried to ask Aunt Darlene about it, but you know your mum. Anything to do with s-e-x always made her squirm. She said she never meddled in Carolyn's 'doings,' and I should leave well enough alone. I always wondered if she knew more than she let on. Anyway, we can't ask her now."

"No," said Morgan sadly, thinking of her poor mother's addled memory. "But even if Carolyn didn't tell her sister, she would have written about him in her diary. An event like that!"

Sarah smiled wryly. "I just hope it was an event unusual enough to record." She stacked the journals neatly beside her and opened the one on top. "This is 1977 here. I wonder if she—look! Look at these drawings, Morgan."

Morgan leaned over while Sarah turned the pages. Carolyn had used the Hilroy scribbler as a sketchpad as well as a diary. Delicate pencil drawings of trees and boats and a portrait of a man they recognized as their grandfather. Then an old photograph, pasted in, of two grinning children.

"That's you and Sam!" Sarah said. "In front of your house on Walnut Street." There was Sam, eight or nine years old, posing on a blue scooter. Behind him, Morgan hung on tightly to her big brother's waist. Sarah looked at the house, which was not many blocks from where she lived now, and recalled the bright, sunny rooms where she'd gone to live after her mother died. Her early years there had been sad and lonely, despite the best efforts of her Aunt Darlene. She flipped the pages quickly to the end of the scribbler, but there were no more pictures, only writing.

"I'll leave you alone to read," Morgan said. "Sleep tight." She kissed the top of Sarah's head and carried her copy of *Midnight Feast* to bed with her.

Sarah turned back to the photo of her cousins and began reading the accompanying page.

MEMORY IS A wild thing, fleeting, like an animal in the forest. Dad died seven days ago, and already he's disappearing into that colorless space where Mother descended long ago. I cannot see his face.

The Dead of Midnight

Darlene wouldn't come here to the island after the funeral. She drove back to Winnipeg right away, still crying so hard at the church she could barely say goodbye. Leaning on her husband, as if she might faint. I gathered Sam and Morgan up in my arms and did not want to let them go. It will be desolate here now. I felt it keenly when I came home alone with Sarah. No one to greet the boat, no fire in the kitchen, everything still and hushed. Everything mine now, and the sense of responsibility is overwhelming. Sarah to care for all by myself, the whole island to watch over, garden, cabins, boat, and the dark forest at night. No moon tonight, and the statue is invisible, black against the black forest. My inheritance. Rocks, trees, water.

When Evan Knight read us the will, Darlene was shocked. The pitiful balance of a life measured in stone. Three small trust funds for Sarah and Sam and Morgan. Nothing else, except the island and the house in Wolseley, which will be Sarah's when she grows up. Darlene thinks I should move to Winnipeg and live in it, but I could never afford the taxes or the upkeep. No. I will have to keep renting it out. I suppose I am a landlord now. Absurd thought. Darlene can't understand why there is nothing else. Nothing for her but trinkets—Mum's mirror, and her jewelry, a few plates and books. But Darlene left us long ago. She wasn't here to see the way things went. Money always flowing out and nothing coming in. For years now, the rent money barely paid expenses on the house. Nothing else but Dad's old-age pension, the odd carving he'd make and sell in town, the tiny checks from my readings and books.

I have to rest now, gather my strength. Work on the new book and hope that it sells. Dad always said work was the best medicine. The struggle to survive. I thought of that this evening when an eagle came down and perched on Persephone's stone shoulder. Watched the surface of the lake carefully and then swooped down to catch a fish. Life goes on. A cliché, but it's true. And I will have to stop writing now, and feed the fire, because there is no one else here to do it. Everything is in my hands now, small hands, and unworthy of the task.

Chapter Fifteen

ALFRED WAS SURPRISED EARLY Monday morning to find Cady Brown sitting in his second-floor office, chatting with Gregory. She must have come in while he was taking a shower.

Gregory snapped his briefcase shut and jumped up as Alfred entered. "I thought you left early this morning. I was just telling Ms Brown you were unavail—"

"Ms Brown," Alfred said curtly, "I apologize for missing our meeting last week. I was called to Toronto suddenly."

"Yes, I know. It's too bad. I'll have to file my story without the author interview. The deadline's tomorrow. Perhaps in the future—"

"What brings you here this morning, then?"

"I, uh, I missed the launch of the new book last night. *Midnight Snack*, is it?"

"*Midnight Feast.*"

"Oh, yes. I thought I might get a promo copy from you? I could mention it in my article."

"Certainly. Greg, hop downstairs and get Ms Brown a copy, will you?"

Gregory hopped.

"Now," Alfred said. "Why are you really here? Still after Gregory for Walter White's telephone number? It's unlisted, and we can't give it out. He's not to be disturbed. He's quite sick at the moment."

"Sick, eh? How sick?"

"Sick enough."

Cady considered mentioning her visit to Bill Wesley, just to observe his reaction. But she didn't want anything to interfere with her plans to visit Wesley again this afternoon. She was determined to get some information from him this time. After what Gregory had just told her, she knew Alfred would never help her find White.

Gregory returned with a book for Cady, and Alfred ushered her to the top of the stairs. "My wife will see you out," he said. He returned to the office, where Gregory sat twisting an empty candy wrapper between his fingers.

"Cady Brown, girl detective," Alfred remarked.

"I'm sorry, Alf. She just barged in here."

Alfred waved a hand, dismissing Gregory. "Don't worry about it. Just don't let her in the office again, unless I'm here. She's a snoop."

"I won't," Gregory promised.

"Now, can you help me out with this new e-mail program?" Alfred asked. "I can't access my messages."

DOWNSTAIRS, BETTY PUSHED aside a stack of *Midnight Feast* books and held Cady's briefcase out for her.

But Cady did not notice. She was leafing through the book Gregory had given her. "Oh, look at the list of recipes in the back!"

"Here's your purse," Betty said, offering the briefcase again. She wanted Cady out of here so she could get back to planning her dinner party, but Cady's comment intrigued her. "What do you mean, recipes? In a novel?"

Cady put the book down and reached for her shoes. "It's one of those mysteries with recipes in it. You know—a culinary mystery—a very popular sub-genre."

"Sub who?" Betty picked up a copy and turned to the back. Why, it was like a little cookbook, with everything from Appetizers to Desserts. She studied the recipes while Cady put on her shoes. Now, this looked like a book she might actually like. Clam Chowder, Lamb Stew, Pumpkin Soup.... That sounded great. She flipped to the page with the soup recipe.

She was so absorbed in reading the list of ingredients that she didn't even notice when Cady gathered her things and left the house. She walked into the kitchen, still reading, to check her pantry for nutmeg.

"SARAH'S GONE HOME for a bit," Morgan said. She was standing before the mirror in her living room, brushing her thick, auburn hair, which never behaved itself on Monday mornings. "But she'll be back soon."

Alfred shot a regretful look at her in the mirror. He was reclining comfortably on her couch, sipping a cappuccino in a sugared glass. "So Sarah figured out how to drive her car?"

"Her ankle's a lot better now, so yes. She's just gone to pick up a few things. She'll be back any minute."

Alfred sighed. "Anyway, I came to give you girls these. They're for our dinner party on Saturday—Betty made up invitations."

"Oh, how sweet," Morgan said as she took them. "How am I going to live through this?"

Alfred shrugged. "It's better if you come. Betty specifically asked me to invite you and Sarah. I was just going to invite a few business connections, but Betty feels more comfortable with—"

"Comfortable! What about me?"

He stood up and walked toward her. "You can bring a date," he said. "It'll be okay."

When the telephone rang, he grabbed her hand. "Ignore it," he said, but Morgan pulled away.

"I'll just be a sec." She stepped around him and entered the kitchen.

Alfred tipped his glass up and finished the cappuccino. He glanced at his watch. As soon as Morgan got off the phone, he'd talk to her, reassure her. He didn't want her flying off the handle now. Maybe he could take her out for breakfast. Then he heard her shouting into the phone. Alarmed, he hurried out to the kitchen.

"What are you saying?" Morgan asked her caller. "Calm down." She held up her cigarette to show Alfred the long ash.

"Who is it?" Alfred mouthed, but Morgan only glared at him. He brought the ashtray from the living room and leaned against her refrigerator, listening.

"I didn't take them anywhere!" Morgan cried. "What are you talking about?" She listened for a moment. "Of course not!" She listened again, said, "I'll be right over," and hung up.

"You'll be right over where?" Alfred asked. "You can't leave now!"

"It's Sarah. She's in a state. I don't know what she's done, but she's lost her mother's stuff." Morgan was pulling on her sandals.

Alfred straightened up. "Not her mother's papers?"

"Yeah. I don't see how—there were boxes and boxes of them. It's impossible."

"The Carolyn Yeats papers?" Alfred said. "How could she lose them?" He started to put on his own shoes. "I'll come with you."

SARAH HAD OBVIOUSLY called the police as well, because Daniel was already there when Alfred and Morgan pulled up. Morgan didn't know exactly what she expected, probably tears and confusion. But she was surprised to see Sarah absolutely energized with rage. A palpable anger emanated from her as she related the details of the theft to Daniel.

Sadly, there weren't many details to relate. Sarah had been at Morgan's apartment overnight. The porch was easy to enter. Someone had simply slit the screen beside the door and reached in to turn the lock.

Daniel nodded at Morgan and Alfred, then resumed writing in his notebook.

Alfred examined the torn screen and the flimsy lock. "This is all you had on here? Of all the stupid—anyone could—"

"Don't blame Sarah!" Morgan cried. "She's the victim here!"

Sarah turned on Alfred. "I never had anything of value out here. Nothing! Just a few sticks of furniture." She indicated the battered old chairs and the table.

"You had the Yeats papers out here," Alfred accused. "You left them sitting out here where anyone could—"

"Who would want them?" Sarah cried. "Who in the world could possibly want them besides me?"

"Who would want them enough to *carry* them?" Morgan asked.

"Oh, you ignorant people!" Alfred threw up his hands.

"Let's be civilized," Daniel said. He turned to Alfred. "These papers are valuable?"

"They very well might be, yes. Depending what's in there. Which we didn't get to see! Carolyn Yeats might be obscure to your average Canadian." He glared at Morgan and Sarah. "She might be held in low esteem among her own family." He turned back to his stepson. "But her papers represent a period in Canadian poetry that would be of great interest to scholars."

"Or someone interested in my estate," Sarah said.

"Peter?" Morgan asked. "You think he did this?"

"Who else? He's either looking for deeds and titles and stuff—he always believed Grandpa had untold wealth stashed away somewhere. Or, like Alfred, he thinks that they're worth something."

"And if they're worth something," Morgan said, as she started to understand, "they'll be part of the divorce settlement."

"Have you started divorce proceedings?" Daniel asked.

"Not yet, but we've discussed it. We've already argued over this house."

Daniel scribbled this down.

Morgan sat down in the armchair and tuned out the conversation. Peter? Yes, it was possible. And if he did this, he might have broken in last week as well. Done all those wild, outrageous things that happened to Sarah, right down to the trick with the lightbulb. But why? To make Sarah look crazy? If so, it had worked. Morgan watched Sarah speaking to Daniel. Sarah stood up straight, barely leaning on her crutches at all. Her cheeks were flushed with anger, and her voice was raised, but she was perfectly lucid. She looked almost . . . powerful.

"That's it, then," Daniel said. He handed Sarah a card. "Your complaint number is on there. Refer to it if you need to call the station." He turned to leave.

"That's it?" Sarah asked. "Aren't you going to talk to Peter?"

"I'll talk to him," Daniel said. He pointed at her. "You stay away from him. Leave it to me." He waved to Morgan, said, "See ya, Al," and walked out to his car.

"I'm going to call the neighbors," Sarah said. "Maybe somebody saw him." She went inside and Morgan started to follow.

"Morgan, wait." Alfred tugged at her arm. "We should talk."

"You've said enough," Morgan snapped. "And I don't see what we could possibly have to talk about, seeing I'm so terribly *ignorant!*" She slammed the door in his face and followed her cousin inside.

Chapter Sixteen

IT WAS A GOOD THING ALFRED wasn't home, because Betty needed a drink. She'd been all over town today, looking for her sister, and although the search had included at least ten different seedy bars, Betty hadn't even had a beer. She had not stopped long enough anywhere. She dragged a chair over to the kitchen cupboard and stood on it to reach the back of the top shelf. Ah. There was still half a bottle of the good stuff left. She took one slug, still standing on the chair, and then climbed down and poured herself a few ounces in a proper glass.

She sat at her kitchen table and reread the ominous note she found this afternoon: *He doesn't know what you did in Kenora. You'd better keep your mouth shut about AFM, if you don't want him to find out about your little trip there.*

Who could have written it? She ran over in her mind again the names of everyone who had been in the house today. Zina Schwartz dropped by on business, and Alfred's stepson Daniel looked in for a few minutes as he passed by on his beat. That Cady person was here early this morning. Who else? Gregory was here all day, helping Alfred catch up on his long-overdue correspondence. Betty's own mother, of course, and the boy who delivered the groceries. It couldn't have been any of those people. But Betty was pretty sure the note had been placed in the book some time earlier today. She had only started reading it today. Then she tucked it away with her cookbooks when she went out to the hairdresser. When she returned—she cringed when she remembered the moment she opened the book and the note fell out. She'd had the idea to try some of the recipes in the novel, and she'd found the anonymous threat.

Thank God Alfred hadn't found it.

Who, besides her sister, even knew about Kenora?

And AFM? What was that? She threw back her head and gulped the whisky. AFM. AFM. The letters had been running through her head all day. All she could think of was the Alcoholism Foundation of Manitoba, and that didn't make any sense.

What was it she was supposed to keep her mouth shut about?

GINGERLY, SARAH STEPPED over the two remaining boxes of Carolyn's papers, the ones that had been in Morgan's car. All that was left of her mother's memories. At least they'd be safe here, in Morgan's apartment. Sarah felt badly, remembering her initial reaction to receiving so many papers. She'd wanted to be rid of the responsibility. But now that almost all of them are gone, she wanted them back. Well, she would get them back. They were the only link she had to this lost woman she was only now beginning to know.

It had been a rough day. Sarah and Morgan speculated angrily for hours on Peter's methods and motives, but came up with no solutions. Then they canvassed the entire street for witnesses, hoping someone had seen Peter entering the porch or loading the boxes into his car. Mark Curtis offered to help, going door-to-door with Morgan, while Sarah stayed home and telephoned all the neighbors she knew. They met with no luck, though. The street lamp by Sarah's house was still not repaired, and the night had been pitch black. No one saw anything, or no one would admit it.

She wondered if Daniel had spoken to Peter yet, or if he had called with any news. She decided to check her home messages.

As she pushed her code into the telephone, she could see Morgan lying in her bedroom, where she had retired earlier to read her new mystery novel.

"You have one new message."

Sarah listened as Cady Brown's voice came over the line. "It's now urgent that I get in touch with you. . . ."

"What a nuisance," Sarah said aloud.

Morgan looked up. "What's a nuisance?"

Sarah listened to a few more words and then hung up. "It's Cady again, sounding desperate now. Says she 'needs' me. I guess it's deadline time."

"She shouldn't have procrastinated so long. Are you going to call her back?"

"Too tired tonight," Sarah said. "I'm going to bed."

"Me too." Morgan turned back to *Midnight Feast.*

All seemed in order in the kitchen. The pheasants roasting slowly on their spits were approaching a rich, burnished perfection. A kitchen maid was pinching the dough round the last of the apple tarts. And the soup! The butler sipped from a tasting spoon and pronounced it delicious. A delicate blend of pumpkin and sweet potato, subtly flavored with a hint of nutmeg. Ahh. It needed only one addition. He put his hand in his pocket and glanced round to see if anyone was watching.

Morgan groaned. If the butler did it, she was going to throw the book across the room into the wastebasket.

This book wasn't nearly as exciting as the previous two. In fact, the only thing keeping Morgan going was the romantic subplot. The heroine, an heiress in danger, was falling in love with a young beekeeper on the lavish, southern Ontario estate where she was hiding out, disguised as a lowly maid. The poor beekeeper had no idea how wealthy she really was. Or did he?

The table was set for twelve. The butler performed a final inspection. White linen, silver, crystal, and the finest bone china. Candlesticks of pure gold. A centerpiece of red roses. At the end of the table, a single bloom in a cut-glass bud vase complemented the setting for the guest of honor. A very special guest indeed.

Morgan could barely keep her eyes open. The novel was full of descriptions like this that slowed the pace to a crawl. She wanted some action. So far, there were motives all over the place. Lots of means and lots of opportunity. But not a single murder. She decided to try reading one more chapter. Surely something had to happen soon.

Chapter Seventeen

ZINA, LETTING HERSELF OUT QUIETLY at dawn, was reminded of an old episode of *The Twilight Zone* about a man who woke one morning to find himself alone on the planet. Westminster Avenue seemed artificial, like an abandoned movie set. The little grocery stores and launderettes were locked up. The ragged posters, stapled in thick layers onto every telephone pole, flapped in the breeze, advertising concerts and yard sales and Zina's book-club meetings. On the side streets, the large old brick and clapboard houses were still dark. The sense of unreality was heightened by the bright sunshine and the silence. She heard only the cooing and chirping of unseen birds somewhere above, and even they seemed—or was it her imagination?—strangely subdued.

Zina turned down a back lane, a shortcut to the café. In contrast to the well-kept front yards of the neighborhood, the lanes were a mess, especially in spring. Old plastic bags and soggy newspapers lay tangled among the bushes. The gravel was littered with broken shards of beer-bottle glass and cigarette butts and, oddly, a discarded ski mask, lying face up on the ground, its two stitched eyeholes staring at the rising sun.

As she turned out of the back lane, Zina was startled by the sight of flashing lights down the street from her café. Two black and white police cars, a fire department rescue truck, an ambulance. What was going on?

She joined the small crowd gathered across the street to watch the drama unfolding. A couple of people glanced up, then quickly looked away. Zina expected excited gossip, the offer of some kind of information. But everyone was silent. She turned toward the scene. The lawn and sidewalk in front of the River Point apartment building were swarming with men and women, both in plain clothes and in uniform. The entire yard was cordoned off with yellow crime-scene tape, the kind she had seen only on television. Through an open window, she could hear a man inside barking orders in a frantic, authoritarian voice. But from which apartment? Zina felt a sudden, nauseating premonition.

As she stood there transfixed, she felt a hand on her arm. It was Alfred Carriere, dressed for a morning run in track shoes and a sweatsuit. He squeezed her elbow tightly.

"Alfred? What happened?"

He merely shook his head.

Beside him, his wife Betty burst into tears.

DANIEL BRADLEY BARELY took time to button his shirt and tie his shoelaces before he raced out of the house and into his car. Swinging onto Osborne Street, he reached out his window and placed the portable siren on the roof of the Jetta. He shook with excitement.

He could picture what was happening at this moment. He knew the steps. Secure the scene, send in the identification unit, the detectives. Hell, the detectives would be there already. He'd missed almost everything. He went over in his mind the statistics he'd studied. They'll assume it's a domestic, he told himself. A domestic or a drinking party. Winnipeg, though known in recent headlines as the "murder capital of Canada," was also a city with a ninety-eight percent conviction rate for murder. Strangers didn't kill each other here. No. They'd look first at those closest to the victim. Interview the neighbors, question the family.

He sped north across the Osborne Street bridge, siren flashing and bleeping. His palms were sweating, and he took them off the wheel one after the other to wipe them on his pants. He had to appear calm and collected. He didn't want his behavior this morning to stir up any memories of his fainting spell and his waffle-like bruise. Everyone had almost forgotten about that, and if he wanted it to stay that way, he'd have to act cool. Prove that he was in control.

He exited the bridge, zig-zagged around the meridian, and made an illegal left-hand turn onto Mostyn, accelerating past the curling club. Almost there. "Take ownership of the neighborhood," the chief said. Well, if Daniel was going to own this neighborhood, he'd have to take charge.

He glanced at his watch. Six twenty-six a.m. He hoped the investigation hadn't progressed too far.

PETER PETURSSON COULD not stop crying. He sat hunched on a stool in the kitchen with a box of tissues on his lap and blew his nose for the eleventh time.

Detective Vishnu Maharaj waited, watching him closely. Was the guy faking? He wondered if it was possible to fake so much snot. The guy seemed honestly broken up.

Detective Kayla Petrovitch wasn't wondering at all. She was convinced he was faking. Or, if the tears were real, it was only because he regretted hanging around and insisting the police break in to search the apartment. The trail of blood had led them straight to the body, and Petursson had put on a pretty good imitation of shock as soon as he saw it.

Arrogant scum had thought he could pull it off, but now he could see the net closing in on him. No alibi. Plenty of motive. He even had keys to the apartment in the pocket of his blue jeans.

Kayla turned away in disgust. "I'll be right back," she told Vishnu. She left the building and walked out to use the radio in her car. She popped a piece of bubble gum in her mouth and chewed hard, thinking. The apartment door had been chained from the inside. That was one element of Petursson's story that checked out. But Petursson could have done that himself, either before or after the fact. You didn't have to be a brain surgeon to latch a chain from the outside, if you had the right tool. She radioed in to the station to check up on some other queries she had.

Yes, Jeannie the dispatcher told her, Petursson's 911 call came from the booth at Westminster and Evanson, just as he said. A neighbor had also called in a disturbance at two thirty-three a.m., complaining that a guy was hollering and banging on apartment 303. But it had been a busy night. The complaint was given low priority, and no car was dispatched.

So he probably did holler and bang first, Kayla thought. The Distraught Lover: Act One. Then, when he attracted no audience, he used the 911 ploy. Trying to make himself look innocent, the injured party. Some of these guys were un-believable, the scenes they set up. But Kayla and her team would cut through the bull soon enough.

She re-entered the apartment block just as Johnny Wolverine was exiting with the identi-kit. "Any good prints?" she asked.

"Lots. But we haven't tried to match any yet, except the victim's."

"And Petursson's?"

"Kayla," Johnny said, "you know his prints are probably everywhere."

Kayla nodded wearily. Yes, she knew all too well. That was the whole problem with domestics.

DANIEL COULD SEE at once that it was impossible to pull up in front of the apartment block. He didn't think he could maneuver his car down the front street at all, with so many vehicles there. He decided to use the back lane, parking in the carport next door. Then he walked around the front of the building and ducked under the crime-scene tape.

"Hey—Bradley!" It was his old partner, Jay Kilroy. "What are you doing here?"

"This is my beat," Daniel said. "Jeannie called me just a few minutes ago. What's going on?"

"A stabbing. Woman's cut to ribbons in there."

Daniel saw Johnny Wolverine coming around the side of the building, sweeping the lawn with a metal detector. "Who's on it?" he asked Kilroy.

"Maharaj and Petrovitch."

"Damn," Daniel said. The two most ambitious detectives in the city. Vishnu Maharaj viewed every big case as an opportunity to get his name in the news. And the ego of Kayla Petrovitch was legendary. She had transferred here from Toronto a few years ago with a chip on her shoulder that no one had knocked off yet. She had no patience for those she considered inferior, a category that included just about everyone in town except Vishnu Maharaj. Daniel would have a devil of a time with those two on the case.

"Are they inside?" he asked.

Kilroy nodded. "Go on in."

"Okay." Daniel drew a deep breath, trying to fill his lungs with fresh air.

"It's bad," Kilroy called after him. "You better watch your waffle-head in there."

MORGAN WAS DEEP in a dream of pumpkin soup and pheasant under glass when the telephone rang. It was seven a.m., for goodness' sakes. She reached across the bed and answered.

"This better be good."

136

"Morgan? It's me, Zina. Listen, something awful has happened. You know Cady?"

"Cady Brown? Of course I know her."

"She lives in the River Point apartments?"

"I guess so. I don't know."

"Are you sitting down right now?"

"I'm *lying* down, Zina. I just woke up."

"I'm serious, Morgan. Something terrible has happened. Cady Brown has been murdered. Right in her own home!"

Morgan sat up. "What are you saying?"

"I just walked past her place. It's swarming with cops. Everyone in the neighborhood is out there, reporters, too. They say she was stabbed to death."

"Oh my God," Morgan said slowly. "I don't believe it."

"If you don't believe me, turn on your radio."

Morgan was silent.

Sarah appeared at the bedroom door, leaning on one crutch. "What is it, Morgan?"

Morgan handed the receiver to her cousin and watched her face turn pale.

DANIEL'S MIND WAS reeling. He sat on the front steps of the apartment block, his head between his knees, gasping for air. He had never seen anything so horrible. Not even the autopsies he had witnessed were as bad as what he had just seen. At least in the autopsies, the eyes had been closed.

Why hadn't they at least closed her eyes!

Cady Brown's tiny body lay upstairs above him in a pool of frozen blood. She had stared right through him. Her face a vivid blue. Her expression paralyzed with horror. The pupils of her eyes fixed and dilated and reflecting back to him an expression he could only imagine existing in the depths of hell.

He would never forget it, not as long as he lived. He would never forget.

137

Chapter Eighteen

ALL MORNING, CADY BROWN'S murder was the only topic of conversation in the Mystery Au Lait Café. Alfred and Betty had been in the café since Zina opened, retelling the events of the morning to every customer who entered. Half of Zina's regulars were there, including Joe Delaney, who lived across town in St. Boniface and usually came by only on weekends. But somehow he'd heard the news. Somehow everyone had heard the news. The café was jammed and buzzing with shocked voices. Zina bustled about behind the counter. The murder was bringing in the best day of business she'd seen in weeks. Even the cops were spending a bundle on coffee and pastries.

Byron Hunt sat at the counter and stirred his steaming bowl of mushroom soup. "What do you think could have happened?" he asked Zina. It was a question everyone was asking, and Zina had no answer. She left the counter to make the rounds of the café, refilling coffee cups. Every table was full, and a number of people stood by the window, balancing plates and cups in their hands.

"Miss Brown was writing something subversive?" Javier asked.

"No, no, Javier," said Alfred. As the first one on the scene this morning, he'd taken on an air of authority about the matter. "She was an entertainment reporter. You know, theater, books, movies. She wrote about art."

"Art is subversive," Javier ventured.

"Not in Canada," Alfred replied. He turned toward his wife. "Betty, you want to have breakfast here? Or brunch, I guess. We might as well."

"Might as well," Betty agreed. She read the menu on Zina's blackboard, although she knew it by heart. She had already consumed two cheese croissants, but she ordered a clubhouse sandwich and a large side of fries.

Joe Delaney stood at the window, peering down the street, trying to see what was happening in front of Cady's building. "They're still milling around out there," he reported. "Looking for clues. They're dragging the ground with a vacuum or something."

"Metal detector," Byron said. "Looking for a weapon."

He stood to join Joe at the window. "I can't believe this is happening here," he said. "Right in my own back yard."

"Murder's Half Acre," Joe muttered. "Wasn't it Cady's newspaper that gave this neighborhood that nickname?"

"That's east of here," Byron told him.

"Way east," Zina agreed. "Five, six blocks east."

"Eight blocks at least," said Alfred decisively. "Up past the Big Sky Tavern. It's a completely different neighborhood up there. There's an invisible line running right down the middle of the street. One side it's a jungle. This side it's safe."

"It *was* safe," Byron said sadly.

"Oh, come and sit down," Zina called. "There's no point staring. The coffee's ready."

Byron sat and picked up his coffee cup, but he didn't drink. Like everyone else, he had already consumed far too much coffee. But like everyone else, he kept ordering things.

He looked at the line-up of orders on the counter—bowls of soup, omelets, sandwiches. Nobody wanted to leave. They were all drawn together, he thought, eager for any scrap of information they might glean, anxious to analyze every known fact about the crime, as if by understanding it, they might somehow undo it. He ordered a blueberry muffin.

"Could I get some service over here?" a woman called. Zina turned to see Dr. Adele Allard waving a menu at her.

Zina hurried over. "Sorry." She smiled. "I didn't see you come in. We're so busy in here today."

Dr. Allard didn't seem to care whether Zina was busy or not. "Does soup come with the special?" she asked.

"Yes. Mushroom soup today."

"Is coffee included?"

"Yes," Zina said wearily. Dr. Allard didn't come in often, but when she did, she fussed over the price of the books, the quality of the food, the speed of the service—and she never left a tip. The only thing she ever gave Zina was a headache.

"They found something!" Joe called from his lookout at the window. "They're marking off a spot under her window."

Byron got up again to look, and Alfred and Betty followed him.

"Where?" Betty asked.

"I'll take the special," Dr. Allard decided. But Zina's attention had been drawn to the small crowd at the window. She peered out over Betty's head. Down the block, she could see a police officer marking the ground with a little orange flag. Another officer crouched low with his hands held up to his face, and Zina saw the flash of a camera bulb. They were photographing the site.

"Can you tell what it is?" Betty asked.

"Not from here," Byron said. "But I'm going to go see what I can find out." He strode to the door, with Joe close behind him. "Stay here," Byron said. But Joe followed him right out of the café. Several more customers gathered at the window to watch them hurry down the street.

"The cops won't tell them anything," Alfred said.

Dr. Allard rapped a teaspoon against the table and asked again loudly for the special, Greek salad and falafel.

Zina nodded impatiently, then hurried back to the counter, where people were lining up to pay their bills. The door opened and another four customers entered. Two of them carried camera bags. Reporters, Zina thought. It was getting to be a circus in here.

"How about dessert?" Dr. Allard called after her. "Is dessert included?"

"Pie is included," Zina answered without turning around. She smiled at the first customer in line as she took his bill. She rubbed her neck, which was sore from tension and fatigue. She felt she'd been cooking for an army. Crime seemed to make people hungry. It seemed the more they discussed the murder, the more they ate. The café just kept filling up. She rang up one sale after another and tried not to be happy about all the money accumulating in the cash register. Cady was dead.

MORGAN USUALLY OPENED her clothing shop at ten-thirty on weekdays, but today she was still sitting in her pyjamas at ten, biting her nails and worrying. Sarah was dressed and stood at the stove, scrambling eggs. They were both quiet, listening to the local news on the radio. But they learned nothing they didn't know already. Just the fact of the murder and some background information about Cady. There were no details yet.

Sarah set a plate in front of Morgan, and Morgan groaned.

"Come on," Sarah said. "You have to eat. You have to get ready for work."

"I don't know if I'll open up today," Morgan said. "It doesn't seem right, with Cady killed just down the street."

"Well, you have to eat, anyway," Sarah said.

Morgan picked at the eggs with her fork. "What are you going to do today?"

"I thought I'd keep going through my mum's papers—what's left of them. I was going to call Daniel Bradley today, to see if he's talked to Peter yet. But now. . . ."

"Yeah. Now he'll have more serious things to do," Morgan agreed.

"Maybe I should call Peter myself."

"You should wait," Morgan said. "Daniel told you to stay away from him. Let Daniel handle it."

"Well, Daniel never called back yesterday. When I checked the messages last night, there was nothing but Cady's—oh no, Morgan! I wonder when it happened. She could have been dead already. Lying there dead while I was listening to her voice!"

"Did you save that message?" Morgan asked. "Did you save the time it came in?"

"I don't know. I just hung up. I didn't even hear the whole—"

"Check it," Morgan said. "Check it out right now. It might be important. You might have been the last person to talk to her."

"To listen to her," Sarah said. She moved toward Morgan's phone and dialed in her code.

"DETECTIVE KAYLA PETROVITCH, line two, please." Jeannie's voice crackled through the intercom in the interrogation room, interrupting the silence that had descended ever since Peter Petursson asked for a lawyer.

Kayla scowled. How many times had she told Vishnu to turn that damn thing off when they were questioning suspects? She glared at him, but he only shrugged. Kayla motioned him to follow her out into the hall, and they left Peter sitting at the table with nothing to do but trace his thumb through the gouges on its scarred surface over and over again.

"We're through, anyway," Vishnu told her. "The guy

wants a lawyer. He's not going to give us any more information now."

"Any more bull, you mean."

"Kayla, you're pushing too hard. You scared him off."

"Get real, Vishnu. He's practically got *guilty* tattooed on his forehead. His story is so full of holes you could strain cheese through it."

"Don't start closing your mind yet," Vishnu warned. "It's too early. Anyway, we have to back off now, and get going on background stuff. I'm heading out to see if they turned up anything more at the scene."

"Daniel Bradley's still waiting for you," Jeannie called from her desk.

"Tell him to keep his pants on," Kayla yelled. "I've got to take that call first."

She turned and stalked down the corridor toward her desk and snatched up the phone.

"Petrovitch," she barked.

A diffident voice replied. "Hello? My name is Sarah Petursson."

VISHNU MAHARAJ STRODE quickly out through the reception area, his mind focused on his partner. Kayla was getting tunnel vision. He'd seen it before, and it worried him.

"Hey! Maharaj!"

Vishnu turned to see the beat officer—Daniel Bradley—from Wolseley. Another one who liked to jump to conclusions. Impulsive. He'd been hanging around the crime scene this morning, getting in the way. "What?" he asked.

"Heard you made an arrest in the Brown murder."

"Not yet."

"Jeannie told me you got Petursson in there." Daniel jerked his thumb toward the interrogation room.

"We're holding him. But he's clammed up. Asking for a lawyer."

"You didn't charge him?"

"No." Vishnu jingled his keys impatiently. "Look, Bradley, I gotta go. You got something to say, spit it out."

"I had him in here ten days ago," Daniel said. "You don't know about that?"

Vishnu frowned. "We ran him," he said. "He's clean."

"Not entirely." Daniel smiled. "Take a read through this." He handed over his notebook.

LINDA SAT AT her lathe in the workshop at the back of her store and examined the fiddle bow with her expert fingers. Almost perfect. It was past quitting time, and she was supposed to meet Byron for dinner at Zina's café, but she decided to finish this job first. The customer wanted to pick it up tomorrow morning. And anyway, she admitted to herself, she didn't want to hear any more about the murder of Cady Brown. When she'd picked up her afternoon coffee at Zina's, she'd been sickened by the atmosphere of excitement and curiosity surrounding Cady's death. She hoped the café had cleared out a little by now. The crowd made Buttercup nervous. The poor dog was still restless, pacing the floor.

Buttercup gave a soft bark and Linda told her to settle down. She started up the lathe and continued shaping the bow. But Buttercup barked again, loudly. Linda took her foot off the treadle of the lathe. Had someone entered the store?

"Hello?" she called. "Who's there?"

She heard the delicate tinkle of the bells on the front door. Darn! She must have put the "Closed" sign on backwards again. She should have locked the door. Heavy footsteps sounded on the shop's hardwood floor, and Linda's stomach turned over, as she thought of Cady. She'd have to start locking her door all the time now.

"Anybody home?" A deep male voice.

Linda rose. "Who's there?"

"Channel 9," the voice said. The footsteps entered Linda's workshop. "Wow. This is quite the set-up you have here."

"Who are you?" Linda asked.

"Channel 9. You know, News Every Hour on the Hour. You got a minute? I just have a few questions."

"About what?"

"I heard you're a member of the Mystery Book Club next door. I'm putting together some background on Cady Brown," the reporter said. "How well did you know her?"

"Not very well, really," Linda said. "I only met her recently, through the book club."

"You know Peter Petursson?"

"Well, yes. He's a long-time customer. Plays guitar."

"When was the last time you saw Peter? Sorry—when was the last time you talked to him?"

"Oh, maybe a couple of days ago. Why?"

"Just trying to get some background. You know, Cady Brown's boyfriends, her activities. This is a big story. Anything you can tell me—"

"Peter wasn't her boyfriend," Linda said. "There's no need to go making up rumors."

"Hey, hey." He laughed a little. "Come on. The word is, Petursson was her main squeeze. And now that they're holding him for questioning—"

"For questioning? Why?"

"That's where they look first," the reporter said. "The boyfriend or the husband. And you gotta admit, they're usually right."

Linda bit her lip. Peter? A suspect? She remained silent. She didn't want to give this sleazebag any quotes.

He wandered around the shop, touching things. "Nice place you got here," he said. "Who owns it?"

"I do."

"You're kidding! I mean, that's great. Who does the handmade instruments?"

"I do."

That seemed to shut him up for a minute. But only for a minute.

"Tell me, did Peter ever show up at this book club? I understand his ex-wife was a member, too. Did Peter belong? Did he read the books?"

"What does that have to do with anything?"

"Well, you know—a love triangle, a bunch of people reading murder mysteries. It's a possible angle."

Linda told him to get out.

Chapter Nineteen

By the time Linda entered Zina's Café, the crowd had thinned slightly. Only the regulars remained, and though they had not yet exhausted the topic of the murder, they were reduced to repeating themselves. But Linda's news about the Channel 9 reporter got them going again.

Linda recounted her conversation with the reporter. "So Peter was dating her," she concluded. "Who knew?"

"Not me," Zina exclaimed. "I never would have guessed that."

"But here's the bad part," Linda said. "The Channel 9 guy says Peter's in custody."

Alfred stood up suddenly. "Arrested?"

"I don't know," Linda said. "He said 'held for questioning.' Whatever that means."

"Petursson," Alfred mused. "I never did like that guy."

"I'm sure he's not a suspect," Zina said cautiously.

"Then why would they hold him?" Joe asked.

Alfred thumped his fist suddenly on the counter, and Betty jumped. "Of course! It *had* to be Petursson!"

"But I *know* him," Byron Hunt interrupted, as he approached the counter and thrust his cup toward Zina for a refill. His hands trembled as he received his third cup of Colombian. "I've known the guy for years. No way he'd do something like that. The man's a musician. He's an artist, for God's sake."

"So was Burroughs an artist," Alfred remarked dryly. "And Pound. And van Gogh. Doesn't mean he's not crazy."

"I know Peter, too," Betty put in. "And I agree with Byron. I used to see Peter working in the yard, when he was still with Sarah, and he was always friendly. I remember when he painted the house. He was always whistling, up there on his ladder. You could hear him way down the street."

"Oh," said Alfred. "He *whistled*. Well, then."

"Alfred, come on," his wife admonished. "You don't really think . . ."

"I know more than you do," Alfred said. "The guy's no angel, believe me. He broke into Sarah's house—"

"Hey, hold on!" Byron said. "You mean the Yeats papers? That could have been anyone. Probably a book collector. Some jerk who views fine art as a commodity." He pointed a finger at Alfred. "Probably some *publisher*."

"Go to hell," Alfred muttered. "Petursson's been harassing Sarah—"

"They're getting divorced!" Byron said. "Of course there's harassment. It doesn't mean—"

"He's been terrorizing her!"

"Terrorizing?" Byron scoffed. "Where do you get these dramatic ideas?"

Alfred was silent. He looked guilty, as if he'd said too much already.

"He's making it up," Byron said scornfully to no one in particular. He carried his coffee back to his paper-strewn table by the window. "He's been reading his own murder mysteries and now he's trying to write one."

"This Peter," Javier asked, "he was the killer?"

"Nobody knows, Javier," Zina told him. "People are just speculating."

"Spec-u-lating?"

"You know, guessing."

"Oh. Guessing. Yes. And the police? They are guessing, too?"

Joe Delaney laughed. "They're always guessing. As usual, they haven't got a clue."

"I don't know about that," Zina said, still cautious. "That cop on the beat—you know the new one? He had some pretty sharp questions this morning. I think he's on the ball."

"That guy? The one with the baby blues?" Joe asked. "I saw him last week trying to help Linda across the street. Practically got her run over." He snorted. "That guy? If he had brains, he'd be dangerous."

Javier muttered to himself, "Brains or no brains."

"What did you say?" Zina asked him.

"Brains or no brains," Javier said darkly, "the police are always dangerous."

KAYLA PETROVITCH CHEWED the end of her ballpoint pen and thought hard about the call from Sarah Petursson. This wasn't the first call she'd received about Cady Brown's actions on the day she was killed, but it was certainly the most interesting. An urgent message to the suspect's wife from the suspect's girlfriend—the night before the girlfriend was killed! Sarah had hung up in order to forward the voice message directly to Kayla's phone, and Kayla was eager to hear it, tape it, and rush it down to Anthony Sinclair, the tough new prosecutor.

While she waited for the call to come through, Kayla flipped through the notes she'd made. In typical Winnipeg fashion, anyone who had ever heard of Cady Brown felt compelled to call in a tip. Wolseley residents were practically falling over each other to volunteer the slightest bits of useless information. In the days before her death, Cady had phoned the university, asking for a retired professor. She'd been seen in Kenora. She'd been seen jogging along the riverbank. So what? Kayla held out no hope for these snippets of maddeningly irrelevant information, but she had dutifully entered them in her notes. Until now they were all she had to go on. Investigators had so far turned up a lot of background information on the victim, all of it disappointingly boring.

When Sarah phoned back, Kayla turned on her recording device before she picked up. The dead woman's voice came across clearly, and Kayla relished every word. "Sarah? Cady Brown again. It's now urgent that I get in touch with you as soon as possible. I need to speak with you, about something that concerns you—that concerns your life. Maybe you already know. . . . Well, I'm not sure, but call me, anyway, as soon as you can. We need to talk."

What was that, Kayla wondered, if not a warning—or a plea for help—from one woman to another? Kayla knew about the book-club story Cady wanted to do. But it was obvious this message had nothing to do with any book club. Anyone—any jury—could tell from Cady's voice that she was nervous as hell—distraught, even. Kayla wrote the word "distraught" on her notepad. She imagined the prosecutor playing the message aloud in court. Petursson was toast.

A knock on the door interrupted her thoughts.

"Come in."

Vishnu entered, a grin on his face.

"Guess what," Kayla said. "I think we got him."

"Oh, we got him all right." Vishnu's grin widened. He thumped Daniel's notebook down on Kayla's desk, open to the relevant pages.

AFTER MORGAN FINALLY left, an hour late, for the clothing shop, Sarah carefully bolted and chained the apartment door. Then she washed the breakfast dishes and settled down in

Morgan's living room with the two remaining boxes of her mother's papers at her feet. She tried to push the murder of Cady Brown out of her thoughts. She had done all she could, told the police all she knew, and there was no point dwelling on it. The idea that a murder had taken place mere blocks away was too creepy to bear. It had upset Morgan terribly, and Sarah was worn out from trying to convince Morgan to go about her life as usual today. Morgan was full of theories about a serial killer on the loose.

"Like that nut in *A Chill at Midnight*," Morgan had said. "He did in seven women. Seven total strangers. Just because they were blue-eyed blondes!"

But that was absurd, Sarah had argued. The murder probably had something to do with Cady's personal life, about which, she reminded Morgan, they knew very little.

After days of leafing through the journals at random, Sarah had decided to sort through them methodically and try to find the journals for 1975 and 1976—the dates of her own conception and birth. She hoped those entries had not been among the stolen papers. She opened a small, black, pocket notebook and looked inside. 1980. Under that was a large hardcover journal, the kind used for keeping accounts. Carolyn had written right across the pages, ignoring the vertical columns meant for rows of numbers. 1974. Now where had Sarah put that other one from 1974? She was finding it hard to focus.

She opened a couple of journals and checked the dates inside. She'd have to start again. Concentrate. She cleared a space on the coffee table, pushing aside a copy of *A Chill at Midnight*. The terror-stricken blue eyes of the shivering blonde on the cover seemed to meet her own, as if appealing for help. Sarah shuddered.

Psychopathic serial killers were not likely to be lurking around Wolseley, she told herself, and even less likely to step off the pages of a book and enter the living room. Nevertheless, she shoved the book into a drawer. Then she rose and swung on her crutches over to the balcony door, remembering that Morgan often forgot to lock it. Good. It was secure. On her way back, she accidentally caught a glimpse of herself in Morgan's mirror—her small frame swinging by on the crutches, and her blonde hair, freshly washed, hanging loosely around her shoulders. Get a grip, she told herself. But she could see the hunted look in her own blue eyes.

Chapter Twenty

THE LOCAL DAILY, WHERE CADY had written a weekly entertainment column, splashed the story of her murder across the entire front page. When Sarah went home to pick up some clothes on Wednesday morning, the delivery boy was tossing the paper onto her porch. She tipped him, then unfolded the paper and stared at the huge, black headline: BODY FOUND IN DEEP FREEZE. She sank into the armchair on the porch and forced herself to read, though she did not believe she could really be awake. This had to be a dream.

Residents of the River Point Apartments were in shock yesterday after learning that one of their neighbors had met her death in their building. Cady Brown, columnist for the Manitoba Daily*, was the victim late Monday night or early Tuesday morning of what police describe as a "brutal attack." Detective Vishnu Maharaj refused to release any details of the slaying, citing the importance of tight security during the investigation. But an unnamed source confirmed rumors of bizarre crime scene details.*

Ms Brown's mutilated, fully clothed body was discovered in the deep freezer in the kitchen of her apartment. A common ice pick, believed to be the murder weapon, is said to have been found in the vicinity of the victim's apartment block. Detective Maharaj would not confirm whether an arrest had been made. "We are questioning a number of persons in connection with this crime," he said. "We are pursuing every avenue, and we are confident that justice will be done."

In the meantime, the lack of information is keeping apartment residents on edge. "It's frightening," said a mother of two who lives directly below the victim's apartment. "I don't feel safe here any more."

A university student who lived down the hall from Ms Brown witnessed police entering her apartment Tuesday morning. "It was chained from the inside," he said. "It was creepy, as if she was murdered by a ghost." He said he heard no commotion during the night, although he was up late studying. "She was pretty quiet," he said. "She was always busy. I saw her come in and out a lot, but we didn't talk much. She kept to herself."

Ms Brown was born in Ottawa and earned her journalism degree from Carleton University. She moved to Winnipeg in 1992 and was building a reputation as a talented journalist, with her weekly column for the Manitoba Daily, *as well as freelance work in numerous newspapers and magazines across the country. In 1995, she was the recipient of the Press Association's silver medal for her series "Winnipeg: Where the Arts Never Sleep."*

Could this be real? The ink left very realistic, silvery black smudges on Sarah's fingertips. The chattering squirrels raced up and down the trunks of the elms, and the girls across the street, too little to go to school, played a clapping game, just as if they were real little girls in an ordinary city on an ordinary summer morning.

Sarah raised her head to see her cousin's car pull up at the curb. Morgan emerged slowly, as if in shock, with a crumpled newspaper clutched in her hand. Sarah remained in the armchair, watching her approach. She could hear the girls chanting, "He has forty-eight toes and a pickle in his nose." She wasn't dreaming. All around her, everything was terrifyingly, sickeningly real. Cady Brown had been murdered by the exact same method outlined in such gruesome detail in *A Chill at Midnight.*

THE BARTENDER ADMIRED his handiwork as he set down the two lime margaritas in their frosted glasses. Betty noticed they were the same color as Anna's fingernail polish. She paid the bartender—no one was allowed to run a tab at the Big Sky Tavern—and fiddled with the straw in her drink. It was eleven in the morning, no time to be drinking, really, but she reasoned she'd had a rough few days. She twisted on the bar stool, trying to get comfortable, and glanced at the television. Wrestling. She looked at the long rows of bottles instead. Jack Daniels, Canadian Club, Southern Comfort—she remembered Southern Comfort very well—Wild Turkey, Ballantyne's. Finally she asked Anna the question she'd come to ask her.

Anna seemed to ponder it for a while. She ran her fingers through her short, unwashed hair and chewed thoughtfully on the frayed denim of her jacket cuffs. She lit a cigarette, then finally shrugged.

"AFM? Never heard of it."

"Is it some kind of drug? Like MDA? LSD?" Betty watched her sister's reaction closely, but Anna did not react.

"Not that I heard of," she said. "Hey look! There's gonna be a Disco Revival Night here." She pointed to a poster on the cooler behind the bar. "We should go to that. I've got these neat boots—"

"Anna, I'm serious. Think! AFM. What is it?"

Anna leaned her elbows on the bar, laced her fingers together, and rested her chin on her hands. She *looked* as if she was thinking, but Betty couldn't be sure. She waited. Anna leaned forward and, without touching her glass, sipped her margarita through the straw. Finally she spoke.

"Why so serious, Bets? What gives?"

Betty pulled the note out of her purse and laid it on the bar. "Someone sent me a threat," she said.

Anna read it. "Oh, man. Oh, no. Where'd you get this? In the mail?" She wiped her hands across her face, smearing her mascara.

"Someone came right into my house and delivered it to me personally. In a book I'm reading. Like a bookmark."

"In your own house?" Anna thought for a minute. "Maybe it's Alfred."

"Alfred? No!" Betty sucked hard on her straw and drained her drink.

"Maybe the old man knows something, and he wants to keep you on edge, you know? Who knows how his mind works? Maybe he suspects, and he's trying to smoke you out." Anna waved at the bartender and made a circle with her finger to order another round.

"He doesn't know anything," Betty said. "If he did, he'd accuse me outright. He wouldn't leave me a note."

"I wouldn't put it past him. Maybe he's known all along. After all, you met him in Kenora. He has connections there. Who's to say he didn't hear it from someone there?"

"You don't know Alfred. He's a very respectable type. He'd never have married me if he'd known."

"Respectable!" Anna laughed. "Wise up, Betty. The guy's out late every night—"

"He has a very demanding business," Betty said. She paid for the second round as the drinks appeared before her. They really were a very pretty color, so frothy and pale. So cold and sweet. "Let's not talk about Alfred. It can't be Alfred. It's not his handwriting." She took a large pull on the straw.

"Someone could have written it for him."

Betty ignored this. She was thinking. Sipping and thinking. Anna removed a lipstick from her purse and applied a hot pink slab of it. She blotted her mouth with a bar napkin and took a long drag on her cigarette.

Betty looked blankly at her. After a long while she said, "It must be some sort of blackmail plot."

"Blackmail!" Anna read the note again. "But it doesn't say anything about money." She signaled the bartender for two more margaritas. The bartender looked skeptical. With her slurred lips and smudgy eyes, Anna appeared a bit deranged. But he'd seen worse. He mixed the drinks.

"And give me a shot," Betty said. "Southern Comfort."

"Me too," Anna said.

The two sisters concentrated on their drinks for a while. Betty's scalp itched. The hairdresser had lightened her brown curls yesterday and frosted them with white-blonde tips. Her head felt as if it was encased in cellophane. She realized she hated the hairspray that kept her tight permanent wave in place. She rubbed and scratched at her hair until it stuck up in stiff little tufts all over her head.

When she ordered another shot, the bartender raised his eyebrows, and Betty realized she'd probably ruined her hairdo. She tried to see herself in the smoky mirror behind the bar.

"Do I look okay?" she asked Anna.

"You look like a lemon meringue pie," Anna said. She crushed a lipstick-stained cigarette into the ashtray and rolled up the sleeves of her jean jacket. "Let's figure this out. What the hell is AFM?"

"Somebody's initials?" Betty guessed.

"An organization?" Anna asked. "Some kind of, um, an Alliance?"

"Alliance of what?"

"Alliance of Federated Monkeys," Anna suggested.

"Alliance of Fried Mushrooms," Betty said. She hiccuped and then giggled. Anna looked extremely blurred, as if she were rushing by at sixty miles an hour. "A Fine Marmalade."

"A Freak Martian."

"A Fricasseed Moose."

"A Fucking Mystery," Anna said.

They drank for a while in silence. The bar filled up with customers. Occasionally the room tilted to one side or another, and then it began to spin.

"IT *CAN'T* BE coincidence," Zina whispered furiously to Alfred across the counter. She'd called him as soon as she read this morning's paper, and the two of them were having a heated conference in the café, trying not to attract attention to themselves, and failing.

"I'm telling you, it has nothing to do with your book club. It's Petursson. He must have—"

"That's *ridiculous*!" Zina hissed. "Cady was reading these very books." She gestured vehemently at the display rack. "And she gets killed the exact same way!"

"It's got nothing to do with the books or the book club," Alfred insisted. "And don't start saying it does."

Zina fixed him with a piercing glare. "Come on, it *had* to be someone who's read this book!"

"Shhh. Look, I'll tell you something. It's Petursson. I know it for sure. He tried the same thing with Sarah, not two weeks ago—snuck into her house and tried to recreate the scene from *Bloody Midnight*. He's gone berserk."

"What? You mean he—" She broke off suddenly as Linda Rain entered the café, calling her name.

"Over here," Zina called. Linda charged across the room so fast that Buttercup could barely keep up.

"Did you hear the news this morning?" Linda asked. Her face was flushed with excitement. "They said on the radio Cady's body was found in a freezer!"

"Calm down," Alfred told her. He glanced nervously around the café. Every customer was staring at them.

"Give up, Alfred," Zina told him. "You might as well face it. The story's going to be all over town in a matter of hours. Tell us what Peter did to Sarah."

KAYLA PETROVITCH SAT in her office, chewing bubble gum to quiet her hungry stomach, and reviewed the suspect's statement again. Peter Petursson, boyfriend of the deceased, said he received a strange "muffled" phone call from Cady Brown's number the night of May 28th, at approximately midnight. He tried to call her back several times, but she did not answer. After a couple of hours, he got worried. He drove across town from his East Kildonan home, knocked loudly on her door and called her name, with no result. He used the key that Cady had given him and discovered that the door was chained from inside. He grew frightened and called for help from the nearest phone booth. That was his story. It was Kayla's job to disprove it.

Well, step one in disproving it was staring her in the face—the photocopy of Daniel's notes on his arrest of Peter Petursson in the early hours of May 20th, when Petursson had told exactly the same story to explain his presence at the scene of Sarah Petursson's "accident." Sarah had called him, her voice had been "muffled," her line had gone dead. Was the guy really dim enough to use the same flimsy excuse twice?

Kayla snapped her gum and read over Daniel's account of Sarah's statement, taken from her in the hospital. It didn't make much sense. "Victim confused," Daniel had written. Kayla had seen that phrase before—and always in reports by male cops about female victims. She knew what it meant— the cop didn't have the patience to listen. But she noted that Sarah did mention a phone call and a dead phone line. Kayla resolved to pay a visit to Sarah Petursson as soon as possible.

She returned to Peter's statement and studied it more carefully. When did he say he had received the call from Cady? Midnight. They needed a time of death, that's what they needed, and they'd have it by the end of the day, she hoped. Then they needed to prove he was in Cady Brown's apartment at that time. Or at least that he wasn't elsewhere. Petursson said he'd heard Cady's voice at midnight. If they'd made a connection, even for a second, there would be a phone record. And if Petursson had kept dialing her number, phone records could possibly establish he had been at home—maybe even at the time of death. She could call the phone company. . . .

Hell. That wasn't Kayla's concern. That was one for the defence lawyers. If they noticed it.

Kayla worked her jaws and shaped her wad of gum into a thin film. She blew very slowly until she had created a huge, pink bubble. Then she popped it and flicked it back into her mouth with her tongue. If there was one thing she liked better than a stupid perp, it was a stupid lawyer.

BACK AT THE Public Safety Building, Peter Petursson was sobbing again. Nate Donovan from Legal Aid had just played him the tape of Cady's phone call to Sarah. Detective Vishnu Maharaj had already played it for Peter in the interrogation room, over and over, trying to "crack" him. That was a mistake on the detective's part, Nate thought. He'd made it easy for Nate to get a court order making the prosecution turn over the tape. He continued to question Peter in a quiet, gentle tone.

"So what does Ms Brown mean here on the tape when she says she knows something that concerns Ms Petursson's life?"

"Cady had a plan," Peter said. He was trying valiantly to compose himself, to tell his side of the story. "She thought Sarah was trying to set me up, make me look like an abusive husband, so she'd get a better divorce settlement."

"Sarah was trying to keep everything, including the house, isn't that right?"

"Yes. I wanted her to sell it, so we could split the proceeds fifty-fifty. But Sarah made some dumb promise to her cousins that she wouldn't sell. She wouldn't budge—so we were fighting—"

"You were *negotiating*," Peter's lawyer said carefully.

"Negotiating. And Cady had a plan to get Sarah to admit she was trying to cheat me. She was going to, well, cosy up to Sarah, get her talking, you know, woman to woman sort of thing, and see if she'd admit it."

"And Sarah was unaware of your relationship with Ms Brown?"

"Do you think we can get another bail hearing?" Peter asked. "How long do you think it will be?"

"Don't worry about that right now. Right now we need to prepare a new argument. The more information you can give me, the stronger our case. Try to focus. Did Sarah know about your affair with Cady Brown?"

"No. We kept it quiet, because of the divorce."

"No good."

"What?"

"Looks like you're deceiving your wife," Nate said.

"I was—hey—who's side are you on?"

"I'm trying to prepare you for questions from the prosecution. That's what they'll say. That's what they'll hammer on. That you kept the affair a secret—that it was adultery. That you and Sarah were fighting. They'll zone in on the, uh, the incident of May 20th." He shuffled some papers. "Let's go over this statement of Sarah's again. She says you broke into her house—"

"God help me," Peter said. He buried his face in his hands.

"Now, about this weapon Sarah says you were carrying—"

"That's one thing I didn't tell them," Peter said into his hands.

"Speak up."

Peter lifted his head and looked at Nate with fear in his eyes. "I couldn't tell them. It looked so bad for me, I just kept my mouth shut about it."

"You did have a knife?"

"It was a—sort of a letter opener—like she said. But it wasn't mine. I found it inside the house. It was stuck in the door to the basement—right in the middle, as if someone had stabbed the door. I pulled it out. It was like a clue, you know—an arrow pointing the way. That's what made me look in the basement. I was scared, I'll tell you. I carried the blade with me down the steps for protection. I called her name. Then when she saw me coming at her, with that thing in my hand, she started screaming—so I dropped it."

"Where is it now?"

"I don't know. I heard it land on the floor, and then—I don't know what happened to it."

"The police never found it," Nate said. "Are you sure you don't have it?"

"I'm sure."

"You're telling me the truth?"

"I swear it."

"All right, then." Nate wiped his brow with his sleeve. "Let's hope it doesn't show up with your prints on it."

"God help me," Peter said again. He lay his head down on the grimy surface of the table and wept.

Chapter Twenty-One

DANIEL ARRIVED AT SARAH'S house to find Sarah and Morgan both shaken. Morgan was sitting balled up on the couch, biting her nails and hugging a quilt like an infant with a security blanket. Sarah was more dignified, but her face was tense and drawn as she motioned Daniel to a chair.

"I have some information about Cady Brown," she began. Daniel whipped out his notebook and pen.

"There are certain, uh, similarities between a book she was reading and, uh, what—what—"

"What happened to her?" Daniel supplied. "Yes, we know."

"You do?" Morgan asked.

"Yes. Zina Schwartz called from the bookstore this morning." He flipped backward in his notebook. "She gave me a list of details. The freezer—"

"The freezer!" Morgan moaned. Even her orange freckles were pale. "I can't bear thinking of it. The ice pick. I think I'm going to faint." She leaned forward and placed her head down between her knees.

"Are you okay?" Sarah asked. She felt queasy herself.

"Yes, the freezer," Daniel repeated. "The ice pick, the door locked from the inside. Ms Schwartz also reports seeing a ski mask in the lane nearby."

"Who is doing this?" Morgan wailed. Her hands shook as she tried to light a cigarette.

"Don't smoke, Morgan." Sarah took the cigarette away. "Breathe."

"And then there's the details of your case," Daniel continued, pointing a finger at Sarah. "The ladder and the cut phone line and the letter opener. Ms Schwartz claims these are all details straight out of this book." He picked up a copy of *Bloody Midnight* from the coffee table. "She says you were reading this when it happened."

"Zina said that? That's why I called you over—I was going to—Zina said that? How could she know? We didn't tell—" Sarah looked sharply at her cousin. "Morgan, you didn't tell anyone, did you? What happened that night?"

Morgan was looking closely at her fingernails, which were almost non-existent.

"Morgan? Tell me you didn't—"

Morgan looked up, and the color returned to her face in full force. "I told Alfred," she said.

ALFRED SUPERVISED THE loading of the latest shipment into his newly rented storage locker. Betty was right. The Midnight Mystery series was such a huge success that he could no longer operate entirely out of his own home. As he signed the receipt for delivery, he felt an intoxicating sense of accomplishment. In the west alone he had doubled his usual sales. The first three books were selling like hotcakes, thanks to the media blitz. On trains and on airplanes and in waiting rooms all across Canada, everyone was reading Midnight Mysteries. And soon they would hit the beaches.

There'd be plenty to celebrate at the dinner party

tomorrow night. He was relieved Betty seemed to be over the flu that kept her in bed yesterday. He wanted everything to be perfect, and he was used to relying on Betty to make it so. She'd come up with a truly creative plan for the theme—a pleasant surprise. And she was always a dependable cook. As long as the dinner conversation didn't veer toward the murder case that was on the tip of everybody's tongue, he'd be happy. He worried that it might, especially with his stepson Daniel there. People loved to talk shop with the cops. But he hoped the presence of the suspect's wife would keep the guests politely off the topic. And he hoped that Morgan would behave herself.

He slit open two boxes and pulled out copies of the fourth and fifth novels in the series, to admire them. Beautiful. The most enticing covers of all. These final two books would sell even better than the first three. Once they hit the stands, he'd be reprinting the whole series, he bet. At the bottom of the cover of the fifth book, a small hand holding a pen added a flourish to a note in cursive script: *The Last Midnight Mystery.*

A nice touch.

It wasn't really the last Midnight Mystery. But Alfred was the only person who knew that yet.

LONG AFTER MIDNIGHT, Sarah lay upstairs in her bed, reviewing the events of the day. Morgan, in the guest room down the hall, was also still awake. Sarah knew, because she could hear the occasional clink of a bottle against glass—Morgan's cure for insomnia—and smell the cigarette smoke drifting down the hall.

She was still stunned by the news of Peter's affair with Cady Brown and his arrest for her murder. When Detective Kayla Petrovitch joined Daniel at her house this afternoon, the unpleasant woman had been blunt. Sarah grimaced as she remembered Kayla Petrovitch in her severely tailored clothes and aggressively short haircut, stalking across the living room, her leather boots squeaking as she inspected the curtains, the lamp, the statues and books, as if trying to size Sarah up by her furnishings. She grilled Sarah mercilessly on the events of May 20th, and positively barked at her when she couldn't provide proof that Peter had read the Midnight books.

Kayla's theory was clear. Peter attacked both Sarah and Cady in methods copied from the Midnight books.

The only thing Kayla couldn't explain was why.

"I don't ask why any more," Kayla said in response to Sarah's question. "I've been in this business too long to ask why. I'm just interested in who, and we know who. Peter Petursson."

Sarah was undecided. On the one hand, it seemed unlikely. If her husband was a homicidal maniac, why had she never seen it? On the other hand, there was the business of his cruel teasing, his jumping out at her, his ghost story. Maybe it was a progressive disease, she thought now, like alcoholism. A sadistic streak that started to emerge a few years ago and just got worse and worse.

She heard the floorboards creak as Morgan got out of bed and walked down the hall toward the bathroom. She heard her shaking the window frame, securing the lock. Poor Morgan. She'd been literally trembling tonight as she chain-smoked at the dining room table, refusing to eat any dinner. Sarah was unable to calm her. Morgan was obsessed with the notion that an unknown killer was loose in Wolseley, stalking murder-mystery fans.

As for Sarah, she wasn't sure what to believe. She couldn't really see Peter as a killer, but she had to admit she was glad he was safely locked up.

And she was glad she had survived. She sent up a quick but heartfelt prayer of thanks for her life. She was lucky to be here, breathing the air—even the foul smell of Morgan's cigarettes—instead of lying on a slab with a letter opener through her heart.

Chapter Twenty-Two

THE SECOND DAY OF JUNE dawned warm and breezy, so Sarah took her coffee out on the front porch and read all morning. Morgan, who had lain awake most of the night, was sleeping in. It was a Saturday, and the street was quiet. Sarah opened one of Carolyn's notebooks and began to read an entry dated September 6, 1980.

I was so grateful to Roger today that I gave him two baskets of berries when we came over. Such a sweet man. When we got to the top of the lift, poor Sarah was so frightened she was weeping, and I couldn't calm her. "Look in my eyes," I told her. "Mummy's here. Mummy's right here with you," but she wouldn't be comforted. Roger stopped the lift and stepped right out on the railing and took her in his arms, out of the boat, and carried her down to the little garden. She waited for us there, quietly enough, and by the time we got over, she was all smiles again. She knows how to amuse herself. She picked every pink petunia out of the garden, she loves the pink ones best, and dug out an earthworm, whom she insisted on naming (Frankie) and bringing home as a pet.

Roger says she's just like I was—tears one minute, smiles the next. I know he misses the old days, misses our long talks and our good, long, easy silences, lazing about on his dock, watching the pelicans dive and soar. I miss it too, sometimes, the simplicity and peace of those days, Roger with his line in the water, pretending to fish, and me sometimes with a notebook in my lap, pretending to write. If he could accept that those days are over, it would be better for both of us. But he pleased me today with his kindness, and I think he knew it. I hope he makes good use of the berries. It was hot picking today, and the flies were hellish. Sam has bites all over his ankles, but he would insist on going barefoot.

I don't know why Sarah is so fearful of the boatlift. Even as a baby she didn't like it. I'd tuck her head into my breast, so she couldn't see, but still she cried and cried, as if she could sense it— that great drop below her—the void.

The boatlift! A sudden, visceral memory gripped Sarah's body, the sensation of being pulled up and up and up until her stomach seemed to drop right out of her. The rushing water and the sharp rocks far below. Yes, she could see again that shady little channel cut through the rock, brambles on the shore, the high white metal rails of the boatlift and the wires that even a child could see were not strong enough to lift a boat out of the water. But it worked. The pulleys pulled and the gears turned and the elevator carried you out of the lake and set you down in the Winnipeg River.

She could visualize it. She could see her mother pulling up at the dock on the lake side and letting her out of the boat, so she could walk across. "If you don't want to go up, you can portage," her mother would say.

Sarah leaned back in her chair and stared at the sky. She remembered. She remembered her mother, her mother's words. Her voice. "You can portage," she'd say, and laugh. Her blonde hair blowing in the wind, her sun-browned hands on the wheel. The green, wooden boat. Her mother's thick-knit sweater—it must have been a cold day, fall, maybe. Yes, the maple trees were turning color. She stood at the foot of the lift and tilted back her head and watched her mother in the green boat rising high above her while the white gulls dipped and the red and golden maple leaves drifted through the air.

"You can portage." Sarah searched in her purse and found a pen and her daybook. She wasn't sure exactly why, but she wanted to write those words down.

A moment later, she looked up as the steel-gray head of Dr. Allard appeared above the hedge.

"Good morning," Sarah called. "How are you today?"

"Worried about you," Dr. Allard said immediately, as if this should be obvious. She crossed the lawn and stood on Sarah's steps, toying nervously with the gold-framed spectacles that she wore on a chain around her neck. She spoke to Sarah through the screen. "I read in the paper about your husband. Are you all right?"

"I'm fine," Sarah said. It was partly true—or maybe she had just said it so many times it was coming true. "I'm getting over it."

"Nonsense. You don't get over something like that! To think that he lived with you— Didn't you see any signs?" Dr. Allard raised the spectacles to her eyes and scrutinized Sarah closely, as if looking for signs of dementia.

Sarah tried to be polite. "I *am* in the process of divorcing him," she said. "So I must have seen something."

Dr. Allard gave her a condescending smile. "I'm serious," she said. "If you ever need to talk about it, you just come on over. I'm a professional, you know. I can help."

"Uh . . . thanks."

"I'll see you tonight, I suppose?"

"Tonight?"

"At the Carrieres'."

Sarah looked blank.

"The dinner party."

"Oh, that's tonight!" Sarah clapped her hand on her forehead. "I completely forgot."

"That's perfectly understandable," Dr. Allard murmured. "No one would take it amiss, dear, if you didn't—"

"I'll be there," Sarah announced suddenly. She didn't have a date yet, but she'd think of something—someone. She didn't want the whole neighborhood patronizing her.

As Dr. Allard returned to her garden, Sarah picked out another journal from the box. When Morgan woke up, she'd ask her to suggest a date for dinner. In the meantime, she immersed herself once again in her mother's words and forgot about the world around her.

June 30, 1968. Dad and his friends caught a fine batch of pickerel yesterday, and they all came back here for a feast—Evan and Bill and Cam and Cam's two sons.

Sarah knew that Cam's two sons must be Alfred and his brother Quinn. She hadn't realized Alfred had known her mother when she was so young. No wonder Carolyn published her first book with Carriere Press. She read on, curious to see what Carolyn might say about Alfred.

When we heard the boat returning, Darlene ran down the hill and then she ran halfway back and yelled, "Get a fire going!" So I knew they had a good catch. They cleaned the fish on the beach and then came up with them wrapped in paper like bouquets of flowers for Darlene and me to cook.

After dinner, Dad opened a bottle of whisky and the six of them talked all night in the kitchen. Darlene went to bed, but I sat in the corner by the stove and listened.

Dad started bragging about me being already finished high school at age sixteen. Bill said he had his doubts about home-schooling, and Dad gave him his philosophy about fresh air being better than chalk dust for the brain. Nature is the best teacher, and the girls learn as much from the birds as they do from the books, etc. etc. He said if Bill had kids of his own, he'd understand.

Then Bill asked if I was going to go to university and Dad got all quiet. He said he didn't know if I'd like that, but he didn't ask me. None of them asked me or even glanced at me, except for Quinn, though I was sitting right there. They had one candle burning in a coffee tin, and the kitchen was dark, as if they didn't even want to see each other. Dad said that maybe the city wasn't a place he'd like to see me grow up in, and Bill said I was grown up, or almost, and there comes a time when young people have to take their place in the world. He said there were kids a lot more immature than me in his freshman classes.

Cam Carriere said his sons liked university and Quinn was top of his English class and would be a great novelist some day, and then Alfred started in about the history course he's taking and the state of the country and Canadian values and passing them on to the next generation and they all slapped him on the back and said he was the hope for the future, and they forgot all about me. The candle sputtered in the can and drowned in its own wax, and the kitchen got even darker, but they didn't notice. They just kept drinking in the dark and discussing the country as if they were in charge of it, and I must have fallen asleep, because suddenly the dawn light was coming in at the window and I could see that Dad had the shadow of whiskers on his face. If I had watched him more closely, I might have seen his beard growing.

I got up and went into the bedroom and lay down in bed next to Darlene. They didn't say good night to me, or good morning. It was as if I was invisible to them.

Sarah turned the page and was disappointed to find it stained and wrinkled, as if something—coffee?—had been spilled across it. She could make out the words "next morning," but the rest was illegible. The ink had run a long time ago, and the words blurred into soft blue waves. The pages had once been stuck together and later forced apart, for in places, the surface of the paper was abraded. She turned to the next page and read what must have been the end of the ruined entry for June 30, 1968.

I showed him two poems, and he said they were beautiful and "crisp." I've been thinking about that all day—"crisp"—what does it mean and is it a good thing? Sometimes I want the words to flow gently so that the sounds all string together and sometimes I want them to stand apart, so I can hear their shapes clearly, and maybe that's what he means. I don't know. He said he would bring me a book next time he comes. They are planning a fishing trip to Clearwater Bay next month, and he will bring it then, if not before. A new poet, he said. A Canadian lady. I said I didn't know there were any Canadian ladies writing poems, and he said there's a lot I don't know, living out here, and he's going to do his best to change all that.

It must have been Quinn or Alfred who brought the book for Carolyn, Sarah thought. They must have seemed like sophisticated, worldly men to her, though they were only undergraduates and not much older than Carolyn. She turned a few more pages and laughed at a description of Evan Knight falling off his water skis. It was hard enough to imagine Mr. Knight, the dusty old lawyer, fishing and staying up all night drinking, let alone water-skiing. But Sarah supposed he had been a lot livelier thirty-three years ago.

The entries for the summer of 1968 continued with many long poetic descriptions of the wildlife on the island, interspersed with records of visits from Luke's friends—Bill and Evan, and sometimes Evan's son Steve, who would be Jacob's father, Sarah realized. And Cam Carriere and his sons. At sixteen, Carolyn seemed to have no friends of her own, except for her sister Darlene, who was soon to leave home. It seemed cruel that Luke had kept his daughter so isolated, so lonely that she'd stay up all night just to eavesdrop on her father's friends.

Most of the journal was filled with observations of the weather and the light on the lake and the various birds that Carolyn obviously adored. These descriptions were lovely to read, because Carolyn was a keen and reverent observer of nature. Sarah was more interested in the entries with people in them, but they were few and far between. Most of the time, the writing took her deep into the very private world of Carolyn Yeats, a world populated only by pelicans and loons and the high lonely cliffs of her home overlooking the sparkling vista of Lake of the Woods.

Sometimes, reading these journals, Sarah felt she was actually there in the past with her young mother, as if she knew nothing but Persephone Island, and the rest of the world was a kind of dream, a place far, far away.

Chapter Twenty-Three

IT WAS IMPOSSIBLE TO FIND a pumpkin in Winnipeg in the month of June, but Betty had finally decided that pumpkin soup wouldn't really be appropriate, anyway. The tomato bisque would do. She turned to page 78 and read the recipe again, making sure she had all the ingredients handy. Butter and onions, yes. Paprika and parsley in the spice rack.

Alfred had finally carted the books out of her kitchen, and it was heaven to move freely in here again. Betty had scrubbed the floor and polished every surface until it gleamed before she began the final preparations for tonight. She'd worked like a demon to recover lost time from her little slide the other day, and everything was very nearly ready. Let's see, there were twelve in all, if Morgan and Sarah brought dates. She hoped they'd bring suitable dates—or at least educated ones. Most of the guests were book people—Gregory, Zina, Linda, and Professor Dawson. There was Dr. Allard, who was, after all, sort of a book person, as she'd published a sort of a marriage manual, which Betty had long intended to read—maybe she could skim it quickly before Dr. Allard arrived. Then, of course, Alfred had invited his stepson Daniel who, as a cop, didn't really fit in, but he could be counted on to join in any conversation smoothly enough. Betty liked her dinner parties to go smoothly.

The more literary chatter there was, the less likely anyone would notice that Betty didn't join in. Life with Alfred was a constant struggle to keep her roots from showing. She remembered a chapter title from Dr. Allard's book: "Mixed Marriage: When You're from the Other Side of the Tracks." She would read that carefully one day, she promised herself.

In the meantime, the important thing was to shine at the things she truly *was* good at—cleaning and cooking and setting a fine table. She stood at the entrance to the dining room and surveyed the table; every detail, down to the red roses, was straight out of *Midnight Feast*. And the menu—she hoped people would notice—followed the novel's final dinner party to a T—from the shrimp cocktail appetizers to the apple-tart dessert. It was true that the tomato bisque came from an earlier chapter, but, aside from the pumpkin availability problem, it had seemed wise to make that one little substitution, seeing as the pumpkin soup in the novel was, after all, laced with poison.

"I FORGOT ALL about it, too," Morgan said, when Sarah reminded her of the dinner party. She sat on the porch in her pyjamas, drinking coffee at one o'clock in the afternoon and trying unsuccessfully to glue on a set of false fingernails. "Darn these things!" she said.

"Who am I going to ask at this late hour?" Sarah asked. "I promised I'd bring a guest."

"There's always Joe Delaney," Morgan said.

"Seriously, now."

"I'm bringing Mark Curtis," Morgan said. "We could ask him if he has a friend."

"I wonder if Mark's home." Sarah stood up and saw a blue

Thunderbird convertible pull up behind Mark's rusty green Gremlin. "Oh," she said. "We have company."

"I'm not dressed!" Morgan cried. But she stayed where she was, curious about the visitor.

Sarah watched as the driver expertly parallel-parked and emerged from the T-bird. Even in casual clothes, Jacob Knight looked very lawyer-like, she thought. He wore a gray linen suit jacket over blue jeans and a white cotton shirt. He glanced at his watch and straightened his tie as he walked up the path. For some reason she didn't quite understand, Sarah was not at all surprised to see him.

"ALFRED CALLED THE office last week," Jacob explained. "But I was out of town. I talked to him this morning, and he told me about the theft. I was just sick about it. To think that we kept those papers safe for nearly twenty years, and now—I came as soon as I could. What happened?"

Sarah explained about Peter and the divorce and, though she didn't want to, about Peter's recent arrest. "So I expect we'll be getting the papers back soon," she concluded. "The police will be searching his apartment, if they haven't already, and they'll notify me—"

Jacob shook his head. "I had no idea you were going through so much. I heard the news of that murder, of course, but I didn't realize it involved your husband."

"Ex-husband," Morgan put in. She'd been unusually quiet during the conversation between Jacob and Sarah. But she could no longer contain her curiosity. "So you're Evan Knight's grandson?" she asked, almost shyly.

"That's right. Why, I'm practically family, which is why it's all right that you're sitting here in your pyjamas." He grinned, and Morgan blushed.

"And you know Alfred?"

"Sure," Jacob said. "Or I used to know him. His father was one of the gang, you know."

"What gang?"

"Cam Carriere, Luke Yeats, Bill Wesley, and Evan Knight," Sarah said.

Morgan looked at her in surprise.

"They were friends practically from childhood," Sarah continued. "They vacationed together on Lake of the Woods and liked it so much they all bought cabins out there. Evan Knight moved there permanently when he set up his law firm."

"Wesley and Carriere moved there permanently, too—when they retired from the U of M," Jacob added.

"That's right," said Sarah. "Cam Carriere's cabin isn't right on the lake, though. The Carriere place is just north of the lake, on the Winnipeg River."

"How do you know all this?" Morgan asked Sarah.

"It's in the notebooks," Sarah told her. "My mother wrote down everything. There isn't much about Cam Carriere, though." She turned to Jacob. "Tell me about him."

"He was a great fisherman," Jacob said. "He was the first to get a cabin out there—on the river, as you say. A much more rugged place than my grandfather or Bill Wesley would ever live in. Cam was a fanatical outdoorsman, the driving force behind all those fishing expeditions." He laughed. "I think he was mainly trying to get away from his wife. He often brought Quinn and Alfred along, but I never knew them well. They were more friends of my father's—and Carolyn's."

"Alfred and Quinn published Aunt Carolyn's first book," Morgan remembered.

"That's right. Her second one, too. Then she went with a Toronto firm, Laurentian Shield."

"Are there any more of her things in Kenora?" Sarah asked. "We only have the two boxes that were left behind in Morgan's car—and the photographs and things your mother gave me—thank you for that. Is there something else at the law office? Anything else held back?"

Jacob shook his head. "No. That's it. Unless there's anything left on the island."

"The island," Sarah said. She fell silent, thinking. After reading so many of her mother's descriptions of Persephone Island, it was starting to seem very real to her.

"Have you been to the island?" Morgan asked Jacob.

"I've been past it. Often."

"Is the green cabin still there?"

"Yes. You can see the roof through the trees, from the water. It's still standing. Grandpa Evan sends someone around every once in a while to check up on it. Wesley's son, I think. He does small repairs, keeps the dock up."

Sarah looked surprised. "Wesley has a son? There's no mention of him in my mother's diary. I thought Bill Wesley had no children."

"Well, poor Bill became a father late in life. Twin boys. Little hellraisers, according to my mother. Last time I saw them they were still in kindergarten. Anyway, Evan hired one of them a few years back to keep an eye on your property. He was out of work and the place was getting run down. As far as I know, he's still taking care of it. Doesn't do much, but at least he keeps it painted. I noticed the roof had been repaired a while back, and—"

"So you go there?" Sarah asked. "You visit the island?"

"Why? Do you want to go see it?"

"I think I do," Sarah said slowly.

"Sarah! You'll go?" Morgan jumped out of her chair in excitement. "You mean we can go?"

"I think I just might," Sarah said.

"I'm driving back to Kenora tomorrow afternoon," Jacob said. "You're more than welcome to come with me. My mother has plenty of room at the house. If you stay with her overnight, I can run you out to Persephone Island Monday morning. You could catch the evening bus back to Winnipeg."

"I could get away for a day!" Morgan said eagerly. "Sarah, let's!"

"All right," Sarah agreed, and Morgan let out a whoop.

"I'll phone my mother," Jacob said, "and tell her to expect us for dinner tomorrow. She'll be thrilled." He was obviously pleased himself.

Morgan and Jacob continued to talk, making plans for the trip to the island. As Sarah listened quietly, with a serene smile on her face, she sensed Jacob's interested glances at her. He was no doubt wondering why she'd changed her attitude so radically since he first met her.

Sarah knew why. It was the power of Carolyn's words drawing her toward the island, toward the past, giving her the strength to face the memories that were surfacing.

WHEN THE DOORBELL rang at six o'clock, Betty removed the pot of blanched endives from the heat, quickly wiped her hands on her apron, and glanced nervously in the mirror. Her hair wasn't fixed yet, and she didn't have a speck of lipstick on. She hoped the dinner guests weren't starting to arrive already! The invitations said seven. She patted her hair into place and hurried to answer it.

But it was only Daniel, who didn't really count. "Come on in to the living room. Would you like a drink? I'm busy in the kitchen, but Alfred's—"

"Hey, Dan." Alfred descended the stairs and shook Daniel's hand. "Betty, get Daniel a drink, will you?"

After accepting a glass of iced tea and a coaster from Betty, Daniel took his notebook and pen from his pocket.

"How's the investigation going?" Alfred asked him.

"It's been a tough few days. Gathering evidence, interviewing. This link to your Walter White mysteries gives the case an odd twist. I thought you might have some insights there."

Alfred shrugged. "Not really. Seems obvious that Petursson's gone mad."

"So you think it was Petursson? Any reason why you think so?"

Alfred looked surprised. "He's been arrested, hasn't he?"

"Yes, but I thought you might have another point of view. After all, they're your books—"

"Now, look," Alfred said quickly. "It's hardly the fault of the publisher if some reader goes mad. Those books are bestsellers. I don't have any control over who reads them."

"Of course not," Daniel said. "But I thought there might be a link if, say, if someone was trying to ruin your business?"

"Who would want to do that?"

"I thought you might tell me," Daniel said. "Can you think of anyone who might want to hurt you? Any particularly jealous rivals, for instance?"

"Nobody *that* jealous!" Alfred protested. "No!"

"Where's your brother Quinn these days?" Daniel asked.

"He's in Toronto—hey, Dan, come on. When he left the business, we parted as friends. Quinn's no killer! Don't get crazy on me here."

Daniel scribbled, then looked up, his pencil poised. "I heard you were first on the scene—how'd that happen?"

"I was out jogging." Alfred smiled proudly. "I still do two miles every morning. Rain or shine."

"You went with him?" Daniel asked Betty.

"Betty came later," Alfred said. "When I saw the commotion down the street, I called her on my cell."

"So"—Daniel flipped a page—"you knew Cady Brown?"

Alfred laughed a little. "Hey, Dan, what is this? An official visit? I thought you were here for dinner."

Daniel shrugged. "We're building a case. Every bit helps. What can you tell me about Cady Brown?"

"I didn't know her well," Alfred began.

Betty left the room. She didn't want any part of this conversation.

BACK IN THE kitchen, Betty tried to remember whether she'd added lemon juice to the sauce yet. It was almost time to put the endives in the oven to braise. But Daniel's questions unnerved her. For the past few days, she'd tried to convince herself that Alfred was right. Peter killed Cady Brown in some kind of fit of rage. But she still couldn't quite bring herself to believe it.

Worse, she couldn't help wondering if the murder of Cady Brown was in any way related to the threatening note she'd found in her kitchen. It seemed unlikely, and yet the words of the note kept echoing in her mind. "*Keep your mouth shut about AFM, if you don't want him to find out. . . .*"

Who could have written it?

Betty sliced up lemons, but her mind was not on the task. Cady Brown? Cady *was* in the house that day. She *was* seen in Kenora lately, according to Daniel, and she *was* nosy— well, she was a reporter. Was it possible Cady had uncovered the facts of Betty's past? Would such a story interest her? Maybe not for the news, but for purposes of telling Alfred. Betty remembered the way Cady held on to Alfred's arm. She remembered that Cady telephoned Alfred at his brother's house in Toronto. Had Cady been after Alfred for herself? Trying to ruin Betty's marriage by dredging up the past?

Maybe Cady had been asking the wrong kind of questions —about the wrong kind of people.

"I CAN'T BELIEVE they denied him bail!" Byron lamented. "Whatever happened to *innocent until proven guilty?*"

"I know, I know," said Linda sympathetically. Byron was walking Linda and Buttercup home. He insisted on walking them home every evening now, and Linda had to admit to herself that she enjoyed the company. "Don't worry," she told him. "I'm sure Peter will be cleared at the trial."

"But his lawyer told me they might hold him for months before trial. It's a travesty. I've got to do something to get him out."

"I don't see what you can do," said Linda. They had reached her apartment door, and she took her keys out of her purse.

"Are you all right by yourself?" Byron asked. Do you want me to come in?"

"I'm fine." Linda didn't want to mention the party she was attending at the Carrieres' house tonight. She knew Byron didn't like Alfred. "Don't worry about me. And don't worry about Peter. There's nothing you can do right now."

"I'll think of something," Byron said as he walked away.

Linda locked the door behind her and let Buttercup out of her harness. She flipped open her watch and read the time with her fingers. Just after six. She should get ready for the dinner party soon, but she figured she had time to read just a little before she got dressed. This morning, she'd had to leave for work in the middle of a chapter, and all day she'd been wondering what would happen next.

She turned her tape recorder on, and Joe Delaney's voice filled the room, reading from *Midnight Feast*.

"She could see the beekeeper leaning against the side of the stables, gazing at her bedroom window. But she wasn't up there. She was crouched in the gaze, in the gaze—oh sorry—*in the gazebo, down low where no one could spot the glow from the candle she'd lit to write a secret letter to her sister.*

"She glanced over her shoulder. A tall shadow was moving across the lawn between the apiary and the beekeeper's shed. Who could be out here in the middle of the night? And why? She saw him enter the shed and disappear inside for a few minutes. Then he emerged, hurrying. Coming right at her!

"She must not be found here! She extinguished the candle with a quick exhalation and sat still as a statue, save for the trembling of her bosom."

Linda was annoyed by the tone of Joe's voice at this point. It was the word *bosom* that had done it. His barely suppressed laughter very nearly ruined the mood of the scene. But he recovered himself and read the rest of the chapter with a fine dramatic flair: "*With a gasp of terror, she realized it was the cook. Why would he be sneaking among the beehives? Surely there was nothing of value in there. Nothing but sleeping bees and chemicals and supplies. So what was he up to? Was he looking for her? She ducked low and held her breath. She had never completely trusted the cook.*"

Chapter Twenty-Four

THERE WAS SOMETHING SO EXACTLY right about Jacob showing up on this day, at this hour, at this time in her life, that Sarah didn't even protest when Morgan manipulated the conversation so that she was forced to invite him to Betty's dinner party.

She sat on the sofa beside him in the Carrieres' living room and accepted a whisky and soda from Zina, who was helping Betty to serve. Betty herself made only a brief appearance before scurrying back to her kitchen to check on the roasting pheasants. It was past seven, and everyone had arrived except Linda Rain.

Dr. Allard stood near the mantel, examining the cluster of photographs and knick-knacks. She picked up a china figurine of a young shepherdess and sheep and turned it upside down. Sarah smiled to see her expression of approval. Apparently Dr. Allard was impressed by the name on the bottom.

"Betty's toys," Alfred remarked. "I tell her she's like a little girl with a set of dolls."

Dr. Allard quickly replaced the figurine. "Quite a collection of photos," she said. "Family?"

"Family and friends," Alfred said. "Jacob, have you seen this one of your grandfather?" He reached across Dr. Allard and handed the picture to Jacob. Sarah looked on. It was a picture she had seen before, on previous visits to the house, but she had never really studied it.

Alfred pointed out who was who. Evan Knight, Bill Wesley, and Luke Yeats stood in a row, with their arms linked across each other's shoulders. Cam Carriere stood slightly to one side, with his hands on the shoulders of his two young teenaged boys. The younger one, Quinn, was shielding his eyes against the sun, so his face was obscured. The older one was Alfred, proudly displaying a prize-winning bass. Sitting cross-legged on the dock was Carolyn Yeats, looking shyly at her own hands.

"There's your mother," Jacob said to Sarah. "She looks about ten, there."

"That was the bass derby," Alfred said. "My father talked about that fish for years. My first big catch. Quinn was sick with envy."

The doorbell rang, and Linda arrived, bearing a gift of homemade chocolates and a gaily wrapped bottle of wine. The party broke up to reassemble in the dining room.

ALFRED SEATED HIMSELF at the head of the long, carefully arrayed table and directed his guests to their places. Betty's place was at the far end, near the entrance to the kitchen. She and Zina were in there now, arranging twelve tall glasses of shrimp cocktail on a tray.

Sarah sat at Alfred's right, with Jacob beside her and Professor Dawson across from her.

"That's a handsome dog you have there," Jacob remarked to Linda.

"Yes, Buttercup's a true beauty," Linda said. "I hear that all

185

the time. Go on, girl, get under there." She urged Buttercup
farther under the table, out of the way. "Now stay."

Professor Dawson was an affable man, bulky and robust,
with a keen intellect that shone clearly in his bright hazel
eyes. He immediately entered into a lively conversation with
Dr. Allard and Alfred about his latest project, a study of the
influence of one Canadian novelist upon another. Linda, a
former student of Dawson's, joined in. Jacob and Sarah soon
found themselves in the midst of a spirited literary debate.

"But isn't it true that he was a tortured soul?" Linda asked
about one of the authors under discussion.

"One always wants to look at the psychology of the author,"
Dr. Allard pronounced as Betty served the appetizers. "The
unconscious forces at work in the author's psyche will always
reveal themselves in the writing."

"Ah, but how can you ever know the author's psyche?"
Professor Dawson challenged. He swept his left arm above his
head and made a circular motion, encompassing every guest
in the gesture. "Why, even here, sitting at the very same table,
we cannot see into each other's hearts."

"Yes, but a novel is much more intimate than a dinner
party," Linda argued. "When the reader spends hours alone
with the author's words, it's like entering his mind."

Dawson leaned forward and wagged a thick finger at her.
"But why would you *want* to know his mind? Why would
you *want* to be intimate with him?" He sat back tri-
umphantly, as if he had scored a point. "That illusion of
intimacy is probably the single most misguided reason for
reading."

"It sells books," Alfred said. "And speaking of selling
books, please excuse me for a moment. I just remembered
something I forgot to do." He stood up and headed toward
the stairs to his office.

Professor Dawson continued. "The sophisticated reader
knows that literature is about language, not personality. The
text itself. . . ."

Betty, removing the empty cocktail glasses, said, "Come right back, Alfred. We're about to serve the soup."

Jacob turned to Sarah. "How about you?" he asked quietly. "Are you a sophisticated reader? Or a misguided one?"

Sarah smiled. "Oh, definitely misguided. I haven't read any serious literature since college. Just popular novels."

"Well, at least it's fiction," Jacob said. "Better than a case-book of contract law, which is what's been keeping me up nights lately. Not much intimacy involved in that, I assure you!"

Across the table, Morgan was leaning her right hand on Daniel's shoulder and giggling while she whispered something in his ear. Mark was stuck between Morgan and Dr. Allard, who was still arguing with Dawson. He looked across to Jacob for conversation.

"Morgan tells me you have a law practice on Lake of the Woods," he said. "It must be great out there."

"Yes," Jacob said. "Nice work if you can get it, as they say."

"Aren't there a lot of tourists out there?" Mark asked. "What's it like, working in a vacation town?"

Alfred re-entered the room with a frustrated frown on his face. "Greg, can you give me a hand for a minute?"

Gregory rose instantly from his chair.

"Alfred, dear," Betty said. She was collecting the soup plates. "It's time for the main course." She said it sweetly, but nobody missed the undercurrent of irritation.

Alfred paid her no attention. "I still can't get into my e-mail," he complained to Gregory. "It's been screwed up for days. Now I'm getting a message that the configuration has errors or something."

"Just use the configuration from the previous session," Gregory advised him. "Just click on the—"

"Can you show me?"

Betty placed a hand firmly on Gregory's arm and pushed him gently toward his chair. "You can do that after dinner," she said. She looked straight at Alfred. "Right now, we have guests."

Everyone turned to look at Alfred, and he was quickly shamed into resuming his seat. Sarah heard him grumbling under his breath. "Doesn't anyone know what it's like to run a business?'

IN THE KITCHEN, Betty glazed the endive dish with butter while Zina arranged the pheasants on individual plates.

"Those tarts look lovely," Zina remarked. "You really outdid yourself, Betty. You must have been cooking and baking for days."

Betty smiled modestly. She'd been too hungover earlier this week to do everything herself and had bought the tarts at the Flax Fields Bakery down the street. Not that she could afford it. Anna had wheedled another hundred dollars out of her for rent again.

"You're a marvel," Zina said. She carried four of the plates into the dining room.

"The area was originally called *Waszuch Onigum*," Jacob was saying in answer to a question from Mark about the history of Kenora. "That means 'the road to muskrat country.' It refers to the land along the north shore of the lake, where it meets the Winnipeg River."

"The river flows into the lake? Is there a waterfall?"

"No. The lake drains into the river, actually. The lake is some eighteen feet higher than the river, so it was necessary to portage there. There were three main portages in the area. Three waterfalls—but of course they've all been harnessed now. There's a power house at Kenora and a dam at Norman—"

"I remember the Norman Dam!" Morgan suddenly turned away from Daniel and spoke to Jacob. "We used to fish there."

"Yes, a popular spot." Jacob smiled at her. "And then there are the falls at Keewatin, where I grew up—the Keewatin falls were harnessed as hydro power for the old flour mill." He turned to Sarah. "You know, that photo we were just looking at was taken there."

"I remember when that flour mill burned down," Alfred said. He had resigned himself to socializing, at least for the time being, and was slicing his roast pheasant determinedly, as if to get it over with. He tasted the endives, and his mouth puckered. Too much lemon juice.

"Pass the butter, please," Linda said. Under the table, Buttercup thumped her tail, believing that Linda was talking to her. The smells of the feast tantalized her, but though she remained hopeful, she was too well trained to beg.

DR. ALLARD AND Professor Dawson continued their discussion in the living room after dinner. Dawson described his research, his discovery of an author's letters, hidden away in a neglected cabinet of the university library. "The letters confirmed my theory," he said. "He wrote the book ten years before it was published!"

At the mention of author's letters, Sarah turned her head to listen.

"Fascinating," Dr. Allard murmured. "And where did the letters come from?"

"The author's wife had kept them in her attic. A sentimental old woman, fortunately for me. When she died, her heirs donated them to the archives."

"Donated them? For free?"

"Yes, luckily for us. We're so underfunded these days—"

"How much would letters like that be worth?" Dr. Allard asked.

"Oh, well, it depends on the author," Professor Dawson said. He sipped his coffee thoughtfully. "These were the letters of one of Manitoba's first published writers. They'd be worth several thousands, at least. We were lucky to acquire them."

Sarah wanted to ask how much her own mother's papers might be worth, but decided this was not the time or the place.

"So Canadian authors are going up in stock?" Dr. Allard mused. "I've a few first editions of Canadian novels, and some other things in my own collection. Perhaps you could come to look at them some time? Give me an appraisal of their value?"

"Ah, you collect rare books?"

"Sarah?" Linda was asking. "Where are you?"

"Right here. On the couch across from you," Sarah said loudly across the chatter of the room. Linda was looking abandoned. In her corner of the room, Morgan was flirting even more energetically than usual, dividing her attention between Mark and Daniel and ignoring Linda completely.

Sarah crossed the carpet and guided Linda over to join her on the couch. She glared at Morgan, to reprimand her for her rude manners, but Morgan was oblivious. Oh well. Sarah was glad Morgan was having a good time, even though she knew Morgan was tipsy. The color was high in her cheeks, and she was laughing for the first time since the murder.

When she returned, the topic had changed. Alfred was questioning Professor Dawson about the tastes of his students. Dr. Allard had fallen silent, and was again fingering the miniature china shepherdess on the mantel.

"Which genre do they prefer?" Alfred asked.

"What *is* a genre, anyway?" Betty asked quietly.

"*Genre*," said Linda, rolling the R. "It's from the French, meaning a type, or—"

"It's a literary term," Alfred said quickly to his wife, dismissing her question. He turned back to Dawson. "What do you think the most popular genre is today, Professor?"

"Oh, the biography, without a doubt," Dawson said.

A lull in the chatter caused Linda's voice to carry loudly throughout the room. "Oh no!" she said. "Without a doubt it has to be the mystery!"

Chapter Twenty-Five

THE GUESTS ALL LEFT RATHER EARLY, Betty thought as she wrapped the leftovers tightly for freezing. There was a time not so long ago when they would have stayed past midnight, drinking and talking, but she supposed they were all getting older now. Except for the early hour—it was only eleven—the party was a success. The guests mingled well, and even Daniel seemed to fit in. She was especially grateful that Sarah had brought along Jacob Knight, whose presence helped to steer the conversation away from the grisly topic of Cady Brown's murder and onto the slightly less unsettling topic of Kenora.

Alfred had left his glass of wine untouched on the kitchen counter. Betty had asked him to sit in the kitchen with her while she tidied up, so they could discuss the party. But Alfred was up in the office with Gregory. Lately, he was consumed with work. She looked at the buzzer on the kitchen wall and considered summoning him. But she didn't want to annoy him while he was working. He was an absolute bear when interrupted.

She scraped the good china and washed it carefully in the sink, then piled everything else into the dishwasher and turned it on. The gentle hum relaxed her. The sound of things being cleaned always soothed her nerves.

UPSTAIRS, GREGORY RUBBED his eyes and tried to stay awake. He'd eaten too much again, and the heavy meal was making him drowsy. He could swear Betty was trying to kill him with all that wine and—what was it? Seven courses? And the detail! She had every detail out of the book—even the color of the tablecloth. He guessed she was too dumb to realize how tasteless it all was. Either that or she was crazy.

Gregory tapped at the keyboard. He'd promised Alfred he would get the correspondence up to date before he went home, even if it took him until midnight. Lately, Alfred had been turning more and more work over to him. This was a good sign, Gregory supposed. It proved that Alfred trusted him. He grinned to himself.

He fixed the problem with the configuration easily, and logged on to Alfred's e-mail account. Whoa. There was a message from Cady Brown. Sent on Monday night, the night she was murdered! Gregory listened carefully to make sure Alfred was still upstairs. Yes, he could hear the sound of the shredder at work. Alfred was busy. He clicked on the e-mail, read the first few sentences, and deleted it right away. He went into the computer's trash basket file and deleted it from there as well. Gregory knew it was still technically retrievable, but Alfred would never figure out how to get it.

He skimmed through the other e-mails, barely knowing what they said. He was fuming with anger at the dead girl. He had told her to keep her mouth shut. He had very specifically warned her in the note he'd placed inside her promo copy of *Midnight Feast*. But she'd ignored him. It was just as well she was dead now. Eventually she would have cost him his job.

Gregory finished answering the e-mails, printing out the ones that needed a personal response from Alfred. Then he shut down the computer and turned to the regular mail. These days Alfred was barely able to keep up with his published authors and their agents, let alone the slush pile of unsolicited manuscripts that grew nearly a foot every week. It seemed the more successful the press became, the more submissions they received.

Alfred had lately instituted a system to save himself time. He scribbled short comments on Post-it Notes and attached them to the unwanted manuscripts he passed on to Gregory. Then Gregory typed up letters and forged Alfred's scrawl of a signature at the bottom, preserving the illusion that Alfred Carriere was in control of every detail, even the slush pile.

The evil slush pile. Sometimes Gregory's stomach turned over when he looked at it. But Gregory always did whatever he was paid to do.

He picked up the first manuscript and read Alfred's note: "Be polite—son of the justice minister." Gregory didn't feel like dealing with that one right now. He turned to the next one. "No encouragement please!" the note read. "Repeat offender—fourth submission this year!" Gregory had to grin. He looked at the next one. "Illiterate—suggest she take up some other occupation." Sometimes, when Alfred's notes were so outrageously nasty, Gregory was tempted to leave them stuck on the manuscript. But he knew that could cost him his job. He couldn't afford to lose this job.

Gregory didn't hear the first timid knocking on the door of the office. When it came again, it startled him so that he cut his tongue on the envelope he was sealing.

"Come in," he called.

Betty entered with a glass of red wine and some of Linda's homemade chocolates on a tray.

"Oh, Gregory! You're still here?"

"Almost done," Gregory said.

"I just thought I'd bring Al a little refreshment." She

glanced around the office, as if Alfred might be hiding somewhere among the stacks of books.

"Alfred's working up on the third floor. He said not to disturb him."

"Oh, well." Betty hesitated. She glanced around again, as if looking for something hidden. "I'll take it up to him."

Gregory took the tray and placed it firmly on the desk beside him. "He really doesn't want to be interrupted," he told her.

"All right, then. How about you? Shall I bring you something?"

"I'm fine," Gregory said. He pretended to concentrate on typing the rejection letters with a great show of concern until Betty finally left. When he had printed all the letters, he prepared the works for mailing. He shoved each manuscript into its own stamped, self-addressed envelope, making sure he returned each rejected piece to its rightful owner. He weighed in his hand the hefty submission from the son of the justice minister and estimated it was short on postage. Too bad. Not Gregory's problem. He licked the flap, sealed it, and tossed it in the "out" basket.

He was very sleepy now, and slightly nauseated. This was vile, boring work. As he sealed the envelope of the repeat offender, he nearly gagged. He could feel a thick build-up of glue on his tongue. Yuck. He reached for the wine Betty had brought for Alfred and gulped thirstily.

BETTY HAD VACUUMED the entire main floor, dusted the baseboards, and washed the kitchen floor. Then she set the breakfast table, and finally there was nothing left for her to do. She sat at her island counter and leafed through the pages of the latest cookbook, hot off the Carriere press. She hoped to find some creative new way to cook turnips. But turnips, apparently, were beneath the notice of the author. There was not a mention of them, even in the index. Turnips must be passé, Betty thought. Maybe there's something for zucchini, though. She was just turning to the "Z" section, when she heard the buzzer from the second-story office sound in the kitchen.

It was about time!

But the next thing she heard was Alfred calling her name—shouting frantically, almost screaming, for her to come.

Something was terribly wrong.

Betty sat still for a second, steeling herself for whatever had happened. Then she rushed upstairs to her husband.

"What is it?" she cried as she entered the office. But she could see what it was. Gregory lay collapsed on the floor, and Alfred knelt beside him, slapping his plump red cheeks, trying to rouse him. Betty watched as her husband leaned over and put his ear to Gregory's chest.

"He's barely breathing," Alfred told her. "Call 911."

"What happened?"

"Just do it. Call 911 and tell them to send an ambulance. He's had a damn heart attack or something."

Chapter Twenty-Six

How THE HELL WAS HE SUPPOSED to take ownership of the neighborhood, Daniel wondered, when nobody would tell him what was going on? Neither of the detectives would return his calls, and he'd had to stake out Jeannie in dispatch to get any news on the search of Peter Petursson's apartment. According to Jeannie, there were no boxes of papers matching the description Daniel gave. No diaries or notebooks of that kind at all. In fact, the apartment was virtually empty—the typical detritus of the divorced male littered the floors—socks, pizza boxes, unopened junk mail—but nothing of interest had been discovered.

Daniel tried again to reach Sarah, but she wasn't answering her telephone. He checked his watch. Nearly seven. Sarah was probably at the café for the book-club meeting.

THE MYSTERY AU Lait Café was jammed. Daniel could see one empty chair across the room, but he didn't want to walk in front of Byron Hunt, who was standing at the podium, reading to the crowd from a sheet of paper. So Daniel edged away from the door and stood with his back to the windows. A small group of people was standing there also, and he recognized Sarah's next-door neighbors—Mark Curtis and his landlord, Dr. Allard. He waved at them and Mark waved back, but Dr. Allard made a shushing movement, as if Daniel had interrupted the lecture.

He listened, but it didn't seem like a lecture. In fact, it sounded for all the world like poetry. Daniel tuned it out and scanned the faces of the audience, looking for Sarah. He wanted to ask her a few more questions about her husband, now that he'd read the mystery books she'd lent him. Now that he'd seen the coincidences for himself.

The coincidences were so marked, they were obvious. Too obvious. Daniel had spoken to Peter Petursson several times, and though Daniel didn't like the guy, he had to admit he seemed sane. Detective Kayla Petrovitch was positive the case was closed, but Daniel wasn't so sure. It didn't seem likely that the guy would murder his girlfriend according to *A Chill at Midnight* when he knew full well that his own wife would tell about his trick with *Bloody Midnight*. The similarity was too pat. And how did the stolen papers fit into all this? Or did they?

Daniel stood on his toes and craned his neck a bit, until he could see the whole audience. No Sarah, and no Morgan. Byron was still droning on, and Daniel continued his meditation on the case. Peter didn't seem like an uncontrolled maniac who just couldn't stop himself, which was the only kind of perp Daniel could see for two such copycat crimes. Nobody in his right mind would do something so incriminating, unless driven by wild compulsion. Daniel imagined some obsessive-compulsive type, driven to recreate the crimes in the fiction he read. Probably a long-time murder mystery fan, maybe even someone in this very room. . . .

A small spurt of applause made him look up. Only one

person was clapping enthusiastically—Linda Rain. The rest of the customers slapped their hands together once or twice.

"Thank you," Byron said. "So, as you can see, there is room for poetry at our Sunday night meetings. I hope we can institute it on a regular basis."

Daniel saw some members of the audience look at each other with grim expressions.

"But now," Byron continued, "to keep in tune with the tradition of the club, I will read my review of *Midnight Feast*."

Daniel hadn't read this one yet. He decided to pay very close attention.

"You are what you eat," Byron began, and the mystery fans perked up as a wave of renewed interest passed through them.

KEEWATIN WAS NOW officially part of the town of Kenora, but it retained its distinctive air of a small village. Built on the Precambrian Shield that had forged the lake, Keewatin was marked by steep, rocky hills, and the houses were built at various heights along the streets. Some were perched at the tops of small cliffs, others were tucked into hillsides, and all of them boasted well-tended gardens.

"It's a little like a fairy-tale village," Sarah remarked.

"Yes. Tourist towns are all like this," Jacob said. "Everything's kept up. It makes a simple trip to the grocery store a pleasure. That's my place, there." He pointed to a solid red brick bungalow, half-hidden by an enormous fir tree. Sarah turned her head to get a better look, but it was gone. "I've been there six years now, and I love it. It's a five-minute walk to the harbor where I keep the sailboat. I'll show her to you tomorrow."

"We're going sailing!" Morgan cried.

"Not tomorrow. Sorry. We'll take the old Lund to the island. It's more practical."

"What a sweet little cottage," Sarah said, as Jacob pulled into his mother's driveway.

Morgan leaped out of the car to admire the flower beds, overflowing with petunias and pansies. The house was small and neat, white stucco with marine-blue trim and a matching blue door. White curtains hung at the picture window, and Sarah saw some movement behind them. Mary was watching.

"I can't wait to hear all the family stories," Morgan said to Jacob as he helped Sarah out of the car. "There are so many connections between our families. Our grandfather, your grandfather. Sarah's mother, your mother . . . what about your father? Did he know Carolyn, too?"

"You won't be hearing anything about my father," Jacob said. "Mum doesn't talk about him."

"Why not?" Morgan asked, and Sarah poked her hard with a crutch.

"Ouch! Sarah!"

Jacob laughed. "It's okay, Sarah. It's Mum who's the sensitive one, not me. He left when I was only a kid, so I don't remember him. But it's a sore point with Mum."

"Maybe she wants to talk about him," Morgan said. "To us. To women. I'll bet she—"

"Best not to ask," Jacob replied. "Believe me." He knocked on the blue wooden door of the cottage.

MARY KNIGHT TOOK one look at Sarah and embraced her tightly.

"You're just like your mother. Oh, Jacob, I can't believe it. And this is Morgan—so grown up! I'd recognize that fiery hair anywhere. How is your brother? Do you remember me? Come and sit down." She led the way into the living room, talking non-stop, asking questions without waiting for answers. "Jacob, bring some wine from the fridge," she ordered. She settled herself on the edge of the couch, leaning forward, her green eyes shining eagerly. Her brown hair was beginning to silver, but she had obviously made no effort to dye it. It fell in soft, loose waves to her shoulder, framing her rosy cheeks. The red sweater she wore seemed to suit her personality, bright and warm. Her excitement was contagious, and Sarah liked her immediately.

"Now tell me all about yourself," she said to Sarah. "What do you do? Are you a writer?"

"A writer? No. I'm an accountant, and Morgan has a clothing store."

Mary looked surprised. "Your mother always thought you'd grow up to be an artist of some kind. You were such a creative little thing."

"She was a great mud-pie maker," Jacob said, as he returned with the wine.

"Morgan went to art school," Sarah said. "But I thought I'd do something more. . . ."

"More practical," Morgan finished. "Sarah's the practical type. Good with numbers. Did Carolyn ever say what she thought I'd be?"

"Oh you!" Mary exclaimed. "Oh, yes, we were all convinced that you and Sam would be sailors. Run away and join the merchant marines or something."

"I wish! What else did Aunt Carolyn say about me?"

Mary related tale after tale about the days she and Carolyn spent with the four children. As Sarah listened to the stories of picnics and trips into town, and the time Sam cut his knee, she started to remember some of those incidents for herself. It was amazing how much she could remember, she thought, now that she was open to it.

ALFRED WALKED PAST his wife without even answering her. She was mumbling something about a lost shepherdess, but he paid no attention. He climbed the stairs wearily. It was eight p.m., and he still hadn't done a lick of work all day. He'd slept past noon, after spending all last night in Emergency, anxiously awaiting news of Gregory's condition. When the doctor finally appeared, it was only to tell him that Gregory had died.

Then Alfred had spent altogether too much time today trying to calm Betty, who claimed she believed it was her own cooking—too much cholesterol—that contributed to Gregory's death. Alfred reassured her that she had never forced Gregory to eat, that he ate all day, whether at Betty's table or elsewhere. He was more worried about the loose ends of the business he'd entrusted to Gregory. He couldn't be sure what his assistant had and hadn't taken care of. Alfred always felt uneasy when things were beyond his influence. How could he know how much progress had been made on the correspondence, for instance? He regretted not making Gregory give him a daily report. He should have thought of that.

Up in the office, Alfred righted the chair that had tipped over when Gregory collapsed. He looked through the envelopes in the "out" box. At least they were not yet mailed, so Alfred could make a note of them. He tidied the desk, sorting phone messages and emptying the dregs of a wine-glass into the bathroom sink. He placed the glass on the windowsill by the stairs, to remind himself to take it down to the kitchen later. He picked Gregory's jacket off a chair and saw Gregory's briefcase beneath it. It was locked.

Alfred hung the jacket on the stair railing beside the wineglass and tried to open the briefcase. He retrieved a pair of tweezers from the bathroom and began to pick the lock. He would turn the case over to the boy's parents, of course, though he dreaded the idea of facing them—he'd managed to slip past them in the hospital this morning. But in the meantime, he needed to see if there was any-thing important in here. The lid snapped open suddenly, and Alfred pawed through the jumble inside. Chocolate bars, postage stamps, and, yes, some papers related to Alfred's business. Press releases that should have been faxed on Friday. Incompetence.

But then Alfred found something that shocked him. Concealed in the flap on the inside of the lid, there was an envelope with Cady Brown's name written on it. He tore it open and gaped at the bright orange and red design of the picture he knew so well. The color mock-up of the cover for the sixth Midnight mystery—the one Alfred had kept so carefully secret. Paper-clipped to the top was a tiny note, in Gregory's hand, reading, "This ought to be worth a month of steak dinners." That dirty rat! So he'd been selling secrets to the girl detective!

How did Gregory find out about this? No one knew about it except the graphic artist. Alfred had worked with her for twenty years and trusted her completely. She wouldn't tell a soul; he knew that with confidence. The image of Morgan crossed his mind. He regretted a conversation he'd had with her when they were drinking one night in her clothing shop, after hours. When Morgan expressed regret that the series consisted of only five books, Alfred had hinted broadly that he had a little surprise hidden away in his private filing cabinet. A little Christmas present. Did Morgan catch his drift? He wasn't sure. But he didn't think Morgan would tell Gregory anything. She hated Gregory.

Betty? No way. She'd never dare to interfere with the business. But Gregory—

A tremor seized Alfred. He raced upstairs to his private office, fumbled with the keys to the file cabinet, got it open and reached for the small, fireproof box in the back. He nearly broke down crying with relief when he saw that its contents were still there, safe and sound. Still unread by any-one but Alfred. But what if Gregory had told others of its existence?

Alfred looked over his shoulder as if expecting an intruder. He didn't feel comfortable up here any more. His own personal, private space had been violated. It was no longer safe to keep the manuscript up here.

It was time for some serious precautions. He would stash

his treasure into the safety-deposit box, as soon as the bank opened tomorrow. He'd been an idiot not to do that earlier.

He actually kissed the brittle, yellowed pages before he hid them away again in the filing cabinet.

AFTER DINNER, MARY served cake and hot chocolate, and the conversation continued. Sarah enjoyed hearing about Carolyn from the point of view of someone who knew her as a close friend. It gave Sarah the sense that she was sharing Carolyn with someone who loved her the way Sarah was coming to love her. But there was something more she wanted to know.

"To be honest," Sarah said. "I was hoping you could tell me something about my father."

Mary shook her head sadly. "I'm real sorry, honey," she said. "Carolyn wouldn't say. She kept the pregnancy a secret until she started to show, and when I asked her, all she'd say was that I'd find out some day. She told me to be patient, and she'd tell me when the time was right. After you were born, and she wrote *father unknown* on the birth certificate, I asked her again. She said the time wasn't right yet. The years went by, and she never did tell me."

Sarah thought of the man named Roger in her mother's journals, the one who had pleased Carolyn with his kindness. "Did you know my mother's friend Roger?" she asked Mary.

"You must mean Roger Lariviere, the man who used to run the boatlift."

"That's the one. In my mother's diary, she wrote about Roger carrying me out of the lift because I was afraid of heights when I was little."

"You're still afraid of heights," Morgan said.

"Roger Lariviere was a close friend to your mother for years," Mary said warmly. "Especially when she was younger, oh, in her late teens and early twenties. When I first met Carolyn she was absolutely thick with him. I remember when we went across on the boatlift, he'd always give her a bouquet of flowers from the garden there."

"Oh wow." Morgan sat up straight. "It was a romance?"

Mary smiled sadly. "It might have been. I mean, it might have developed into one. But something went wrong between them. His attitude changed. When she was pregnant, I remember, we went over the lift and he'd just nod, kind of cold, you know, as if she'd hurt him somehow."

"She didn't tell you why?" Sarah asked.

"No." Mary sighed. "I guessed they'd quarreled. But Carolyn never explained. She could be very, well, infuriating sometimes—extremely private."

"Do you think he could be Sarah's father?" Morgan asked.

Mary looked at Sarah. "I doubt it. Besides, Roger's not the type to abandon a child. Sarah's father, I'm afraid, well...I've always wondered...."

"What?"

Mary fidgeted with her wineglass and looked at her son.

"It's all right, Ma," he said. "Just say it."

"I just wondered if maybe it was a married man. I can't think of any other reason she wouldn't tell me his name. Maybe she was waiting for him to leave his wife. I'm sorry, Sarah, it's not really my place to say it, but why else would she keep it a secret?"

Sarah sat quietly, wondering the same thing. "But who?" she finally asked.

"I don't know," Mary said. "I'm sorry."

"I THINK I'M going to sleep for the first time in days." Morgan snuggled under the covers in Mary's guest room. "It is such a relief to be out of Winnipeg and away from all that ugliness. It almost seems like nothing but a bad nightmare."

"Mmm hmm," Sarah said. "It's nice to see you happy, Morgan. Get a good rest now. We'll have to be up early."

"Sure," Morgan said. She closed her eyes and was fast asleep in minutes.

Tired as she was, Sarah lay awake. She could hear Mary and Jacob chatting in the kitchen, long after Morgan fell asleep. Sarah snapped on the bedside lamp. She crept out of bed quietly, so as not to waken her cousin, pulled the notebooks out of her suitcase and began to read where she had last left off, August 1978.

You are gone from me again and when you are gone the lake grows cold, the color of iron, and the sky is iron, oppressive. Words so weighted today they sink beneath the surface of the mind with a sound like stones dropping through thick water. The poems lie flat on the page. They will not take wing.

"AND SO THE novel ends with everyone getting his just desserts," Byron concluded.

Zina noticed the applause was more sincere this time, and Byron beamed. He'd been reluctant, almost shy in fact, to do this week's review. But aside from the long introductory poetry reading, he'd done a good job. As Zina passed around a plate of cookies, she saw Linda praising Byron and Byron actually blushing. Byron was certainly changing, Zina thought. The Midnight books, which he'd once scorned, seemed to excite him. Who would have thought Byron Hunt would ever read one of Alfred Carriere's crass, commercial books? She wished Alfred were here to see it. Where was he, anyway? Neither he nor his usual entourage had shown up tonight. The new books had arrived via courier.

Mark Curtis waved to Zina, and she carried the plate of cookies toward the window where he stood with Dr. Allard and Daniel.

"Hi Mark," Zina said. "Hi Daniel." She nodded stiffly at Dr. Allard. "Sorry you couldn't get a seat."

"That's okay," Mark said quickly. "We enjoyed the review.

I think *Midnight Feast* is my favorite book so far. Wasn't that a great ending?"

"It gave me the creeps," Zina confessed. "I know he was the villain, but what a horrible way to go! Swarmed by bees!"

"Served him right," said Dr. Allard. "Most appropriate."

"True enough," Mark agreed. "The punishment fit the crime."

"Have you seen Sarah?" Daniel asked Zina.

"She's out of town."

"I'd like to ask you some questions. Do you think I could talk to you for a few minutes?"

"Now? I'm kind of busy." Zina indicated the crowd with a tilt of her head.

"We could talk in the back, in the kitchen."

"Go ahead, Zina. I'll pass these around," Mark offered. He took the tray and headed toward the tables.

"Wait a minute," Dr. Allard said. "Let me help." She reached over, took a dozen cookies off the plate, and began to wrap them in a napkin.

Zina led Daniel into the kitchen. She paused to hold the swinging door open for him, and as she turned around she saw Dr. Allard stuffing the cookies into her purse.

"Is this as private as we can get?" Daniel asked quietly. He glanced around at Javier, who was loading dishes into the washer. He didn't seem too happy about the presence of a cop in his kitchen.

"This is it," Zina said. She directed Daniel to a stool. "What did you want to talk about?"

"Well. I'm wondering . . . about the book club. The last two mysteries you've featured. Can you tell me anything you've noticed about the people who've been reading them? Anything strange?"

"Strange? Like getting murdered, you mean? Of course I've noticed something strange! I told you last week. First Sarah, then Cady. Both of them avid fans."

"Yes." Daniel opened his notebook. "We're grateful to you

for coming forward. Now I'm interested in the other people who've been reading the books. The members of the book club."

"The members of my book club are perfectly normal people," Zina said. "Most of them live right here in this neighborhood."

"Yes, I know," he said, as gently as he could. "But we're obviously looking for someone who's been reading these books."

"Or someone who's been writing them," Zina said.

Daniel looked up sharply. "Why do you say that?"

"Well, I've been thinking. Cady was after him, researching him."

"Researching who?"

"Walter White! She was trying to track him down for an interview. Just a simple little interview for a simple little promo piece, and guess what? He can't be found. It's like he's a ghost."

"And you think Cady's search for this author had something to do with her death?"

"I don't see what else. Oh, I know you all think it's Peter, but I don't buy it. You know what I think? I think Peter might have pulled that trick on Sarah, trying to scare her, and then somehow this Walter White found out about it, and when Cady got too close to him, wham—he killed her and framed Peter for it, just like that." She snapped her fingers angrily.

Daniel nodded, careful to show no reaction. He wondered why Alfred had never mentioned Walter White.

"And Walter White also wrote this *Midnight Feast* book?"

"He wrote the whole series, including the one launched tonight."

"Can I take a look at it?"

"Sure. Come on." Zina led him out to the book rack and handed him a copy. They were selling faster than ever. She'd have to get Alfred to restock tomorrow.

Daniel studied the cover, then turned the book over and read the back. "There's nothing about Walter White here," he said. "No information on the author at all."

"I told you—he's like a ghost," Zina said. "It's probably a pen name."

"Maybe I should take one of these," Daniel said. "And the third one, too—*Midnight Feast.*"

Zina led him to the cash register and rang up the sale.

"It's too bad I missed Sarah," Daniel said. "Where did she go?"

"She and Morgan went to the lake for a couple of days."

"To the lake?" Daniel looked up at her and then turned the latest book over again. He and Zina both stared at the cover. *A Midnight Swim* was illustrated with a beach scene. A woman's belongings lay scattered on a deserted stretch of sand in the moonlight. Out in the water, a single, desperate hand waved wildly as some drowning person sank out of sight.

Chapter Twenty-Seven

IN THE MORNING, JACOB DROVE the cousins to the Keewatin marina. It was a hot, sunny day, and Sarah rested on a bench in the shade, while Jacob took Morgan to see his sailboat. Sarah didn't feel like clambering around on the docks with her crutch. She was only using one crutch now, but she was still unsteady on her feet. She was content to watch the flotilla of pleasure craft heading out for a day on the lake. Most of them were motorboats, puttering slowly out of the crowded bay. There were a few sailboats as well. Their fluttering sailcloths of white, yellow, and blue stirred memories of her cousin Sam and his passion for sailing. A train rumbled by, stopping traffic on the tall bridge that spanned the bay to Sarah's left. To her right, the wide dock in front of the marina was full of activity. An attendant was kept busy pumping gas, a mechanic was hauling the damaged prop of a motor into the shop, and a group of children threw crumbs to a paddling mother duck and her brood. Everywhere, people moved slowly and happily. It was early in the season, and not yet crowded with tourists. When school let out at the end of the month, those with cabins would move here for the summer.

"Sarah!" Jacob's deep voice boomed across the docks, and she could see him waving. He stood beside a sixteen-foot, aluminum, Lund fishing boat. Sarah rose to join him.

Jacob and Morgan had loaded the Lund with the overnight bags, a basket of food from Mary, and Sarah's suitcase of Carolyn's papers.

"You're becoming a nut," Morgan teased her. "Hauling those around everywhere."

Sarah just smiled. She had lost her mother once, and she didn't want to lose her again.

Jacob untied the bowline as the women climbed into the boat. "We could go straight out to Persephone Island," he said, pointing toward the open water at the end of the bay. "Or I could take you first to see the boatlift you were asking about." He pointed in the opposite direction. "It's just under this bridge and around the bend."

"Let's see the boatlift," Sarah said.

Morgan jumped into the captain's seat. "Can I drive?"

"Sure." Jacob got into the seat beside her and pointed the way. "Just keep it real slow. Around those buoys, there, and through that archway. There's a little channel there, see?"

MORGAN STEERED THE boat slowly into the cool, narrow channel. Willow trees and berry bushes overhung the steep rocky banks on either side. The waterway had been blasted out of the granite with dynamite, Jacob explained. At the corner of a sharp turn, the crooked limb of a tree hung out over the water like a bent arm, bearing a sign that warned, "Slow." Morgan laughed. "As if you could speed through here."

As they rounded the turn, they could see the dock and the high cement foundation of the old mill rising out of the water.

"The Lake of the Woods Flour Mill," Jacob said. "Or what's left of it. Let's get out and walk around."

Morgan docked, and Jacob jumped out easily to tie up. "It's a great view from up there," Jacob said. In a minute, he and Morgan disappeared up a flight of cement stairs to the top of the foundation, the highest point around. Sarah got out of the boat more slowly. She looked at the boatlift. Jacob had told her it closed down two years ago, with no date set for its reopening. It still worked, but it was too expensive to maintain, according to the town council, so they had ceased its operation, despite protests from residents who lived on the river side and now had no easy access to the lake. Sarah looked up at the white railings that she had recalled as she'd read her mother's journal. The huge wooden crate that held the boats was parked high on the rails on the lake side, about twelve feet above the channel. Sarah shuddered. She knew that the drop from the lift to the water was even higher on the other side, where the lift raised and lowered boats in and out of the lower-lying Winnipeg River.

A cracked sidewalk ran up a small grassy hill to a little white building, and Sarah followed it, without looking back or waiting for the others. Roger Lariviere must have used this little shed for shelter when he was working here in bad weather. She stood on her toes and tried to look in the windows, but they were covered with white curtains. Flower gardens surrounded the shed. Someone had kept them up, though the lift was not in use. More willow trees flanked the edge of the cut lawn, and beyond them was untamed bush, covering the steep incline to the river. She could see part of the ruined mill—a crumbling brick building on the very edge of the riverbank.

As Sarah started toward the old brick building, she could make out a jagged hole in the side of it, about nine feet high and three feet wide—a strangely human shape, with shoulders, as if a giant had walked right through the wall. Could she get in there? She made her way along the bank through the bushes, grabbing at the trunks of young trees for leverage. There was a wide gap in the chain-link fence that surrounded the ruins. Sarah ducked her head and slipped through to the other side.

She entered the building and found herself on a small platform above the flooded floor of an enormous, underground room. A metal staircase descended into opaque water, where floating beer bottles and cans clanked eerily against each other as the water trickled slowly out a hole in the brick on the other side, down the steep wall into the river. At the far end of the room, huge toothed gears and axles, red with rust, rose out of the water. This must have been the generating station, Sarah realized. The turbines themselves were probably rusting in the cavern below her. She could sense the hollow space below the floor and hear the loud rush of the eighteen-foot waterfall that had once provided the horsepower to run the mill. The room was cold and dank, long abandoned.

Twisted and rusty mechanical devices of every shape and size lay about, both in and out of the water, but Sarah could not identify any of them. Mangled dials and gauges, massive bolts, broken tools, and smashed glass lay at her feet. On the wall beside her, a curious, white metal box was attached to a disintegrating water pipe. Its door dangled open on broken hinges. Sarah pushed it closed and saw the sign "100 Volts" stamped on the front. It must have been a fuse box of some kind. She took a closer look at the wall and felt uneasy. From somewhere behind it, she could hear the steady drip, drip, drip of more water. The brick foundation she stood in was badly crumpled. It was slowly collapsing under the weight of the dirt that seemed to push against it, sinking it into the earth. Tree roots climbed in at the broken windows.

When she heard Morgan calling her name, she was happy to leave the dark, chilly ruins and get back out into the sunshine. She climbed along the bank and up the stairs to join her companions at the top of the foundation, on a cracked cement surface that must, once, have been the floor of the mill.

Morgan was leaning out over an old iron railing that threatened to give way and send her plunging fifty feet down onto the rocky riverbank. Unconcerned, Jacob rested his own weight on the railing beside her, and they both calmly surveyed the wide, rushing Winnipeg River below. Sarah approached cautiously, staying far from the treacherous edge. "When this mill burned down in '67," Jacob was saying, "half the town of Keewatin was thrown out of work. Hard times for everyone. I think that's when my dad really started to go downhill. At least that's what Grandpa Evan told me. He and my dad didn't get along."

"Where is your dad now?" Morgan asked.

Jacob shrugged. "California, last I heard. But that was years ago. He could be anywhere now."

"Why didn't he get along with his father?" Morgan asked. Sarah shot her a warning look, but Jacob just smiled.

"Oh, that I know. It's about the only thing I do know. Evan wanted him to go to college, law school, of course, and join the firm. But my dad was just not interested. He took a summer job at the mill when he was in high school, and I guess he liked the money. He never went back to school in September. Never graduated. And Grandpa Evan never forgave him."

"I guess Evan is proud of you, though," Sarah said kindly. "He must have been glad when you joined the firm."

"Oh yeah," Jacob said. He turned to smile at her ironically. "Fatted calf and all." He looked up at the sky, which was clear and blue. "Beautiful day to be out on the lake. Let's get going." He straightened up and stretched, then headed down toward the dock, with Morgan close behind, scrambling to keep up with his strides and peppering him with questions about his family.

Sarah followed slowly. Before she climbed back into the Lund, she turned and looked up once more at the white rails of the boatlift. In her imagination, she saw the green boat going over, her mother waving goodbye.

DETECTIVE KAYLA PETROVITCH was twenty minutes late getting to the hospital, because she'd let herself get caught up in an argument with Daniel Bradley. By the time she arrived, Vishnu Maharaj was finished his interview with the medical examiner and was fuming impatiently in the corridor, waiting for her.

"We might have another one in Wolseley," he said, as soon as he saw her. "Another death, not two blocks away from the last one."

"Homicide?"

"The ME thinks it might be." Vishnu read to her from his notes. "Gregory Paul Restall, twenty-seven years old. Publisher's assistant. Single. Collapsed at work Saturday night. Young, but overweight. Dead on arrival. Resuscitation efforts failed, blah, blah, blah. Autopsy concluded this morning. Cyanide poisoning."

"Cyanide? Confirmed?"

"Not yet. The ME sent blood to the lab this morning. But she says she could smell it when she opened him up."

"Is it true it smells like almonds?"

"Apparently."

"She ruled out suicide?"

"*I'm* ruling it out," said Vishnu. "There's one other detail. The guy worked for Alfred Carriere. Remember him?"

"With the ponytail? The mustache? The guy on the scene at the Brown murder? The one who wouldn't shut up?"

"That's the one. And here he is again. He brought Restall into the ER. Says Restall was assisting him in his home office. What they were doing there at midnight on a Saturday is beyond me. We'll have to have a talk with him."

He strode off toward the exit, and Kayla followed.

"Carriere's the publisher of those books!" Kayla said to

Vishnu's back. "Daniel Bradley was just in talking to me about him. Bradley claims there's some connection between Carriere's business and the MO in the Brown murder."

"Interesting." Vishnu stepped out into the parking lot. "What kind of connection?"

"Something about the books Carriere's selling," Kayla said. "The ones Petursson copied for his crimes. Bradley's been after me for a couple of days about them. And now he has some theory the author's involved. It sounded wacko to me. I didn't pay much attention, but now—"

"But now," said Vishnu, "you'd better go hear him out." He opened his car and got in. "Meet me at Carriere's house in one hour. Bring Bradley. And don't be late!"

"Right," Kayla said. She stood in the parking lot for a minute, trying to remember everything she knew about murder by poison. It didn't take her long. During her years in Toronto, she'd worked stabbings and gunshot wounds and vehicular manslaughter and plenty of blunt trauma, but she'd never seen a single case of poisoning. She'd have to do some serious research.

"THANKS, ZINA," ALFRED said. He hung up the phone and made a notation. Two more cartons of *A Midnight Swim* for Zina.

Zina was surprised at how well the books were selling, but Alfred wasn't. He'd known in advance that interest would be very high in this series. At first Zina had been afraid to risk featuring a single author for five whole weeks, but Alfred explained that was how he was selling them. Five weeks or nothing. With a display. He chuckled to think of the calls coming in lately from bookstore managers across the country who'd initially refused to take that deal. They were changing their tune mighty fast. He smiled as he tossed the order for Zina on top of a growing stack. She'd actually said she was sorry there were only five books.

But there were six. Alfred got up from his chair to lock the door—Betty was getting so nosy lately—and made rapid calculations on a piece of paper, imagining the public's reaction. He had to time it perfectly. Let's see. He scribbled down his ideas as he brainstormed. He'd drop a few well-placed hints over the summer, just as a teaser, and then sit back and let the rumor spread. When the fall book season was at its height, and all the publishers were competing for media attention, he'd launch a special hardcover edition. The perfect Christmas gift for any Midnight Mystery fan. It would be just like the return of Sherlock Holmes, the resurrection of Superman. This particular book had never been published before, and Alfred had worldwide rights. He would sell it in every state of that great union to the south, in every country in Europe, in Japan— And the movie rights!

Bill Wesley would be dead, and Alfred would reap one hundred percent of the profits.

He roughed out a production schedule and reworked the budget for the hundredth time. He'd need a bank loan to pay the printer, but how much? How many copies should he print? A hundred thousand at least, to start. Then millions. Oh, he was going to be rich. He was going to be rich beyond his wildest dreams.

"POISONED? WITH CYANIDE?" Daniel stared at Kayla. When he'd seen her coming, he'd braced himself for another humiliating dressing-down from the arrogant detective. But nothing had prepared him for this. Cyanide. In Alfred's own house? Very slowly he handed Kayla the paperback he'd been reading at his desk.

"*Midnight Feast?* Another one of Carriere's books?" she asked. "A murder mystery?"

Daniel nodded. But he was still temporarily speechless.

"So what do you want me to do?" Kayla asked. "Sit down on my butt and start reading? I got to get over to Carriere's house to meet Vishnu. If you think you can contribute something, you can tag along." She didn't mention that Vishnu had asked for him. She didn't want Bradley getting cocky.

"But Kayla, Detective Petrovitch, you have to read it, to see—"

"To see who done it? Too bad, Bradley. Real detectives don't work that way. You coming or not?"

Daniel cleared his throat and rose out of his chair. He was taller than Kayla, and he felt a little more confident standing. "The murder in the book is a pumpkin," he announced boldly.

She raised one eyebrow.

"I mean a poison, a poisoning. Cyanide in the pumpkin soup."

It took her a second to comprehend. Then she pointed to the book again. "Bring that along," she said. "And find me the page. You can read it to me in the car."

A FULL YEAR had passed since Alfred first hatched his plan. He remembered distinctly the day Bill Wesley first came to him and proposed that Alfred take over the Canadian distribution of a new series by one of Bill Wesley's long-time clients. The books, Bill explained, were not really new. And they were not really a series, at least not originally. Bill gave Alfred five old paperbacks to read. Dog-eared and faded, their bindings cracked, the books seemed, at first glance, to have nothing in common. There was no mention of midnight in the titles. They were published by five different American companies and written by five different authors. Pen names, Bill explained. The author, now unfortunately confined to a psychiatric institution, was an eccentric who preferred to keep his identity a secret. Each book had been popular in its day. Each book had made money. But because of their scattered publication history, and the lack of name-recognition, they had never reached their full commercial potential. If they were marketed properly, Bill argued, they would sell again, better than before. Walter White couldn't write any more, poor man—his eccentricities had progressed into full-blown lunacy. He was quite mad now. Raving. But Bill was still representing him—for the sake of White's family, he said. They were nearly destitute. The mystery books were White's sole literary achievement, and reprinting them was the only way to squeeze any income out of his estate.

Alfred checked the copyright pages. The years of publication ranged from 1975 to 1984. "Kind of dated," he said.

"These are timeless classics," Bill proclaimed. "Good writing and well-drawn characters never go out of style. The human heart is constant throughout the ages. Think of Shakespeare!" He launched into a literary lecture, heaping so much praise on the novels that Alfred began to suspect Bill had written them himself. This made him nervous.

"I'll have to read them before I decide," Alfred told him. "I'll get back to you next week."

Alfred had started to read without much hope. But as he turned the pages of the first novel, he began to see that Bill was right. The book was amazingly timeless. Except for a few details of technology—the lack of bank machines and cell phones, for instance—it could have been written yesterday. Walter White, sane or insane, must have been a genius. Alfred spent the next two days in a state of excitement, reading through the series and fantasizing about a marketing plan that would make him rich. As a series, the mysteries had a wonderful coherence. A clever thread of subplots, involving minor characters, ran from book to book. The recurring themes of darkness and mistaken identities tied them all together. Plus, a murder at midnight occurred in every story. Alfred thought he could use that as a selling point.

It was not until he'd started to read the last book that Alfred experienced a sense of discomfort that grew steadily as he turned the pages. The style of writing became progressively more sophisticated as Walter White improved his skills with each new book. Alfred was starting to recognize it, but from where? It was uncanny. And one of the minor characters in the story, a sinister millwright with a case of pyromania, gave Alfred a sense of déjà vu. Yet he knew he had never read this book before.

Where had Alfred read Walter White's work before? Bill claimed that White had written only these five books. But somewhere. . . . A memory had flickered in Alfred's mind and sent him searching through his old files. What a relief he'd felt when, after days of searching, he found what he was looking for. A long-forgotten manuscript, typed on an old Remington with a ribbon that was none too new, even then. Walter White had submitted it to Carriere Press long ago, a couple of years before the last Walter White novel was published. This puzzled Alfred. White must have been under contract to Bill Wesley's agency at the time. Why had he sent out a manuscript without his agent's knowledge? Bill Wesley obviously didn't know—even now—that the book existed. If he knew, he would have sold it—because it was the best, and the scariest, thriller of them all. Alfred remembered it well.

He had read the whole manuscript when it first came in. He recalled his secret shame when he found himself unable to put it down. He'd read the whole thing in one night and even now he shivered to remember the eroticism and the suspense. But of course he hadn't considered accepting it. That was back in the days when Alfred regarded his press as a high-minded cultural institution and wouldn't dream of dealing in mystery novels. He published only Literature with a capital L. He'd been a starry-eyed fool. He remembered his own pompous lectures to his brother Quinn about nationalism and Canadian identity and duty to the artistic community. He'd been an idiot.

But he had done one thing right. In his arrogance, he'd made the decision that would now make him a millionaire. He had kept the manuscript. It was a point of pride with him to refuse to enter into correspondence with the authors of

unsolicited manuscripts that didn't come up to his standards
—especially when they arrived without sufficient postage for
return.

Alfred had never heard from the eccentric Walter White
again—and never heard *of* him, either, until Bill showed up
with the idea to reprint the mysteries.

Now, Alfred was in sole possession of the one and only
truly final Midnight Mystery. There might be a copy somewhere, but Alfred had good reason to believe there wasn't. Bill
had access to all White's work, and he had never so much as
mentioned it. No. The book had been submitted to Alfred. It
was his by rights. And this morning at ten o'clock he had
stashed it away in the bank.

Alfred grinned. He imagined the manuscript glowing in
the darkness of the safety-deposit box like a bar of pure gold.

Chapter Twenty-Eight

SARAH CLOSED HER EYES and took pleasure in the sensation of the wind on her face, cooling her eyelids and forehead and, she knew, tangling her hair into knots that might never yield to a comb again. Over the sound of the motor, she couldn't catch what Jacob and Morgan were saying in the front seats, but she didn't care. Jacob was driving now, because he knew the way, and he was driving fast. It was exhilarating. The lake was calm, but once in a while, when they crossed the wake of a motor-boat, Sarah had to hold tight to the gunwale as the Lund slammed hard against the waves. Whenever this happened, Morgan shrieked with glee and turned around to grin at Sarah.

Sarah lost track of the number of islands they passed. There were over 14,000 islands on the entire lake, according to Jacob, many of them here at the northern tip. She was amazed at his ability to navigate through them, for to tell the truth they all looked the same to her. Water, rocks, trees. Trees, rocks, water. The only distinctive features she could recognize were the variety of beautiful cabins dotted among the trees, with their porches and gleaming windows facing the lake, their docks and elaborate systems of decks and gazebos rising above the rocky shore.

When Jacob slowed down to pass through a turbulent narrows, he turned around and pointed, directing her attention to the shore. "Here's Devil's Gap."

On a boulder, someone had painted the snickering red face of a black-bearded devil. The grotesque figure guarded the entrance to the passage beyond where the Hades Islands lay scattered in a confusing pattern Sarah had seen on the charts.

Jacob speeded up again slightly, past the narrows, but kept the motor at a reasonable pace as he started to peer carefully ahead and behind him, a little less sure of the way.

"Persephone is just around that next bend, I think," he said. "It's not named on the chart. Too small, I guess."

"It was Grandpa who named it," Morgan said. "I don't know why—there it is!"

Through the woods on the shore to their right, they could see the roof of the little green cabin and its clapboard walls, a brighter green than the trees, as though recently painted. Jacob steered the boat toward the dock. Sarah felt a wave of excited happiness flow through her, and she recognized it. It was the feeling she'd always had when returning home.

Persephone Island. Sarah guessed it was the location, so near the Hades Islands, that gave Luke the idea for the name. And maybe the separation of his daughters from their mother. But she didn't say so. She felt it was not something she could say out loud without her voice breaking.

As soon as Jacob cut the motor, Morgan leaped out onto the dock and tied the bowline to the cleats. Then she hurried up the dirt path toward the cabin.

Jacob tied up the stern, then offered his arm to Sarah, saying, "The path's a bit steep."

"I'm all right." Sarah used her crutch to make her way up, keeping her eyes on the rocky, root-strewn ground.

At the top of the path, she raised her head. Morgan was standing on the site Luke Yeats had chosen for the big log cabin where he raised his daughters. He had cleared the site and built the cabin himself, with logs he'd felled himself. But now, few signs of his labor remained. After twenty years, a few charred logs were barely visible under the lush green growth of ferns and bracken that covered them. Scraggly young pines dotted the clearing where once, Sarah remembered, there had been a meager lawn and a vegetable garden. The only signs of human cultivation were the drooping leaves of tulips and daffodils that were past flowering and an unruly hedge of rose bushes that were not yet budding. Rosehips still clung to their thorny branches, and Sarah twisted one between her fingers. It was hard, shriveled after the long winter, and she wondered that the roses had survived all these years. The young pines cast shade on the hedge. Soon the encroaching trees would block the flowers from the sun entirely. The forest was reclaiming its territory.

"Oh my gosh," Morgan said. "The green cabin looks in great shape." She rushed right past the blackened, overgrown ruins toward the smaller cabin Luke had built later in his life, for his grandchildren.

Sarah stayed where she was. She looked up at the blue sky and let the sun warm her face, let the memories flood through her. Beside her, Jacob coughed slightly and shifted from one foot to another. Then she felt his hand on her own. A brief, warm squeeze, quickly withdrawn. He followed Morgan's path toward the green cabin.

Sarah wandered closer to the ruins. Beneath the fronds of the ferns, she could see the rusted hulk of an ancient stove and the half-burnt carcass of a wooden desk, lying on its side. Toadstools sprouted from its open drawers. She imagined for a moment she could smell the smoke. She imagined for a moment that her mother's spirit still hovered.... A blue-black raven lifted suddenly from the undergrowth and took wing across the clearing toward the lake.

Sarah looked in the direction of the green cabin, but she did not want to join the others. She wished she were alone. She walked across the clearing, leaving the site of the fire and her greatest loss behind. At the edge of the woods, she could make out the entrance to a tangled, overgrown path, and she decided to explore the island on her own.

ALFRED FELT A twinge of loneliness because he had no one to share his secret with. Eventually, of course, the book would be published and public. Alfred had changed Walter White's original title and scribbled in a new title with the word "Midnight" in it, the magic word that would make the book famous, mark it as part of the series. But there was only one other person who could ever comprehend the book's true value, and that was Bill Wesley. Alfred sat at his desk in his private office and thought about Bill Wesley's secret.

Just before Bill had been diagnosed with cancer last fall, he'd proposed a merger of his Pen and Ink agency with Carriere Press. Alfred had agreed; he was leaning toward the promotion end of things anyway. He liked the idea of representing authors instead of haggling with them. He simply asked to go over the agency's account books first. Bill had stalled him—for good reason, as Alfred now knew. But then Bill was rushed into surgery. While he was in hospital with his wife at his side, the Wesleys' maid let Alfred into his study and Alfred got a good long look at the books.

At first, everything seemed legitimate. Alfred was particularly interested in the accounts related to Walter White, and he'd whistled aloud when he saw the huge amounts paid to the Pen and Ink agency by the various publishers of Walter White's novels in the seventies and eighties. He noted the long list of checks drawn on the account to pay Walter White his share. Whenever the mystery novels earned revenue, Bill had kept fifteen percent and paid the remainder to the author. According to the books, there was nearly $15,000 left in the account. Quite an asset for the agency—and Alfred wondered why Bill had not disclosed it to him. Curious, he searched through the bank statements in Bill's desk until he found a recent one with the identical account number. The balance was in excess of $100,000. Hoping to explain the discrepancy, Alfred began a systematic study of Bill's financial records. What he found astounded him.

Bill kept two sets of books for every transaction related to Walter White. One set recorded royalty checks made out to White. The other told a different story. None of the recorded payments to Walter White had ever been removed from the account. Instead, Alfred found payments to Bill's real estate agent, his travel agent, his stockbroker. Bill Wesley had been spending extravagantly from Walter White's account for years.

Alfred had spent a lot of time since then trying to figure out the story behind the Walter White account. Was Walter White dead? Was he fictitious? Had Bill actually written the novels himself after all? Or was Walter White simply incapacitated? Unable to cash the checks? This was the most likely scenario, Alfred thought. Bill had said White was recently confined to an institution, but maybe he'd been in one all along, too ill to take care of his own business matters. In any case, Bill had simply kept the money; and now the unspent portion of accumulated royalties from five best-selling paperbacks was gathering interest in Bill's account. With the books about to be reissued, the balance would soon start to swell all over again. Alfred had been shocked. But as he'd stood above the mess of paperwork on Bill's desk that afternoon, he'd also experienced a slowly dawning glee. His secret sixth Midnight book was worth a lot more than he'd originally realized. He could pocket every cent of the profits. He was publisher, agent, and author. There was no one with the motive to ask any questions. Except Bill Wesley. But Bill was now so sick he'd never live to see the last book launched.

Whenever Alfred's conscience bothered him, he reminded

himself that Bill had been keeping the money for years and no one, apparently, had ever missed it. Maybe Bill had even written and mailed the checks. It wasn't Bill's responsibility to make sure they got cashed. Sometimes Alfred remembered the destitute White family Bill had mentioned, but he convinced himself that Bill had invented them. Most of the time, Alfred felt quite justified in his secret plan. The book had been submitted to him, and it was his. It wasn't his fault if the author had mysteriously disappeared. Still, on occasion, he was gripped by unexpected dread. The worst crises of conscience came when, like now, he was suddenly haunted by the image of a bearded and emaciated Walter White, languishing in the filthy cellar of one of those ancient lunatic asylums on the late movies, clanking his chains and moaning. That was ridiculous, he told himself. If White was alive, he was in a nice, clean, modern hospital somewhere. Hopefully a locked ward.

His thoughts were interrupted by the buzzer from down below. "What is it, Betty?" he answered.

Betty's hysterical voice was barely audible through the crackling intercom. "You'd better come down, Alfred," she said. "The police are here."

THE TWISTING PATH that Sarah followed opened into a smaller clearing, where two majestic maple trees rose high against the pine forest. Sarah turned to look at them and gasped. For an instant she thought she had come across a real person. But it was a statue. In the middle of the clearing, a life-sized young woman of stone sat beneath the massive trees, her legs tucked demurely to one side under her stone dress. Sarah approached her. The folds of her dress and her wavy hair were expertly carved. Sarah could see only one side of her face, for the statue's head was bowed, her attention focused on a large volume that lay open across her lap. She was reading.

She was the woman from Sarah's dream.

Sarah circled her slowly. It hadn't been a dream, she realized now, but a memory. She bent her knees slightly, to get a
better look at the face, and recognized it instantly. From the
photographs she'd been recently studying, she knew it was
her own mother. Probably about eighteen years old. Luke
Yeats must have used Carolyn as a model for the sculpture.
Sarah leaned over and examined the book. In minute script,
Luke had actually carved words onto the open pages. The
delicate lines that formed the letters were weather-beaten and
caked with dirt, but Sarah could still read them.

She had been hungry, wandering in the gardens,
Poor simple child, and plucked from the leaning bough
A pomegranate, the crimson fruit, and peeled it,
With the inside coating the pale rind showing,
And eaten seven of the seeds.

Sarah wished she could turn the page to read the rest of the
verse, but the pages, of course, were stone.

She recognized the poem, though. It was from the story of
Persephone in Ovid's *Metamorphoses*, a poetic version of an
ancient Greek myth. In college, Sarah had read several versions of the myth with interest, because of the name of the
island. One day, when young Persephone was innocently
picking flowers, she was kidnapped by the Lord of Hades, the
dark underworld, who held her hostage in his shadowy realm
beneath the earth. Persephone's mother, Demeter, searched
the whole world over for her daughter, sorrowing and
grieving her loss. Demeter was a kind of nature goddess,
Sarah remembered, and because of her grief, the land turned
cold, the plants all withered and died. The myth explained
the changing of the seasons, and this was the topic of the
verse Luke had chosen for his stone book. Zeus decreed that
the Lord of Hades must set Persephone free, to return to her
mother—so long as she had eaten nothing in the underworld. But Persephone had eaten those seven seeds, and so

she was forced to stay there seven months of every year. That was winter, when Demeter mourned.

Sarah sat down beside the statue and felt a rush of memories flooding through her. Her mother's scent, her strong arms lifting Sarah, her laughter. She heard again the soothing voice that comforted her when she lay at the bottom of the laundry chute. "It's all right now. You can face it."

A rustling in the bushes told her that Morgan and Jacob were coming for her. It was time to return, to catch the bus to Winnipeg. How was Sarah going to explain to them that she wasn't going with them, that she wasn't ready to leave the island?

BETTY WAS RATTLING off the menu by heart so fast that Vishnu had to ask her to slow down.

"Braised what?"

"Braised endive and a currant rice pilaf—"

Vishnu scribbled as fast as he could. The list of things that Gregory had eaten prior to dinner already filled half a page in his notebook. The dinner menu was a phenomenon.

Kayla was striding around in the kitchen, opening and closing cupboard doors. They hadn't been able to get a search warrant, at least not yet, but she was making the best of the Carriere's cooperative attitude. She lifted the lid of the sugar bowl and sniffed. Betty glanced at her nervously.

"He had a plate of chocolates up there in the office," Alfred said. "I don't know where that went. And he'd drunk a glass of wine—I think my wife brought it up for me, actually, didn't you, Betty?"

Betty's eyes shifted from Kayla to Alfred. "I don't remember," she said.

Alfred acted as if she hadn't even spoken, Kayla noted.

"It must have been for me," he said. "I'd left it downstairs on the counter. I remember. It was in that French glassware. We only have one of those left."

"Where is the glass now?" Vishnu asked.

"I left it on the windowsill upstairs," Alfred said. "I meant to bring it down, but—"

He stopped, surprised at Kayla's reaction. She was charging up the stairs toward his office.

Daniel patted Betty's arm gently. "I know it's upsetting," he said. "But these are merely routine questions." His role in the house at the moment was uncomfortable. As Alfred's stepson, he was part of the family. As a guest at the dinner, he was a witness of sorts. And as a cop, he was allied with Vishnu and Kayla in a way that made him a little suspicious of Betty at the moment. Now, the news that Gregory had drunk from a glass intended for Alfred weighed heavily on Daniel's mind.

KAYLA DECIDED TO start on the third floor and work her way down. When she arrived there, she looked around the office and shook her head. Any office had excess paper, but this one was unbelievable. The walls were lined with stacks of paper. She tugged at the handle of a filing cabinet marked "Private," but it was locked. She wouldn't know what to look for in there, anyway. Instead, she made a practical search of the room for foodstuffs. She found one bottle of pop. It was unopened, but she snagged it anyway. A bag of peanuts, too. Nothing else.

She searched the second-floor office more carefully. This was where Gregory Restall had died. The cyanide could have been in his dinner, but Kayla doubted it. No one else had been poisoned. Of course, no one else probably consumed as much food.... No. If it had been in the dinner, they'd all be dead.

She lifted an open newspaper off the desk and found the plate of chocolates—stale. And the wineglass was right where Alfred said it would be, on the windowsill. She poked through a wire basket full of envelopes, all sealed and ready to mail. Strange. Each had been addressed in different handwriting, some in blue ink, some in black, some in block letters, some in flowery script. The filing cabinets down here were unlocked, and she snooped a bit, just for the sake of snooping, but quickly gave up. If there were any paper clues in here, they'd take months to find. She picked up the stale chocolates with a pair of tweezers that were lying on the desk and dropped them into a plastic evidence bag. Then she bagged the wineglass and headed downstairs.

"What's the story on the mail in your out basket up there?" Kayla asked Alfred.

"The story?"

"Who addresses the envelopes for you? Gregory?"

"Those are self-addressed," Alfred explained. "When writers submit manuscripts, they send along a stamped envelope, addressed to themselves. So if we reject it, we don't have to pay the postage."

Kayla raised her eyebrows. Clever way to do business.

"Let us know if you're planning to leave town," Vishnu was telling Betty. Betty was nodding fearfully. That was one suspicious-looking woman, Kayla thought. Kayla would bet her last dollar that Daniel Bradley's hunch was way off base. The stupid books had nothing to do with this poisoning. If there was a connection to the books, it was only a cover-up. After the attack on Sarah and the murder of Cady Brown, the whole neighborhood knew about the copycat angle. Betty Carriere might have decided to follow suit.

Daniel had taken Alfred aside for questioning. "Look," he said. "Are you sure you've told me everything? If you know anything more, if you have any reason to suspect anyone at all, now is the time to speak up."

Alfred's eyes remained fixed on his own shoes.

As Byron Hunt rode past Alfred's house on his bicycle, he saw Daniel Bradley, in his blue uniform with the red stripe down the legs, emerging from the front door. A man and a woman followed him out. They had to be plainclothes detectives. He braked and walked his bike onto the sidewalk, intending to see what was going on.

"What's up, Officer Bradley?" he asked.

Daniel waved at him. "Busy right now, Byron."

"Any news on Cady Brown?" Byron called, but Daniel didn't answer. It must be Cady Brown's case they were working on, because . . . wait a minute. . . . Byron had heard the rumor that Alfred's assistant died suddenly Saturday night of a heart attack. But maybe the cops didn't believe that. The guy was awfully young to have a heart attack. Maybe the cops knew something. He wheeled a little closer to the car, where Daniel was talking to the detectives.

They clammed up when he got too close, but Byron could see what the woman was holding. It was a fancy wineglass in a plastic bag.

SARAH WATCHED THE boat speed away without the smallest regret. She had not argued with Jacob and Morgan, but merely stood her ground, refusing to budge, until finally they'd had no choice but to leave her here. Jacob had emptied his store of emergency supplies from the boat—tinned food, sleeping bags, kerosene lantern, candles, first-aid kit—and promised to return to check on her. But Sarah wasn't worried. She felt perfectly secure here. Persephone Island was only twenty minutes from Kenora, but it seemed light-years away from Sarah's other life. She felt strangely as though she'd been traveling a long, long time, and her journey was finally over. She was home. There was something she was meant to do here, and she intended to discover what it was.

Besides, she had nothing to return to.

Chapter Twenty-Nine

BACK AT THE STATION, VISHNU was on the telephone to a friend in the forensics lab, begging for a favor—a rush on the testing of the wineglass and other items seized from the Carriere house. He knew it was a lot to ask, because the RCMP labs were booked up months in advance. But Vishnu's network of contacts usually came through for him. He'd long ago mastered the art of the favor exchange.

Kayla sat across from him, typing the names of Betty's dinner guests into the computer. So far, the only one with a suspicious past was Adele Allard, the psychologist, who apparently had a bit of a shoplifting problem. None of the others seemed to have any criminal record. In fact, some of them seemed to have no records at all. Mark Curtis, for instance, didn't even have a driver's licence. And Professor Dawson seemed never to have owned a credit card—strange. Stranger still, she could find no evidence that Professor Dawson had a degree of any kind from a North American university. She logged on to the website of "Canadian Who's Who," because most eggheads, she knew, couldn't resist listing their credentials there. She was just typing in Dawson's name, when a knock came on the door.

It was Daniel Bradley. Kayla looked up in annoyance. Ever since Bradley had come up with the dope on the mystery-novel connection, Vishnu had been giving him far too much attention. "What do you want now?" she snapped.

"I want to see the files on Cady Brown," Daniel said.

"When did you get promoted?" asked Kayla.

Daniel squared his shoulders and faced her. "I still think it's the same guy. Both murders."

"A stabbing and a poisoning? Those are completely different crimes."

"No, they're not," Daniel said. "They are both in the Midnight books. It's a pattern."

"Maybe it's a fake pattern," Kayla said. "In this business, things are seldom what they seem."

"I just want to take a look at the Cady Brown file," Daniel said. "What would it hurt if I took a look?"

"Oh, let him." Vishnu sighed as he hung up the phone. "What difference does it make?"

Kayla looked up, astonished. "Let him?"

"Why not? Give the kid a break."

Kayla stared.

"Nobody ever gave you a break?" Vishnu asked. He snatched the files from Kayla's desk and thrust them at Daniel. "They don't leave this room, you understand? You got thirty minutes. We're going for coffee."

"Coffee?" said Kayla. They had just come back from a coffee break. But Vishnu was already pulling on her sleeve and leading her toward the elevator.

"No more coffee for me," Kayla said when they reached the cafeteria. "I think the ulcer's back."

"Oh, is that what's eating you?"

"Nothing's eating me—I just think the kid should mind

his own business. Take care of the truants and the lost dogs and let us worry about the real stuff."

Vishnu spooned sugar into his coffee and waited.

"He's a damned nuisance," Kayla said.

Vishnu waited.

"He's a waffle-headed kid!"

Vishnu sipped the coffee, added more sugar. "He seems very bright," he said quietly. "Maybe if we let him in on the case a little, he might learn something."

Kayla looked at him. "You don't think he's actually on to something? Come on! Some writer killing his own readers?"

Vishnu shrugged. "Bradley gave the mystery books to the ME's office and to the prosecution. They've both called me already."

"To say what?"

"That Bradley might be right," he said softly. "There are too many coincidences going on. It's a definite pattern. And now that there's been a death in the publisher's own home. . . ."

"But Petursson! I mean, we got him!"

"Shh," said Vishnu. He waved at Jeannie, who was passing by with a bag of take-out sandwiches for the switchboard crew. He lowered his own voice. "Petursson was locked up during the poisoning. What do you think he did? Phoned it in?"

Kayla sat up, suddenly rigid. "Or mailed it in!" she said.

"What?"

"Come on," she said. "We're going back to Carriere's."

NEWS TRAVELED FAST in Wolseley. A rumor from a nursing student at the Health Sciences Centre where Gregory died had started it. A tidbit here and a tidbit there added up, and Byron's report on the wineglass cinched it. Gregory Restall had been poisoned. By cyanide. Just like the guy in *Midnight Feast*.

Everyone at Zina's café was discussing the murder.

"This proves that Peter is innocent," Linda was saying.

"Yes, it does," Byron said. "They've got to let him go now, or at least give him bail. And I intend to bail him out. I can mortgage the house."

"You'd do that for Peter?" Linda asked. "You're a true friend."

"Do you think that's a good idea?" Joe asked nervously. "What if he's guilty?"

"He's innocent," Byron said. "I've said from the first he's innocent. It's clear now that someone is out to kill people according to the books."

"But who *is* it? Who could he be?" Morgan asked. Her eyes met Zina's, then slid away. The two women glanced surreptitiously at their friends.

"Petursson was involved with both Sarah and Cady," Joe argued. "Isn't he the obvious—"

"The obvious suspect, right," Byron said. "You see? It's a frame-up."

"But what if it *is* Petursson?" Joe challenged. "What if he gets out and goes after Sarah again?"

"You really think the same guy who killed Cady Brown could have poisoned Gregory?" Mark asked Byron.

"Who else?"

"But poisoning is a female thing," Mark mused. "It's usually a woman's method."

Morgan shifted uncomfortably in her chair. "Maybe it's some angry girlfriend of Gregory's," she suggested.

"It might have nothing to do with Gregory—or Sarah or Cady," Linda said. "Maybe it's just some crazed mystery-novel fan, picking victims at random."

"Or maybe it's not a fan at all," said Mark. "Maybe it's someone who *hates* mystery novels."

"Or hates book clubs," Zina said miserably.

"Or hates Alfred," said Byron. He stared out the window and watched as the rain began to fall against the glass. "Maybe it's someone who hates Alfred."

KAYLA PETROVITCH LEANED back in her chair and massaged her temples. Daniel Bradley might be cute, but his impenetrable silence was giving her a major headache. If Vishnu wanted to play mentor, why didn't he pick someone a little swifter? Bradley had been hunting through the files for over an hour and still hadn't offered any observations.

Vishnu and Kayla had sped to Carriere's house, only to find that Alfred Carriere had already mailed every envelope Gregory Restall had licked. Alfred had a record of the addresses, but he didn't know which ones Gregory had sealed on Saturday night. He'd provided Kayla with a photocopy of his record book, but what she really wanted was the envelopes themselves to send to the lab. She glanced at Alfred's list of sixty-two addresses and sighed. If she was right, poison by self-addressed envelope was nearly a perfect crime—the evidence went straight back to the killer, courtesy of Canada Post.

She still hadn't eliminated Betty Carriere as her main suspect in Gregory Restall's death. The poison was no doubt a botched attempt to kill her husband. But Kayla's recent idea that Petursson had mailed a poisoned envelope intrigued her, too. He could have mailed it before he was arrested. Or he could have an accomplice on the outside—someone trying to throw them off his trail. She wanted to start tracking down the sixty-two addresses, to get the long process of elimination underway, even if it was a wild-goose chase. But first she'd promised Vishnu she'd talk to Daniel Bradley.

"What have we learned?" she repeated. "Damn it, Bradley, are you *reading* this stuff?" She swept out an arm to indicate the mass of files spread across the desk. "Are you *looking* at these pictures?" She gestured toward the ugly crime-scene photographs.

"Well," he said, "according to the ME's report, the body was placed in the freezer no later than midnight."

Kayla drew in her breath sharply and accidentally swallowed her gum. "So?" she managed to say.

"So did anyone check out Petursson's claim that he talked

to Cady Brown at midnight? That he tried calling her back for nearly two hours?"

Kayla crossed her arms tightly across her chest and tried to look casual. How did Bradley pick up on that so fast? "Anything else?" she asked.

"Well, here's what I think," said Daniel, encouraged by her apparent interest in his ideas. "I think that someone has a big stake in keeping Walter White's identity a secret. It could very well be Walter White himself. He found out about Petursson's terrorizing Sarah with a recreation from the novel plot, and he decided to copycat it."

"Copycat the copycat?"

"That's right. As you said, the pattern could be fake. He probably thinks it's clever, acting out the scenes from his own books."

"But why these victims?" Kayla waved her hand across the scattered files of evidence. "Why these two?"

"Simple. Cady Brown was tracking him down. She might have discovered his identity already. Look at the way the killer trashed her place." Daniel pointed at a photo of Cady Brown's apartment, depicting overturned bookcases and a smashed computer. "Where are her papers and files?"

Kayla didn't answer him directly. "We did a thorough search of her place," she said. "Fingerprints, blood samples, fibers, everything. It's all at the lab."

"I think we should look at her papers and—"

Kayla coughed.

"I think you should, then," Daniel corrected himself. "See if you can find the story she was working on. And I hate to say it, but I think you should search Carriere's office, too. He's holding something back. And he's in danger. That poison was most likely meant for him."

Kayla thought of the mountains of paper in Alfred Carriere's office. Bradley was dreaming if he thought she was going to have it all carted downtown on his say-so. It could take years to sift that much material for clues.

"Just supposing for a minute that you're right," she said, "why would a writer want to poison his own publisher?" She tore the wrapping off another square of gum and stuck it in the pocket of her cheek. "Doesn't make sense."

"No—but this guy doesn't make sense," Daniel said. "If he's obsessed with protecting his identity, and if Alfred somehow leaked some information to Cady Brown, he might have become enraged."

Kayla picked up the list of dinner guests from the night of June the second and scanned it while she opened up another package of gum.

"So you think one of these people is actually Walter White?"

"Maybe," Daniel said.

Chapter Thirty

BYRON HUNT WHISTLED AS HE cycled home from the grocery store with his basket full of fresh pasta and the makings of a rich Italian dinner, including a celebratory bottle of Chianti. For the first time in over a year, he would have a guest for dinner. A good chance to practice his cooking skills, he thought, for the day he got up his nerve to invite Linda over. But it wasn't the lovely Linda Rain he was cooking for tonight. *Linda Rain*. He loved to say her name out loud. But no, his guest tonight was Peter Petursson, newly released from jail, thanks to the banker who'd arranged a quick mortgage on Byron's childhood home.

Byron smiled in satisfaction as he remembered the hearing this afternoon. That legal-aid lawyer, Nate Donovan, was pretty sharp. With a little espionage and a little luck, Nate had discovered enough facts about the investigation to convince the judge that Peter had been railroaded. Nate seemed to have inside information at the police station. Byron had heard rumors he was dating a certain switchboard operator there named Jeannie.

When Nate outlined the connection between the break-in at Sarah's, the murder of Cady, and the Midnight mystery books, the judge looked skeptical. When he described the cyanide poisoning of Gregory Restall and its connection to the third mystery novel, she looked intrigued. She listened intently as Nate explained that the medical examiner, the prosecution, and Officer Daniel Bradley were working on a theory that all three crimes were the work of the same man. With the news that there might be a serial killer running around, that a similar crime had been committed while Peter was in jail, well, Byron could tell by the look on the judge's face that she was considering setting Peter free.

"So Officer Bradley actually said to you that he suspects the author of these books?" the judge asked Nate.

"Yes, your worship," Nate had answered. "He told me so himself when he was questioning Mr. Petursson."

Then Nate produced phone records showing the calls from Peter's house to Cady's apartment, both during and after her time of death. The judge agreed to set a reasonable bail.

Byron turned onto Westminster Avenue, riding past Zina's café and Linda's Handmade Harmony shop. A man he'd never seen before was standing in front of Linda's display window, watching her through the glass. Byron slowed down, then came to a stop and waited. The man glanced over his shoulder warily and then moved on. Everyone seemed uneasy lately, Byron thought as he pedaled on. Byron had been excited about the serial-killer theory because it seemed to clear Peter. And he wanted Peter out of jail. But he hadn't thought about the implication of this theory for his neighborhood until now. He pictured Linda alone in her shop, nervous every time the door opened, imagining a masked villain coming at her with a letter opener or an ice pick. Like everyone else, Linda would be on her guard these days.

Wolseley had always been such a peaceful neighborhood, which was why Byron stayed here. Well, that and the fact he'd inherited his parents' house. He glanced at the innocent wares in the shops he passed, wholesale health food, incense, books of Zen poetry. The front yards of the houses were works of art, the wooden porches painted burgundy and turquoise and hung with wind-chimes from the corner store. The gardens were blooming, spilling out from the yards onto the grassy boulevards. Byron knew the people who lived in nearly every house he passed: playwrights, philosophy professors, hip young mothers, and a truly alarming number of publishers. It was a neighborhood where people walked, and usually Byron was calling out greetings to many friends as he rode his bike home. But now, his attention was captured by another stranger—that young woman crossing the street up ahead, her tie-dyed skirt swishing around her legs. Was she eyeing Byron with suspicion? And that kid on the corner seemed to scurry away from Byron in fear.

He turned onto Ruby Street. But he could not enjoy the sense of contentment that usually cheered him as he arrived home. All along the sidewalk, he suddenly noticed, the cement was badly cracked. And despite the sunshine, he could not see the neighborhood clearly. It began to waver in the summer wind. The narrow brick houses, with their over-lapping eaves, took on a gothic, haunted cast, and the neat picket fences creaked ominously. A dark, translucent film descended from the sky and settled like a fine dust on the rooftops, the children's bicycles, the flower beds. The elm trees stretched taller, their high, warped branches forming a tangled net that blocked out the sky. The wind picked up. Byron hurried. He could almost feel the crime rate rising, and the property values plummeting through the ground.

HOW I LONG to be free of this secrecy. I want to open myself to the world the way I opened myself to you on the beach in the rain, the warm sand on my back so I felt I was part of the earth, and the electricity came crashing through us. I felt it was cutting me in two, the way you cut me in two, the way you showed me the world. Electrified me. I felt I could let the lightning bolts spear me and sink me into the earth and never regret it, as long as I could feel you with me. In me.

Sarah's breath caught in her throat when she read this passage, and the blood rushed to her face. *You cut me in two.* Sarah had never felt that way about anyone. Certainly not Peter. *Electrified me.* Sarah wondered what that felt like.

Then, a few minutes later, she wondered why it was she *didn't* know what it felt like.

She turned quickly to the next entry.

Mary came over with Jacob today, and I was longing to tell her, but I will have to wait. Not long, now. Not long! He left me another note in the white box yesterday. He calls me "Darling," precious, sacred name. Darling.

He wants me to burn the letters, but I won't. I promised I would, but I can't. They are all I have of him, something his hands have touched. When I feel that he doesn't exist, that I don't exist without him, I have something to press against my face, a place I can read our love, and it seems real to me. Because nothing is real unless it is written.

This final sentence almost made Sarah laugh out loud. It was too close to the truth. Sarah had no way of knowing anything about the past unless Carolyn had written it down. From 1978 to 1980, when Carolyn was at the height of a wildly obsessive passion, she had made diary entries nearly every day. And yet there were never enough clues about her lover to identify him. He was older than Carolyn, it seemed, for she referred to his career as though it was well established.

He seemed to travel a lot. And he was a literary person, for she often referred to the help he gave her with her poems. Sarah wondered if he was a writer. Or maybe a publisher, someone from Laurentian Shield perhaps.

Whoever he was, he had neglected Carolyn badly, leaving her alone on the island with little Sarah, with nothing but continually broken promises. There were many references to promises received in letters retrieved from the "white box," which must have been a secret mail drop of some kind for the lovers. Mary Knight's guess must have been right. Sarah's father was married to somebody else, and Carolyn, blind with love, had loyally kept his secret, despite the cost to herself. Where were those lost letters now? In Peter's apartment? Had the police found them? She would find out when she went back home. But she was not yet ready to return, although Jacob had begged her to today, when he dropped off more supplies.

She regretted not asking Jacob for more kerosene. When the sun was low in the evening, the little green cabin grew dim, and the lamp was nearly empty. She lit a candle and continued to read by its flickering flame.

When the wind sweeps through the tall pines like this, it's almost as if I can hear the island whispering to me. Perhaps it is the island's lullaby for our little daughter. I just looked in on her and she's sleeping curled up like a flower bud in May. Nights like this, I am tempted to wake her, just to hear another human voice.

The wind swept through the very same trees outside Sarah's window and she felt at one with her mother and her mother's loneliness.

BY SUNSET, SARAH realized she had read through everything except the journals covering 1982—the last year of Carolyn's life. She stacked them in chronological order and settled down at the kitchen table with a cup of coffee and the plate of Mary's cookies Jacob had brought yesterday. She lit another candle and opened the book on top, a blue scribbler. February 14, 1982. Sarah braced herself. Many of the entries were heartbreaking. But the winter ones were always the bleakest.

It was so good to spend an evening with Roger again. He walked out on his snowshoes all the way from shore and brought us mountains of food on his back, and coffee. I have not had coffee for days! He brought Sarah a teddy bear, and she will not part with it. Now that things are changing, I feel closer to Roger than ever before. In the years when we were apart from each other, something very fundamental was missing from my life. He is like the compass that keeps me traveling in the right direction. I feel like I've been lost, off course, for so long now, I am not certain whether I can find my way again. But as long as the north star. . . .

What was "changing," Sarah wondered. Why did Carolyn seem so happy? And what did she mean by being "lost, off course"? Was it a reference to the love affair that had possessed her like a form of madness for the past few years? Was it a love affair with Roger? Mary had said Roger seemed to pull away from Carolyn when she was pregnant. Possibly Roger and Carolyn had been estranged—maybe Roger had been with another woman, neglecting Carolyn except for his missives sent through the white box. Maybe Roger was the cause of all those outpourings of unrequited passion—and maybe on Valentine's Day in 1982, Roger had begun to come back to her. Sarah kept reading eagerly, hoping that something really had changed for Carolyn before her death, hoping that Carolyn had found happiness at last.

IN BYRON'S LIVING room, Peter Petursson downed one beer after another and plotted his strategy. He had to get the cops off his tail. Nate Donovan made it plain at the bail hearing that the cops were single-mindedly intent on nailing Peter, to the point of ignoring other evidence. It occurred to Peter that he'd better come up with some of this ignored evidence himself, and fast.

He needed to find out more about Cady. She had to have secrets. Everyone had secrets. She was always tight-lipped about her frequent absences. She'd say she was writing. Four, five hours a day. No one spent that much time writing! Peter thought she must have had another lover stashed away somewhere. The day she was murdered, he couldn't reach her anywhere. Yes, there had to be another man. If Peter could focus the cops in that direction. . . .

He wished he could talk to Cady's friends, but Byron said most of her friends believed he was guilty. They'd probably scream if they saw him coming. Maybe if he could get into Cady's apartment, late at night, take a look around. . . .

He stood up and walked into the kitchen. "Hey Byron."

Byron looked up from the sauce he was stirring.

"You want to help me with a little project I'm planning?" Peter asked.

DANIEL WAS OFF the case. He was too embarrassed to tell Marnie what Kayla Petrovitch had said to him. It seemed that his ideas counted for nothing with Kayla now, since Peter Petursson's lawyer had used them to get his client released. Daniel didn't understand her attitude. Wasn't it their job to get at the truth? Daniel had appealed to Vishnu, but even Vishnu seemed disgusted with him now. They would share nothing with him. He was back on his beat, no further ahead. He'd have to continue his investigation on his own.

Marnie was explaining her own theory of the killings as she strolled beside Daniel along Westminster Avenue at two in the morning. Marnie thought it might be Zina Schwartz herself, trying to drum up publicity for her book club. Daniel thought this was absurd. Zina ran a very small business. No matter how much publicity she gained, she wasn't going to earn enough to make it worth her while to kill people.

"She's not going to commit murder just to sell books," Daniel objected.

"You've obviously never worked in a bookstore," Marnie told him. "I have, and let me tell you—hey, what's that?"

She pointed to the alley. Daniel saw a tall shadow flit across the lane, right behind the apartment block where Cady Brown was murdered.

"Someone's in the lane over there. Let's go take a look."

They approached swiftly and cautiously. The dark lane appeared empty.

"Anyone there?" Daniel called. No answer.

"Maybe he turned into the back lot of the building," Marnie suggested. She pushed open the gate that led to a grassy lot behind the apartment block. Turning on her flashlight, she searched the yard, looking under the trash-can stand and a car that was up on blocks. When her light landed on the back door, she said, "What's this?" The lock was smashed.

"This is new," Daniel said. "It wasn't like this yesterday."

"What were you doing here yesterday?" Marnie pushed open the door and began to climb the stairs. They both knew where they were going. To the third floor. Cady Brown's apartment.

The empty, carpeted stairwell smelled of the stale cigarette smoke and cooking grease that had stained the walls yellow. The muffled sound of a television could be heard on the second floor. Otherwise, everything was quiet. When they reached the third floor, Daniel and Marnie pressed their backs against the wall of the stairwell and listened. Through the fire door, they could hear the repetitive scraping noise of metal on metal. Daniel nodded at Marnie, and she took a stance to cover him. Daniel drew his gun. He stepped into the corridor.

Daniel had the element of surprise on his side, and it worked for him. Peter Petursson looked up from picking the lock of Cady's apartment and stood stock-still in the middle of the corridor, staring at the barrel of the gun.

"Freeze," Daniel said. "Put your—"

But Petursson bolted. He turned and ran down the flight of stairs toward the front entrance of the building. Daniel raced after him, gun drawn.

Marnie rushed down the back staircase, hoping to catch up with the suspect before he fled through the front door. But Petursson was fueled by adrenaline. He ran faster than either of them expected, and by the time Dan and Marnie reached the front door together, Petursson was running across the road, about to disappear between two houses on the other side of the street. He was not alone. Marnie glimpsed the dark outline of another man escaping just behind him.

Daniel yelled, "Stop!" He gave chase.

Marnie followed him between the houses and into the darkness beyond.

SARAH'S DREAMS, USUALLY peaceful and soothing here on the island, woke her in the middle of the night with a start. She had dreamed that someone was standing out in the clearing, beckoning her. Was someone really out there? She pulled back the curtain as slowly as she could. She peered out at the clearing until her eyes adjusted to the darkness. Gradually, the landscape took shape. Nothing but the trees and the wind in the trees. Nothing but her own imagination. Too many cookies and eye strain from reading too much. She turned over in bed and tried to sleep again, but she soon gave up.

She lit the last candle in a holder on the bedside table. She pulled the next notebook into bed with her and flipped the pages, until Roger's name caught her eye. June 2, 1982, very near the end of her mother's life.

We came back from the river just as the lift was closing. I caught nothing all day, and Roger teased me, saying we'd have to come to his place tonight, if we wanted to eat. "That's fine with me," I said, and I thought he would fall off the dock, he was so surprised. But I pulled the boat around and waited while he locked up the little house, and Sarah was happy. She's always glad to see Roger.

Roger raced us back, and of course he won. I passed him by Coney, but he caught up to me through the French Narrows and waved as he flew by. By the time we got to his island, he had a fire going on the beach.

He opened a bottle of crabapple wine, and we grilled his pickerel on the fire and talked and smoked. Sarah fell asleep all rolled up in Roger's sweater by the fire, and we carried her inside and lay her on the couch. "That only leaves one bed, you know," he said. And I said, "I know." And then we went back outside and drank some more wine.

It was a slow, simple night, with a thin moon shining on the water and the otters scampering up the bank for the leftover fish. I walked for a while down the shore by myself and watched the light dancing on the waves, and I felt I'd been released somehow, as if I'd been lost in some house of bright mirrors, some maze of smoke and fire, and finally broken free to stand there on the low rise above the lake and feel the night air on my skin, and just breathe. I felt that way all night, with Roger's long, cool hands on my body. Blessed.

Roger Lariviere. Could he possibly be her father? She wondered if Roger still lived on the same island and how hard it might be to find him. She reread the page and noted the reference to the French Narrows. Maybe Mary or Jacob would know where he lived.

Her mother had felt released by this man, blessed, she wrote. *Blessed.* The word stayed with Sarah all night, like a kind of prayer.

MARNIE WAS PANTING heavily as she tore through the bush along the riverbank with the beam of her flashlight dancing crazily on the path and the branches before her. She stopped and bent over, her hands on her knees, and tried to catch her breath. She had lost Daniel long ago, and she knew she should give up and radio for help. She started back along the path toward the street. Daniel was too impulsive. Surely he had seen that second figure, running along behind Petursson. It was madness, even with a gun, to chase two suspects into the dark woods without calling for back-up first.

"Marnie!"

It was Daniel, puffing almost as hard. He came up the bank from the river, holding his empty palms skyward in a gesture of failure. "Lost 'em," he said. "But at least we know who one of them is. Let's call it in."

They called in an all-points bulletin on Peter. "This will send him back behind bars quick enough," Marnie remarked. "Maharaj and Petrovitch will love you for this."

Daniel merely grunted. He was staring up at the window of Cady Brown's apartment. "Let's go see how far he got with his lock-picking."

Daniel stepped over the mangled coil of yellow police tape on the floor and tried the doorknob. The lock was broken, the door swung open easily. The kitchen was much as he had seen it before, the blood dried on the floor. The living room and bedroom seemed untouched.

"Let's get out of here," Marnie said. "We'll call the shop and get them to put on a new lock."

But Daniel wanted to examine the trashed study he had seen only in the crime-scene photos. He walked through the living room and opened a door. Chaos.

"Daniel," Marnie hissed. "Let's go!"

This was the site of the initial attack, Daniel saw. A chair and a bookcase were overturned, books were scattered across the floor and marked with footprints and blood. There were lots of papers, too—he could see that Kayla had never taken his advice to search through Cady's notes. The computer at the desk was smashed completely. Daniel knew from the files that the hammer that did the damage was locked in the evidence room. It had yielded no prints.

"Man!" Marnie said as she entered. "Look at this mess."

"She must have been sitting right here," Daniel said. "At the computer, with her . . . let's see . . . with her back to the door when he entered."

"Don't touch anything," Marnie warned.

Excited, Daniel moved about the room, recreating the scene for himself and his partner. In spite of her misgivings, Marnie found herself caught up in his enthusiasm.

"And then," Daniel finished, "he took a hammer to the computer, to destroy whatever she was working on. Damn it! We'll never know what she was writing!"

Marnie had walked around the back of the computer and was taking a close look at it. "If he was trying to destroy her work, he didn't know very much about computers," she said. From her pocket, she pulled out a package of plastic gloves and began to tear it open.

"What do you mean?"

"Look. He smashed the monitor and part of the casing, but the hard drive should be intact. Why didn't they take this in to the shop?"

"Because they think they have a jealous boyfriend case," Daniel said. "Are you telling me this thing still works?"

"If we hooked up the monitor from that other computer, we might be able to access her files." Marnie donned the pair of gloves. She unplugged the broken monitor and set about reassembling a working unit.

Daniel waited impatiently while Marnie typed. The monitor lit up, and the machine made promising noises.

"Is it working?"

"Hold on." Marnie tapped some more keys.

"Look for an article on Walter White," Daniel said.

After an interminable amount of typing, she cried, "Yes!"

Daniel looked over her shoulder at the screen. A box labeled "Sent" listed a series of names. He saw Alfred Carriere's name at the top, across from the date, 28 May, 11:30 p.m.

"That's her e-mail?"

"You bet," Marnie said. "I can't read any of her articles right now. Can't access her word-processing files—they're password-protected. And I can't get into her unread e-mails. But she hasn't protected the messages already sent and received."

"Read that first one," Daniel said, and Marnie opened it.

Hi Alfred. Did you know you have a spy in your house? Your attempt to keep me off the trail of your precious Walter White and his secret book didn't work. I found Bill Wesley without your help, and I've been to see him twice. When I asked if White had any family, he managed to croak out a few words. So! Now I know that Walter White is the father of our very own mutual friend and neighbor! Is that why you're hiding him? You might as well tell me now, because

The message ended there. Cady must have pressed "Send" before she finished composing it. Probably interrupted by the intruder who killed her. Daniel and Marnie stared at each other. Daniel's mind was clicking like the tumblers in a safe being cracked, so fast he couldn't even follow his own thoughts.

"Walter White *is* involved!" Marnie said. "But who's the friend and neighbor?"

"Is there any reply from Alfred?" Daniel asked. He was humming with tension. It sounded as if Cady had discovered some secret of Alfred's just before she was murdered. That didn't look good.

Marnie scanned the messages in the "In" box, but none of them was from Alfred. And the only references to Walter White came from publishing companies regretting they could not give Cady the information she sought. She went back to the "Send" box. No luck there, either. Cady had sent out a lot of inquiries, but no information.

"Can you get into her files?" Daniel asked. "We need to see the story she was writing."

"Without the password, it could take me days. We should take the whole machine in to the shop, let the computer guys crack it."

"No," Daniel said. He was thinking of Kayla Petrovitch and her sarcastic tongue. First she'd bust him for contaminating a crime scene. Then she'd put the computer in a back room somewhere to gather dust. He couldn't let that happen.

"Who's Bill Wesley?" Marnie asked.

"I don't know," Daniel said. "But I'm going to find out. Turn that thing off and let's get it over to your house right away, before our shift is over."

"My house! We can't take it to my house!"

"Didn't you tell me your foster son is a computer whiz?" Daniel asked. "Don't you want to know who Walter White's son is?"

"Or daughter," Marnie said.

"Or daughter." Daniel was gathering the stray pieces of paper from the floor and shoving them into a plastic bag. "Someone who knew Cady. Someone who knows Alfred. Someone in this neighborhood."

"We can't do this," Marnie was saying. But she was already shutting down the system in preparation to move it out.

Chapter Thirty-One

Jacob sat with his chair tilted back and his feet on a rung under the table. He folded his hands behind his head and looked out the window toward the clearing where the Persephone statue was concealed behind the bushes. His hastily towel-dried hair had lost its part. His rumpled suit jacket hung open, and his tie was askew. But even a boat ride in a morning rain shower hadn't ruffled his lawyerly look completely. He tipped his chair forward and sat up straight with a serious air, his hands clasped on the table in front of him.

"So what do you think?" Sarah asked. She poured him another cup of coffee.

"I think you're crazy," he said calmly. "I think you should come back to civilization. With me. Today."

"No, no. What do you think of what I just read you? About Roger?"

"You need wood," he said. "You need candles. Groceries. More blankets—"

"Couldn't you bring those things for me?" she asked.

He sighed. He covered his face with his hands. Then he looked up and straightened his eyeglasses. "I already did," he said. "It's all in the boat."

Sarah smiled. "Thank you! I just want to stay until I've finished the journals. It seems right, somehow, to read them here, where she wrote them. Now listen this time." She picked up the notebook she'd been reading from and repeated the passage for Jacob. "*Roger has been a true soulmate, seeing me through rough weather and despair. If he still feels the pain I caused him when I turned away from him, he does not show it.*"

Sarah closed the notebook. "What do you think?"

"Roger Lariviere again," Jacob said. "I have to admit, he sounds like a promising lead." He grinned. "Soulmates, huh? I like that."

"I want to talk to him," she said.

"Well, he's still around, as far as I know. He was still operating the boatlift a couple of years ago. I don't know him myself, but I know where his place is. He's got an island even smaller than this one. Little log cabin, big Canadian flag out on the dock. It's not far. If you really want to see him, I'll take you."

Sarah leaned over and kissed him on the cheek so energetically she knocked his glasses right off his face.

DANIEL FIDGETED IN the vestibule of the Wesley house, somewhat in awe of the elegant atmosphere. Although he had wiped his feet vigorously on the mat, he dared not set foot in the living room, with its immaculate cream and white Persian carpet. He took what he could see from the hallway. The living room reminded him of something out of a magazine—lifestyles of the rich and famous, maybe. It was the size of a ballroom and full of highly polished cherry wood furniture, including a grand piano on which stood an enormous crystal vase holding dozens of pale yellow roses and a number of photographs in gold frames. Daniel examined the one closest to him, a family portrait of a self-consciously handsome man with a younger woman and two little boys. The woman caught his attention. She was a tall, strikingly beautiful brunette, but her posture was stiff. She posed in a formal manner, wearing white gloves, a strand of pearls, and a forced smile. She was dressed to the nines, and he suspected she was the one responsible for the decor. His eyes traveled around the room. An enormous bank of windows, graced with white lace curtains, swept across the back wall. The other cream-colored walls were hung with landscape paintings. Yet, despite all the care that had gone into the decoration, the room was uninviting. He couldn't imagine sitting on any of this furniture. The pale green sofa was covered in some kind of shimmery, slippery material—satin? Surely not. He wished Marnie were here. She would know. He reached out his hand across the threshold and was just about to touch it when a small cough at his shoulder made him jump.

It was Mrs. Wesley. About twenty years had passed since the photograph was taken, but he recognized her. She was nearly sixty now, he guessed, and still beautiful. The top of her perfectly coiffed head was at Daniel's eye level, and she was trim as a twenty-year-old. She wore a beige dress and sunhat, with matching gloves—subdued colors, suitable for a woman whose husband is so ill, he thought.

"What is this about?" she asked quietly. One hand rested over her heart, as if she were preparing herself for a shock. "Why have you come? Is it one of the boys?"

"No, no," Daniel reassured her quickly. Mothers were all the same, he thought. As soon as they see a policeman at the door, they think the worst. "It's nothing to do with your boys. I've come about some business matters of your husband. I have some questions, and as you know—well, I went to the hospital, and he wasn't able to speak to me."

"He's dying," she said simply.

"Yes, well, do you think you could spare me a few

minutes?" Daniel hoped she could. He was running into dead ends everywhere. Marnie's foster son wasn't having any luck cracking Cady's password, and Alfred had been no help at all. He claimed to know nothing about Walter White and nothing about Cady's e-mail. Gregory had handled all the e-mail, he said. When Daniel mentioned a child of White's, Alfred's eyes widened, but he claimed to have no idea who it might be. He'd told Dan to ask Bill Wesley, who was in the Lake of the Woods Hospital. So Daniel had driven out here. But Alfred hadn't warned him how sick the old man was. The nurses wouldn't even let Daniel into his room.

"We're working on a case in Winnipeg that may involve one of your husband's business associates," he explained now to Mrs. Wesley.

"Come in," she said. She led the way into the living room and gestured toward a chair upholstered in embroidered tapestry. Daniel wiped his feet again on the mat in the hall and ventured inside the intimidating room. He felt clumsy and dirty and completely out of place.

Mrs. Wesley rang a bell, and the maid who had answered the door appeared instantly to take her order for tea.

"Now what is all this about?" Mrs. Wesley asked. She perched herself at the edge of the green sofa and looked at him with an expression of mild concern. "How may I help you?"

Daniel relaxed a little. "I understand your husband is a literary agent," he began.

"Yes, he is—or he was. He hasn't been actively engaged in the business for quite some time now."

"Since his illness?"

"Yes. He was diagnosed with cancer last fall, and since then he's spent all his energy fighting it."

"But up until last fall, he worked as a literary agent, isn't that right?"

"Well, yes, let's see . . . since he retired from the university."

"He retired early?"

"Yes, he was—we were rather lucky with some investments and he was able to devote himself full time to his passion— promoting Canadian literature." She smiled. "The Pen and Ink agency was small but very successful."

"What can you tell me about your husband's relationship with Alfred Carriere?" Daniel asked.

"They have been business associates for years," she said. "Bill helped Alfred get started in publishing back in the seventies. Once Alfred expanded his business, Bill steered several of his finest authors in Alfred's direction. And more recently—" She paused a minute, thinking. "Recently, as Bill got older, you know, he was cutting his list. I believe Alfred was representing some of the authors himself."

This was news to Daniel. "Alfred's becoming an agent?"

"Well, not officially—not yet, anyway. But if, I mean to say, when Bill's gone, Alfred will take over the business entirely."

"He'll inherit it?" This was even bigger news.

But Mrs. Wesley was smiling wryly. "Not inherit it," she said firmly. "Bill has a family of his own, you know. No— Alfred will buy us out. At a reasonable price."

"I see." Daniel made a note of this.

"Is Alfred in some kind of trouble?" Mrs. Wesley asked. "What is this case you're working on?"

"We're trying to locate one of the authors your husband represents," Daniel said.

The maid entered, bearing a silver tray with a fine china tea set. Mrs. Wesley received it with a pleasant smile and a firm nod of dismissal. The maid retreated.

"Honey in your tea? Or sugar?"

"Sugar's fine."

"Are you sure? This is the finest local honey. My neighbor makes it himself."

"One lump of sugar, please," Daniel said. "We want to talk to the author Walter White. Do you know him?"

Mrs. Wesley was bent over the tea tray, intent on pouring. "Walter White? Not really."

"He's a mystery writer?"

"The Midnight Mystery man, yes," she said.

"So you do know him?"

Mrs. Wesley was busy with the sugar tongs. She made a vague gesture with her left hand. "I haven't seen him in years," she said. "Milk? Or some nice fresh cream?"

"Just a little milk. Do you know where we might be able to locate him?"

"Heavens no," she said. "He always was a traveler, if I recall correctly. He's no doubt in the States somewhere." She looked regretfully at Daniel. "New York, perhaps?"

Daniel sighed.

"He might be in Europe. He's rather famous at the moment, and he doesn't like the limelight."

"Could you describe him?" Daniel asked. "There's no picture of him on his books."

"Oh, let's see. . . . He was stout, if I recall correctly. Handlebar mustache. A bit stooped. Have you spoken to Alfred? As far as I know, Alfred is handling all Mr. White's books now. Bill has turned over nearly every aspect of the business to Alfred, by now."

Daniel wondered how true this was. Surely "every aspect" would include the authors' addresses. He decided to fish some more. "So, Alfred and Bill are pretty close, then?"

"Alfred's always been good to Bill. And lately, since Bill's been sick, he's been a great comfort to us."

Daniel nodded. "He visits you?"

She sighed sadly. "He doesn't visit *here*. Not at the house. He used to come to dinner, though. He was always welcome here in the old days."

"The old days?"

"Well, before. . . ." She lowered her voice to a whisper. "Before Alfred's *divorce*."

"His divorce from Dorothy?" Daniel asked. He colored. As a police officer, he was well versed in covering his motives during questioning. But Dorothy was his own mother, and he couldn't help feeling a bit ashamed at his pretense of ignorance.

"No. From his real wife. The first one. It was such a shock." Mrs. Wesley leaned forward confidentially. "We had two small boys at the time—impressionable children. I explained to Bill he'd simply have to tell Alfred he was no longer welcome here. We couldn't allow an adulterer into our family home, to sit at the same table with our children!"

"But surely, after all these years—"

"After all these years, Alfred has landed in the marriage he deserves," Mrs. Wesley said. "He's been married three times, each woman worse than the last. Now he's shackled himself to that awful—that little juvenile delinquent—that Betty. I wouldn't trust her in my house for a second."

"Delinquent? She's a juvenile delinquent? Betty?"

Mrs. Wesley leaned forward and passed Daniel a cup of tea. "Oh, yes," she said. "Don't you know she killed a man?"

Daniel dropped the cup, spilling Earl Grey tea all over the Persian carpet.

WHEN JACOB PULLED the Lund up to Roger Lariviere's dock, the air was still. The Canadian flag hung limp on its pole. Sarah could see a thin line of smoke rising straight up from the chimney of the small log cabin on the low rise above the water. The island was tiny and seemed nearly submerged by the lake. She clenched her hands together and tried to compose herself.

"What should I say to him?" she asked.

"I'll do the talking," Jacob offered.

"No, you stay here. Wait in the boat. I have to do this myself." She climbed out onto the dock and, without letting herself think too much, started up the path toward the cabin.

He had heard the motor and was coming down the small hill to greet her, a giant of a man, with an axe in his right hand.

"Are you lost?" he asked.

"I'm Sarah Yeats," she blurted. "Carolyn's daughter."

He took a minute to find his voice. "Ah, the little voyageur, eh? Carolyn's daughter? My God." But that was all he managed. His lips trembled. He turned away and hid his face.

Sarah realized with alarm that he was crying. The reaction had been immediate—as if she had struck him. She waited, feeling awkward, while he gained his composure. He ran a sleeve across his face, but when he turned around, the tears were still visible in his eyes.

Sarah had been right about one thing. Roger had loved Carolyn.

But she doubted he could be her father. How could Roger Lariviere have fathered such a small, pale, blue-eyed child as Sarah? He stood about six foot six. His skin was deep brown, his long hair thick and black and perfectly straight. His eyes, when he finally wiped them and turned to look at her, were so dark they were nearly black. Surely those dark brown eyes would have dominated her mother's blue.

She felt a sense of loss, mingled with relief. She was disappointed he wasn't her father—this sweet man, whom she'd come to know through her mother's writing. But she was also glad to feel her muscles unclench and to regain control of her shaking hands. She would not have to endure any emotional father-daughter reunions today.

Instead, it was Roger who was in distress. "Why have you come here?" he asked. "So many years. . . ." He could not continue.

"I'm sorry," Sarah said. "I didn't mean to upset you. I just wanted to talk, if it's all right with you. I know you were a good friend to my mother, and I never really knew her, you see, so—"

"Of course," he said. "Of course. Come in. Tell your friend to come up and I'll put on some coffee. We'll talk."

"You're sure it's okay?"

"I'm sure," he said, and he seemed to mean it. "I'm glad you've come." He pointed uphill at the cabin. "Do you remember this old shack?"

"Not really."

"Well, you were here many times when you were small." He smiled at her. "Welcome back."

She watched him stride easily away. A strong, handsome man. She'd been expecting somebody older, and she realized with a pang that, if Carolyn had lived, she would still be under fifty years old today.

"She sure had a way with words, your mum." Roger carried a teapot from the wood stove to the table, a journey of about two feet. The cabin was cramped and too small for its contents, which hung on the walls—saws, snowshoes, maps, and cooking utensils.

Sarah smiled. "Yes, she did."

"But she had a way with secrets, too. She never told you anything about your dad at all?" He poured tea into Jacob's cup and Jacob nodded his thanks. He was listening quietly to the conversation without interrupting.

"I was little," Sarah said. "I didn't even know I was sup-posed to *have* a dad. We were there on the island, just the two of us. It all seemed normal to me."

Roger nodded. "You didn't know any other way of life."

"No. When she died—" Her throat seemed to close. It was that gaping loss again, threatening to swallow her whole. The feeling she sealed up so tightly when she was a child, the spot she couldn't bear to touch.

She felt a hand on each of her arms. Both Jacob and Roger were touching her gently. She sensed that their eyes were meeting over the top of her head.

Roger raised his eyes to the ceiling. "Ah, Carol," he said, as if he were speaking directly to Carolyn. He patted Sarah's arm and then withdrew his hand to pour her tea. "I'm sure she never meant to do this to you. She wouldn't have hurt you for any reason. She would have told you eventually, I'm sure, when you grew up."

"I can't believe she didn't tell anyone at all!" Sarah said. "She doesn't even name him in her diary."

"She wouldn't tell me," Roger said. "Far as I knew, she was my best friend. I hoped she'd be my wife someday. Next thing I know, she turns up with a baby." He sighed. "I never met a woman who drove me so crazy."

"Didn't she say anything *about* him, though? Where he worked? Anything?"

"Near the end, there, when she was getting ready to break it off with him, she said a few things." Roger looked at Sarah. "Look, I hate to say this, 'cause he's your father and all, but he was not a good man. She was a lonely young girl when he met her. She thought he was smart and educated—he was all the things I'm not, I guess. He knew all about books and all about the world—that's what she called any place that wasn't on the lake—*the world*—like as if we weren't part of it. Anyway, near the end there, she told me all that, and she said she guessed she'd been dazzled by the wrong things. She guessed there were more important things than the world. I think that was her way of apologizing to me, you know. Or I took it that way. She'd always wanted to get off that island, ever since I first met her, when she was a girl. But near the end, she said she was happy there. Said she was going to quit waiting to be rescued. She was working on a new book. She was—" His voice broke. "She was happy."

Sarah watched him, amazed at the power of her mother to bring a man to tears twenty years after her death. She waited a minute before asking another question.

"You must have had some idea who he was," she said. "Who was she seeing? You must have seen her with someone."

Roger sipped his tea. "Oh, there were a few I wondered about," he said. "There was that fishing buddy of Luke's, Cam?"

"Cam Carriere," Jacob said.

"Yeah, Cam Carriere. He had two kids who were always around. The younger one, Quinn Carriere, he took an awful interest in Carol. I used to see her talking to him, down by the boatlift. She was always exploring there, down by the old mill, picking up rocks and stuff." He shook his head and laughed softly. "I used to think she was hanging around to see me. Then one day I followed her into the wreck of the mill and found her stuffing a letter in the old fuse box in there. Must have been leaving someone a message—"

"The white box!" Sarah cried. She remembered the white metal fuse box she'd seen in the mill's power station, with "100 Volts" stamped on its door. "She talks about a white box in her journals. And she *was* using it as a mailbox—for letters to her lover. You mean Quinn Carriere used to meet her there?"

Roger began to clean his fingernails with a match. "I'd go talk to Quinn, if I were you," he said without looking up.

ON THE RIDE back, Sarah didn't talk much. If Quinn Carriere was her father. . . . She looked at Jacob. He was concentrating on navigating.

"Alfred's brother Quinn?" she said. "You don't think. . . ."

"The thought crossed my mind," Jacob said. He steered expertly through a rock-infested channel and made a sharp turn toward Devil's Gap. "It crossed Roger's mind, too."

"But Quinn was a family friend. She knew him since she was a child! How could he just abandon her?"

"It happens," he said. "It's been known to happen."

Sarah wondered if he was thinking of his own father.

"Quinn is in Toronto, as far as I know," Sarah mused. "He moved there with his wife and kids a long time ago. I think it was—" She stopped, suddenly realizing exactly when it was—when the Carriere Press split up. Just after Carolyn's death.

Chapter Thirty-Two

MORGAN FOLLOWED JOE DELANEY to Linda Rain's Handmade Harmony shop, bearing muffins and coffee from Zina's café. Joe opened the door for her, and they both jumped in surprise at the jangle of bells and the loud shriek of a buzzer that greeted them.

"Hello?" Linda called from behind the counter. "Who's there?"

"Joe and Morgan," Joe said. "What are you trying to do, deafen your customers?"

"Hi there. Sorry. I just felt, with everything going on around here, I needed a little more protection. Sort of an alarm system."

"Right." Joe set the coffee and muffins on the counter.

"Mmm," said Linda. "Thanks. Is that cranberry?"

"The nose knows." Joe unpacked the muffins and took the lids off the coffee. Buttercup's toenails clicked on the hardwood floor as she came over to investigate. Zina was her favorite cook.

264

"I think it's a good idea, that system," Morgan told Linda. "I don't know how you can work alone in here. Even with Buttercup. I'd be petrified to work all alone if I couldn't see."

"You're petrified and you *can* see," Joe said. "You must have paid out a fortune in overtime lately, just to get someone to stay with you all day at work." He laughed.

"You can't be too careful," Morgan said. "It's all right for you to make fun. You don't have to live here. Nobody feels safe on these streets any more."

"Nobody trusts their neighbors, either," said Linda. "Everyone imagines the killer is lurking right next door."

"Zina thinks it's Walter White himself," Morgan said.

"Weird," said Joe. Despite his carefree attitude, he couldn't suppress a shiver. "To think he might be spying on us as we read his books. I can just picture him, all grizzled and mean, up in the attic of some Wolseley mansion, laughing maniacally—"

"Stop that!" Linda told him. "It's bad enough as it is, with all the negative attention focused on our neighborhood. That Channel 9 reporter has been coming in almost every day to pester me. He's been broadcasting the most awful stories, making it sound as if Wolseley is haunted. It's bad for business."

"It's not bad for Zina's business," Joe replied. "She's packing them in, and *A Midnight Swim* is flying off the shelves."

Linda clucked in disapproval. "Curiosity seekers. Ghouls."

"Have you read it yet?" Morgan asked.

"Oh yes, I'm reading it right now," she said. "Byron finished reading it for me this morning, and I was just listening to it when you came in."

"Isn't it scary? It's giving me the creeps."

"Yeah right, Morgan," Joe said. "You're afraid you'll be working away in the clothing store and someone will pop up behind you and *drown* you!"

"It's no joke," said Linda. "People are afraid. I heard there's nobody jogging down by the river these days."

Joe said, "That's just foolishness. You know what I'm really afraid of? I'm afraid Peter Petursson's going to get himself another girlfriend while he's out on bail. Now *that* would be frightening."

"Have you seen him?"

"No. But I heard Byron's been looking all over for him. Apparently he's lying low. If he skips bail, Byron'll lose his house!"

"Isn't he staying with Byron?" asked Morgan. "I thought Byron was sort of, you know, keeping an eye on him." She began to chew on her thumbnail.

"He was, but Byron says last time he saw him he was—uh oh!"

"What?"

"He was down by the riverbank," Joe said.

"Oh Joe, cut it out!" Linda said.

"No, really!" Joe protested. But the women wouldn't listen to him any more. Finally he sighed and, with a great jangling and buzzing, left the shop.

"Who's reviewing *A Midnight Swim* this Sunday?" Morgan asked Linda.

"Dr. Allard. It should be interesting. I heard she's going to discuss the role of the reader in the text—you know, the way everyone's always reading a book in that book."

"That's true," Morgan said. "Now that you mention it, they are." She finished her coffee and tossed the remains of her muffin to Buttercup. "I have to get moving. I'm going over to the Carrieres' house to borrow a photograph Alfred showed us at the dinner party. A picture of Sarah's mother as a girl. I want to get a copy made for her. She's sort of rediscovering her mother these days."

"How is Sarah?"

"She's great, as far as I know. She's out at her place on Lake of the Woods, lucky girl. She doesn't have a telephone or TV. She doesn't even know about the poisoning or Peter being out on bail or anything."

"Do you think she's safe out there like that? With no phone?" Linda asked.

"Oh sure. It's sort of a family tradition to rough it like that. Our grandpa raised his daughters out there, all by himself. It's probably safer than the city, especially right now. Anyway, a friend's looking out for her. You remember Jacob Knight from the dinner party?"

"Oh yes, the handsome lawyer," said Linda.

"How can you tell he's handsome?" Morgan asked.

"I can tell. Really, Morgan," she teased. "Didn't anyone ever tell you about *inner* beauty?"

"Yeah, I guess so."

"Beauty is only skin deep," Linda said.

"Okay, okay," Morgan said. The cacophony of noise told Linda she had opened the door.

"More to a man than meets the eye!" Linda called.

"Goodbye, Linda!"

Linda chuckled to herself. She fed the leftovers to Buttercup and turned her tape-recorder on again.

"It was nearly midnight when she tiptoed out of the hotel and made her way across the moonlit beach to watch the high wild ocean whitecaps rolling in to shore. She breathed deeply, filling her lungs with the cool, salty air. The violent seascape thrilled her blood. She sat at the very edge of the water, wrapping her arms around her bare knees. Her toes tingled in the cold foam that rose and receded as the waves slapped and broke against the sand. Linda, I'd love to be at the seashore with you—"

What? Linda stopped the tape. Was that part of the story? She pressed *rewind* and listened again. Byron Hunt's voice repeated, "Linda, I'd love to be at the seashore with you, to walk along a beach with you, hand in hand, with Buttercup running along beside us." Linda stopped the tape again and sat in silent astonishment. Byron Hunt had interrupted his reading of *A Midnight Swim* to . . . well . . . to make a pass at her!

ALFRED HUNG UP the phone and turned to watch his wife as she carried the throw rugs out the front door and began to beat them with a wire racket. He found Daniel's story hard to believe. Daniel seemed to assume that Alfred knew all about it. He'd accused Alfred of concealing Betty's past from the police. But Alfred had known none of it. He stared at his wife. Betty looked exactly the same as she always did on a cleaning day, her permanent wave protected by a dotted kerchief, her movements brisk and efficient. Could she really be a killer? The thought was preposterous, and yet, and yet . . .

There was a certain logic to it, Alfred thought. A certain, dare he say it, poetic justice. If Betty was going to kill, that was the way she'd do it. And to think that she'd done it before! True, she was only seventeen at the time, but perhaps if she'd discovered Alfred's affair, she'd reverted to her former ways.

Little Betty mixed up with a gang? Mild-mannered Betty a biker chick? According to Daniel's information, Betty and her boyfriend were heavily into dealing drugs some twenty years ago in Kenora. When an addict had crossed Betty's boyfriend on some deal or other, he'd taken revenge by cutting the fellow's mescaline with arsenic. The poisoning was slow. The dealer kept feeding it to him week by week, until he ended up in hospital. It was a painful and lingering death, with plenty of time for the dying man to point the finger. The boyfriend been sentenced to life in prison. Daniel didn't know if he was still behind bars or not. Betty, in consideration of her age, had done her time in a Kenora juvenile detention center.

Betty returned to the house with the clean rugs, and as she passed, she smiled at her husband as if nothing had changed.

Alfred watched her familiar back, with its bow of pink apron ribbon, disappear into the kitchen. Betty in jail? Alfred couldn't quite wrap his head around that one. She had never breathed a word of it in all the years of their marriage.

When she passed him again, carrying a bucket of water and a brush, she looked at him strangely.

"Daydreaming?" she asked. She went outside to scrub the front steps.

"Come back here," Alfred said. Betty set the bucket down and returned.

"Whatever's the matter?" she asked, alarmed.

Something in him snapped.

"You're a liar," he said. "You've been lying to me all these years."

Betty blanched and dropped the scrub brush.

"You're a poisoner," he said. "You killed a man, and you went to jail and you never told me!"

Betty had to sit down immediately. As there was no furniture in the vestibule, she chose the floor.

"And now you're trying to kill me!" he cried, the full implications of Daniel's phone call settling in at last.

"No, Alfred, I swear it," she managed to say. "It wasn't me."

"Who else could it have been? You served the wine. You brought it upstairs for me, as usual. You were planning to do away with me! And then poor Gregory—" For the first time since Gregory's death, Alfred actually felt sorry for him.

Betty slowly rose to her feet and tried to compose herself. She felt she would suffocate if it weren't for the fresh air coming in at the open door.

"Alfred, think!" she reasoned. "Why on earth would I want to poison you?"

Alfred regarded her warily. She looked so prim and innocent. She looked like one of those singing evangelists on Sunday morning television.

"I love you," she continued. "We have a good life together. You treat me well. Why would I want to harm you?"

"Because you found out about Morgan, I guess," he said.

"Morgan?" Betty seemed genuinely puzzled. "What does Morgan have to do with any of this?"

AS SHE WAS coming to the end of the journals, Sarah found herself reading more slowly. She was thinking, piecing Carolyn's story together from the fragments she'd read and the scraps of information she'd gathered from the people who knew her. It seemed that Carolyn had begun to write poetry very early. At the age of twenty, she'd given a collection of her work to Carriere Press, and over the next ten years, she'd written and published four more. All well received and highly praised. Yet despite her success, loneliness and poverty were the constant themes of her life. She had begun an affair with her mysterious, unnamed mentor at the age of about twenty-two and kept it up, as far as Sarah could tell, until shortly before her death, bearing his child and taking his literary advice and loving him madly, while never breathing a syllable of his name to a single soul. It almost seemed as if he had enchanted her. Even when he stayed away for months at a time, she remained deeply committed to him, completely under his spell. Then, as Roger had said, something changed. Near the end of her life, Carolyn seemed to wake up.

He came last night and I told him I wanted to break it off. He was devastated, begging. When he left, he asked for the latest poems, but I told him I want to take care of my own business now. I want to make a clean break, start fresh. I thanked him for all his support over the years and told him honestly I couldn't have done without him, but I have to live my own life now. If I'm going to care for Sarah all by myself, then I have to learn how to manage my own life and my own work. The look in his eyes nearly made me break down, but I held firm. After he left, I wept all night, but this morning I'm stronger. It's for the best. Perhaps my life is finally going to begin.

Sarah felt like cheering when she read that. But it was sobering, too. The date was early June, a mere two weeks before her mother's death. Sometimes, she thought, it takes us too long to wake up.

MORGAN PLANNED TO make a copy of Alfred's old photo of the fishing derby, then enlarge it and cut out the figure of ten-year-old Carolyn. She'd frame it and give it to Sarah as a birthday gift—a late birthday gift, but Sarah was used to that.

As she approached the Carrieres' house, Morgan saw that the door was wide open. A pail of soapy water sat on the front steps, as if Betty had been interrupted in her chores. A heated argument was clearly audible from within. What was going on? Morgan cautiously crept up the steps, keeping well out of sight.

"And all this time you were sleeping with her? All this time?"

"It was nothing." Alfred's voice.

Morgan cringed. Nothing?

"It didn't mean anything." He was actually pleading with his wife.

"It's not nothing to me," Betty's voice declared. "How could you get mixed up with that flighty little—"

"I know, I know," Alfred said. "She's nothing. It was just a fling. It was only sex." Morgan nearly gagged. "Betty, listen to me. Don't leave!"

Morgan quickly pressed her back against the stuccoed wall beside the door, hoping Betty wouldn't come storming out. She was disgusted to hear Alfred's whining. She knew this marriage was convenient for him. She'd long known he would never leave his subservient old Betty. She was too easy for him to control. But Alfred and Morgan had something special going, something fun, or at least Morgan had believed so. Now, listening to him describe their love affair as a dirty little fling, she was revolted.

"If that's the kind of cheap stuff you prefer, then you can have it," Betty screeched. She was closer to the door now. But Alfred was apparently gripping her by the arm, because she cried, "Let me go!"

"Honey, wait. You know I don't prefer her. It's you I'm

married to. Not her. I could never love a woman like that. Not seriously. With those second-hand clothes and that cheap perfume? She was only a diversion, a little indulgence. I'm sorry I was tempted, but—Aaargh!"

Alfred and Betty both howled as the cold, soapy contents of the pail came flying through the door and hit them full in the face.

Chapter Thirty-Three

SARAH IS PLAYING "KING OF THE CASTLE" with Sam and Morgan on the beach and Sam has finally let her be the king. I can see her from here, crowing on top of the little sand heap, victorious at last. Sam is so tall now, it's hard to believe. And so mature. He'll be thirteen in a few days, and must find it tiresome stuck out here with the girls all day. But he's kind to them, patient. This morning he even made breakfast for them while the rest of us slept in, and he's played with them all day long, keeping them so amused I was able to get ten whole pages done this afternoon without interruption. And now—miracle of miracles—I have a few moments to myself.

Darlene's gone into town for the day to shop. I asked her to stop by Knight's and pick up some empty cartons—Evan insists I use his cartons so that they will be "uniform in size." Such a fuddy-duddy sometimes! Tonight I will begin the task of sorting everything. The thought makes me groan. So many years and years of words. Who could have guessed they would accumulate like this, become so heavy? At least I am not a sculptor, like Dad!

If the words were stone, they could weigh down the moon. But of course, if they were stone, they would not have to be protected. They would be impervious as Persephone's book.

Perhaps I should be glad to get rid of it all. It feels lately as if every burden is dropping from me, as if I am becoming weightless, unmoored, preparing for a journey.

This was the theme of nearly every entry in June 1982. Freedom, weightlessness. It all sounded very liberating, but from Sarah's point of view, knowing Carolyn's days were numbered, there was a sad irony to it all. And Sarah wasn't sure whether she was imagining it or not, but there seemed to be an undercurrent of dread. Something unspoken, just below the surface of the words, that Sarah couldn't read.

ALFRED STILL COULDN'T tell if Betty was truly shocked or if she deserved a Gemini award for acting. She was moving through the house at an uncanny speed, opening and closing drawers and closets, choosing clothing and cosmetics. She found every item with an unerring precision that chilled him. Within minutes, it seemed, she had tidily packed a complete matching set of luggage, called a taxi, and was waiting on the front steps, fuming in a state of silent rage so intense that Alfred could feel it through the door, although she had slammed it most definitely.

She's probably telling the truth, he thought. She's innocent. Where would she get cyanide from, anyway? If only Daniel's phone call hadn't caught him off guard. If only he'd had time to think before launching into a full-blown confession. He'd been an idiot. If Betty didn't want to poison him before, she'd be wanting to now.

"What have I done?" he moaned softly to himself. "What the hell have I gone and done?"

THE BIG SKY Tavern was not a place where Morgan usually hung out, but it was open earlier than any other bar she knew, and today she needed a drink before noon. She sat in the back near the pool tables and watched the big-screen TV without paying much attention to it. She was thinking about Alfred.

She was thinking about all the times she'd sneaked out to meet him at her clothing shop in the middle of the night, all the lies she'd told to Zina and to Sarah and to Linda, and, well, to everybody. And for what? So that he could criticize her clothing and her perfume! After everything she'd done for him, listening to his stories about his cold, cold wife and his business problems and his little plans for the future which never, she recalled now, included Morgan.

She was drinking Bloody Marys because they had vitamins in them and she hadn't eaten breakfast. Also because the name of the drink suited her mood. She lit a cigarette and contemplated how best to get her revenge. Nobody criticized Morgan's taste in clothes and got away with it.

At one o'clock, the Channel 9 News came on, and Morgan saw a huge graphic of the cover of *A Midnight Swim* on the screen. She strained to hear the announcer's voice. Something about the last book in the series being launched on Sunday, but she could hear nothing else. The clack of cues on the pool table, and an argument over the placement of an eight-ball, drowned out the television. But the item made Morgan think. Alfred had hinted pretty obviously one night that he had something up his sleeve for the fall, something about more Midnight books, it sounded like. He'd sworn her to secrecy, but then, that was his little mistake, wasn't it? She picked a quarter from the pile of change on her table and staggered toward the pay phone.

"Linda?" she said, when her friend answered. "What's the name of that Every Hour guy? That Channel 9 reporter who's been bugging you for dirt on the book club?"

ON THE LAST few pages of the very last of Carolyn's note-books, there were several pencil drawings. Most of them of a sleeping child, who must have been Sarah herself. The writing continued after the sketches.

Sarah has my mother's face. I could never see that, before, looking at her. But sketching her tonight, I can see it clearly. The soft rounded cheeks, the high forehead. I remember my mother standing by the window, twisting her hands in that anxious way, as if she knew she would have to leave us soon.

When our father told us the story of Persephone and Demeter, I wept. I thought only of Persephone, separated from her mother, the way I was separated from mine. I pictured her wandering the dim landscape of the underworld, imprisoned, homesick. Abandoned.

But I see now that it is Demeter's story, after all. How she mourned for her lost daughter until the flowers all withered and cold winds swept the earth, the way they do across the prairies in November, when the sun barely rises above the horizon, until at the lowest point of winter, the midnight of the year, all life is hidden, tucked tight below the earth. Swallowed, consumed by Hades. When I think of what might happen, what might be taken from me, it seems that darkness could swallow me, too.

I have packed everything and soon it will be safely stowed. A relief. But what will I do with the new book? I have to keep it here with me, to keep working on it. It is unbearable to think that Sarah might never read what I have written, that she might never know.

It seems right to consign my work to my daughter. Let her protect it, with the shade of her right hand. I don't know why I feel this strange misgiving. In the stories, Persephone always returns. The earth spins on its axis and light floods back across the sky.

The journal ended there. Sarah turned the pages carefully to the end of the notebook, but found nothing else. No drawings. No loose notes. Every page was blank. Her task was complete.

The shade of her right hand? Sarah looked down at her own right hand and turned it over, examining the palm. It must be some saying, but from where? From the Bible? She remembered something in there about the right hand of God. But *shade*? Perhaps it was a phrase from the myth of Persephone. The whole story seemed to be about light and shadows, summer and darkness. Maybe if she looked through Ovid, she could find it.

THE GLEE THAT Morgan felt when she'd heard the Channel 9 News at four was short-lived. The announcer had used her little snippet of information, and even embellished it wildly, telling the entire city that "a sixth and final Midnight Mystery is rumored to be in the works for fall. But the man-uscript is locked tightly away in the private files of Carriere Press. Plans for its launch, and even its title, are shrouded in secrecy. With the recent murders linked to the mystery series, residents of Wolseley are clamoring for details of the plot. But those details, even though they may save a life, are being kept strictly under wraps. Publisher Alfred Carriere refused to return our reporter's calls. . . ."

Revenge was sweet, for a while. But the sting of hurt pride quickly returned, and the high from the Bloody Marys had worn off, leaving her with a headache.

She needed some company. Sarah was away and Zina was too busy lately to have time to chat. She decided to drop in on Mark Curtis, for a little tea and attention.

SARAH PLACED THE final journal back in the suitcase and tidied the cabin. Birdsong at the window made her smile. It was a gorgeous day. Jacob would return for her on Sunday, and until then she had two days and nights to enjoy the beauties of the island. Time to stop reading and start living her own life again, instead of her mother's. She should walk a while, forget the past.

She didn't need the crutch any more. She was adept at walking with the cast, even on the uneven ground of the island. She made her way through the woods and found she could ascend without too much trouble the gradual slope of the hill to the north of the cabin. When she reached a point above the lake, she eased herself down on a rocky outcrop of the cliff edge. She sat watching the gentle whitecaps, letting herself be lulled by the soft slap of the waves against the rocks. The breeze was slight, even here on the exposed ledge above the lake. But far up in the sky, the wind currents were blowing furiously. The white clouds were speeding across the sun so swiftly that the mottled pattern of sunlight and shade on the water shifted constantly.

Sarah wondered if the high wild wind presaged a storm. She shaded her eyes with her hand and looked out across the water. A line from the journal repeated itself in her head: *When I think of what might happen.*

She tried not to dwell on it. Enjoy the day, she told herself. Live in the present. She leaned back on her elbows and looked up at the tall, scraggly pines behind her. She marveled, as she always had, at the way they survived here on the rocky edge of the island. There seemed to be no soil where they could fasten their roots. The trees swayed gently, and she heard the whisper of the poplar leaves gathering themselves in the forest, as if they were about to speak.

When I think of what might . . .

What might happen, Sarah asked the trees. What?

DR. ALLARD GREETED Morgan with a smile, but told her that Mark was not at home. "He's on campus, doing research for his thesis proposal. He phoned to say he won't be home until late. Would you like to come in? You look like you could use a little company."

"Well, maybe." Morgan looked at Dr. Allard's outfit. Instead of her usual jeans and threadbare cardigan, the doctor was dressed in a smart tweed skirt and green silk blouse. "Are you going out somewhere?"

Dr. Allard glanced at her watch. "Not for an hour or two. I'm addressing the Historical Society at seven. I was just about to put on the kettle. Why don't you join me for tea?" She opened the door wide and led Morgan down the hall, past her rare book collection and into the dining room.

The jacket that matched Dr. Allard's skirt was on a hanger on the doorknob.

"Nice outfit," Morgan commented. She felt the material. Expensive. An emerald pin was attached to the lapel, obviously carefully chosen to match the blouse.

"Yes, I don't usually splurge on clothing," the doctor said. "But this is a special occasion. I'm giving the anniversary lecture of the society. Dinner and dance to follow."

"How nice," Morgan said. How boring, she thought.

"Excuse me while I set out the tea things."

"Sure," Morgan said. "Do you have any aspirin?"

"I'll bring you some." Dr. Allard entered the kitchen and Morgan sat down at the dining-room table in front of an old-fashioned typewriter. She hadn't seen one of these for a while. It wasn't even electric. She poked sulkily at a few keys to amuse herself. Then she stood up to investigate the contents of Dr. Allard's china cabinet. The figurine of a little boy with a pair of floppy-eared rabbits caught her fancy, and she admired it for a while before turning to the others. There was a ballerina, a jolly tramp, and a shepherdess with a sheep that looked awfully familiar. Morgan looked closer. Yes! The sheep's ear was chipped. It was a minuscule nick, but Morgan knew it well, because she had nicked it herself one day when she'd placed her beer mug carelessly on the mantel at Alfred's house. It was Betty's shepherdess. What was it doing here?

A fit of irrepressible giggling hit Morgan right in the solar plexus. Dr. Allard must have stolen it at the dinner party! The thought of the distinguished psychologist pilfering a coveted bauble from the home of a respected publisher made her want to hoot. Who would guess that Dr. Allard was a petty thief, a kleptomaniac!

When Dr. Allard returned with two aspirins and a glass of water, Morgan could barely choke them down.

"Are you sure you're all right, dear?" Dr. Allard inquired. "Have you been drinking?"

"Yes," Morgan managed to sputter. "I'm a bit giddy. Sorry." She snorted loudly.

"Sometimes it helps to talk," Dr. Allard said. "Just let me get the tea and we'll have a little chat and you'll feel better. I'm a professional, you know." She returned to the kitchen.

You're a professional, all right, Morgan thought. A professional thief! She forced down another spurt of laughter and moved across to the other side of the table, where she would not have to look at the shepherdess while she had her little chat with the doctor.

She pushed aside a pile of papers to make room for her teacup, and as she did so, she caught a glimpse of the transparent sheen of onion-skin tracing paper. She tugged it out of the pile and her heart began to race as she recognized the drawing on it. It was Aunt Carolyn's map of her boat trip to Massacre Island with Grandpa, showing the route from Persephone Island. The rattle of the tea things in the kitchen threw Morgan into action. She began to insert the map back into the pile, then thought better of it and stuffed it instead into the pocket of her jeans. She wanted proof.

"Here we are," Dr. Allard said soothingly as she sailed back into the dining room with a tray. "There's nothing like a nice cup of tea."

"Uh huh," Morgan said. Dr. Allard got the map out of the orange notebook, Morgan was thinking. And if she's got the orange notebook, she's got everything.

"Honey?" Dr. Allard asked. "Or lemon?"

Instead of an answer, Morgan let out another snort. But this time it wasn't laughter that was the cause. It was fear.

"SO SHE LEFT me," Alfred concluded.

Daniel nodded. He wasn't taking notes this time. He had come over to Alfred's house strictly as a friend, out of uniform, off duty. He'd hidden his disappointment at the news of Alfred's affair with Morgan. Daniel had been planning to ask Morgan out, but now. . . . Anyway, he was also furious with his stepfather for concealing the affair while a murder investigation was under way. Couldn't Alfred see that he was only placing himself in danger by keeping secrets from the police?

"I knew you were hiding something," he told Alfred. "I just didn't know what it was. I'm sorry you're upset over Betty's leaving, but it's better this way. Until we can eliminate her as a suspect—"

"No," Alfred said. "I've thought about it and thought about it, and I can't believe she's guilty of this thing. Even if she did get mixed up with a bad crowd when she was young, she's changed. You should have seen her face when I confronted her."

"You still need to be careful," Daniel warned. He stood up. "I have to get back to work."

"Thought you had a few days off."

"Oh, just a little thing I'm working on with Marnie." As Daniel walked toward the door, he spotted Alfred's bulging suitcase in the hall. "Going somewhere?" he asked.

"I have a meeting in Toronto," Alfred said. "Just because my personal life's in a mess doesn't mean I can let the business fall apart."

"You were asked to notify the police if you left town, Alfred," Daniel said. "We take that seriously, you know."

"All right then," Alfred said impatiently. "I'm going to Toronto. There. I've notified the police."

"So we can reach you at Quinn's house if we need you?"

"No," Alfred said. "The Sheraton Hotel. Quinn's away on vacation with his family."

"Which Sheraton?"

Alfred grumbled under his breath, but he gave Daniel the address.

"One more thing," Daniel said before he left. "I have to ask again. You're sure you have no idea where Walter White might be."

"I told you, Dan. I've only ever contacted him through his agent. I'm sure when I take over the agency, we'll find him. But right now the man has a right to his privacy."

By the time he took over the agency, Alfred hoped, the murders of Cady Brown and Gregory would be solved, and Daniel would forget all about Walter White.

Daniel regarded him closely. "And you're *sure* you don't know anyone in the neighborhood who might be related to Walter White?"

Alfred shivered. "I'm positive," he said.

"You can't think of anyone at all with a motive to keep Walter White's identity secret?"

"No," Alfred lied. "No, I can not. What is this crazy idea of yours, Dan? What's this obsession with Walter White, whose only crime is a desire to be left *alone*?"

"I'm not so sure that's his only crime," Daniel said. "Somebody's acting out the murders in his novels, and we have reason to believe—"

"Reason?" Alfred exploded. "Look here." He stood up and poked an index finger at Daniel's chest. "This is a free country. You can't go arresting people for *writing* about crime!"

MORGAN GULPED THE tea as quickly as she could, pretending to listen to Dr. Allard's summary of her lecture for tonight. Some nonsense about the pathology of the 1919 Winnipeg strike. Oedipal something. But all Morgan could think about was getting out of there. She could feel the heat of her anger creeping up her neck and inflaming her face. The map seemed to be burning a hole in her pocket. She had to calm down, get control of herself, before she gave herself away. She drained the still-scalding cup of tea and rose from her seat, making an excuse about a forgotten appointment.

Dr. Allard seemed a bit offended, but she remained polite. "I'll see you out," she offered.

"That's okay," Morgan said quickly. "I'll let myself out the back." Dr. Allard protested, but Morgan bravely ignored her and marched through the kitchen, down past the back landing, where she knew there were several spare keys hanging on hooks. She was formulating a plan. It was still a bit fuzzy, but she figured she'd work it out, if only she could get rid of this pounding headache. She grabbed a set of keys and fled out the back door, crashing through the hedge to Sarah's house. She opened Sarah's door with her own spare key and concealed herself behind the curtains, to see if Dr. Allard had followed her. No. The yard was empty.

Morgan paged Daniel, then entered Sarah's home office, where she could watch the house next door. The top of Dr. Allard's gray head was visible through her kitchen window, bowed over the sink. Washing up the teacups, no doubt. Then the doctor left the kitchen. Was she going into the dining room? Morgan left the office and slid down the hall. She concealed herself behind the curtains of Sarah's kitchen. She could see Dr. Allard's silhouette clearly through the lace curtains. She was bending down, tugging at something heavy. The boxes were hidden under the dining table! They'd been right under Morgan's nose the whole time! Dr. Allard straightened up, her hand full of papers. Morgan saw her raise her glasses to her eyes and sit down to peruse them. Morgan rummaged through Sarah's cupboards until she found a bottle of wine. Then she drank and spied through the window for nearly an hour, as Dr. Allard turned pages. Coldly appraising the dollar value of Aunt Carolyn's most private thoughts! The injustice of it! Morgan felt her face burn with indignation. She would like nothing better than to rush over there right this minute and confront her, but Dr. Allard might be dangerous. She might be the Midnight maniac! Morgan thought of calling Alfred for help and then instantly remembered that she hated him.

The phone rang, and she dashed to answer it.

"Daniel?"

But it was Linda, wanting to gossip about Byron Hunt.

"I can't talk now," Morgan said. But Linda said something about Byron wanting to re-enact a scene from *A Midnight Swim*, so Morgan felt compelled to listen. Was Byron the Midnight maniac? He was showing a bizarre interest in mystery books lately—and he'd always hated Alfred. Maybe he was engaged in some sort of poet's revenge against popular novels! Morgan's mind was cloudy. She couldn't even remember how much alcohol she'd consumed since eleven o'clock this morning. But eventually, as Linda chattered on, Morgan realized the news was only about Byron's unique way of asking Linda for a date. By the time she hung up, it was seven o'clock. Past time for the Historical Society lecture.

Was Dr. Allard gone? Morgan returned to the window. The light in Dr. Allard's dining room was off. She must have left while Morgan was on the telephone.

Morgan was growing too tense to wait for Daniel, and the wine was fueling her courage. She crossed over to Dr. Allard's back door and rang and knocked loudly for some time, to make sure she was out. Then she tried several of the keys she had stolen until the door opened. She headed straight for the dining room.

Sure enough. A box of Aunt Carolyn's papers was stashed under the dining-room table. But where were the others? Morgan crept through the main floor, searching. She doubted that Dr. Allard could have carted the boxes up or down the stairs. The sound of voices from the den did not alarm her. The familiar canned laughter told her Dr. Allard had left the television on. She had also left on the lights in the front hall. Morgan crossed the hall and entered a room furnished with a massive oak desk and lined with bookshelves. Dr. Allard's study. A glance under the desk revealed nothing. There were two doors off to one side, and Morgan opened one. Just a bathroom. The other door was locked, and Morgan quickly found the right key. The door opened, but she could not step inside. Bingo! The long, narrow closet was completely blocked by Aunt Carolyn's boxes. She counted nine. All accounted for.

Morgan had figured out how the papers were stolen from Sarah's porch with nobody spotting the culprit. It seemed obvious in retrospect. She planned to employ the same method to get them back. Finding the key to Dr. Allard's shed, she pushed the wheelbarrow out through the clutter of gardening tools and ladders, and used it to haul the boxes. She dragged them one at a time across Dr. Allard's house and out her back door, and then wheeled them two at a time in the barrow across to Sarah's, carrying them up the steps and leaving them inside the house, locking Sarah's door securely behind her each time.

The boxes were heavy, and the whole process took a lot longer than expected. Her back ached and her head was pounding again. But she kept going. She re-entered the study and stepped into the closet for the second-last box.

Bong!

Morgan's heart nearly stopped.

Bong!

The grandfather clock in the hall was telling the hour. It tolled nine times and then fell still. Dr. Allard's lecture had begun at seven. How much time did Morgan have left? There should be plenty, with dinner and dancing . . . but somehow Morgan couldn't picture Dr. Allard doing a lot of dancing. She'd better hurry.

Another sound made Morgan pause again. Was that a key in the lock? She held her breath. Yes, someone was opening the front door. The doctor was back! Morgan was trapped.

There was no way to cross the hall without being seen from the front entrance. She backed away quietly toward the bathroom, hoping the doctor would go upstairs to bed, so she could make her escape. She hated to leave the final two boxes behind. She wished she had the nerve to step forward and accuse the doctor openly. But what if—

Oh no.

Footsteps approaching. Heading for the study! Morgan slipped into the bathroom and pulled the door closed. As she turned around, her feet skidded on the slippery floor, and she went sliding across the wet tiles, straight toward the toilet, waving her arms madly to keep herself upright. Desperately, she grasped on to the shower curtain and managed to stop herself from crashing. Morgan held still and listened, but heard nothing. Her feet grew cold. Water was seeping through her thin canvas shoes into her socks. The floor was one big puddle. The shower curtain, though closed, was hanging outside the tub, and Morgan figured someone had been careless in the shower. But why hadn't Dr. Allard mopped up? She heard the footsteps move in the study again. Had Dr. Allard noticed the missing boxes? Would she be searching for an intruder? Would she come into the bathroom?

Morgan decided to hide in the tub, behind the shower curtain, just in case. She drew back the curtain and stepped backward, placing one leg into the tub. She plunged into cold water up to her knee. The scream that rose up from her belly seemed to lodge in her throat.

Morgan's leg had disturbed the calm surface of the water, and Dr. Allard's body bobbed up and down slightly as her open green eyes stared accusingly up through the water. Her gold-rimmed spectacles floated on the surface, still attached by their gold chain to the doctor's neck. Her tweed jacket, dark with water, billowed out around her. At first, Morgan was paralyzed. But when the cold, stockinged leg of Dr. Allard bumped against her own leg, the scream that was caught in her throat escaped.

Chapter Thirty-Four

DETECTIVE KAYLA PETROVITCH knew for a certainty that her ulcer had returned. With a vengeance. A small, hot coal ate away at the empty pit of her stomach as she listened to the babbling of Morgan Wakeford and watched her pulling papers from the boxes that littered Sarah Petursson's living-room floor. Morgan was waving the papers in Kayla's face and rattling on incoherently about maps and archives. Papers again! What was with these people and their papers? Three murders had been committed within a two-block radius of this house, and always among a mass of bloody papers!

"Look," she said to Morgan. She wanted to slap the young woman in the face. "You absolutely *must* calm down." She turned to Mark Curtis, who had his arm protectively around Morgan's shoulder. "Can you calm her down? I need some straight answers here." She wished she were next door with Vishnu, investigating the crime scene. At the moment she'd prefer a dead body to this hysterical live wire of a redhead.

"Morgan," said Mark. "Take a deep breath. Try to be quiet for a minute. It's all over, now. You're safe."

"But I'm probably next!" Morgan cried. "She'll be coming after me next!"

"Shh, shh. It's okay. Nobody's coming after you. Here. Take a sip of water. That's it." Mark turned to Kayla. "I'm sorry, Officer—"

"Detective."

"Sorry, Detective." Mark stroked Morgan's shoulder gently. "She's just had a horrible shock. I found her standing right in the bathtub with the—with the doctor's—"

"That much I've gathered," Kayla said. "You got home at nine o'clock from the university. How long were you there?"

"I was there all evening. I'm doing research."

Morgan hiccuped, and Mark turned back to her. "Are you going to be all right?"

Morgan nodded. She was still shaking, and her face was pale and blotchy, but at least she was keeping quiet.

"Anybody see you there?" Kayla asked Mark.

"Where? At the university? Of course. Lots of people saw me."

"Any of those people have names?"

"Oh! Well—of course they do. There's Luis and Chin-Li and—I don't know their last names, though." He bit his lip. "But there's Professor Dawson, of course. I was working near him all evening, in the carrel right across from him in the library. He was facing me for hours."

"And you never left?"

"Not for more than five minutes," Mark said. "I was there from about four o'clock on. Until the library closed at eight-thirty. He'll remember. He knows me."

"Fine," said Kayla. "He's the head of the English department, right?" She remembered the name from the infamous dinner party. What a strangely inbred lot these people were in Winnipeg. Kayla had learned that these kinds of coincidences usually meant nothing here. She made a note to phone Dawson to verify the story. Then she turned to Morgan. "Now," she said. "Do you think you can answer a few questions?'

"Uh huh."

"Who is this person you think is after you?"

"Betty Carriere, of course. She tried to kill Alfred and now she'll be going after me. You see we were—"

"Having an affair. Yes, I know. But what does this have to do with Dr. Allard?"

"Dr. Allard stole Betty's sheep!" Morgan said. "The one with the chipped ear!"

The coal-fire in Kayla's stomach ignited into a full-blown blaze.

It was long after midnight by the time Mark left Morgan at Sarah's house. He hated to leave her, but she had surrounded herself with friends—both Linda Rain and Zina Schwartz had promised to spend the night at Sarah's with her, and the three women were all camping out together in sleeping bags on the living-room floor. With the dog.

Morgan's friends had tried to help her contact her family. Morgan's brother Sam had been so alarmed by his sister's hysterical state that he'd promised to take the next flight out. He would arrive tomorrow morning and then, Mark thought, there would be a man in the house. As for Sarah, she couldn't be reached. Morgan wanted to leave an emergency message for Sarah with the Knights, but her friends had advised against it, fearing it would only cause panic.

"What's the point of sending Jacob out there with a message like that?" Zina asked Morgan. "Imagine how she'll worry riding back in the boat, not knowing what's wrong. Wait until you can tell her the whole story. Let her hear your voice. Once you've calmed down, of course."

Mark himself had not yet calmed down. What a traumatic experience! He could still hear Morgan's scream in his ears.

He'd nearly had a heart attack when he walked in on that. He stood on the sidewalk and looked back at Dr. Allard's house. The door sealed with yellow police tape. The detectives had escorted him in and let him pack a small bag of belongings under their suspicious eyes. They had taken the phone number of his mother's house, where he would sleep tonight—and probably for some time to come. His mother would not be pleased. But there was no way he could move back into a house with a dead landlady, even if he wanted to. He wondered when the police would let him back in for the rest of his things. In his nervousness, he had forgotten to bring his backpack with his research notes. Ah, well. He sighed. He didn't think he'd be able to concentrate on the thesis for a while, anyway.

He opened the door of his Gremlin and took one last look at the lighted windows of Sarah's house before he sat down and locked himself in.

SARAH WOKE TO the hoarse caw of a raven outside her window, and the rapid beating of wings. She lifted the curtain and looked out at the moonlit clearing where her mother's cabin had burned to the ground.

Someone was standing out there. Beckoning to her.

She closed the curtain and remained sitting up in bed, perfectly still. Who could be out there in the middle of the night? She had heard no motorboat. Or was it the sound of an approaching boat that had wakened her? She pulled back a corner of the curtain and looked again. Yes. A woman in a white dress stood in the center of the clearing, clutching a large book in her hands. . . .

As if drawn forward by an unseen hand, Sarah moved across the cabin and opened the door. In the light of the bright, swollen moon, drops of dew glittered on the broad leaves of the ferns and on the spiderwebs that feathered the grass. They glittered also among the pale halo of braided hair on the head of the woman who stood among the burned ruins. A breeze stirred the trees and rippled through the long white gown of the apparition. But Sarah felt no fear.

"Mother?" Sarah called faintly. "Carolyn?"

Sarah took a step forward, holding out her hands. "Mother?"

The woman began to glide toward the forest.

"Wait!" Sarah called, but the woman moved gracefully further away, entered the path through the trees, and was gone.

Sarah followed her into the black woods.

The moonlight barely penetrated the high, thick branches. Scattered patches of light skipped erratically across the ground, revealing only at random the tree roots and stones among the thick carpet of pine needles. But she knew the way. She realized vaguely that she was walking easily, barely aware of her cast at all. The knee had healed completely. She strode on through the darkness, determined to find the woman again. If only she would speak to her!

The statue of Persephone gleamed whitely in the moonlight of the clearing, and Sarah could clearly see the pale woman there, restlessly circling the statue, as Sarah herself had circled it earlier.

"Mother? It's me. Sarah." The woman came to rest in front of the statue and turned to look in Sarah's direction. Not only her eyes, but her whole face and body—even the book she carried—seemed translucent now. She was fading.

"Don't go!" Sarah cried. But the woman was backing away. She raised her right arm and placed her hand over the hand of the statue, and Sarah saw the two hands become one. Then the woman settled down, as if to sit in the statue's lap, and Sarah saw her sink gradually into the very stone and become absorbed. She was gone. Only Persephone remained, patiently reading the same stone verse, over and over.

Vishnu Maharaj did not even raise his eyes from the computer screen when he said to Kayla, "You've got to be kidding."

"I'm serious. Morgan Wakeford and her cousin are mixed up in everything."

Vishnu shook his head. "Ridiculous." He continued to type. "You were right the first time. It's got to be Petursson."

Vishnu and Kayla had cut short their investigation into Mark Curtis once Professor Dawson verified Mark's alibi. Mark had been at the university from four to eight-thirty. Dr. Allard had been seen alive at five o'clock by her neighbors across the street. Morgan Wakeford had seen her between five and approximately six-thirty—she wasn't sure—and then lugged boxes in and out of the house from seven to nine. So Allard must have died sometime between six and seven, give or take. But why? Professor Dawson had been co-operative enough to answer a few questions about the nature of the papers Dr. Allard had allegedly stolen. They could be valuable, he said. Add to that the fact that her house was a veritable treasure-trove of rare china and silver. . . . Vishnu guessed that Dr. Allard had surprised a burglar in the act. Probably Peter Petursson, who couldn't be found anywhere. He pressed a button, faxing Petursson's description to every police force in the country. He yawned. He would have to go home soon, or he'd fall asleep with his head on the keyboard. Not that it would be the first time.

"At least hear me out," Kayla tried again. "They're looking pretty good to me right now, the two of them. The ones you'd least suspect."

Vishnu looked up. "Okay. I'm listening."

"Good. Now concentrate. First off, they both belong to the book club. Zina Schwartz says they're the most devoted members. So they both know the books. The first incident supposedly happened at Sarah Petursson's house in May. But there's zero proof that anyone broke into her house that night. We know there's no evidence, because that's why we had to let her husband go in the first place. No ladder, no letter opener, no nothing. What if she made it up? Motive? To set up a phony pattern. And the night of Cady Brown's murder, their only alibi is each other! They claim they spent the night together. Motive? Frame Sarah's husband, get rid of his girlfriend. Then they were both at the poisonous dinner party. Motive? Get rid of Morgan's boyfriend, or maybe get rid of the boyfriend's wife—but something went wrong there. The wrong guy bought it. And tonight? The redhead finds the body of her cousin's next-door neighbor and tries to pin it on her boyfriend's wife. You don't think that's all a bit suspicious?"

Vishnu sat with his arms crossed over his chest, in an attitude of deep thought. "Hmmm," he said.

"You don't think that all adds up?"

Vishnu let his head weave slightly back and forth as if undecided. "Well, actually, now that you put it like that. . . . No. I don't."

Kayla let out a blast of air in frustration. "Fine," she said. She returned to her own computer, where she was tracing the credit record of Morgan Wakeford. It was hard to believe that someone so young could rack up a debt so high.

Her stomach ached. She hadn't eaten for hours, and she couldn't think of anything she wanted to eat now. She searched in her desk for some gum. Nothing but empty wrappers. The screen before her was blurred, illegible. She rubbed her eyes and glanced at the clock. Four-thirty. For a moment, she had no idea whether it was day or night.

She stared out the window. The moon was full. Or nearly full. Or it had recently been full. Or something.

Chapter Thirty-Five

SARAH SAT SIDEWAYS IN the passenger seat of Jacob's Lund and watched Persephone Island disappear behind her. She was ready to leave now. She'd felt at peace ever since her mother's spirit had visited her the other night. In the light of day, Sarah knew she had been dreaming, walking in her sleep, but it didn't matter. She believed the visitation was her mother's way of saying goodbye to her. And it wasn't hard to say goodbye, not any more. Not when Sarah knew she could return.

She smiled at Jacob, and he returned the smile with warmth. "Am I ever glad to be taking you back," he said. "Maybe my mother will let up on me a bit."

"She's been nagging you to bring me back?"

"She's been impossible."

Sarah laughed. "I guess I'll have to stay and visit for a while. I can tell her about the diaries. What I've learned about my father so far."

"Oh, definitely," Jacob said. "You'll have to tell her everything." He reached out and covered Sarah's hand with his own, squeezing gently. Sarah expected him to take it away again, as he usually did. But he left it there. He steered with one hand all the way back to Keewatin, and though they did not speak again, they smiled whenever their eyes met.

At the marina, Sarah walked along the dock while Jacob gassed up the boat and chatted with the owner. She entered the little store beside the marina and wandered the aisles, amused by the mishmash of merchandise—raincoats, laundry soap, fishing lures, candy, and maps were all jumbled together on the shelves. She chose some cold drinks and pastries to take back to Mary's house, and as she was paying for them, she noticed the paperback book rack.

A dozen copies of *The Midnight Strangler* were stuffed into the top rows of the metal rack. The cover of the fifth and final book in the series depicted the hooded head and shoulders of a looming figure, holding a knotted noose above a scantily clad and quite unconscious young woman, who lay sprawled across a bed, completely at the mercy of the vile intruder. It was the most blatantly sexist cover of all. Marketing, she thought wryly. Alfred. She added a copy to her purchases.

As she waited for Jacob, she opened the book to Chapter One. *When the death penalty was outlawed,* she read, *the hangman was out of work. He was too young for a pension, and he had nothing to put on his resumé. His work, at which he considered himself a consummate master, had spoiled him for any menial labor. So he decided to go into business for himself.*

WHEN ALFRED RETURNED from the airport on Sunday afternoon, he harbored a small hope that perhaps Betty had returned. But no. The house was silent. She must be staying with her sister. He dropped his suitcase in the hall and went to the kitchen to check his messages.

Alfred had nineteen voice mails. None of them from Betty. All of them related to the Midnight books and the murders. Most were from reporters or bookstore owners frantic for more Midnight mysteries. But two were from Daniel, asking about the secret manuscript he'd heard about on the Channel 9 News. Zina had called, too, sounding anxious and exhausted. There would be no book-club meeting tonight, she said. There had been line-ups at the café since the murder of Dr. Allard hit the news yesterday. She'd sold out of *The Midnight Strangler* in half an hour. The café had been inundated by curious customers and media types—including a man from the American television show *Unsolved Mysteries*. She was going to close up shop for a while, "until things blow over."

Alfred already knew about the murder of Dr. Allard and the subsequent media frenzy. He opened again the newspaper he'd read at the airport this morning. The leading Toronto paper, which liked to call itself the "National" paper, had covered the story in an in-depth feature on the front page of its Entertainment section. "Murders Linked to Mystery Novels," the headline read.

Members of a murder mystery book club in Winnipeg, Manitoba are living in terror as events from their favorite novels appear to be coming true, right in their own neighborhood.

So far, a break-in, a stabbing, a poisoning, and a drowning in the quiet Winnipeg neighborhood of Wolseley have all seemed to mimic the plots of the wildly successful Midnight Mystery series that has swept the continent this summer in a phenomenon that one New York reviewer has called "bigger than Stephen King." The mystery is compounded by the reclusive nature of the author of the books. Mr. Walter White, said to be a Manitoba resident, could not be reached for comment . . ."

Alfred closed the paper. Of course Walter White could not be reached for comment. That was no surprise. Alfred noted that the White family was not mentioned. If they existed at all, they would surely have come forward. Daniel's theory that White's child lived right here in Wolseley could not be true.

Alfred opened the cupboard and pulled out his good

whisky from the top shelf, then frowned when he noted its diminished contents. Had he been drinking that much lately? He put the bottle back, untouched.

It was time to make a decision. His original plan to wait for fall to unveil the final Midnight book might have to be changed. Since Channel 9 had broadcast the news of the book's existence, Alfred could no longer rely on the surprise factor he'd planned. In fact, he didn't need the surprise factor any more. The murders had provided more publicity than he could ever afford. If he launched the last book right now, sales would be phenomenal.

He was certain that Walter White had no family members who would challenge Alfred's right to the royalties. But what about Bill Wesley? Bill was most likely too sick at the moment to have heard anything about the final Midnight mystery. But the possibility still made Alfred nervous. He wished the man would hurry up and die.

"SO SHE LEFT him near the end," Sarah said. She had showered and washed her clothes, and now she was finishing the telling of her mother's story for Mary, while they prepared a vegetable soup for dinner. "She broke it off, just like Roger said."

"And she was happy about it?" Mary asked. She handed Sarah a bowl of potatoes to peel.

"She seemed to be . . . but there was something wrong." Sarah looked at Mary. "Tell me, did you notice anything different about my mother in the last few days of her life? Did she seem sad or, well, frightened to you?"

"Frightened?" Mary frowned as she chopped the carrots. "I don't know. I met her in town a few days before the fire. She came in to see Evan. We went swimming at Coney Beach. That's how I got the necklace and ring I gave you. She forgot them in my beach bag. That wasn't like her." Mary put down her knife and rubbed her temples. She closed her eyes. "Now that you mention it, maybe she *did* seem a little distracted. We ran into Quinn Carriere and his wife at the beach." She sank down into a kitchen chair. "Yes. I'd forgotten that. They invited us—"

Jacob entered the kitchen and stole a slice of carrot off the cutting board. "Don't you think that's enough reminiscing for now?" he asked.

The women ignored him. "Did she seem uncomfortable around Quinn?" Sarah asked Mary.

"I can't really say. Quinn and his wife invited us back to their place on the river for dinner. But Carolyn insisted on leaving in a big hurry. She said she'd left Darlene with the kids all day and she had to get back to the island. I wasn't paying much attention to her reaction. I didn't know it would be the last time I ever saw her."

"Maybe she knew," Sarah said. "Sometimes, reading her diaries, I felt. . . ." Sarah's voice dropped to a whisper. "It's almost as if she sensed what was coming."

Jacob reached across and rested his hand lightly on the back of Sarah's neck. "Don't do that to yourself," he said.

"But maybe she had a premonition," Sarah continued. "Maybe she was clairvoyant. I mean, she was a poet, her mother was mad, saw visions. Maybe my mother foresaw her own fate."

"No," Jacob said. He withdrew his hand and stepped back abruptly. "No. Don't start thinking that way."

"Don't you believe in premonitions?" Mary asked her son.

"No," he said firmly. "You know I don't. Not if you're talking about fate. What I believe in is intuition. I believe in intelligence. If you think you're in danger, you probably are. You've picked up on some clues, maybe subconsciously. But that doesn't mean you're doomed. It means you're fore-warned. You can protect yourself."

"She couldn't," Sarah said softly.

But the telephone rang, and Jacob, on his way to answer, did not hear her.

"Maybe he's right," Sarah said to Mary. "Maybe it wasn't clairvoyance, but intuition. Maybe she sensed some very real danger—"

"I believe in premonitions," Mary said. "I get them myself. I didn't want to say anything, but all day I've had an uneasy feeling—"

Jacob appeared again at the kitchen door. He was wearing his jacket. "That was Grandpa Evan," he said. He pulled a tie from the jacket pocket and began to knot it around his neck. "I have to go visit a client."

"But, Jacob, it's Sunday!" Mary protested.

"I have to go. I have to pay a condolence call on Mrs. Wesley. Her husband's passed away."

"Oh dear," Mary said. "I knew something was wrong." She covered her eyes with her hands.

"I won't be long," he said. "I'll take the boat. Wesley's place is fifteen minutes up the lakeshore. I'll be back before dark."

"TRY IT ONE more time," Marnie coaxed. Her foster son Henry had tried three days in a row to hack into Cady Brown's computer, and Marnie and Daniel were getting desperate.

"Okay," Henry agreed. He obviously wanted to please Marnie. He often said she was the best mother he'd ever had. But Marnie could tell he was starting to lose confidence in his ability to crack this particular code.

She looked over Henry's head at Daniel and saw him nervously running his fingers through his short hair. Their plan to replace the computer before the detectives noticed it missing had failed miserably. Since the murder of Adele Allard, Maharaj and Petrovitch had revisited Cady Brown's apartment, and when they found the computer missing, they'd posted a watch on the place.

The detectives knew Peter Petursson had been spotted there—Daniel and Marnie had called in that information themselves the night they chased him away. And now the detectives were furious with the beat officers for not checking on the crime scene that night. Daniel and Marnie couldn't admit they'd been in there, so they were taking the heat. And it was hot. Daniel was two inches away from a suspension. The only saving grace was that the detectives were convinced Petursson himself had taken the computer.

But it was here in Marnie's basement. And unless it yielded some absolutely fantastic clues, Daniel and Marnie were going to lose their jobs.

I CAN TELL she knows. Today, I caught her snooping in this very diary.

Was that my mother, Morgan wondered, snooping in her sister's diary? Darlene and Carolyn rarely argued, and Morgan was intrigued by the scene, though she was finding it hard to focus. The letters seemed to merge together on the page.

She claimed to be looking for her husband, and I said, "What would he be doing in here?" and she didn't answer. But she made a gesture as if to throw my diary into the stove. I snatched it back and she laughed, as if she was only kidding. But I remember what she said at my last book launch. That the poems were dirty and should be burned.

Morgan looked up as Sam entered the living room. "Still reading?" he asked. "Aren't you getting hungry?"

"A little." Morgan closed her Aunt Carolyn's diary and placed it back in the box. She yawned. She was perfectly tranquil, now that her beloved brother was here to protect her. And to give her Valium. "Is there anything for dinner? Or have we eaten poor Sarah out of house and home already?"

Sam smiled. "There're lots of casseroles in the freezer," he said. "Shall I heat one up?"

"Sure," Morgan said. "If you don't mind." She stretched out on Sarah's couch and let her thoughts drift aimlessly for a while as she listened to Sam preparing dinner in the kitchen. She felt removed, detached. The events of the last few days seemed to float above her, encased in a bubble, with no power to hurt her at all. She had triumphed. Rescued Aunt Carolyn's papers. She imagined herself stepping up to a podium, receiving a gold medal for bravery before an admiring crowd. Applause filled the auditorium.

Then the ring of the telephone broke into her daydream.

"Sarah!" she heard her brother say. "I'm so glad you called. You won't believe what's been going on around here!"

"HEY!" HENRY SAID. The monitor flickered, then went black. A second later, a menu popped up on the screen. Daniel and Marnie leaned in close, over Henry's shoulders. *Correspondence, Notes, Articles, Birthdays, Columns.*

"Try *Articles*," Daniel said.

"No. Try *Notes*," Marnie told her son. "She never finished the article," she explained to Daniel. "Let's just skim over her notes."

The files in the *Notes* folder were dated, with the latest date at the top: May 28. Henry clicked it open, and Daniel rubbed his hands together in excitement.

"Thank you, Henry!" He pushed the boy gently on the shoulder. "You can go play now. We'll take over from here."

"No way," Henry said. "I'm gonna read this!"

So the three of them read it together.

Hit the jackpot today. Went back to Bill Wesley's & found out he was in the hospital. They're taking better care of him there. I said I was his granddaughter & they let me in to see him. Should describe the whole scene—the way his eyes lit up when he saw me. He's quite the tough old guy—should make him a character in the article. Make my search part of the story—like a mystery. I could write the whole introduction tonight—if Sarah would get back to me!

Notes for the scene—Wesley in bed & the bed cranked up, nurse with one glass eye (weird), crucifix on wall, Wesley's little crack of a smile when he saw me (the Bible thing), his blue eyes—a bit of a sparkle. The tube in his arm. The green bruise.

Me sitting down. Asking questions. Why is WW's sixth book such a big secret? Why won't Alfred talk about it? Does WW still live in Kenora? Does WW have any family? He finally talks (his hoarse little voice), "Walt—Walt—" Hard to talk. Give him water. Then wife comes in, gives me hell for disturbing him. But suddenly he spits it out—"Ag ag a daughter—Sarah Yeats." I scribble the name down quick & then she kicks me out. Nice lady, but overprotective, acts like she owns him. I think he wanted me there, he likes me. I get back in car, pull out of parking lot & then it hits me—Yeats—That's Sarah Petursson's maiden name!

Why didn't Peter tell me? And how did Alfred think he could keep that quiet? I'll have to e-mail him right away.

"Oh, man," Daniel said. "I don't believe it."

"Is it good?" Henry asked. "Is it a good clue?"

"It's a great clue, honey," Marnie said. "You're a genius." She looked at Daniel. "So. What do we do now?"

SARAH PROMISED HER cousins she'd be home as soon as possible—tonight or tomorrow morning. Then she hung up the phone and wished she had someone here to talk to. Mary was in her bedroom resting, and Jacob had still not returned, although the evening was creeping on. She looked out the window and hoped he would keep his promise to return before dark. She wanted to get back home to Winnipeg. Poor Gregory. Poor Dr. Allard.

And poor Morgan! She'd sounded calm enough on the phone, but Sam had told Sarah privately that Morgan was suffering terrible nightmares, waking up from her sleep with visions of stabbed and drowned bodies dangling before her eyes. How awful! Sam said Peter had been released because the police suspected Walter White. But now Peter was missing! Was there some connection between Peter and Walter White? What twisted person could be acting out the murders in these books?

She glanced at the cover of *The Midnight Strangler* she had bought this afternoon, and a bubble of fear rose through her. She had been the intended victim of the first murder. Who would be the target of the last?

She considered phoning Jacob at the Wesley residence, but just as she opened the directory, the telephone rang.

"Hello?" she answered.

"Is Sarah Petursson there?"

"This is me," Sarah said.

"Sarah, it's Dan Bradley. From Winnipeg. I was wondering if you could answer a few questions about your father."

"My father?"

"Yes. Where is he? We need to talk to him about his books."

Sarah sat down.

"Sarah? Are you listening?"

She managed a faint "yes."

"Can you tell me where your father is?"

"I don't know where he is," she whispered. "I don't know *who* he is."

"Your father isn't Walter White?"

"Walter—what? What do you mean? Walter White is a mystery writer. He's the author of the Midnight—"

"We know that," Daniel interrupted. "We need to talk to him about these murders in Wolseley."

"But I don't *know* Walter White!" Sarah cried. "And I have no idea who my father is. That's what I've been trying to find out." She told Daniel the story of her search for her father's name.

Daniel listened with interest. "So you don't think your father's a writer?" he asked her.

"I—I don't know."

Daniel noticed some hesitation there. "Do you think it's possible he might be?"

"But—but you think Walter White is connected to the murders!" Sarah exclaimed. "What makes you think my father might be Walter White? Did Alfred tell you that?"

"No." It was Daniel's turn to hesitate. "Just checking on a hunch."

"What kind of a hunch is that?" Sarah demanded.

"I'll keep you posted," Daniel promised. He hung up, frustrated. He couldn't tell Sarah he'd discovered her father's identity in the files of a computer he'd stolen from a murder scene.

Chapter Thirty-Six

SARAH THANKED THE MAID, then waited a minute at the front door before she decided to enter. She didn't have any time to waste. She walked down the carpeted hall from the vestibule and found the living room, then stood in the doorway for a moment and surveyed the lavish decor. Mrs. Wesley sat poised on a green satin sofa, her ankles crossed neatly, and her black-gloved hands folded in her lap. Her head, covered in a black hat with a half-veil, was bowed as if she was praying. Sarah hated to intrude like this, but she had to.

As she entered the room, Mrs. Wesley let out a delicate gasp and jumped to her feet.

"Don't get up," Sarah said. "Why, what's the matter?"

"You startled me," Mrs. Wesley said feebly.

"I'm sorry," Sarah said. "I thought the maid announced me."

"Yes. You're Sarah Yeats." Mrs. Wesley sank back into her chair.

"I'm very sorry to disturb you at a time like this," Sarah continued. "Please accept my condolences on your loss."

"Thank you, dear." Mrs. Wesley regained her composure. "You're Carolyn Yeats' daughter, aren't you?"

Sarah nodded.

Mrs. Wesley gestured for her to take a seat, but Sarah remained standing.

"I'm looking for Jacob Knight. Is he still here?"

"Jacob's been a great comfort to me," Mrs. Wesley said. "He's a dear boy. So you're friends. Your mother would have been pleased."

"Yes, I'm sure." Sarah smiled politely. "But I have to find him right now, and I was wondering—"

"Would you care for some tea? I've some nice, fresh honey."

"No, really, I can only stay a minute. If Jacob isn't here—"

"He's a busy young man. He'll be head of that firm some-day soon, mark my words."

Sarah tried not to let her impatience show. "Mrs. Wesley," she said. "It's important that I talk to Jacob. I have to tell him something. You see, he was helping me to find my father—"

"I see," Mrs. Wesley said. "Quinn called here tonight. For Jacob. He said he had some important news. And Jacob went rushing off." She gestured out the wide windows that over-looked the lake and smiled sadly. "He's in demand tonight, it seems."

"Jacob's gone to meet Quinn? Quinn Carriere? Right now? Where?" Sarah stood poised, as if to run. "Where are they meeting?"

"Down by the old mill," Mrs. Wesley said. "The old flour mill, do you know it?"

Sarah nodded, stunned.

"I thought you would. After all, that's where Quinn used to meet your mother. They had a sort of game of postman going on down there."

Sarah stared.

Mrs. Wesley seemed amused. "Oh yes, it was quite the affair for a while there!"

"You mean Quinn Carriere—and my mother? And you knew about it all along? You knew about the letters?"

"Why, everybody knew," Mrs. Wesley said, surprised. "My dear, it was the worst-kept secret in town."

SARAH TURNED JACOB'S Thunderbird onto the road that led to the boatlift. Although the sun had not yet set, the sky was dark with rain clouds. She parked at the edge of the little garden and got out of the car. She gazed over at the old mill, remembering its dark, dripping interior. She didn't want to go any closer. But there was no sign of Jacob.

Instead, she saw Roger Lariviere coming up the bank from the mill.

"Hi there!" Roger called. "What are you doing here?"

"Have you seen Jacob?" she asked.

"Sure. He just took off ten minutes ago. Up the river to Carriere's place."

Sarah was confused. "With Quinn?"

"By himself. He was in a big hurry. He borrowed my boat. His Lund is docked on the lake side, over there." Roger pointed at the dock in the channel, and she saw the Lund.

She tried to process this news. Jacob had come here to meet Quinn. Then he had gone up to Quinn's place alone? Something was wrong. Had Quinn invited Jacob out to his place for some awful purpose? If Quinn was her father, and if Daniel Bradley was right . . . if he was the author of the books, and possibly involved in the murders . . . and if he thought that Sarah and Jacob knew who he was. . . .

"We've got to go after Jacob," Sarah said. "He could be in terrible danger."

"Weather's not that bad," Roger said. "He's in my brand-new Glastron. Fourteen feet, with ninety horses on her. If he gasses her up at the Riverside Marina, he'll be fine."

"It's not that," Sarah said. "I think Quinn Carriere might be—he might be my father after all, and—" She hesitated, unsure how much to tell. "I just *have* to talk to Jacob before he gets to Quinn's. Do you think we could catch up to him before he gets there?"

Roger shrugged. "I don't have a boat. I'm sorry." Then he looked at Sarah's face again. "You're really anxious, aren't you? I suppose we could go after him in the Lund. We'll put her on the lift."

"But how?"

He produced a set of keys from his pocket. "I know how to run her."

Sarah backed away from him. "I'm not going up there," she said. "I hate that thing."

"Well, if you want to catch up with Jacob, you'll have to go up in it. Someone has to stay in the boat, and I have to run the controls."

Sarah tried to think. There must be some other way! But she could not think of one. The Lund was moored on the lake side, eighteen feet above the surface of the river. To drive into town and rent another boat would take at least an hour, and she had to warn Jacob.

"It's already starting to get dark," Roger said. "Wind's picking up. If we're going to go, we have to go now."

"Okay," she agreed. "I'll do it."

"STEER HER RIGHT in," Roger directed from above, where he was operating the controls.

Sarah maneuvered the sixteen-foot Lund between the massive wooden sides of the open box, or crib, in which the craft would sit for the ride up and over the rocky spit of land that separated the lake from the river. She cut the motor and tilted it up as high as it would go to protect the prop. Then she gripped the wooden edge of the crib to keep the boat steady.

Roger set the lift in motion and the whole crib, with Sarah and the boat inside, began to rise like an elevator. As the

Lund came out of the water, it tipped sideways until the starboard gunwale rested against the side of the crib, and the hull settled firmly on the bottom.

"You okay?" Roger called down to her.

"I'm fine."

Raindrops began to fall, and Roger pulled the hood of his jacket over his head. "You want to put the top up on the boat?" he asked.

"I'm fine," she repeated. The thought of standing up and struggling with the canvas top while she was way up here made her head spin.

"Okay then." Roger returned to the controls, and Sarah's stomach dropped as the pulleys lifted the crib higher and higher above the channel, up to the level of the white guide rails that stretched over the rocky spit. The wind shifted to the north and the machinery creaked ominously. Sarah felt as if she were at the very peak of a rise on a roller coaster, about to plummet toward the earth. Then the gears spun and she began the mechanical portage that would take her to a point over an even longer drop to the river below. A mild shimmer of sheet lightning lit up the clouds, and she saw before her nothing but the long white rails that seemed to lead to nowhere but the middle of the sky. She closed her eyes.

Suddenly, the grinding gears squealed and the whole frame of the lift seemed to lurch forward. A crack, like the sound of a whip, hit the air behind Sarah. She braced herself against the wheel as the lift came to a shuddering halt, about twelve feet from the end of the ride. The Lund stood still in its wooden crib high above the shore.

"What happened?" she called.

"Something snapped," Roger said. "Cable maybe. I can't see a thing. Hold on."

She waited as he moved back and forth along the wooden walkway. The sky darkened and the rain began to fall steadily. Roger returned with a small flashlight, which he shone across the esoteric workings of the machinery.

309

"I need a stronger light," he yelled to her. "And my tools. It may take a while. Sit tight."

"But, Roger!"

"Don't get out of the boat," he warned. He disappeared down the steps toward the shed.

"Roger!" she called, but her voice was lost among the downpour and the rumble of thunder.

"Damn this rain," she said.

As if in answer, the rain began to fall more heavily.

WHEN THE RAIN falls like a curtain of silver birds, Morgan read as the rain began to tap on the window beside her, *it seems to veil the future from my eyes. It descended like that all day today, and the work was difficult. The words came so thick and fast this morning I could not see beyond them. Sometimes the world of the book seems more alive to me than this world of trees and stone. If it weren't for Sarah, I believe I would step right into it and become lost among the sentences, sink into their soft folds and tangles. Another fork of lightning just zinged across the top of the cabin. If it should hit us, we'd be out of this mess at last. So weary tonight, I am writing nonsense. Of course I don't want us to be hit by lightning, but I do want to claw my way somehow out of this drudgery of work and work and work, with barely a dollar to show for it. Poor Sarah. She played with her teddy bear all morning, making him a little house with blankets and chairs. At lunch time, she said to me, "I was good today, Mama. I didn't 'sturb your typing." I felt so guilty I left the book and made up a game of fairies with her. We let Teddy play too, naturally. And then when she lay down for her nap, I could not enter the book again. It had shut itself down, jealous of Sarah, I guess, and would not let me in.*

Lightning again, and thunder. Like the night Sarah was born. Persephone sits reading unperturbed by the storm, but Sarah is frightened and has crawled into bed beside me here, as I write.

Chapter Thirty-Seven

SURELY A METAL BOAT, thirty feet above the water, was the worst possible place to be in an electric storm. Sarah called again for Roger, but he was busy somewhere in the darkness far below and did not answer. She waited. Nothing was happening, except that the storm was increasing in intensity. A bright bolt of lightning was followed quickly by a low roll of thunder. The lightning was close. It was dark now, and blowing hard, and Sarah doubted they would make it to the Carriere place tonight.

She touched the wet, splintered boards of the crib and considered trying to climb out. But the sides were too steep and slick with rain. She walked to the stern, looking for another way out. Then, as her eyes adjusted slightly to the night, she spotted a movement in the bushes below.

In the downpour, a black figure was walking through the bushes from the ruins of the old mill. He stopped and seemed to be looking up at her, but in the darkness she could not see his face at all.

The stance of the man was familiar, though, the broad curve of his shoulders. Was it someone she knew? Not Roger—it was someone shorter. Her first impulse was to call out for help, but some deeper instinct made her hold her tongue. The figure disappeared below the lift.

LIGHTNING FLASHED AGAIN, and she could see the stranger more clearly this time. He was climbing up the cement steps toward the controls of the boatlift. But something was wrong. He was stealthy, secretive, as if trying to advance on her undetected. With horror, she saw that he carried a length of thick rope across his shoulders.

He looked up then, and her heart thudded as she saw the black executioner's hood that covered his entire head.

The midnight strangler!

She scrambled back through the boat to the bow and perched there, wild to escape, but not knowing where to go. He was closer now. She had no choice.

She crawled from the prow down to the floor of the crib and out onto one of the slippery metal guide rails of the boatlift. She crouched low, clinging tightly to a vertical pole beside her. The rail she balanced on was only eight inches wide, and the rubber soles of her running shoes were worn and wet. Above the sound of the rain, she imagined she could hear the waves slapping furiously against the stony shore. Directly beneath her, the river was shallow, and if she slipped.... She thought of the sharp, jagged edges of the rocks she'd seen beneath the water there. The farther out she moved, the deeper the water would be, and the greater her chances for survival if she fell. But she'd have to let go of the pole. She clung to it with both hands, and the cold metal stung her skin.

The next streak of lightning revealed him standing in the stern of the boat with a flashlight, peering over the side of the lift, as if he thought she might already have fallen. The bow of the boat kept her hidden from him. He aimed the beam of light at the ground, where it darted and bounced wildly along the shore, providing brief, jerky glimpses of the cliffs, the dock, and the spindly trees far, far below. Sarah, overcome with dizziness, closed her eyes. Rivulets of rain poured down the open collar of her jacket and streamed down her back. Her hands were now completely numb.

She opened her eyes and saw nothing. She could not tell if he was still searching or if he had spotted her.

About twelve feet away, she knew, there was another upright post that reached down into the river. If she could make it there, farther out over the water, she might be able to climb down it into the frigid safety of the river. She forced herself to unfold her cramped, icy fingers from the metal pole. Lowering her heavy plaster cast over one side, and her right leg over the other, she balanced herself, straddling the rail. With her hands, she inched her body forward, praying.

Keeping her eyes fixed on the white metal of the narrow rail, she tried not to stare into the black, gaping void below, tried not to let the lightning or the thunder shake her. She thought only of her goal, ten feet, nine feet, eight feet away. Her hips ached, and she shivered involuntarily in her soaked clothing.

Where was he? She turned to look back.

In the next instant, she was blinded by the beam of his flashlight in her eyes.

He had found her.

And he obviously had no fear of heights.

He walked forward quickly and steadily, balancing himself easily with his long arms outstretched. Sarah, straddling the rail, was now only two feet from the vertical pole. But it was too late to escape into the river. He was right behind her, leaning above her. Stretching his arms over her head, he grabbed onto the pole. She could hear him breathing heavily behind the mask. He swung his right leg around her. One steel-toed boot, caked with mud, came down on the rail inches from her hand. Then the other.

Sarah bent her head back to look up at him. When he turned toward her, she could see the faint mist of his breath, the beads of water that clung to the dark woolen hood. She couldn't see his eyes behind the two blank holes that stared at her.

"Who are you?" she demanded.

He was silent. He tucked the flashlight into his belt. Then slowly and deliberately he pulled the rope off his shoulders, secured one end to the pole, and began to knot the other end into a noose.

He was going to hang her! From the boatlift railing! The image of her own body hanging there in the morning light, like some victim in the novel, enraged her.

He was lowering the noose, as if intending to catch her head in it.

She looked closely at his feet. He was standing with one behind the other like a tightrope walker, and though he was holding on with one hand, she knew he'd have to loosen his grip momentarily to secure the knot, and when he did—

He shifted slightly and she knew he was temporarily off kilter. She crossed her legs beneath the railing, hooking her right foot securely behind the plaster calf of her left leg. Then she let go of the rail and grabbed him above the ankle with both hands. His foot slipped, but did not leave the rail. He was heavier than she'd expected. She gripped the rail firmly with her thighs for leverage and twisted his ankle hard. He grunted and tried desperately to kick her away, but she was wrapped tightly around the rail. Maintaining her hold on his leg, she pulled with all her strength and twisted again, harder.

The violent movement sent them both off balance.

She felt herself teetering as he began to slide. The weight of his falling body wrenched her to one side, and she let go of him. She opened her arms wide and felt him drop past her.

By the time she realized what had happened, she was hanging by her crossed legs under the rail.

If there was a splash below her, it was drowned out by the sound of the storm.

But she felt he was gone. It was over.

Or almost over. She was still upside down and freezing, suspended thirty feet above the river.

Chapter Thirty-Eight

MARY WAS ALARMED AT HER son's appearance. When he rang her bell at eleven at night, she looked out and saw him on the front stoop in the rain, wet and bleeding from a cut on his forehead. Lightning crashed across the sky above his head. She hustled him in and closed the door against the thunderstorm.

"What happened to you? Where are your glasses?"

"Had a little boat trouble. Where's Sarah?"

"She went to meet you at Wesley's house. She had a phone call from Winnipeg that upset her. She went rushing off to find you without any explanation. You're absolutely soaked through! Did you fall in the lake? Get out of those clothes at once, or you'll catch your death." Mary hastened to the bathroom for towels.

Jacob dried his face and rubbed a towel through his hair, wincing when he touched the wound.

"When did she leave?"

"About eight. She took your car. Didn't you see her?"

"No. She hasn't come back here?"

"Not yet. I'm going to get some antiseptic for that cut."

"I'll do it." He was shivering. "You'd better call over to Mrs. Wesley and find out if Sarah's still there."

In the bathroom, Jacob took off his jacket and shirt and examined the bruise that was spreading over his chest and ribs. He threw his clothes in the dryer and wrapped himself in a robe. Then he examined his face. The cut was long, but not too deep. He opened a bottle of hydrogen peroxide and dabbed at it with a ball of cotton. It stung, and he could see he was going to have a hell of a bruise over one side of his face as well. Probably a black eye, too. Damn.

Well, he should be thankful there were no broken bones.

As she hung upside down in the darkness, Sarah felt her legs begin to shake. She was losing her grip on the guide rail. She bent at the waist and stretched her arms as far as possible, trying to reach the rail. Her fingers merely grazed its cold, slippery surface. She could not grasp it. Cautiously, she began to swing her upper body back and forth like a pendulum, gathering momentum until, with one mighty effort, she heaved herself upward and managed to wrap her arms around the rail, just as her legs came loose. For a minute she clung there, too exhausted to haul herself up. Then she realized she had no choice.

She raised her right leg, hooked it over the rail, and pulled herself up into a sitting position. She inched her way back along the railing and finally walked shakily down the stairs to Roger.

He was lying unconscious beside his toolbox by the open door of the shed. Sarah was unable to pull him inside. The rain was still coming down, and he was as wet as she was. Shaking uncontrollably from cold and shock, she gathered every available blanket and piece of clothing she could find, even the curtains from the shed windows, to cover him. She knelt beside him, rubbing his wrists and speaking his name, urging him to waken. Loathe as she was to leave him there, she had just decided to go for help when his eyelids began to flicker.

"Roger? Can you hear me?"

He groaned and opened one eye.

"Roger? Can you move? Talk to me."

He opened his other eye and lifted a hand to his head.

"Wait here a second. I'll be right back." Sarah grabbed a ball-peen hammer from his toolbox and hurried across the lawn toward the car as fast as she could, her feet slipping on the wet grass. She approached the car carefully, the hammer raised and ready to strike. No one appeared. She got in and locked the door. Her hands were shaking so violently she could barely turn the key in the ignition, but she got it started. She drove across the well-manicured lawn, parking as close to Roger as she dared. He was sitting up now, dazed.

"What's happening?" he asked her.

She knelt beside him. "We're taking you to a doctor," she said. "Can you stand?"

Roger was able to walk, but he was too disoriented to co-operate. With a great deal of difficulty, Sarah guided him to the car and got him into the back seat, locked all the doors, and started the car again. She stepped hard on the gas, and the vehicle lurched forward, tires skidding on the wet grass and tearing the sod to mud as she gunned the motor and sped up the hill.

"She's been gone over two hours." Mary was worried now. "Mrs. Wesley says she went to meet you at the old mill. What were you doing there?"

Jacob grimaced as he raised the cup of hot tea to his cut lip. "I went to meet Quinn Carriere. Mrs. Wesley told me he's here on vacation, up at his dad's place on the river. She said he wanted to see me about something important. I thought it might have something to do with Sarah, so I took off right away. But I must have missed him at the boatlift. Roger was there, just coming in from the river, and he lent me his boat. But I never made it to Quinn's."

"What happened?"

Jacob shook his head. "I ran out of gas. I thought I could make it, if I gassed up at the Riverside Marina, but they were closed. I ended up paddling back in this storm. Got blind-sided by a wave, and you don't want to hear the gory details, believe me. I lost a paddle and ended up in the lake. Not very pleasant. Don't you think we should look for Sarah? Who phoned her from Winnipeg?"

But Mary didn't know. They decided to take her car and drive around town, to see if they could spot the Thunderbird.

Jacob sat in the passenger seat, trying to see through the pelting rain, but without his glasses, he could barely dis-tinguish one dark shape from another. Mary drove slowly, up and down the streets, unable to imagine where Sarah could be.

"Maybe she had car trouble?"

"Drive into town," Jacob said. "If she got stuck between Keewatin and Kenora, she might be stranded on the highway."

They were just approaching downtown Kenora, when Mary suddenly turned and headed up the hill toward the Lake of the Woods Hospital.

"Just in case," she said. But when she reached the hospital parking lot, she cried, "Jacob! Your car!" The Thunderbird was parked at an erratic angle in front of the building.

SARAH DECIDED TO try phoning Mary's house again. She was starting to calm down. She had survived again. And Roger's prognosis sounded good. The X-ray showed no fracture to the skull. He'd been admitted for observation and was lucid enough to give Sarah the number of a girlfriend, who was on her way to see him. Sarah was still shivering in her hospital robe and slippers. The first thing the nurses had done was take away her wet clothes, and she was waiting to get them back. She'd emptied her pockets first, and she still had her wallet and coin purse. She dug out a quarter and padded down the hall to the front lobby to call again. She wanted to talk to Mary and Jacob before she called the police. The phone rang and rang. Was Mary taking a shower? Sleeping? Sarah tried to tell herself that Jacob was in no danger. He had gone to Quinn's place, and if Quinn was the midnight strangler, he wasn't home. As she stood in the phone booth, listening to the endless ringing, she wondered exactly where the midnight strangler was. Sarah wasn't sure exactly how far out over the river they'd been when he fell. Would he have hit his head on the rocks? Drowned? Or did he survive, pull himself up on the banks? Was he lying there, injured and possibly freezing to death? She hung up, deciding to call the police right away, after all.

The flash of a red raincoat hurrying past the phone booth caught her eye. Mary! And Jacob was behind her. They were talking to the receptionist at the desk, right outside the phone booth. Thank God! Sarah raised her hand and was about to tap on the glass.

Then Jacob turned his head, and she saw his face. A long gash ran from under his hairline to his jaw. A dark bruise was forming on his cheekbone. She turned around quickly and backed out of sight, her heart pounding.

She moved away from the reception desk. Where to go? Behind her, the doors to the hospital, the pouring rain. Should she take Jacob's car? She glanced outside and saw a taxi pulling in. Without thinking, she dashed out into the rain in her robe and slippers and threw open the passenger door. She slid inside, surprising the elderly passenger who was still in the back, fumbling with his wallet to pay his fare.

"Take me to the bus depot," she told the driver. Hurry!"

Chapter Thirty-Nine

ALFRED WAS WAITING OUTSIDE the bank when it opened on Monday morning, and he was first in line. When the teller left him alone with the safety deposit box, he made room in his briefcase to receive the manuscript. Mrs. Wesley had called last night with the news of her husband's death, and now there was no reason not to take full advantage of the publicity from the murders. Alfred would begin typesetting immediately. The cover design was already done. The book didn't need much editing. If the printer would cooperate, Alfred could have the book on the shelves by the end of June.

He opened the box and nearly fainted. It was empty, except for Betty's engagement and wedding ring. He shook it, hoping somehow that would help. The rings rattled. He closed the box and opened it again. Nothing had changed. No stock certificates, no bonds, no deeds, no nothing. And no manuscript. Betty had cleaned him out.

He knew where she was. She had to be at Anna's. He

would simply go there and take it back. He would even let her keep everything else—at least for today.

He drove straight there. He'd never visited Anna, but he knew where she lived, a rooming house on Furby Street, down past the Big Sky Tavern. He squealed to a stop, then tried to rein in his anger as he walked to the front door.

"She doesn't want to see you," Anna told him.

Alfred pushed his sister-in-law aside and ran down the hall to the kitchen. It was empty. And surprisingly clean. He retraced his steps and entered the living room. He'd expected to find Betty in a state of emotional ruin, surrounded by wads of used tissues. He'd pictured Anna's apartment as an unkempt hole, with cracked linoleum and cockroaches. Instead, he found himself in a spacious, colorful room. How did Anna afford this place? A fire blazed in the grate, and a little table was set for tea. The walls were freshly painted and decorated with posters. Instead of wailing wretchedly in her sister's arms, Betty was sitting cross-legged on a braided rug, perfectly dry-eyed and calm. The contents of the safety deposit box were spread out in neat piles on the floor around her.

"What do you want?" Betty asked him.

"Oh thank God!" Alfred strode toward the precious brown envelope, his hand outstretched. "Do you know what this is worth?"

Before his fingers could close on it, Betty snatched it away and held it close to her chest.

"*A Fire at Midnight*?" Betty asked. "You mean AFM? Your dirty little secret? I'm beginning to guess."

"It's the last Midnight mystery," Alfred said. "You didn't let anyone read it, did you?"

Anna was leaning against the door frame behind him, her arms crossed over her chest, listening.

"I can pretty well guess what it's worth," Betty said quietly. "And why you were hiding it." She stood up and assumed a dignified stance. "You were planning to leave me, weren't you? You were planning to leave me for that rusty-headed little Morgan Wakeford. And you were hiding your assets. Well, you won't get away with it. I've already called a lawyer and I'm filing for divorce at two o'clock this afternoon."

Alfred stepped forward. "Betty, let me explain."

Betty stood up, gripping the manuscript tightly. "Explain what? That you're a lying cheat? That you think I tried to poison you? That you care more about your little porno book—"

"It's not porno," Alfred said. "Betty, be reasonable."

She drew the pages out of the envelope and began to read aloud. "Chapter One. *Sometimes the fever of their passion rose so high she feared for her own sanity. He said she made him feel alive, but when he touched and ignited her, she knew only that she was mortal.*

"Lovely," Betty said. "Simply lovely." She lifted the page and let it drift down into the fireplace, where it shriveled immediately in the flames. Alfred watched in fascinated horror. What was happening? Betty was completely out of his control. He stepped forward, but stopped when she held the second page high above his head, taunting him. She was too near the fire. He didn't dare move any closer.

"Now, Betty," he said. "It's not pornography. It's a mystery. There's a big difference between the genres."

"Between the what?" Betty asked.

Alfred took another step forward. Betty backed up.

"Be careful," Anna cried. "Or someone's going to get hurt."

"Between the *what*?" Betty repeated.

"Genres. It's a literary term. You wouldn't understand. It means—Betty! Don't!"

She had shoved a whole fistful of the book into the fire. Three chapters at least.

Alfred moved forward, his open palm raised to strike.

Anna jumped on his back. Alfred twisted wildly and threw her off, but he stumbled, and the delay cost him. Betty stared defiantly into his eyes as she thrust the rest of the manuscript directly into the flames.

"No!" Alfred screamed. He lunged toward the fireplace.

Too late. *A Fire at Midnight* was old and very dry. It turned brown, then black, then gray. In less than a minute, it was nothing but smoke.

Chapter Forty

SARAH AND MORGAN HAD A tearful reunion, a long exchange of horror stories, and an exhausting visit to the police station. But nothing was resolved.

Jacob phoned and explained to Sarah about his boat accident. He had hit his head as he fell over the side of the boat, and nearly drowned in the rough waters of the river before he pulled himself up over the gunwale in the storm. When she heard the explanation in Jacob's calm, rational voice, Sarah believed him.

She had also talked to Alfred, who was strangely despondent and unwilling to discuss any theories about Sarah's father. But he claimed he was positive Quinn wasn't Walter White. "Quinn can't write. He tried all his life and could never finish anything. No, the style's all wrong for my brother. I know his feeble efforts well. He's been submitting them to me long enough." Alfred also claimed his brother Quinn wasn't anywhere near Kenora. He had gone on an Alaskan cruise with his family and could not be reached.

So who had phoned Mrs. Wesley, pretending to be Quinn? Who had set Sarah up at the boatlift? Where was he now?

And where was Walter White? Alfred said he had no idea. He was still waiting for Bill Wesley's grieving widow to turn over the agency records.

In the meantime, the murder investigation was no further ahead. The Ontario police had searched the area of the boatlift and found no evidence. No evidence was found in Dr. Allard's house, either. The lab confirmed the ME's theory that Gregory died of cyanide. But no traces of the poison were detected on any items seized from the Carriere house. The wineglass was clean, and Betty was cleared. The only new fingerprints found in Cady Brown's apartment turned out to be Daniel's—and he was suspended from the force. The homicide detectives came by almost daily with new questions for Sarah and Morgan, but nothing they could supply seemed to help. Kayla and Vishnu were not at all sold on the Walter White angle. They were concentrating on a search for Peter. In the meantime, nobody else got killed. Whoever was acting out the lethal plots of the novels stopped when the series stopped.

Sam returned to Vancouver, and Morgan moved in with Sarah on what seemed likely to be a permanent basis. They installed an expensive alarm system and tried to resume their normal lives. The doctor removed Sarah's cast, and she could walk freely again. She was exercising, trying to regain the strength in her legs. She resumed the task of reading her mother's words. With all the boxes recovered, she knew it might take months, but she had Morgan to help her now.

THE TWO COUSINS sat on the floor of Sarah's living room late in the afternoon, with the boxes spread out around them, sorting. Morgan had found an early draft of *Island Songs*, and the cousins had decided to separate the private journals from the poetry that might be of interest to the public.

At the bottom of the fifth carton she opened, Sarah found a flat box of thin, white cardboard, the kind of box a store might pack a shirt in. On the cover, Carolyn had written "100 Volts." Sarah opened it. Inside, in bundles tied with string, were letters. The letters from the fuse box at the old mill.

"Morgan, look!" Sarah untied the top bundle eagerly. A quick shuffle revealed that the letters were all in the same hand, all from the same man. They were not dated, except for the days of the week, and they were not signed. Not too surprising, Sarah thought. If you're going to leave an illicit love letter in an abandoned building, you don't sign your name.

"Let me see," Morgan begged. Sarah gave her a handful of the letters.

"*Darling,*" Morgan read aloud. "*Of course I am longing to see you, and the sooner the better. But you must understand that my work comes first. The poems you sent are marvelous, very promising. I hope to read more when I return. Keep working along at it, darling. I'd write you all that is in my heart, but I leave for New York in one hour. Kiss our little baby for me. XXX.*"

"Oh my God, it *is* your father! These are his letters!"

"Yes." Sarah ran her fingers across the yellowed paper. This was the handwriting of her own father. Who *was* he?

"There have to be some good clues in here," Morgan said. "Let's read them all."

The cousins took turns reading the letters aloud, searching for clues to the writer's identity. Soon they were swept up in the drama the letters unfolded. It was a one-sided story, for Carolyn's letters were missing. But Sarah and Morgan could follow it nevertheless.

"*My Darling,*" Sarah read. "*Your letter caught up to me in New York, and I must say I was rather alarmed at your tone. You mustn't let your imagination run away with you. It's unhealthy. I have promised you we'll be together, and we WILL be together, as soon as I get myself established. So calm yourself.*

"*As for sending your new collection to Alfred, I urge you most* strongly NOT to do so. It's best if I read through it first, as we agreed. Believe me, you don't want to open yourself to criticism before you're ready. That's death to the artistic spirit. It will make you tough, and we want you as soft and fresh and lovely as ever. Until next Sunday, XXX."

"Until next Sunday," Morgan repeated. "Listen to this one. *Darling, I'm sorry I couldn't make it Sunday, but the motor is acting up, and I know you wouldn't have wanted me to chance it in that weather. I enclose a check for the baby's bed. Get Roger to help you bring it over from town. I'm glad you decided to send the book to me first and I will read it as soon as I can. Love and XXX.*"

Sarah grabbed the envelope from Morgan and searched it carefully, hoping foolishly to find a signature on an enclosed check. But of course it was long gone, cashed twenty-some years ago.

She pulled out the next letter and read. *"Darling, Here it is! As you can see, it looks lovely. Laurentian Shield does a better job of cover art than Alfred ever did, I think, and it's turned out for the best. Your book launch will be bigger, too. I'm sorry I'm unable to attend, but rest assured I'll be there in spirit, as proud of my little poetess as ever.*

"As for the other, I'm afraid I can't place it yet. Perhaps it's best if you put it out of your mind and start work on another. It's not good for an artist to dwell too much on the business end of things. Leave that to me. XXX and hugs to my sweet poetess. I am so proud of you!"

"Sweet poetess, my eye!" Morgan said. She was getting the picture. This Walter White, or whatever his name was, was nothing but a condescending jerk. Using Aunt Carolyn to feed his own ego—not to mention other needs. He played mentor, editing her poems and dealing with her publishers as if she were an incompetent. Then left her alone to cope with the baby all by herself. Judging by the references to the baby, Carolyn must have been about twenty-five. Sarah's present age. A grown woman!

"He treated her like a child!" Morgan exclaimed aloud. "Why did she put up with it?"

Sarah sighed. She knew the answer to that one. She had read Carolyn's outpourings of grateful passion for this man who had reached down into her isolated little world and introduced her to literature, encouraged her writing, even helped her get published. "Times were different then," she told Morgan. "The women's lib movement was barely begun. And my mother had probably never heard of it. But let's remember, she did break free of him, finally. She wasn't entirely spineless, after all."

"But she didn't live long after she broke up with him," Morgan said. "Doesn't that seem—"

She broke off, and the two cousins bowed their heads and continued to sort through the letters, not wanting to think the ugly thought.

The letters in the next bundle Sarah opened contained more of the same promises to "be together" and more flimsy excuses why it was impossible. But then she hit a series of letters dealing with the editing of Carolyn's work. Comments on the poems, a quoted verse or two—Sarah could recognize her mother's poetry now—and suggested changes in wording or punctuation. Sarah supposed this was the stuff that was valuable to literary scholars. This was the reason Dr. Allard had stolen the papers.

Then she found something ominous. *"Darling, Don't worry about her! I'm sure it was just a casual remark. She's a bit of a prude, is all. Nobody is going to burn your books. But I must insist that you burn these letters. You are destroying them, aren't you?"*

"Who could he be talking about?" Sarah asked Morgan.

"It might have been my mother," Morgan said. "I thought I found some reference to her reading Carolyn's diary. . . . Where did that go?" She looked at the hundreds of papers strewn across the carpet and gave up before she even started to search.

"Darlene wouldn't burn her books. Would she?" Sarah remembered that Darlene *was* a bit of a prude, but she dismissed the thought. "Don't you think it's possible my mother knew someone else was out to destroy her work? In her journal, she said she was taking it all in to the law office because she wanted to 'protect' it. Protect it from what? Evan Knight talked about dampness and rot, but look at the way she shoved these papers in, such a mess, as if she was rushed."

"She didn't say why, in her journal?"

"No, she just said she was relieved to have it all 'safely stowed'—except for one last book. She was worried about preserving one last manuscript, because she was still working on it."

"What manuscript was that?"

"I don't know," Sarah said. "It must have been lost in the fire."

"Keep reading," Morgan said. "We've got to find out who he is."

"Darling, I miss you too," Sarah read aloud. *"You know I will come as soon as I can get away. My work is all-absorbing at the moment. I want to ask you to think about a few things. I'm having a problem with the amusement park scene in Chapter 19. I can't seem to figure out how the detective can get the roller coaster to work. I'm hardly an expert—"*

"*Bloody Midnight!*" Morgan cried. "He's talking about the roller coaster in *Bloody Midnight!*"

Sarah sat up straight. She remembered that scene from the novel, and she'd seen that same problem with the plot when she read it herself. Here was the proof positive. Whoever her father might be, he was the author of the Midnight books.

"It's him!" Morgan said. "Daniel was right! Walter White is your own father! Read the rest of it!"

"I'm hardly an expert on roller coasters! I'm also having trouble with the ending, which falls flat ... perhaps you could put your mind to it and come up with something a little more exciting for me."

"There's a change in attitude!" Morgan commented. "He's asking Aunt Carolyn for advice about his own writing."

"Yes," Sarah said. "Amazing." Perhaps Walter White's attitude toward women wasn't as bad as she'd thought.

They continued to read to each other, speeding through the letters, looking for further clues to the writer's identity. But the next few letters were mostly about the weather and his apologies for not sending more money. Sarah was disgusted again. By this point in time, he must have been raking in plenty of money. But he always had an excuse—the bank was closed, he had forgotten, he ran out of checks. Sarah began to suspect that he was not simply stingy. He seemed to use money as another way of controlling Carolyn, keeping her childlike, dependent. He was the successful novelist. She was the "little poetess." Sarah realized she didn't like her own father. Not one bit.

And then Morgan found another reference to the Midnight books. *"How could a butler possibly get his hands on cyanide?"* Morgan read. "Good question! *How could he know that the groom would be the only one to eat the pumpkin soup? The plot has to be more realistic. I know these little details don't seem important to you, my dear, but they are! It's the same kind of mistake you made about the maniac in the blizzard. The door's locked from the inside. It's not believable. If you're going to persist with writing these mysteries, darling, and you want me to place them with a publisher, you're going to have to do a little research. I can bring you some books on police procedure . . ."*

Morgan stopped reading. Her eyes met Sarah's.

"Oh my God," they said together.

Everything suddenly fell into place.

Walter White wasn't Sarah's father.

Walter White was her mother.

Chapter Forty-One

JACOB WANTED TO KNOW EXACTLY what it was that Sarah had to tell him so urgently, but she wouldn't give him any hints over the phone.

"I know it's late, but can't you come? It's important."

Morgan stood listening, wringing her hands in excitement. "No, we're fine. Honestly. It's nothing like that. It's just—well, we need some legal advice. From someone we can trust. Yes. Right away."

"Is he coming?" Morgan asked eagerly.

Sarah hushed her. "Thank you," she said. She hung up. "He's coming. He should be here in two or three hours. Do you think you can stay awake?"

"There's no way I could sleep! And I'm suddenly famished. Why don't we put some dinner on?"

"There are casseroles in the freezer," Sarah said. "Why don't you heat one up? I'll clean up the guest room on the third floor for Jacob. It's a mess up there. I haven't done housework for days."

Morgan put a pan of macaroni and cheese in the oven and washed the dirty dishes. She reviewed in her mind the implications of the latest revelation. If the Midnight mysteries were written by Carolyn, why had Carolyn published them under her lover's name? And why had Carolyn been so poor?

Morgan wondered how much of this story Alfred knew.

As she stacked the dishes in the rack to dry, she saw a person carrying bags out of Dr. Allard's house. Mark Curtis. Morgan rapped on the window and waved. He waved back and beckoned her to come out.

Morgan ran to the front door and tore across the lawn to greet him with a hug. "My hero returns!"

He stepped back as if embarrassed, and Morgan saw he was not alone. An older woman stood beside him, in a pink summer dress and matching shoes, holding a flowered carpet bag.

"Morgan, this is my mother," Mark said. "She's come to help me move my stuff." He indicated his duffel bag and backpack, and a waiting car at the curb.

"Oh, hello," Morgan said. Mark's mother smiled and extended a hand encased in a pink glove.

"Mum, this is Morgan Wakeford. She's the one who found the doctor in the—"

"I heard all about it," his mother said. "You poor girl. How absolutely atrocious. Why, just *being* here tonight gives me the willies. I wouldn't go in there!"

"I don't blame you," Morgan said.

"Even though I really do need a bathroom," she added in a confidential tone.

Morgan smiled at Mark. "Why don't you come in and have a drink with me?" she offered. "You can use Sarah's washroom."

She led them up the steps and they followed, bringing their bags. Morgan pointed the way to the bathroom. "Up the stairs, first door on your left."

"You're a lifesaver," Mark's mother told her.

"Well, I owe you," Morgan laughed. "Your son practically saved my life the other night."

"Yes, he's a dear," she said, as she climbed up the stairs, toting her heavy bag. "Such a comfort to me."

SARAH OPENED THE trap door of the third-floor linen closet and tossed another bundle of towels down the laundry chute. She had thrown a mountain of laundry down there already, and there was still more to go. As she bent to gather some sheets and blankets, she thought she heard the click of heels in the corridor. She raised her head and froze. For a moment, the memory of her terror in this closet revisited her, but she shook it off. Would she be shaking it off for the rest of her life? A floorboard creaked in the hall. She straightened up.

"Morgan?" she called.

Morgan didn't answer.

Sarah tried to chalk the sounds up to the settling of the old house. She sent the bedding down, then scooped up a pile of sweaters. She absolutely *had* to convince Sam and Morgan to let her sell this old—

A shadow loomed in the doorway, blocking the light.

"Sarah Yeats?" A woman's voice.

Sarah turned.

"Mrs.—Mrs. Wesley!" she cried. Sarah backed up and felt her sock foot slip dangerously close to the edge of the open trap door to the laundry chute. She steadied herself against the wall. "What are you doing here?"

"I'm here to help my son," Mrs. Wesley said pleasantly. She set down the flowered cloth bag she was holding, and Sarah heard a metallic clunk and a sloshing noise as it hit the floor. "I'm here to spur him on," she said cheerfully. "You might say I'm here to whet his almost blunted purpose."

Sarah could make no sense of this. She dropped the sweaters and stepped toward Mrs. Wesley, but the woman did

not move aside to let her out the door. Sarah stopped, un-
certain. "Who is—where is your son?"

"Oh, he's downstairs having a chat with your cousin," Mrs. Wesley said gaily. "Your little slut of a cousin. It does run in the family, doesn't it?"

Mrs. Wesley's expression had not lost its ladylike charm for a second. She wore the same winsome smile, and for a moment, Sarah thought she must have heard her wrong.

"I beg your pardon?"

"Sluttishness," Mrs. Wesley said clearly. "Promiscuity. Nymphomania. Do you need a dictionary?" She inclined her head graciously and smiled, as if offering a nice cup of tea.

Sarah felt a chill wriggle all the way up her spine.

"I'M GOING TO miss you," Morgan told Mark as she poured him a glass of wine. "What are your plans?"

Mark set his duffel bag down on the sofa and accepted the glass. "There's the thesis to write," he said. He frowned as he sat down and rested an elbow on the bag. "I don't know how long that will take. Writing's not my strong suit, exactly."

"Mine either," Morgan said. She sat down beside him, with the bottle in one hand and an empty glass in the other. She held her unlit cigarette in her mouth and spoke around it. "I'm more of a reader."

"I'm worried about it, actually," he said. "I get—sort of blocked, sometimes."

"Writer's block? I remember that from college." Morgan filled her wineglass and set the bottle down on the table behind her. Then she began a search for her lighter.

"I get frustrated," Mark said.

Morgan nodded sympathetically. She checked all her pockets and found nothing. "Do you have a light?"

"A light? You mean light a match in here?" Mark rose up and moved away from the sofa.

Morgan laughed. "Sit down," she said. "I won't smoke if it

bothers you so much." She raised her glass. "Come on, let's toast." She clinked her glass against his. "May we meet again!" She drank.

"YOUR MOTHER WAS a whore," Mrs. Wesley continued in the same, pleasant, singsong voice. "Now don't look so surprised. Everyone knew it. There she was out on her little island, with her little poems, playing the wide-eyed Miranda, when all the time she was a Circe, turning men into swine. She had my husband so besotted with lust he completely lost his head."

"Your husband!" Sarah said. "Bill Wesley?"

"Yes, poor Bill, rest his soul. He was only trying to help her at first, encourage her, get her published. He thought she was some kind of genius, the deluded man. And then she lured him in. Turned him into an adulterer. It took me years to catch on. They were both so clever at it." Mrs. Wesley shook her head, as if annoyed but amused over some childish prank. "Why, even when she was pregnant with his child, she'd meet me in the doctor's office and smile and smile as if she was—"

"Pregnant!" Sarah gasped. "Pregnant with Bill's child—with—with *me*?"

"Why, yes," Mrs. Wesley looked at Sarah as if suddenly remembering she was there.

"But you—" she sputtered. "You told me—you let me think that Quinn was—"

"But that was a fib, wasn't it?" Mrs. Wesley said. "A whopper, in fact. Oh dear, excuse me." She pulled a hankie from the pocket of her pink dress and held it to her nose as she emitted a minuscule sneeze.

Sarah did not bless her.

"MY DAD USED to help me with my writing," Mark was saying. "But he's dead." He fiddled with the buckles on the straps of his duffel bag.

"I'm sorry," said Morgan. "I miss my father, too. He passed away about five years ago. When did your dad die?"

"Last week."

Morgan looked up, startled. "Oh, I'm *so* sorry. I didn't know."

"I couldn't even attend the funeral," Mark said.

"How sad." Morgan placed a hand on Mark's arm.

"Yeah. My mother wouldn't—"

"Excuse me," Morgan said. The phone was ringing, and she went to the kitchen to answer it.

Mark stood up and casually wandered around the room, looking at the books and the sculptures. He lifted a little stone sparrow from the mantel and pretended to examine it, all the while easing himself closer to the kitchen so that he could listen in.

"No. Everything's okay. We're fine."

Mark put the sparrow down and picked up the raven. Hefty.

"Thanks, Dan, but it's late. And Jacob Knight is coming over." She giggled a little. "No—to see Sarah. Yes. All right. I'll talk to you tomorrow." Morgan hung up.

Mark replaced the raven and moved quickly back toward the couch. He heard Morgan taking something out of the oven. Smelled melted cheese. He looked out the window, wondering how much time he had before Jacob showed up.

When Morgan re-entered the room, he was sitting on the couch, casually sipping his wine.

"Do you think we should check on your mother?" Morgan asked. "She's been gone kind of long."

"I'M NOT HERE to cause any trouble," Mrs. Wesley said, lifting her hands to dismiss any such thought. "Far from it. I'm here to *prevent* any more trouble. You see, my son Mark is in need of help. He's having some difficulties lately. At first, he was sailing along splendidly. I was most impressed when he managed to find a room for rent right next door to you. But then when he botched the first midnight murder, with the letter opener—"

"Oh no," Sarah said. "That's impossible—no!" She stepped forward, but again Mrs. Wesley stood in her path. "Will you *please* get out of my way."

Mrs. Wesley calmly replaced her hankie in the pocket of her dress and withdrew a tiny, silver pistol, which she aimed at Sarah's head.

"My son, you see," she continued sweetly. "He's a little accident-prone. He needs help. First he lost you down the laundry chute—don't think you're getting off so lightly this time. And then he fell off the boatlift. Slipped! What a clumsy—"

"He didn't slip," Sarah said between her teeth. "I pushed him."

"You pushed him!" A spark of anger blazed in Mrs. Wesley's eyes for an instant and then fizzled out. She continued as before. "He was always a little clumsy." She gave a ladylike chuckle. "But he did a good job with that nosy reporter. Now if only *she* had stayed out of it," Mrs. Wesley said. "Everything would have been nice and tidy."

"Cady Brown," Sarah said. "Poor, innocent Cady Brown!"

"Not exactly. Not quite. She was pestering Bill mercilessly. She asked him whether Walter White had any family, and before I could stop him, he let your name slip out. It was very faint, but I heard it. She heard it too, poor girl. And I knew she wouldn't let up. Oh no, she was the tenacious kind. She would have told you and then, eventually, you would have come along clamoring for your share of Bill's royalties. He has two other children, you know." She held up two fingers in a grim mockery of a peace sign. "Two *real* sons—and me, of course. And frankly, the thought of his legitimate family sharing the wealth with his bastard daughter didn't quite sit right with me."

"But Bill did *not* write those books," Sarah said. "My mother did. He stole them from her!"

"Yes, but nobody knows that, do they? And now, nobody ever will."

She bent down to unzip her flowered bag. But Sarah didn't wait to find out what she had in there. She stepped forward, poised to kick the pistol from Mrs. Wesley's grasp. But the older woman was faster than she expected.

"Oh no, you don't." Mrs. Wesley whipped her head up and stood at her full height. Taller than Sarah. She jammed the barrel of the pistol against Sarah's forehead. Right between the eyes. "Get back against the wall."

Sarah calculated quickly. If she pushed past Mrs. Wesley, knocked her over, could she avoid getting herself shot? The cold steel pressed hard against the delicate skin of her forehead. She thought not.

"That's better," Mrs. Wesley said as Sarah stepped backward, mindful of the open chute at her feet. "We have to do it by the book." She shook her head, as if Sarah were a pupil who had misunderstood her lessons. "And you know there *are* no heroic escapes in the books, dear. We have to follow the pattern."

"There are no more books," Sarah managed to say. "*Midnight Strangler* was the last one."

"I'm afraid you're mistaken about that, dear. There's one more story. The story she never showed to Bill. The one about the arsonist. The one that started it all. We're coming full circle tonight, our two little families. And I've brought along just the thing for the occasion."

Sarah looked down at the flowered bag. It was unzipped and folded back to reveal a metal container with a red handle and a nozzle. A bright sticker depicting a fat red flame had been affixed to the side. Sarah knew what it was. She had often seen such containers recently, at the marina. It was a can of gasoline.

"A book about an arsonist?" Sarah whispered. Her throat was dry.

"Oh yes. Her final little effort. She was trying to be independent, you see. But I found it when I was looking through her diaries. I was starting to keep an eye on her. I was getting a tad suspicious, but I had no proof, so I made a few visits to her cabin when she was out—"

"You were the woman snooping in her diaries!"

"Yes, but she was so secretive. Why, her diaries were practically in code! But then I found the carbon copy of her novel. *The Arsonist, by Walter White*, it said. I knew that was her penname—though Bill always changed it whenever he sold a book." Mrs. Wesley tittered. Then she grew serious again. "*The Arsonist!* When I read it, I must admit I saw red. All that flaming passion. All those metaphors for sin and sexuality. Really, Carolyn was so obvious sometimes. The fire at midnight, the burning mill, the letters in the fuse box—it was all rather, well, I'm sorry to say, a bit *tawdry*, my dear. But it didn't fool me for a minute. Tsk. I knew right away, as soon as I read it. When she came home I gave her a piece of my mind."

"And you threatened to burn it!" Sarah cried.

"Yes." Mrs. Wesley shook her head. "I didn't know Carolyn had already submitted the original to Carriere Press. Behind Bill's back! I only found out a few weeks ago, when that reporter Cady Brown came along, asking Bill where the sixth book was. I overheard her say that Alfred was keeping it hidden. What a headache. We had to completely revise our plan in order to take care of Alfred, as well. But that plan didn't quite work out—we'll have to find some other way to stop him from publishing *The Arsonist*."

"Why stop him?" Sarah asked. She slid her foot along the floor, edging closer to Mrs. Wesley, who seemed absorbed in the past.

"Because it's a little too close to the truth, you see. I followed the plot exactly. It took me a few days. I had to wait for Carolyn's sister and her husband to leave the island. Then

I had to buy the gasoline. It had to be done exactly right. I always say—I always said this to my boys when they were naughty—*let the punishment fit the crime.*" She smiled brightly. "I said it to them that very night. I said, *Boys, come along and help your mother, now. It's up to us to put right what's gone awry.* So we took the boat out late. It was nearly midnight—"

"You!" Sarah said. "You killed her!" She took a gigantic stride forward, forgetting about the danger to herself. Fury boiled through her body, and she reached out and shoved Mrs. Wesley out of the closet.

Sarah stepped into the hall after her. She was no longer trapped. But she was still in Mrs. Wesley's line of fire. The two women faced each other.

"Why, you little tart," Mrs. Wesley said. "You little—" She broke off suddenly, as her attention seemed drawn toward the third-floor landing. "Oh my Lord," she said. She dropped the gun, and it bounced once on the carpet before landing behind Sarah's ankles. Sarah turned quickly to retrieve it. And then she saw what Mrs. Wesley saw.

The woman in white again, transparent and wavering, still carrying her book, floating down the hall toward them, closer and closer . . .

Mrs. Wesley squawked in fear and threw herself violently into the linen closet to escape. Sarah watched in awe as the phantom came closer, and closer still, and then, as a wave of warmth suffused Sarah's body, the woman in white seemed to pass right through her.

Mrs Wesley had backed up against the farthest wall of the linen closet. Her little pink high-heeled shoes trembled precariously mere inches from the open trap door. She cowered there, sick and shaking.

Mesmerized, Sarah saw the apparition drift into the threshold of the closet. She felt she was under a spell, probably hallucinating from fear. A small, practical voice from within reminded her she was in danger. She blinked and rubbed her eyes. Keep a grip on reality. Stay alert.

She opened her eyes.

The image of her mother was gone.

The pistol lay on the floor of the corridor, and Sarah bent to scoop it up. But she was still moving in slow motion, as though in a dream.

And then the dream-like mood was shattered by the piercing scream of Mrs. Wesley, a sound that traveled through the whole house, all the way down the chute from the third floor to the basement.

MARK AND MORGAN both jumped to their feet at the sound. The metallic echo of the scream reverberated through the walls. Then they heard the pounding of footsteps coming down the stairs.

"Mother?" Mark cried. He rushed out into the hall and Morgan followed. They reached the bottom of the stairs just as Sarah appeared at the top, a gun in her hands.

"Back off!" she said to Mark, aiming at his chest.

Morgan screamed.

"Get away from him, Morgan," Sarah warned. "Get out of the house." She was rapidly descending.

"Sarah, what are you doing?" Morgan squealed. She hid herself behind Mark, her hands around his waist.

"Morgan, go!" Sarah cried. "He's the killer! Get out!"

But it was too late. Mark had reached behind him and grabbed Morgan's hair. He pulled her in front of him and backed away from Sarah toward the living room, using Morgan as a shield.

"It's Mark," Sarah told Morgan. "It was him all along." She looked Mark in the eye. "I'll bet you killed Dr. Allard, too," she said, as she advanced on him with the gun. "Did she find the papers you stole?"

"But Dr. Allard stole them, Sarah," Morgan cried out. "Mark was at the university that night. You were at the university, weren't you, Mark? Professor Dawson said so!"

"Professor Dawson will say anything I want him to say," Mark bragged. "As long as I don't tell that he's a fraud."

"You see, Morgan? It's him. He's tried to kill me twice. He killed Cady and Gregory, too."

"That was my mother!" Mark objected. "*She* killed Gregory."

"She wasn't even there," Sarah said, steadily advancing. "You were."

"She didn't need to be there," Mark said. "She just mailed in some bad poems with a fake name and address. But first she mixed a little cyanide powder with glue and poisoned the envelope flap. She got it from the honey-maker next door. Pesticide for bees, just like in the novel. Every damn detail had to be perfect." He laughed unhappily. "But even *she* makes mistakes. She wasn't supposed to kill Gregory. It was Alfred she was after. The creep was going to publish the arson book, and she was afraid people might remember."

"Remember what?" Morgan wheezed. Mark was now holding her so tightly around the neck, she could barely speak.

"Remember that she and her sons murdered Carolyn by setting fire to her cabin, nearly killing us, too," Sarah told Morgan. "Make that three times you've tried to kill me," she said to Mark. "There won't be a fourth."

Sarah moved in closer, taking a bead on Mark's left eye. "Let her go," she said.

"I don't think so." Mark dragged Morgan closer to the sofa, where his duffel bag lay unbuckled.

"I'll shoot you," Sarah said. "I'll shoot you right now." She had him up against the sofa now. She was close enough to get a clear shot at him without endangering Morgan.

Mark seemed unconcerned. "It won't be loaded," he said. He reached away from Morgan to put his hand inside his bag. Sarah hesitated. Was he bluffing? Had she been terrorized upstairs all this time by an unloaded weapon? She took a chance. She aimed at the thick upholstered seat of her armchair and squeezed the trigger. Click. She squeezed again. Click.

"She wouldn't risk putting bullets in it," Mark explained. "She wouldn't risk an accident. She wanted this to be done just right." His hand was inside the duffel bag, and Sarah saw his wrist moving rapidly in circles.

"What are you talking about?" Morgan was weeping now. "What are you doing?"

Sarah knew what he was doing. He was unscrewing the lid of a gas can. She could smell it.

"This is one thing I'm not going to mess up," he muttered. "This is one thing I'm going to finish off properly." He suddenly grabbed Morgan's arm and threw her toward the fireplace. She hit her head on the stone mantel and crumpled to her knees, dazed.

Sarah, distracted by Morgan's injury, didn't immediately see him pick up the duffel bag and turn it upside down. Gasoline poured onto the carpet, as Mark moved rapidly around the room, soaking the curtains, the sofa, and armchair.

"Morgan, come quick—we have to get out!" Sarah yelled.

Morgan stood up, wobbling. Sarah held out her arms, encouraging her to come, but Mark stepped between them, a gasoline-soaked cushion in one hand and a cheap, disposable lighter in the other, his thumb on the wheel. "Keep your distance," he said. He looked from one to the other, grinning warily. Sarah knew they couldn't dare try much. Unless she could kill him instantly, it was too risky to tackle him.

"If you light that, you'll never get out of here alive," Sarah told him. "The whole house will blow."

Mark shook his head. "That's all right. The punishment will fit the crime." He flicked the safety catch on the lighter.

Any second now, Sarah thought, we'll be engulfed in flames. She raised her head toward heaven, and as she did, she caught the gleaming eye of her grandfather's raven looking down on her.

"The stone raven!" Sarah cried.

The Dead of Midnight

Morgan understood. She reached for the mantel, and just as Mark turned to see what she was doing, she grasped the heavy stone bird with two hands and lifted it high over her head. When she brought it down hard on Mark's skull, she cringed at the ugly noise it made.

Chapter Forty-Two

IF BETTY HAD A DOLLAR COIN for every lie she'd ever told, she'd be a millionaire. Of course, so would Alfred. So would Morgan, for that matter. The three of them were a pack of liars, and hardly a thing any of them had ever said had been true.

Anna, though, was different. Anna told the truth. Betty glanced sideways at her sister, who sat at the bar beside her with a cigarette dangling from her mouth. Anna was wearing a very pale lipstick, because it was Disco Revival Night at the Big Sky Tavern. Her lips were almost white. She was rummaging through her little beaded clutch-purse for a match.

Betty didn't think white lipstick and beaded purses were disco, exactly. But Anna had her own ideas. She wore thick, black eyeliner, an orange miniskirt, black stockings, and a bright orange, rayon blouse, about two sizes two small. She looked like a combination beatnik and fast-food waitress. The only authentic touch was the disco boots.

"If you can't find it in that tiny bag, it isn't there," Betty said. She plucked a package of matches from a bowl on the bar and lit Anna's cigarette.

"Thanks, Bets." Anna dragged deeply and signaled the bartender for two more.

Betty spotted Peter Petursson waving at her from the stage, where he was setting up the speakers. Since he'd come out of hiding, he'd taken a job as sound technician for the Big Sky. Betty waved back. Maybe she should ask Peter for a dance when the disco music started. She'd always liked Peter, and now, she thought, they were kindred spirits. The falsely accused.

"So, tell me," Anna said. "After all this fallout from the Midnight murder thing, will Alfred have anything left for alimony?"

"It's called maintenance, nowadays," Betty said. "And yes, he'll have enough. The big profits from the Midnight books will go to Sarah Petursson, though."

Anna clucked sympathetically. "You could have been rich," she said.

"I'm just glad my name is cleared," Betty said. "For a while there I thought I was going to land up back in a cell."

MARK WESLEY, ALIAS Mark Curtis, recovered from his blow to the head in the infirmary of the Public Safety Building. His twin brother flew back to Canada from Japan, where he'd been living a normal life, trying to put his dysfunctional family behind him. He tried to bail Mark out, but with so much evidence against him, it was a lost cause. He also tried to contact his new-found half-sister, but Sarah was not returning his calls. As for Mrs. Wesley, she'd been miraculously unhurt by her fall down the laundry chute. Unfortunately, however, she found prison quite disagreeable.

When the whole story came out, the media attention was intense. The news that an obscure Canadian poet was the real author of the Midnight mystery books was full of enough scandal and intrigue to please everyone—the adultery, the tragic betrayal of Carolyn, and of course the real-life murders, all provided enough publicity to launch sales of the Midnight mysteries into the upper stratosphere.

For weeks, Sarah and Morgan pored over the journals, letters, and drafts. They found original notes and drafts for many of the Midnight mysteries. They performed a painstaking comparison to the original dates of publication of the mysteries in the seventies and eighties. The pattern that emerged was diabolical. Every time Carolyn finished a new mystery novel, she was buoyed with hope that she'd finally pull herself out of poverty. A few months later, Bill would tell her it had been rejected and urge her to try again. The cousins were enraged at his encouraging little notes. He undermined her confidence just enough to keep her dependent on him, and encouraged her just enough to keep her writing. Meanwhile, he was selling Carolyn's lucrative mysteries in the States, posing as an agent for various fictitious authors.

Professor Dawson called Sarah, offering to write a biography, using Carolyn's journals. He would write it fast, he said, because interest in the life of Carolyn Yeats was reaching frantic proportions. She knew he was desperate, since he'd lost his position at the university. He'd been fired when it came out that he had no Ph.D. He was, in fact, a grad-school dropout from Florida State.

Sarah turned down Dawson's offer. She had a better one. Byron Hunt and Linda Rain had approached her with a similar idea, and she liked their attitude. With Linda's intellect, and Byron's respect for Carolyn's writing, she believed they would turn out a biography that would do her mother justice.

Sarah and Morgan agreed to give the whole story exclusively to Byron and Linda. Jacob sat in on the interview in Sarah's living room.

"You mean Mark Wesley rented a room right next door to you in order to kill you?" Byron asked Sarah.

"He was supposed to kill me before I turned twenty-five and inherited my mother's papers," Sarah said. "Mrs. Wesley didn't want me reading through them."

"But Mark blew it," Morgan said. "To tell you the truth, I think he couldn't bring himself to kill his own sister."

"Half-sister," Sarah corrected. Jacob reached over to pat her hand, and she smiled at him. "Yes, Mark blew it. He used Dr. Allard's ladder to climb through my upstairs window. Then he called Peter on the guestroom phone—trying to lure Peter over here, to frame him for my murder. But then Mark waited too long. I guess Morgan's right. He couldn't do it. Instead of stabbing me, he stabbed my kitchen door and left the letter opener stuck in the wood."

"Peter found it when he arrived," Byron put in. "But he was too scared to mention it to the cops after he'd touched it. He left it on Sarah's basement floor."

"And Mark recovered it the next day," Sarah added, "when he came over to board up my broken window. I thought he was so helpful!"

Morgan continued. "Mark couldn't kill Sarah, so he did the next best thing—he stole Aunt Carolyn's papers. He hid them in Dr. Allard's closet, and of course she discovered them. She didn't tell anyone. She was probably trying to figure out how she could profit from them. Then Mark came home and found her reading them. He drowned her in her own bathtub, to make it look like another Midnight murder."

"Let's talk about what happened in the past," Linda said. "All those years Bill Wesley was stealing your mother's books? And she never found out?"

Sarah nodded. "Morgan and I have been going through the papers and piecing it all together. Carolyn hit on the idea to write mystery novels to make money. She couldn't support herself—or me—with her poetry. But she never had the confidence to market her own work. She relied on Bill. He told her whenever he placed a collection of her poems—he let her keep the meager revenue from those. But he never told her he was selling her mysteries."

Byron shook his head. "It's the worst exploitation of a poet—"

"The mother of his own child!" Morgan added.

"So Mrs. Wesley knew all about this?" Linda asked.

"She confessed as much. It seems she had no objection to Bill's double dealing with Carolyn, until she began to suspect Bill was having an affair with her. That's when she started to spy on Carolyn. She snuck into her cabin and read her journals. Then one day, she found Carolyn's last mystery manuscript." Sarah covered her face with her hands and shook her head.

Morgan picked up the story. "It was Aunt Carolyn's last mystery. *The Arsonist.* It told the story of her affair with Bill Wesley—in fiction, of course, but Mrs. Wesley recognized the truth. That's when she threatened to burn Carolyn's papers. That's why Carolyn packed them all up and stored them with her lawyer. To protect them."

"Listen to this," Sarah said. She pulled out Carolyn's last journal and read from the final entry: "*I have packed everything away and soon it will be safely stowed. A relief. But what will I do with the new book? I have to keep it with me, to keep working on it. It is unbearable that Sarah might never read what I have written, that she might never know—*"

"That she might never know about her parents' romance!" Morgan interrupted. "That's what the new book was all about. Carolyn was trying to think of a place to hide *The Arsonist* so that Mrs. Wesley wouldn't burn it."

Sarah sighed heavily and closed the notebook. "My mother was afraid for her manuscripts. I don't think she realized, consciously, that she should have been afraid for her life."

"No," Jacob said. "Or she wouldn't have kept you all there on the island with her. Three children. God, when I think—"

"So Mrs. Wesley returned and set fire to the cabin," Byron said. "It wasn't an accident, but murder!"

"Yes," Jacob told him. "A few days after she read Carolyn's revealing manuscript, she came back in the middle of the night with cans of gasoline. She brought her boys in the boat with her. They must have been only six or seven—"

"No wonder Mark is so warped," Morgan said.

They all fell silent, thinking of that awful night. The only sound was the staccato rapping of Linda's stylus as she took notes in braille.

"So nobody else ever read this book, *The Arsonist?*" asked Linda.

"Alfred Carriere read it," Morgan explained. "Aunt Carolyn submitted it to Carriere Press, shortly before her death. It was the first time she'd ever mailed out a manuscript on her own. She was separating herself from Bill, trying to become independent. She sent it to Alfred under her pen name Walter White."

"I can understand that," Byron said. "She had her reputation as a poet to protect."

"Not to mention her reputation as a woman," Sarah added. "If she'd published it under her own name, people would have recognized the autobiographical elements and known about the affair."

"But Alfred never published it," Morgan said. "It sat forgotten in his office for twenty years, until Bill came up with the idea to reprint the earlier mysteries. When Alfred realized he had a Walter White mystery that Bill didn't know about, he planned to publish it after Bill died, under the title *A Fire at Midnight*. But Cady Brown found out about it. She started asking questions. Mrs. Wesley overheard her."

"And Mrs. Wesley knew the novel might implicate her in Carolyn's death!" Linda exclaimed. "So she told her son to kill Cady!"

"Then she tried to poison Alfred to stop him from publishing it," Morgan said. "But Gregory got poisoned instead."

"So why hasn't Alfred published the book?" Byron asked.

"Betty put an end to that scheme," Sarah said. "She destroyed the original."

"What about the copy Mrs. Wesley found in the cabin?" Linda asked. "Didn't Carolyn save it along with the other papers she gave to her lawyer?"

Sarah and Morgan looked at each other. They had been searching through Carolyn's papers for weeks and so far there was no trace of the carbon copy Mrs. Wesley had read so many years ago. Either it had burned in the fire, or Carolyn had stashed it somewhere else. But where?

ALFRED WAS CONVINCED that *The Arsonist* was somewhere among Carolyn's papers. He still planned to publish it as *A Fire at Midnight*, although now, of course, he promised to pay royalties to Sarah. He started a rumor, with the help of Channel 9, that he would soon be releasing the "lost" Midnight mystery by Carolyn Yeats, and this scoop was picked up by wire services all across the continent. Not only was it a Midnight mystery, it was rumored to give all the juicy background about Carolyn's tragic and scandalous life. The book was guaranteed to be a record-breaking best-seller. But the manuscript could not be found.

Alfred telephoned Sarah every day, asking whether she had found the manuscript among Carolyn's papers yet. Finally, growing impatient, he began to accuse Sarah of concealing it from him. He came to her house one day when she was enjoying a private dinner with Jacob and insisted on discussing it.

"I have rights to that book, if you find it," Alfred said. "I'm her publisher—"

"Thirty years ago you were her publisher," Sarah corrected him.

"Right now I'm her publisher! As far as I'm concerned, she's still under contract to me, and I have the paperwork to prove it. Read this." He handed Jacob a photocopy. "It gives me first-refusal rights on all Carolyn's books."

"First refusal?" Sarah asked. "What does that mean?"

"Let me see that," Jacob said. He skimmed the paper, noting the clause that Alfred had highlighted in yellow.

"There's no time limit on it," Alfred said. "She signed it in 1973, when we did *Island Songs*, and it's still valid. Carolyn was legally bound to submit every manuscript first to Carriere Press."

"What the hell kind of a deal is that?" Jacob asked.

"If this is true," Sarah said, "why did you let my mother publish three books with Laurentian Shield?"

Alfred shrugged. "That was just poetry. Worthless. This is different. *A Fire at Midnight* will sell like—"

"Oh, for heaven's sakes," Sarah said. "We probably won't ever find it anyway. We're nearly finished sorting through the boxes, and there's no sign of it. Let's not haggle over it now. We're in the middle of dinner." She stood up and returned to the dining room. "Good-bye, Alfred. You can let yourself out."

When Sarah left the room, Jacob turned angrily to Alfred. "Don't you think enough people have made enough money off the poor woman?" he asked. "All she was trying to do was support her daughter, and it's time to let her do it."

"Look, it's not personal," Alfred said. "It's business. If Sarah goes to another publisher with the new mystery, I'll have to take her to court."

Jacob showed Alfred the door. "I'll see you in court, then," he said.

Chapter Forty-Three

JACOB THREW SARAH'S PACK-SACK into the trunk of his car and hopped in beside her. "You ready?"

"More than ready," she said. "Let's just stop by Zina's café first. Morgan went down there this morning to meet Daniel for coffee, and she never came back. I want to let her know what I'm up to."

Yesterday, re-reading Carolyn's final entry, Sarah had become fixated on a passage near the end: *Let her protect it, with the shade of her right hand. In the story Persephone always returns.* A thrill ran through her. She knew exactly where the missing book could be found.

Jacob turned onto Westminster Avenue. "I had a talk with my grandfather about Alfred's contract," he told Sarah. "He thinks we can beat it."

"Really?"

"Yes." Jacob laughed. "You should see old Evan. He's raring to get back in the saddle again, to defend your rights. He says the terms are so unfair we can probably beat it on the grounds that Carolyn was too young and inexperienced to realize what she was signing—which has the nice advantage of being true. I just love it when my legal arguments are true."

Sarah laughed. "Well, I hope you can beat it," she said. "It's not just the money. God knows I'll have enough money forever, now. It's the principle of the thing. It's, you know...."

"Justice."

"Right."

Jacob pulled up in front of Zina's café, and Sarah stared at the building in amazement.

Byron Hunt had just arrived on his bicycle and he, too, was staring at the front of the café. The blue curtains had been replaced with flowered ones, the brick had been painted pink, and the gorgeous night-sky sign that read "Mystery Au Lait Café" had been taken down and was leaning against the building.

"Is Zina going out of business?" asked Byron. He looked panic-stricken.

"She can't be!" Sarah exclaimed. "Let's go in." Byron and Jacob followed her through the door.

Inside, more surprises met her eyes. The tablecloths were white, and the telephone booth was papered over with a rather tacky design of little cupids. Strangest of all, half the bookshelves were empty, and piles of paperbacks cluttered the floor of every aisle. Morgan and Daniel were down on their knees, sorting through them.

"What in the world?" Sarah tripped over a pile of paperbacks and sent them scattering across the floor.

"Hi, guys," Zina called from the back of the store. "Do you like it?"

Sarah bent to pick up a book. What kind of a cover was this? Against a pearly sunset, a ruby-lipped heroine raved ecstatically in the arms of a well-muscled hunk. The title was *Love Blossoms Slow*.

She handed it to Byron. "Look at this."

Byron raised his eyebrows. "Shouldn't that be *Love Blossoms Slowly?*" he asked.

Sarah scooped up a handful of books and read the titles. *June Bride, Love among the Palms, Passion in Paradise, The Cowboy Who Kissed Me.*

"Zina—what are you doing?"

Zina, assisted by Javier, was coming down the aisle, lugging a new sign. In pink letters, on a white background decorated with red valentines, the sign read: "Zina's Café d'Amour."

"Time for a change," Zina said.

OVER COFFEE AND heart-shaped sugar cookies, Sarah explained to everyone about the clue she'd found to the hiding place of Carolyn's last book.

"Amazing," Morgan said.

"Good detective work," remarked Daniel.

Zina could barely contain her excitement. "It's like something out of *Treasure Island*," she cried.

"Yes," Sarah said. "I even brought a shovel and a trowel. I'll stay with Mary tonight, and then we'll head back to Persephone Island in the morning, to start digging."

"Well, Sarah will be digging," Jacob said. "I have some very important work to take care of at the office."

"Buried treasure," said Zina. "It's so romantic. And it's serious treasure, too. Alfred says a new Midnight Mystery at this point will be worth a few million. Sarah—" Zina put a hand on Sarah's shoulder. "You *will* consider publishing with Alfred, won't you?"

"We'll see," Sarah told her. "I'll have to consult my lawyer." She wrapped her arm in Jacob's and headed for the door.

"Goodbye, Byron," she called. But Byron was engrossed in *Love Blossoms Slow* and did not look up.

JACOB DROPPED SARAH off at Persephone Island at ten in the morning, but he didn't get out of the boat. He had an appointment with Evan to look over contract law and plan their strategy.

"Don't work too hard," he warned Sarah. "If it gets tough, wait for me."

"The soil is shallow here," she said. "If the book's there, I'll find it quickly."

"I'll be back in a couple of hours," he said. "I'll bring champagne and—I hope—we'll be toasting your discovery. If not, I'll help you keep looking."

Sarah waved from the dock until the boat was out of sight. Then she climbed the hill to the clearing and began to dig.

She dug a hole a foot deep beside Persephone's right hand and hit rock. She widened the hole until it was two feet in diameter, but found nothing. Blisters began to form on her hands, and she went into the cabin for bandages before beginning again.

She circled the statue, wondering. This time she tried digging a six-inch trench all around the statue. Nothing.

"Where is it?" she hummed under her breath. "Where have you hidden it? Tell me."

When the sun reached the zenith, Sarah stopped to rest. Seeking some shade, she flopped down in the shadow of the statue, but the sun was still in her eyes. She moved to the other side, where the shadow was longer, under the statue's right arm.

The shadow of her right arm.

The shade of her right hand!

Sarah jumped up, as if shaken awake. Of course. The book wasn't buried beside the hand, but in the *shadow* of the hand, which was right there—no—wait. What time of day would Carolyn have buried it? Instinctively, Sarah knew it had been noon. High noon, just as it was right now. The hour of fullest light, the very opposite of midnight, on June 21st, the longest day of sunlight in the year. *The earth spins on its axis and light floods back across the sky.* Let's see. She circled the statue again, thinking. On June 21st, the sun would have been higher in the sky than it was right now, at the end of August. The shadow would have fallen directly under Persephone's hand. Right up against the very edge of the statue's stone skirt. Right about ... there!

Sarah drove the shovel into the ground and began to dig with renewed energy. Her back ached, and she was sweating so much that the bandages were peeling off her fingers, but she kept going. Six inches, seven, a foot—and then, clang. The shovel hit metal. She used a smaller trowel to loosen her find from the earth until she could pull it out with her hands.

It was a tin candy box, about the size of a telephone book, decorated with Christmas trees and candy canes. Sarah wiped off the dirt impatiently and tried to open it. The lid was wedged on tightly. She carried it into the cabin, sat at the kitchen table, and used a screwdriver to pry it open. Inside, a bundle of newspapers and plastic protected the manuscript. Sarah unwrapped the newspaper carefully, noting the date: June 21, 1982. Carolyn must have bought it that morning in town. Tears of sadness welled in Sarah's eyes as she imagined her mother going about her final day, fearful of losing her writing, but never suspecting the awful fate that awaited her that night.

She pulled out the manuscript. It was surprisingly short. About a hundred pages. Perhaps it was unfinished. Then she saw the title page. In the old-fashioned letters of Carolyn's manual typewriter, the title page read: *Demeter Speaks, by Carolyn Yeats*, and underneath: *for Sarah*.

WHEN JACOB RETURNED, Sarah did not run down to greet him. He hoped this was not a bad sign. He climbed the hill as fast as he could, carrying the champagne in a small cooler of ice.

He found her seated in the shade, across from the statue of Persephone, amidst the wreckage of her digging, poring over a yellowed manuscript.

"You found it!"

She looked up, an expression of wonder on her face. "I found it," she said quietly.

Too quietly, he thought.

"What's the matter?" he asked softly.

"Nothing's the matter," she said. She stood up, holding the book against her chest. "Nothing at all. Everything's wonderful."

The smile on her face warmed his heart. "Sweet justice!" he cried. He kissed her cheek.

"No—sweet irony," Sarah said to him. "Look."

He looked. He turned page after page, slowly, reading with such a bewildered expression on his face that Sarah began to laugh out loud.

"It's—this is it?" he asked. "But this isn't a mystery—it's—"

"Poems!" Sarah cried. She was laughing so hard now that her words came out in short gasps. "Beautiful—marvelous—utterly worthless poems! Even I can tell it's her best work ever—it's all about mothers and daughters, and leaving and coming home again, and oh it's the most precious, unsellable thing—oh sweet, *sweet* justice!" She collapsed onto the ground with laughter.

"Poetry?" Jacob stood staring down at her as she lay at his feet, holding her aching side. He looked at the uprooted tin box, the shovel stuck in the ground, the ground in turmoil, the moat around Persephone's body and the expression of absorbed concentration on her stone face as she ignored them and kept on reading and reading and reading for eternity, and then he began to laugh, too.

AFTER DINNER, SARAH took her mother's book down to the dock to read in the evening light.

"Are you coming?" she asked Jacob.

He shook his head. "No. You go. I'll stay here and pack up." He touched her face lightly with the back of his hand. "I hate to leave, don't you?"

Sarah looked around the kitchen of the little cabin, which had begun to seem like home to her. "We'll come back," she said.

The evening air held a faint chill, but Sarah remained on the dock, turning the pages of her mother's book until there was no longer light enough to read. Evening had fallen unexpectedly, too quickly, as it always did in August. She gathered her things and walked slowly home past the late-blooming roses. All too soon, summer would be coming to a close, and she wanted to memorize their delicate scent. She twisted a flower from its stem, something to press between the pages of a book, something to take with her through the winter days ahead.

To the west, the sun sank below the surface of the lake. But Sarah's path was not entirely dark. Through the gathering twilight, she could see the gleaming white shoulder of Persephone. Inside the cabin, Jacob was lighting all the lamps. From every window, a soft glow blazed, illuminating her way.

photo: Melody Morrissette

Catherine Hunter teaches English at the University of Winnipeg. She has published three collections of poetry: *Lunar Wake*, *Latent Heat* and *Necessary Crimes* and one spoken word CD, *Rush Hour*. This is her second thriller. Catherine used to live in the Wolseley neighbourhood of Winnipeg. She has since moved away.